TAKEN FROM DUNHAVEN CASTLE

A CATE KENSIE MYSTERY

CATE KENSIE MYSTERIES
BOOK SEVEN

NELLIE H. STEELE

CHAPTER 1

*E*verything was different now.

Cate traced a finger over the black print on the paper as though it would make the words more real. She squeezed her eyes shut, realizing those few sentences had altered her life.

Everything had changed when she read those words. Everything was different now.

Everything.

The moment she'd first seen the document flitted across her mind. The decisions she'd made after had been life-altering.

She blew out a long breath, stuffing the papers into a folder and flicking it closed. She tossed it onto the coffee table in front of her.

What's done is done.

She pursed her lips, studying the cold hearth in front of her as she pulled her legs up and nestled into the supple leather of the library's armchair.

She flicked her gaze to the other empty chair in the room, staring at it for a moment before she let her eyes slide closed.

Jack was alive. But the events they had set in motion when they'd traveled to 1942 couldn't be undone. And those events changed history. And her life.

Cate let her head fall back into the cushion behind her. A cold, wet nose nudged at her limp hand that dangled from the chair's arm.

She twisted her neck and glanced down at Riley. His feather-like tail wagged at her. The corners of her lips tugged upward as she ran her fingers through his black-and-white fur. "Hey, buddy. I'm okay."

Bailey wandered over as she spoke, staring up at her tentatively.

"I'm okay, guys, really. It's all going to be okay." She let the words sink in around her, desperately trying to believe them.

Cate pushed herself up to stand and snatched up the folder. She stalked to the fireplace and grabbed a stick lighter. With a click, a flame flared from the tip. She touched them to the corner of the manila container. Fire burst from it.

She tossed the burning papers into the fireplace. They curled as the edges blackened. With her arms wrapped around her, she sucked in another deep breath. She swallowed hard as she considered what she faced later this afternoon. Her palms turned sweaty, and her pulse sped as she contemplated how the events may play out.

Her phone chimed, interrupting her rambling mind. Cate checked the display, staring at the one-word text message on her lock screen.

Ready?

She rested her chin on the top of the device as thoughts flitted through her mind. Was she ready?

She bit her lower lip and typed a response. Her thumb hovered over the send button. She slid her eyes closed, sucking in a breath before she popped them open and pressed the arrow. The lone word floated up. She stared at the simple, three-letter answer.

Yes.

Was it true? Was she really prepared?

The door to the library swung open, cutting off any further contemplating on her part. Molly hurried inside. She tossed a strawberry blonde lock over her shoulder, offering Cate a broad smile.

"Hey, Lady Cate."

"Hi," Cate answered, twisting to eye her. She recognized the pleasant expression on Molly's features. It hid the trepidation behind her pretty face.

Molly clasped her hands in front of her. "Just checking to see if anything else was needed before Mr. Smythe and Gayle arrive later today."

Cate sucked in a deep breath and shook her head. "I don't think so. We should be all set."

Molly forced another grin as she nodded. "Okay. Are you certain they're not staying? Mrs. Fraser is asking. She's surprised they're not. To be honest, so am I."

Cate pressed her lips together, trying to offer a reassuring smile, but sure she wasn't pulling it off. "They aren't."

She let out a shaky breath, biting her lower lip to stop it from trembling. She blinked back the tears forming again.

Molly nodded, her grin fading. She studied the area rug, tilting her head as she drummed her fingers on the back of the armchair. "And neither has said anything about why they're coming?"

Cate shook her head in answer, unable to form words. Mr. Smythe had not told her the reason, but she knew it. She was afraid any verbal response may betray her lie.

"Well, I don't know how you feel about it, Lady Cate, but downstairs we are all in a tizzy. Everyone's nervous. I don't know how you're so calm." Molly flicked her gaze outside the window and shivered. "It sounds so ominous. Especially with him requesting us to be present."

"I'm sure it'll all be settled soon," Cate answered.

"Yeah, but how?" Molly fluttered her eyelids. "I'm sorry. It's not my place."

"No, Molly, it's okay. You should never feel like it's not your place. Dunhaven Castle is your home, too."

"I just can't imagine what this is, but I'm nervous."

Cate approached her friend and housekeeper-in-training, pulling her into an embrace. "It'll be okay, Molly. No matter what he says, no matter what comes next. It'll all be okay. We'll always have each other."

Molly squeezed her tightly before she pulled back. Tears shined in her eyes and stained her cheeks. "I'm sorry," she said, her voice breathy as she waved her hands at her face.

Cate rubbed her arms. "It's okay."

"No, no, it's not." Molly heaved a sigh. "It's just...it's been one thing after another. First Jack's disappearance, then his near-death, and now this."

"When it rains, it pours."

"Yeah," Molly said, wiping at her tears. "But it's poured for you, too. We should be supporting you and instead, I'm crying on your shoulder."

"It's okay, Molly," Cate assured her. "We support each other."

Molly licked her lips and nodded, sniffling before blowing out a steadying breath. "Right."

"Speaking of, I hear Jack's been pestering Mr. Fraser about going back to work."

"Oh, yes," Molly said with a roll of her eyes and a chuckle. "Talking about trimming those hedges out back. He almost died less than two days ago. And he's ready to trim trees."

"Sounds like Jack," Cate said with a laugh.

"We may need to tie him to the bed."

The two women shared another giggle over the suggestion. "Well," Molly said after a deep inhale, "I'll leave you alone. Two hours to go."

"Two hours," Cate said. "I think I'll take the dogs for a walk, and tire them out before the others arrive."

"Enjoy, Lady Cate." Molly offered her a final smile before she disappeared from the room.

Cate stared after her, hoping her words were true. "Everything's going to be okay," she murmured to herself.

With a glance over her shoulder, she called the dogs with her. They strolled around the property, basking in the warm late-spring air. She eyed the castle on the horizon as she sauntered back from the loch.

Dunhaven Castle. Her home. She had to protect it. She had no choice.

She quickened her step, nervous energy pushing her to hustle up the path. The dogs raced ahead of her, galloping into the kitchen as she pushed the door open.

"Well, hello, boys," Mrs. Fraser greeted them.

Molly set out a plate of cookies in preparation for the arrival of their guests.

"And hello, Lady Cate," Mrs. Fraser finished.

"Hello, Mrs. Fraser."

The woman waved a finger in the air. "We're almost ready. If I know Mr. Smythe, he will be on time. Not a moment late."

"We can be sure of that," Cate said with a nod.

Mrs. Fraser shifted a few teacups around on the tray before she clasped her hands in front of her.

"It'll all be over soon, Mrs. Fraser."

"The dreaded visit, you mean?" Jack asked as he and Mr. Fraser pushed into the kitchen.

"Yes," Cate said with a nod. "And what are you doing out there? Aren't you supposed to be taking it easy?"

"Dr. Gresham said I should be getting exercise, not laying around."

"Trimming bushes is a little beyond exercise," Cate said, wagging a finger at him.

"I trimmed nothing. I merely frowned at them as we strode past," Jack assured her.

"Good. No trimming bushes until you're cleared," Cate warned. "I'm going to head up. They should be here in about ten minutes."

Cate's pulse quickened as she said the words.

"Mind if I walk you up, Lady Cate?" Jack asked.

"Not at all. Come on, boys, let's head up to the library."

They strode down the long hall, climbing the stairs to the main level as the dogs scampered up the stairs in front of them.

"You're doing pretty well on these stairs," Cate noted.

"I'm feeling much better," Jack answered as they pushed into the hall.

"Good."

"Cate—"

Cate stopped and shook her head. "Jack, you don't need to say anything. You don't need to thank me again."

"I do. I wouldn't be here if it wasn't for you. There's been so much going on, we've barely had the chance to discuss it. I miss my chair in the library."

Cate smiled at him. "I've missed you being there. We'll have plenty of time to talk after this meeting with Mr. Smythe."

Jack puckered his lips, flicking his gaze down the hall. "I don't like this. Something feels wrong."

"I don't like it either," Cate answered, "but I don't think we have much choice in the matter. Mr. Smythe insisted on the meeting, and he insisted it happen today."

Jack stuck his hands on his hips. "Too much has taken

place since 1942. This just reeks of something blindsiding us."

"I know." Cate pressed her lips into a thin line. "We'll know soon enough, though. Try not to worry about it."

Jack scoffed and crossed his arms. "Yeah, okay, right."

"I'm serious. Jack, you nearly didn't survive. Your heart stopped. I don't want anything else to happen to you. You've got to take it easy."

Jack flicked his gaze to the floor, sliding his eyes closed. He opened them and sucked in a deep breath, centering his focus on her. "I know. Thank heavens the doctor knew what to do."

Cate fluttered her eyelashes, avoiding his stare for a moment before she nodded. "Yeah. Damien said she was the best."

"The best supernatural doctor. Doesn't seem like there would be much competition in that field."

Cate chuckled. "She may have a corner on the market. But her skills were impressive nonetheless."

"Aye, I suppose I do owe her my life."

Cate nodded at the statement as she squeezed his arm. "We all do."

Jack sucked in a sharp breath and stuck his hands on his hips. "Well, I suppose I'll let you go wait on pins and needles in the library."

"I'll call you as soon as they arrive."

"Thanks, Cate. See you soon."

They parted ways, and Cate returned to the library. She chewed her lower lip as she sank into the soft leather of the armchair. Nervous energy stopped her from settling. She studied the bookcases as her leg bobbed up and down.

She rolled her neck around and pulled her legs onto the chair to stop their constant movement. Instead, she drummed her fingers against the arm. Riley approached her again, staring up at her with his almond-shaped eyes.

"I know, Riley. I'm nervous, and you can tell. But it'll all be over soon." She patted his head, and he leapt onto his hind legs, pawing at her.

Cate scooped him up, nestling him in her arms like a baby as she rubbed his chest. He offered a wide yawn. "Looks like you are in desperate need of a nap, buddy. I wish I could nap through what's about to happen."

Riley relaxed in her arms, his eyes closing to slits. The crunch of gravel interrupted any rest on his part.

Cate glanced out the window. A cloud of dust billowed across the garden, indicative of someone driving up the driveway. Her heart thudded in her chest as she set Riley on the rug near the fireplace and strode from the room.

The squeal of a car's brakes pierced the air as Cate reached the front doors. She flung them open to find Mr. Smythe's sleek black rental rolling to a stop.

Cate forced a smile on her face as the passenger door popped open and Gayle emerged. "Hi, Gayle."

"Hello," Gayle said, her forehead crinkling as she tried to smile but worry clouded her face.

Cate peered over the top of the car and offered Mr. Smythe a greeting. His usually set features had an extra-dour tone to them. "Hi, Mr. Smythe."

The attorney forced the briefest of smiles onto his face as he buttoned his suit jacket before pulling his briefcase from the backseat.

"Come in. We'll meet in the library. Let me call everyone else."

Cate waved them toward the large room as she strode toward the servants' stairs. All four of her staff popped from the stairway. "They're here."

"We know," Molly said, worry pinched her forehead.

"We've been standing at the top of the stairs for the last five minutes."

Cate squeezed her hand. "Well, let's go find out the reason behind this meeting."

Mrs. Fraser wrung her hands, blowing out a sharp breath. "Oh, Lady Cate..."

"It's okay, Mrs. Fraser. Let's see what Mr. Smythe has to say. There may be no reason to worry."

"All right," she said. Mr. Fraser wrapped his arm around his wife and led her down the hall.

Jack nodded at Cate and Molly to precede him down the hall.

They entered the library, finding seats as Cate took a post across the room, too nervous to sit.

Mr. Smythe tugged several folders from his well-polished briefcase before snapping it shut and sliding it next to the armchair.

He glanced up, his eyes scanning all of them before lowering to the paperwork perched on his knees. "Let me begin by apologizing for being presumptuous enough to invite the staff, though as this will ultimately affect them as well, I felt it important that they be present."

"Of course, Mr. Smythe," Cate answered, trying to firm her shaky voice. "Can you tell us what this is about?"

"Is there something wrong?" Mrs. Fraser questioned from the sofa across the room, her hands nearly white from gripping each other. Mr. Fraser patted her knee in a silent gesture of support.

Gayle offered the woman a contrite glance from the armchair Jack usually frequented.

Mr. Smythe swallowed hard, running a hand over the folder in his lap as he stared at it. "I am afraid there has been an egregious error made." He paused, his lip bobbing up and down but no sound emerged. "My firm..."

He paused again and shook his head. "I have made a mistake. There was an oversight. I do not know how it happened, but rest assured I am determined to investigate. To be frank, I cannot see how I missed this, but..."

Molly leaned forward, her lips parted as she waited for the news. "What is it?"

Jack leapt from his seat. "If it's about the estate accounts, I've double-checked them—"

"It has nothing to do with the finances," Mr. Smythe interrupted.

"Then what is it?" Molly asked.

Mr. Smythe studied their faces again, his features paler than usual and gaunt. He flicked his eyes downward again as he licked his lips and focused his attention on Cate.

"It seems you, Dr. Kensie, are not the rightful owner of Dunhaven Castle."

CHAPTER 2

*C*ate's heart hammered as the words hung heavy in the air. Gasps rang out around her as she pressed a hand to her chest and swallowed hard.

"What?" Molly shrieked, leaping from her seat on the sofa's arm.

Jack plopped into his chair, his brow furrowing and his jaw gaping.

"But...y-you did a DNA test. You confirmed it," Molly gushed.

Mr. Smythe nodded. "There is no question that Dr. Kensie is a MacKenzie. We did confirm that through a DNA test. She is definitely the closest living relative. In fact, she is the only living relative left of the MacKenzie family."

"Then how could she not be the heir?"

Molly collapsed back onto the sofa's arm, pressing a hand to her forehead.

Jack shook his head. "This is insane. You searched for months, Mr. Smythe. You said she was the right one. We didn't know if anyone was left, and you found her. You assured us Dunhaven would carry on."

"Yes," Cate chimed in, clearing her throat, "when we spoke, you were sure the DNA test would confirm what you were already certain of and that there would be no challenges of any merit."

"Yes, I know, I..." Mr. Smythe slid his eyes closed, pressing his thin mouth into an even tighter line. "There was a codicil. Lady Gertrude added it to the will, and we..."

His voice trailed off, and he swallowed hard. Had the news not been so dire, Cate would have felt sorry for the man.

Mr. Smythe twisted his neck and cleared his throat. "That is, *I* was not aware of it."

"A codicil? What does that mean?" Molly questioned.

"It's an addendum to the original will," Gayle explained. "It modifies it in some way."

"And this addendum changes it so Cate isn't the heir?" Jack asked.

"More or less, yes," Mr. Smythe said.

"Well, what the hell does it say?" Jack asked, lunging forward in his seat. "Because the last we heard Lady Gertrude wanted this to go to family only. It was never to leave the MacKenzie family. So, if Cate's the only MacKenzie, and she's not the heir who the hell is it going to?"

The doors to the library swung open. A curvy blonde in a form-fitting, shin-length dress stood inside. The corners of her full lips curled up into a devilish grin. "That would be me."

Cate's heart skipped a beat as the familiar form of Gianna Caruso sashayed into the room, sticking a hand on her hip as she stopped next to Mr. Smythe's armchair.

"I have the matter well in hand, Ms. Caruso," he assured her with a sour expression on his face.

Gianna lifted a shoulder. "These people deserve answers, and we shall provide them."

"But...she's not a MacKenzie!" Mr. Fraser's quiet voice said.

"No, I am not. But I am, in fact, the rightful heir to this estate and everything in it. And I would like to be upfront about how this affects you."

"I'd like that," Mrs. Fraser said, lifting her chin. "I think we'd all like to know where we stand."

"Of course," Gianna said, her red lips twisting into a tighter grin. She paused, the smile broadening as she scanned all of their faces. "I want you all out by week's end."

"What?" Mrs. Fraser gasped.

"Dr. Kensie is no longer the owner of Dunhaven Castle. She is also no longer your employer. I am. And you are all fired."

Molly's jaw dropped open, and tears filled her eyes again. Jack wrapped an arm around her shoulders.

Cate shook her head at the scene. Her heart pounded as she fought to steady her breathing. Every impulse in her body pushed her to lunge through the air and throttle the woman responsible for so much damage. From the deaths in 1942 to Jack's kidnapping and now this. Gianna Caruso had slashed and burned almost everything dear to her.

Across the room, Gianna continued twisting the knife. "And while we are at it, there is another matter to clear up. Mr. Smythe, would you care to explain it?"

William Smythe's pale skin turned gray as the color drained from his face. He arched an eyebrow as he began. "Any decisions Dr. Kensie has made over the course of her time at Dunhaven Castle–"

"Her illegal time at Dunhaven Castle," Gianna added, pulling one corner of her mouth back in a smirk as she settled her arms over her chest and stared at Cate.

Mr. Smythe fluttered his eyelids before pressing on. "Any decisions Dr. Kensie has made are null. That includes the gifting of the cottage to Charlie and Emily Fraser and…" His voice trailed off again, and he whipped a handkerchief from his pocket and used it to dab his forehead. "Any salaries paid to employees."

Molly's eyebrows knit, and she stared at him with an incredulous expression. "What?"

"You owe me your salaries back," Gianna said, flicking her gaze to the Frasers. "And you owe me your home."

"But surely…" Mrs. Fraser began, a hand pressed to her heart.

"Surely nothing. The cottage is my property. Now, I realize this is a shock—"

"A shock?" Molly squealed. "This is robbery."

Gianna's facial muscles twitched with annoyance. "I'll let that slide since you are upset. However—"

"No! I don't have the money. What do you expect me to do? I got paid. I bought stuff. It's gone! What I do have left is my life savings. I'd be bankrupt."

Gianna arched an eyebrow at the redhead. "I'm a reasonable woman. We can set up a payment plan if you cannot pay the lump sum."

Molly gasped as a tear rolled down her cheek. She started to shake her head, but it turned into a quiver. She pressed a shaking hand to her forehead.

Mrs. Fraser's wrinkles deepened as she wrung her hands and glanced at Mr. Fraser.

Cate slid her eyes closed as the chaos ensued. Her heart broke for her friends. The sudden appearance of Gianna was an unexpected twist. An unwanted nuisance that made her skin crawl. And threatened to ruin everything.

"I can't believe there isn't something we can do," Jack's voice said, bringing Cate back to the reality of the situation brewing around her.

"There is," Gianna said, poking a finger in the air, "you can get out. By week's end, or I will have to use force. Mr. Smythe can handle drawing up arrangements to repay the debts you incurred during the time I should have been in charge of the funds."

"Wait just a minute," Jack growled. "Lady Gertrude *never* wanted this to leave the family."

"And it is just that fear that forced her to write the codicil," Gianna said, crossing her arms.

Jack's nostrils flared, and he held a shaking hand toward the attorney. "Mr. Smythe, can you please explain how this happened? How did Lady Gertrude's desire for Dunhaven to remain in the family force her to add a codicil ensuring it did not?"

"Simple," Gianna began.

"I'm asking him, not you!" Jack shouted.

Cate stepped forward, placing a hand on his shoulder. "Easy, Jack. Let him explain."

Gianna offered him a smarmy smile. "Yes, easy, Jack. You wouldn't want to raise your blood pressure after your illness."

Jack's chest heaved as he gasped in breaths, his face an angry shade of red.

Mr. Smythe held up his hand. "Please, Ms. Caruso, allow me to explain. They deserve that much."

"A matter of opinion," Gianna said, "but proceed."

Mr. Smythe sucked in a deep breath. "Lady Gertrude became concerned that the next owner of Dunhaven Castle may face a situation similar to hers."

"Meaning what?" Jack asked.

"Meaning no clear heir. It was the concern that Dunhaven Castle could pass to someone outside of the family, someone unknown if the new heir had no family. And so, she added a codicil that if the next of kin was not married at the time of inheritance, the property should pass to the Caruso Preservation Foundation, of which Ms. Caruso is the president."

"So, Cate had to be married, or she could not inherit?" Jack questioned.

"Yes," Mr. Smythe said with a nod.

"No, that can't be legal," Jack said, slicing through the air with his hand. "Cate'll challenge it."

"Yes," Molly said, leaping to her feet and threading her arm through Cate's. "Surely, this can't stand up in court. It's discrimination or something. Because she's a single woman, she can't inherit? That's crazy! She's the next-of-kin."

"I assure you it is legal. It will stand up in a court of law. It can be enforced. As archaic as it may seem, this is a standard practice historically in wills."

"I mean, this is the twenty-first century! How can a single woman be denied an inheritance based on her marital status?" Molly asked, shaking her head.

"Because Lady Gertrude wanted this place preserved. And Cate lacks the ability to do that," Gianna said.

"This is crazy!" Jack said, flinging his hands in the air.

"It is," Molly said. "Marriages can fall apart. It doesn't guarantee a future."

"But it does, in most instances, lead to children. And there is a stipulation about the duration of the marriage." Mr. Smythe shook his head. "It's a moot point since Dr. Kensie is and was single at the time of inheriting."

Gianna raised her chin, a smirk on her face. "Which means Dunhaven Castle is mine."

Mr. Smythe pressed his lips together. "Unfortunately, she is correct. And she does have the legal right to enforce you all to leave in a timely manner."

"One week," Gianna chimed in.

"That's hardly reasonable," Molly shot back.

"You don't have that many things. I think you can manage it," Gianna said.

"This is cruel," Molly shouted as she jabbed a finger at the woman. "And heartless."

"Perhaps some leniency could be arranged," Mr. Smythe began, sliding his eyes sideways to Gianna.

Cate's heart pounded in her chest again. She wiped her sweaty palms against her leggings and licked her lips. She cleared her throat and lifted her eyes to the group. "Will you excuse me for a moment?"

Molly wrapped her arm around Cate's shoulder. "Cate–"

Cate squeezed Molly's hand and offered her a slight smile. "No, I'm okay. I just...need one minute."

"Of course, Cate," Gayle said with a consoling smile.

Cate took a step toward the doors when Gianna stepped into her path. "Leave the timepiece. It comes to me, too. I wouldn't want you absconding with any valuable heirlooms."

Cate narrowed her eyes at the woman, her nose wrinkling and her lips settling into a frown.

"That's ridiculous," Jack said.

Cate lifted the pendant timepiece from around her neck. She held it out toward Mr. Smythe, dangling it from her fingers. "I trust this will be safe in your care until we can sort through this mess."

Mr. Smythe accepted the proffered item with a remorseful and fleeting smile before placing it on the coffee table.

"Excuse me," Cate said, skirting past Gianna and darting out the door. She pulled those closed behind her, collapsing against them as she blew out a long breath. She fluttered her eyelashes, glancing upward and blinking away her tears.

The sudden, unexpected appearance of Gianna made this

all the more difficult for her. She fought to steady her breathing. She had to proceed. She had to fight for what was hers. And her staff's. She shook her head at the greed displayed by the woman to require her staff to repay their salaries over the last year.

With a deep inhale, she forced herself down the hall and around the corner to the office. She strode to the file cabinet and tugged it open, digging through it for the documents she sought. She bypassed the green folder containing the copy of the will she'd signed for in Aberdeen. The copy had contained no such codicil. Could she fight it based on that?

She shook her head, pulling the next folder out of the drawer and slamming it shut. She spun on her heel and raised her chin. With the item pressed against her chest, she strode back to the library.

The scene inside remained tense. Jack sat next to Mrs. Fraser on the sofa, his leg bobbing up and down. His hand wrapped around Molly's who perched on the edge of the sofa's arm. She sniffled, biting her thumbnail. Mrs. Fraser and Mr. Fraser held hands, their faces stoic.

Cate swallowed hard and closed the doors behind her.

"Finished with your moment? I'd like to get moving on signing the paperwork," Gianna said as she circled around her to face Mr. Smythe.

"There's no need for that," Cate said.

"Cate," Jack began with a shake of his head.

"Don't give up, Lady Cate," Molly said.

"Not without a fight," Mrs. Fraser said.

Cate twisted to face them and nodded. "It's okay. We'll be okay." She returned her gaze to Mr. Smythe and thrust the folder toward him. "I think you'll find everything you need in here to verify that I am, indeed, the rightful heir to Dunhaven Castle."

Mr. Smythe's eyebrows squashed together as he slowly

pulled the folder from Cate's hand. He shook his head, glancing down at it before returning his gaze to her. "Dr. Kensie, I'm not certain you understand. Unless this is a marriage certificate dated February 1, 2019, you are not the heir. You had to be married at the time of inheritance which is effectively Lady Gertrude's date of death."

Cate lifted her chin, swallowing again as her throat went dry. "As you'll see when you open that folder, I was, in fact, married on February 1, 2019. Actually, nearly five years before that in August 2014."

Mr. Smythe flicked the folder open, studying the contents.

"What?" Molly asked behind her. "You're married?"

Mr. Smythe lifted the certificate, his jaw agape and his eyebrow arching. "Apparently, yes. At least, you were. Are you still?"

"Yes," Cate said.

"No divorce? No separations?"

Cate shook her head before she stalked across the room, taking up her original post.

Mr. Smythe blinked as he stared at the paper, his shock apparent.

"I want that verified," Gianna spat.

Mr. Smythe continued to gawk at the sheet with pinched features. "Y-yes, of course. May I keep this?"

Cate nodded. "It's a copy."

"No!" Gianna shouted. "No, this is a lie. You are not and were not married in 2014."

Cate stared at the woman with a blank expression.

Jack studied her, his features betraying his confusion. "You were married when you came here?"

"Yes," Cate said, sliding her eyes to him.

"To who?" he burst.

"To me," a new voice said from the doorway.

19

All eyes turned to the newcomer. Cate's lips curled at the edges as she stared at her spouse of nearly six years. Silence fell over the room's occupants as he strode into the room and spun to face them. "I do not believe I've met all of you formally, but I am Catherine's husband, Duke Marcus Northcott."

CHAPTER 3

Stunned faces stared at the newest arrival to the room before a few flicked to Cate. Mr. Smythe slow-blinked at the man, then glanced down at the certificate again.

Riley bounded across the room to Marcus who scooped him up and rubbed his head. "Hello, Riley."

"Oh, please. You cannot be serious," Gianna said.

Marcus strode across the room toward the brandy decanter. "I believe you will find all the paperwork in order to clear up this matter, Smythe."

"You are married," Mr. Smythe repeated, as though trying to cement the idea in his head.

"Cate, you're married?" Molly questioned.

Marcus poured himself a brandy and spun to face them. "Yes. Since 2014. Turns out your Lady Cate is actually Duchess Cate." He smiled at Cate, tipping her chin up. "Though you've never been much for titles, have you, dear?"

Cate smiled up at him and shook her head. "No."

"I want this checked into," Gianna said, crossing her arms. "Thoroughly."

"Yes, we will, though this all looks to be in order," Mr. Smythe answered, stowing the marriage certificate in the folder and sliding it into his briefcase along with the other.

"So, just to be clear, we're not all out of jobs, homes, and being asked to repay our salaries," Molly questioned.

"No, that is *not* the case," Gianna said, her nostrils flaring.

"Assuming we can verify the marriage certificate and find no evidence of divorce or separation, yes," Mr. Smythe said as he stood.

Marcus crossed the room and slid the pocket watch from the coffee table. "Thank you, Smythe. You'll find nothing but a happy marriage." He returned to Cate's side and set his brandy on the drink cart before he draped the pendant around her neck. "I believe this is yours."

Cate clutched the pocket watch in her hand and offered him a brief smile. "Thank you."

Gianna's lips curled into an expression of disdain. "You think you've won, but you haven't. You should have given us Dunhaven when you had the chance." She spun on her heel and stormed from the room.

Mr. Smythe rose from his seat. "I will be in touch. We will expedite this as much as possible."

"Until the matter is resolved, that woman should be barred from this estate," Marcus said. "She has upset the staff and Catherine."

"Yes, of course," Mr. Smythe said. "We will advise her–"

"Not good enough, Smythe. Tell her in no uncertain terms that Dunhaven Castle and its grounds are off-limits."

Mr. Smythe pressed his lips together in a thin line as he nodded. "Yes, of course. If you will excuse me now, we will return to London posthaste to begin."

"Mr. Smythe, are you certain you won't stay?" Cate asked. "We'd be happy to have you for the night."

"Oh–" he said, smoothing his jacket.

"Really," Cate said, "it's no trouble and certainly more comfortable than a hotel. There are no trains back today."

He snapped his gaze to Gayle before he nodded. "If it isn't any trouble, that would be most appreciated."

"It's no trouble at all," Cate said.

"Thank you, Lady..." Gayle pressed her lips together and offered Cate an apologetic smile. That is, thank you, Your Grace. *That* will take some getting used to." She gave a small chuckle.

"Really, just Cate is always fine," Cate insisted. "And we are happy to have you stay."

"If you don't mind, I'll step out to make some calls to begin the validation process required by the codicil." Mr. Smythe licked his lips and fixed his gaze on Cate. "For what it's worth, I am very sorry for this mess."

"It's okay, Mr. Smythe. And with any luck, it should be cleared up very soon."

He bobbed his head at her before he strode from the room.

"Well," Mrs. Fraser said, rising along with Mr. Fraser, "I can take you up to your room, Ms. Pearson."

"If it's my usual spot, I can find it with no trouble."

"Yes, it is," Mrs. Fraser answered with a nod.

"Then please don't trouble yourself. I'll find my way up."

"I'll send up a tray with your meal. Given the circumstances, Lady–" Mrs. Fraser stopped, fluttering her eyelashes. "Her Grace thought an informal dinner may be best."

"Of course. Thank you." Gayle offered them all a warm smile before she disappeared from the room.

Mrs. Fraser smoothed her dress and clasped her hands in front of her. Cate recognized the gesture. It betrayed how nervous Mrs. Fraser remained over the recent events. "Well, I suppose we should be returning to the kitchen to finish our preparations."

Cate stepped forward and reached for Mrs. Fraser's hands. She gave them a squeeze and offered her a smile. "It's going to be okay, Mrs. Fraser. Mr. Smythe just needs to finish the verification on his end and everything will go back to normal."

Mrs. Fraser glanced over her shoulder at Marcus before her gaze settled on Cate. "And normal or not, meals must still be prepared or we'll all starve!"

Cate broadened her grin at her. "We wouldn't want that."

"I'll send trays up for you both," Mrs. Fraser said, offering a tentative glance at Marcus again.

"Oh," Cate said, glancing at Marcus for a moment, "I would still like to eat dinner with you."

"Oh, surely you–"

"I have several things to see to this evening. I will dine out," Marcus said.

"Well, then we would be most happy to have you, Lady–" Mrs. Fraser closed her eyes, pursing her lips.

"Good," Cate said. "And there's no need to change how you address me. Lady Cate is perfectly fine."

"But not proper," Mrs. Fraser said, tugging her hand free and wagging a finger at her.

Cate gave the woman's hand another squeeze and smiled.

Molly approached and pulled her into a hug. "We'll talk later?"

"Yes," Cate said. "Definitely."

Mr. Fraser offered Cate a simple pat on her shoulder and a tight-lipped smile.

"Ah, do you mind if we discuss a few estate matters that may be changing given the news?" Jack inquired.

Cate nodded at him. "Yes, I think there are a few things that need to be addressed in the short term while we wait for this mess to clear up."

Molly pinched Jack's chin. "Don't work too hard."

"I'll take it easy."

The majority of her staff shuffled from the room, leaving Cate with Marcus and Jack. Jack pushed the doors shut behind the others before he spun to face them. He focused his gaze on Cate, his chest heaving out a deep sigh.

"Cate–"

She held up a hand, stopping his words. "Jack, please."

"Please what? Please help?"

Marcus sipped at his brandy, offering Jack a stony glance over the rim of the glass. "Catherine hardly needs your help."

Jack's jaw tightened as he fixed his gaze on the man, nostrils flaring.

Cate sighed and held up a hand. "Marcus, please."

Marcus clamped his mouth closed with a huff, busying himself with refilling his brandy and pouring another.

Cate flicked her gaze to Jack. "I can explain."

"I sure as hell wish you would because I cannot understand *this*." He flung his hand at Marcus.

The man handed the second brandy to Cate. She accepted the proffered glass, tapping her fingers against it as she stared into the amber liquid.

Jack pressed his hands against his forehead. "I mean, what the hell happened, Cate?"

"So much," Cate breathed, her features pinching.

"Such as?" Jack inquired.

"Such as she focused her energy on rescuing you instead of saving Dunhaven Castle," Marcus spat. "And this is the fallout of that decision."

Jack's eyebrows shot up as he snapped his gaze at the man.

Cate pressed a palm to her forehead, sliding her eyes closed. "Marcus, can you give us a minute?"

Marcus studied her for a moment before setting his glass down. "Of course. We will speak later about the next steps."

Cate nodded as he strode from the room. He offered her a glance before he pulled the doors closed.

Jack ran his fingers through his hair as the latch clicked, blowing out a forceful sigh. "Now can you please tell me what the hell happened to result in *this?*" He gestured toward the closed doors.

"You were gone, Jack." Cate licked her lips, tears glistening in her eyes as she sank into Jack's usual armchair, her voice lowering to a whisper. "You were gone."

Jack perched on the edge of the chair she usually used. "I know. And I'm sorry."

Cate's features pinched, and she pressed her lips together. "You don't need to apologize. I'm not blaming you. I'm sure it was horrible for you. I can't begin to imagine what happened to you or what those people did to you. But on this end, you were gone."

"And you called him?"

Cate stared into the amber liquid, recalling the panicked moments when she realized Jack had been taken. "I called Damien."

She flicked her gaze up to Jack's face. "They brought Marcus."

Jack's brow furrowed, and he cocked his head. "Damien brought Marcus? Damien? The guy who hated this man the last time we saw him?"

Cate's forehead wrinkled, and she took a sip of her brandy. "Apparently, things in the supernatural world change a lot." Her lower lip bobbed up and down for a moment before she took another sip of the amber liquid.

"Apparently," Jack said, his eyebrows shooting up.

Cate blew out a breath as she considered her next words. She flicked her gaze to him. "He stepped up, Jack."

"He didn't kidnap you this time?"

"He saved my life. Multiple times. And yours."

Jack fluttered his eyelashes, his face betraying his lack of understanding.

"He traded himself for you."

Jack stared at her, unblinking.

Cate nodded at him. "Yes. He traded himself for you. You had temporalysis. You were dying. He traded himself for you. You are alive because of him."

Jack pressed his lips together, lowering his eyes to the area rug. "Sorry, I'm just having a difficult time picturing that man as selfless."

"I was shocked, too. But he did. And he endured a substantial amount of torture because of that."

Jack scoffed. "So he says."

"No," Cate said, slamming her glass down on the table. "Not says him. Says me."

Jack's shoulders slumped. "Cate, I'm not calling you a liar. But I think he's manipulative and–"

Cate shook her head, pressing her hand against her chest. "No. You don't understand, I..."

Jack flicked his eyebrows up as her voice trailed off. "Then help me understand. Because I don't."

"He did something to me–"

Jack leapt from his chair, pacing the floor. "I knew it."

"No, nothing bad."

"I'll believe that when you explain."

"I'm trying but...it's difficult. It's...odd."

Jack rolled his eyes. "Not surprising with him."

"When we were searching for you, Gianna tried to kill me. And she nearly succeeded. Marcus worried something would happen to me. He used some sort of magic to link us."

Jack froze, snapping his gaze to her. "Link you?"

"Yes," Cate said, pressing a hand to her heart again. "He cut my hand and his and mixed our blood. He could feel my heart beating inside his chest."

Jack sank into the armchair again, his features pinching as he tried to understand.

"And, despite me being human, I can feel his heartbeat in my chest, too."

Jack's surprised look turned incredulous. "What?"

"I have two heartbeats in my chest. My own and his. I can feel things that happen to him. Major things. Terrible things."

Jack flicked his gaze to the dark fireplace. "My God, Cate."

"That's how I know they did horrible things to him. I felt them, Jack. He traded himself for you knowing he'd live through that. But he did it. He did it so you could live."

Jack balanced his elbows on his thighs and shook his head. "I'm still having a hard time picturing this guy as selfless."

"Hard time or not, he offered himself. Ask Damien, Michael, or Celine. They were all there when he did it. I was there. Damien had to carry me out of the room. And then when his heartbeat woke me up in the middle of the night…"

Cate's features pinched as her voice trailed off.

Jack leapt from his seat and paced around the floor. "Why the hell would he do that do you? Why would he make you go through that? Are you sure it wasn't a setup?"

Cate lifted a shoulder. "He didn't know I would feel his heart. He was surprised. He thought only he would feel mine. But I did." She pressed her hand against her chest again. "I do."

"This is unbelievable," he breathed, perching on the edge of the armchair again. "I was sick?"

"Dying," Cate said. "You were unconscious by the time we found you, and you wouldn't have survived for much longer."

Jack's features pinched. "I remember…I remember odd things happening. One minute it felt like I was here at Dunhaven. And the next…"

"You were back in some cell somewhere, right?"

Jack flicked his gaze to her and nodded. "Yes."

"You had temporalysis. Like me, only more severe. We are assuming Gianna time-hopped you back to 1810, and that's what caused it. Your case would have been fatal."

"Thanks to Dr. Gresham, it wasn't."

"Thanks to Anna Northcott, it wasn't, *and* Dr. Gresham. And as much as you don't want to hear this…Marcus."

Jack slid his eyes shut as he heaved a sigh. He snapped them open again, focusing them on her. "I'm assuming they cured you, too?"

Cate shook her head. "No. Amelia was still working on the cure. But mine wasn't as severe as yours."

"Did you go comatose?"

"No. Marcus had a treatment that mitigated the symptoms. I still passed out a few times and had weird visions, but I always came to within a few minutes."

"So, do you still have it?"

Cate took another sip of her brandy before shaking her head. "Cured."

"By Dr. Gresham?"

"No, mine ran its course."

Jack jumped from the chair again. "Ran its course? How do you know? How can you tell? Cate, are you certain you're not sick?"

"Yes. Marcus said I'm cured."

Jack flung a hand in the air. "Oh, Marcus said. Well, then it must be true."

Cate pursed her lips, her fingers tapping the side of her glass again.

"I'm sorry," Jack said, spinning on his heel and wandering back across the room. "Did he at least give any proof?"

"He said the visions I kept having were of a moment in my future. Some pinnacle point of my life. And once that passed, if I hadn't fallen into a coma or died yet, I'd survive."

"And you experienced the moment? You lived through it?" Jack asked, sinking into the armchair again.

Cate nodded, lowering her eyes to what remained of her drink.

Jack shook his head, letting his chin rest in his palm. "What was it?"

"What?" Cate asked, flicking her gaze back to him.

"What was your moment?"

"Uhh, a ball at Rosenberg Palace."

Jack's features pinched.

"Marcus's mother was…is…I think, a German Duchess. Rosenberg Palace is his maternal side's home."

"What happened at the ball that was so important to you?"

Cate flicked her eyes from his, her forehead crinkling. She sucked in a breath, her lips parted to answer when she shook her head and shrugged. "I-I-I think maybe the narrowing down of suspects as to who had you and where you may be held? I'm honestly not sure." She forced a nervous smile on her face. "It's all a blur that night."

Jack narrowed his eyes at her. "Cate, did something happen?"

Cate swallowed hard, lowering her gaze to the coffee table.

"Cate?" Jack prodded.

She lifted a shoulder again. "After the ball, I got sick."

"From the temporalysis?"

Cate shook her head, her features pinching as she recalled the painful experience. "Gianna put a poisonous snake in my bed. I…"

Jack lunged forward, his fingers clutching the arms of the chair. "What? Did it bite you?"

"Yes," Cate answered, staring ahead, "and I was sick for three days."

Tears filled her eyes. "I'm the reason you were so sick when we got to you, I think."

"No, Cate, I'm certain that's not true."

"Damien said it wasn't. He said they used the time to find you and assess how we'd plan to get you back, but... had I been awake maybe we would have gotten to you faster."

"You can't think like that, Cate."

"But I do."

"I'm sure for those three days you were pestering everyone for information while you recovered."

Cate slid her eyes closed for a moment. "I wasn't conscious."

"Oh, Cate," Jack said with a sigh. "That woman really did a number on us, didn't she?"

"And she continues to be a thorn in our side," Cate said, setting her glass on the table.

"I assume she's behind this latest...situation."

"The codicil? Yes. Marcus's people caught it when we returned with you. He warned me they'd try something like this. You were just being used as a distraction."

Jack chewed his lower lip as he shook his head.

"And to be clear, I did not do what I did just to keep the castle. I would have traded it for you."

"No one thinks that, Cate. I don't think that. They can't take Dunhaven."

"I know."

Jack rubbed his lips before he shot a glance at Cate. "Just to be clear, you weren't married when you first came here, right?"

The statement elicited a chuckle from Cate. "No."

"Just checking. Your marriage certificate is dated 2014."

31

Cate gave him a broad smile as she nodded. "Yeah. Two days ago, we went to 2014, got married, and came back."

Jack let his head fall back onto the cushion behind him. He stared at the ceiling, sighing, before he picked up his head and stared at Cate. "I guess the only thing left to ask is what the hell do we do now?"

CHAPTER 4

*C*ate slumped in the chair as the question hung in the air. The enigma had plagued her since she'd read the codicil. Marcus had offered her a temporary solution, but it remained just that: temporary. They needed to fix this. To reset the clock. But she had no idea how to do that.

Cate flicked her gaze to Jack. "I'm not sure. I hate to say this, but I think we're going to have to rely on Marcus to take the lead."

Jack dropped his head into his hands. "Words I never wanted to hear."

"I'm sorry."

He raised his eyes to her. "It's not your fault. But I'm damned uncomfortable with this. I don't trust that man."

"Noted, but until we have this fixed and The Agency dealt with, we don't have a choice."

Jack clasped his hands, resting his chin against them.

"Sorry, Jack. But look on the bright side. This is only temporary."

"You sure about that?"

"Yes. We both saw him with Celine in 1792. I'm shocked

he even offered to marry me, to begin with. It must be a huge inconvenience for him."

Jack studied her for a moment. "We both saw him with Celine, yes. But we both also saw Celine with him. She detests him."

"Not anymore," Cate answered. "They're practically civil. Even friendly."

Jack wiggled his eyebrows. "Talk about playing the long game, huh?"

Cate chuckled at the statement and slouched back in the chair. "Yep. So, like I said, I'm certain this is temporary, and he'll want this ended as soon as possible. Maybe this is even designed to impress her in some way."

"Thank goodness for small miracles." Jack offered a laugh. "Impress your future wife by marrying another woman. What kind of world do we live in?"

"It gets stranger by the minute." Cate furrowed her brows, squinting at him. "Did you know there are other universes where we make different choices that result in a different world?"

Jack stared ahead blankly for a moment. "Don't say anything else. I can't handle it."

Cate grinned at him. He shot her a shocked glance. "Wait…are we in one of them?"

Cate chuckled again. "Not to my knowledge. I did not even want to glimpse into one when given the chance."

"We really need to have a long conversation about what happened while I was gone once this mess is over."

"Oh, definitely. I'm glad these chairs are comfortable because we're going to be in them for a long, long time to go over everything that happened while you were gone."

"In the meantime, I better let you have a few minutes to yourself. I'm certain the questions at dinner tonight are going to be brutal."

Cate snickered at the statement as Jack rose from the chair. "I've definitely got some explaining to do."

"I don't envy you that," Jack said. "See you soon." He strolled to the doors and disappeared through them with a wave.

Cate slouched in the armchair, letting her head fall against the cushion behind her. With a long breath, she forced herself to her feet, calling the dogs after her. She trudged upstairs, threaded through the halls to her room, and closed herself inside.

She leaned back against the doors, letting the silence envelop her before she shuffled across to her chaise and sank onto it. She rested her head in her hands as the emotions building from the stressful day threatened to overwhelm her.

She pressed her lips together, tears welling in her eyes. A lump formed in her throat, and a sob escaped her. She buried her face in her hands.

A soft knocking sounded at the door as Riley nudged at her elbow. Cate sniffled, wiping at her cheeks. "Come in!"

"Your Grace?" Andrea said, poking her head in through the door. "Just checking to see how everything went."

"As expected, more or less."

Andrea slid through the small opening and eased the door shut behind her. She approached Cate, clasping her hands in front of her. "Would you like to talk about it?"

Cate glanced down at the area rug, sniffling again. "No, I'm fine, thank you."

Andrea offered her a consoling smile. "Why don't I brush your hair before dinner?"

"Oh, you don't-" Cate began before she sucked in a breath and nodded. "Yes, that would be great."

Andrea led her to the dressing table, and Cate sank onto the chair in front of it. Andrea slid the soft bristles through her long hair.

"Gianna showed up for the discussion," Cate said after a few swipes.

Andrea flicked her gaze to Cate's face through the mirror, arching an eyebrow. "Well, *that* wasn't expected, was it? You thought only Mr. Smythe and Gayle would come."

"Yes. And she made things quite uncomfortable."

"I can imagine. How trying for you."

Cate let her forearm slap onto the table, rattling the perfume bottle, music box, and comb. "Do you know she had the nerve to ask my staff to repay their salaries for the year I was here?"

Andrea froze mid-stroke. "No!"

Cate nodded at her. "Oh, yes, she did. She wants everything repaid to her. She was *kind* enough to offer them a payment plan if they couldn't return the funds in one lump sum. *And* she wanted the Frasers' cottage."

"That woman is a menace. Thank goodness you were prepared."

"Yes," Cate said, lowering her eyes to the piano-shaped music box. She propped it open, allowing the sound to soothe her. "I hope it works."

"I have no doubt it will," Andrea said with a reassuring smile.

Cate heaved a sigh, tearing her eyes from the music box to stare at Andrea through the mirror. "I don't put anything past Gianna and The Agency."

"His Grace will undoubtedly have prepared for everything," the woman said, resuming her steady brushing.

Cate stared at the woman a moment longer, pondering if the statement would prove true. She certainly hoped so.

"There we are," Andrea said as she gathered Cate's hair behind her shoulders. "Would you like to change for dinner?"

"No, that's not necessary. I'm dining in the kitchen tonight with you."

"Oh, how lovely, Your Grace." She hesitated a moment, biting into her lower lip before she added, "Will His Grace be joining us?"

Cate chuckled as she rose from the table. "No. I cannot imagine Marcus eating in my kitchen with the staff."

Andrea giggled as Cate spun to face her. "If I may be so bold, Your Grace, neither can I."

Cate pushed the music box closed and drummed her hands against her thighs. "Well, I guess we should head down."

"Are you all right? I could have a tray sent up."

"No, I think I'd better face the music. I'm sure everyone has questions. I just feel...it feels odd lying to them."

"Does Mr. Reid know the truth?"

Cate nodded. "Yes, he does. I owed him that."

"But the others do not."

"No. And they cannot."

"Of course." Andrea wrapped her arm around Cate's shoulders and led her to the door. "Don't worry, Your Grace, if the questions become too uncomfortable, I will merely spill my soup and cause a scene."

Cate smiled at her, flicking her gaze sideways as they strode through the door. "Thank you, Andrea. I can always count on you."

They made their way to the kitchen below stairs with the dogs in tow. The sweet smell of cinnamon filled the room.

Cate wandered to her seat at the table as Mrs. Fraser pulled a steaming apple pie from the oven and set it on the stove.

"Looks like you've been busy," Cate said, inhaling a deep breath of the delicious scent.

"Indeed, we have," Molly said with a grin as she set a bowl of leafy green salad in the center of the table. "Figured we'd bake a celebratory pie now that we're not all homeless and broke."

Cate squashed her lips together and shook her head. "I am sorry about this."

Molly crinkled her forehead. "Sorry about what? It's not your fault."

"Nay, it isn't, Lady...oh," Mrs. Fraser said, tapping her cheek, "old habits, Your Grace. If it's anyone's fault it would be Mr. Smythe, but I cannae even blame him. He's usually ever so cautious."

"I can't believe something like this would slip past him," Mr. Fraser chimed in.

"I can't believe you're married!" Molly exclaimed, plopping into a seat across from Cate with a grin. "I'm glad. Not only because it's saving our collective rear ends but also for you."

Cate smiled at her. "Thank you."

"Now wait just a minute before we go congratulating her," Mrs. Fraser said as she set a loaded plate of stew in front of Cate. She studied Cate's face with narrowed eyes. "Are you happy?"

Cate smiled up at the woman. "Yes," she said with a nod.

Mrs. Fraser plopped into a seat. "All right, then, I suppose congratulations are in order. Though belated for nearly five years. What in the world has he been doing all this time?"

"Things," Cate said, concentrating on her plate. "We don't have the most traditional relationship."

Molly poked her fork toward Cate after popping a grape tomato into her mouth. "You know, I think I've seen him around campus a few times. He's just one of those men who make an impression. I had no idea you two were married."

"How did you meet?" Mrs. Fraser asked.

"Through friends," Cate answered, shaking the salt shaker with too much vigor.

"Well, even if he hasn't been here the entire time, he seems pretty devoted. I mean, the moment Jack went..." Molly slid her eyes sideways to Jack, the smile slipping from her features. She flicked her eyes back to Cate. "He came as soon as you needed him."

"He did, yes."

"And we are ever so grateful for that," Mrs. Fraser said with a curt nod.

Molly stabbed a carrot with her fork. "Plus, Riley seems to adore him."

The statement brought a smile to Cate's face as she pushed her stew around on her plate. "He does. There is a good reason for that."

Jack snapped his gaze up.

"Marcus gave me Riley. Riley is actually a pup from Marcus's mother's dog, Athena."

"Really? Aww, that's so sweet," Molly said with a grin.

Jack narrowed his eyes at her, and she offered him a subtle nod to verify the truth of the statement.

"Yes. I really needed Riley after my parents died."

"I'll bet," Molly said, reaching across the table to grab Cate's hand.

"Well, we certainly are grateful to him for appearing today," Mrs. Fraser said. "I hope Mr. Smythe can clear this matter up quickly so that horrid woman can go back to whatever foundation she has and worry about stealing someone else's inheritance!"

Cate smiled at her as she scooped up a beef-soaked celery stalk. "My fingers are crossed."

"As are mine. And my toes," Mrs. Fraser said with a chuckle. "The nerve of that woman to act like Dunhaven doesn't belong to you."

"And ask us to pay back our salaries!" Molly exclaimed. "I mean, is she serious?"

Jack scoffed at the statement.

"I am so sorry she's doing this," Cate said again.

"It's not your fault," Mrs. Fraser insisted.

"Let's hope it's over soon enough."

"Mr. Smythe is nothing but efficient, so with any luck, he'll have this wrapped up, and we can get back to planning your first-year anniversary."

Molly's eyes went wide. "Oh my goodness!"

"What?" Mrs. Fraser questioned. "You dinnae forget, did you?"

"No, but…" Molly fluttered her eyelashes. "What do you think Mrs. Campbell will say when she finds out you're married to a duke?"

Cate opened her mouth to answer, but no words came. She crinkled her forehead, trying to imagine Mrs. Campbell's reaction to the news which would surely spread like wildfire through the town. Her eyebrows raised as her nose wrinkled. She slid her eyes closed. They really needed to fix this situation before she ended up at another 1810-like ball complete with blaring trumpets announcing their arrival. Her fork clattered to her plate.

"Oh, she'll likely have the entire event planned around playing up that aspect," Mrs. Fraser said, wagging her finger in the air. "The ninny will become more of a thorn in your side than she already is. That's what'll happen."

"I'm certain His Grace would be most happy to celebrate Her Grace's one-year anniversary at Dunhaven," Andrea said with a smile.

Molly waggled her fork as she eyed Andrea. "So, do you actually work for him?"

"Yes," Andrea said as she raised her water glass to her lips.

"Oh, for how long?" Molly questioned.

"Long enough," Andrea said with a chuckle.

Cate drew in a long breath and licked her lips. "Let's hope

this whole mess is cleared up before the anniversary party and plans can continue as they were. Happy or not, I'm sure Marcus has other things on his plate."

"Well, we'll take it one day at a time. But for now, let's have pie," Mrs. Fraser said, rising from her seat and gathering several plates.

"That sounds like an excellent plan," Molly said as she joined her.

The group shared the buttery, rich dessert before they broke up for the evening. With the dogs in tow, Cate dragged herself up the stairs, ready to stretch out in bed and try to forget the day.

She pushed into the downstairs hall, shuffling toward the main staircase. As she entered the foyer, her eyes snapped to the stairs where a figure leaned against the banister. Riley and Bailey growled. Cate stiffened, her heart thudding against her ribs.

"Hello, little mouse," Gianna said, her lips curling into a derisive smile.

CHAPTER 5

"What are you doing here?" Cate demanded, her muscles stiff and her pulse racing.

The woman crossed her arms and slowly sashayed toward Cate. "You're full of surprises today. Married? To the Duke himself?" She paused, arching an eyebrow. "Well played, Cate. Though it won't help."

"Get out, Gianna."

She positioned herself inches from Cate's face, lowering her voice to a whisper. "You're just staving off the inevitable. We're going to win. And when we do, it's going to leave you in ruins."

The woman smacked into Cate as she stalked past her, knocking her back a step. She grabbed the doorknob and swung the front door open.

Cate glared after her. "Gianna," she called as the woman stepped into the night air.

Gianna twisted to face her, her blonde hair swinging.

"I'll never let you win."

The corner of Gianna's lips turned up on one side. "We'll see."

She spun on her heel and slammed the door. Cate jumped, squeezing her eyes closed as she allowed her heartbeat to slow.

"Catherine, is something wrong?"

The voice startled Cate into opening her eyes. She spun to find Marcus hurrying down the stairs.

Cate sighed, pressing a hand to her forehead. "Gianna was here."

His eyes went wide, and he set his hands on her shoulders. "Are you all right?"

"Yes, I'm fine. She didn't do anything to me outside of her usual threats."

Marcus sighed, flicking his gaze to the floor. "We should go up and speak more privately."

Cate nodded, and they climbed the stairs with the dogs trailing after them. "Our plan is going to work, right?"

"Yes, but it is only a short-term solution. The win will be short-lived as they will be quickly working a new angle," he said as they reached the top of the stairs and continued through the hall.

Cate let her head fall back between her shoulder blades. Short-term solution, just as she suspected. How long before he tired of it? "We need to fix this."

"I'm working on that."

"How?" Cate asked.

Marcus studied her for a moment before stalking away from her. "It may be best–"

"Don't do that," Cate said.

He twisted to face her. "You do not even know what I'm about to say."

"You're about to say it may be best if I stay out of it. And I'm not going to do that. I will not be shut out of this fight."

Marcus's nostrils flared as he clasped his hands behind his back. "You are extremely stubborn."

"Yes, I am," Cate said, lifting her chin. "It's one of those endearing things you can mention about why you married me."

A smile played on his lips. "And how did the conversation go with your gardener regarding our recent yet not-so-recent nuptials?"

Cate's shoulder slumped, and she heaved a sigh. "I don't know what's more maddening. Gianna showing up unannounced twice or you referring to Jack as my gardener."

"If the shoe fits."

"Except it doesn't. He is not only my estate manager, but he is a very good friend. And he also is a very large part of protecting this estate."

"And I assume not only will you not be shut out of the fight, but you will not allow him to be either."

Cate cocked her head, smiling at him. "You are very bright."

Marcus puckered his lips as he sucked in a breath. "Fine, though if he prevents us from doing what we need to do–"

"He won't."

"I'll leave his management to you, entirely, dear."

Cate crossed her arms, drumming her fingers on her forearm. "So, what are our next steps?"

"That remains to be seen, though I have my suspicions that we will be seeking another missing person."

Cate slowed her steps, snapping her gaze at him. "Do you think she'll come after someone else in the house like Molly? Or Jack again?"

"No, I believe The Agency may prefer your predecessor."

"Gertrude?" Cate asked as they arrived outside of her bedroom.

"Yes. It's obvious they've had contact with her. Hence, the codicil."

Cate crinkled her forehead. "And you think they're still in contact with her?"

"I think they will attempt to strong-arm her into changing her will to ensure you cannot inherit, though given her mindset, it will be an uphill battle."

"Given her mindset?" Cate questioned.

"I can only assume they pressured her into changing the will though she found the idea of letting the estate go outside of the family to be less-than-favorable, hence the codicil. The Agency likely allowed it to slip believing it achieved their goal."

Cate pressed her lips together, studying the thick red carpet under her feet. "And now that it doesn't..." Her voice trailed off, and she chewed her lower lip.

"They'll try several angles, I would imagine. One of which will be to pressure Gertrude MacKenzie further. By any means necessary."

Cate flicked her eyes up to his and sighed. "And we both know what that means."

The corners of Marcus's lips turned up, and he rubbed her shoulders. "We'll fix this."

"Should we have done something else?" Cate asked. "Like stop them from taking her."

"We would likely be unable to do that. I'm certain they had unfettered access to Gertrude already. All that remains is to locate her and stop them."

"Won't they just do it again?" Cate pressed a hand against her forehead as her muscles tensed. "This is a losing battle."

"It is not."

Cate pressed her lips together, steadying her breath as her emotions threatened to bubble over.

Marcus put his hands on her shoulders again. "Catherine, we will find a way."

Cate nodded without making eye contact with him.

"Catherine," he prodded, tilting her chin up with his finger, and raising his eyebrows as her eyes met his.

"Okay."

"Your trust in me is most concerning."

Cate crossed her arms, shrugging. "Sorry, I've just never faced anything like this before."

"Which is why I wish you'd let me handle it, but you stubbornly refuse to allow me to do that."

Cate's lips tugged up at the corners, and she eyed Marcus. "I'm not going to do that. This is my problem–"

"*Our* problem, dear, we are married."

Cate broadened her smile, a chuckle escaping her lips. "You really got the worse end of for better or worse, didn't you?"

"I would not change a thing, Catherine. Now, get some rest. You'll need it."

Cate nodded. "Thank you."

He stepped past her, and she pushed her door open, hurrying inside.

"Oh, Catherine," he said, spinning to face her again.

"Yes?" she asked, leaning against the closed second door.

"They will not bang their heads against a brick wall."

Cate crinkled her brow, pulling her chin back.

"The answer to your question of won't they just do this again. They will not bang their heads against a brick wall. They'll move on to another target. We just need to stay ahead of them as much as possible."

Cate fluttered her eyelashes as she attempted to understand the statement. *Another target? When would this end?*

She flicked her gaze to Marcus's dark eyes.

"Just like we did this time," he added, brandishing his wedding band.

Cate forced a smile on her face and nodded. "Goodnight, Marcus."

"Goodnight, Catherine."

She stepped back and eased her door closed. With a sigh, she leaned against it. Fears raced across her mind faster than she could process them. Her face pinched as she worried about the future. She stared down at her ring finger as images of their rushed wedding danced across her mind.

"Trust me," he'd said after she'd read the changed version of the will. He'd offered her his hand, and she'd accepted it.

They'd traveled to 2014. He'd somehow had everything prepared. A dress, a church, even flowers. Their wedding would appear legitimate to anyone outside looking in. There wouldn't even be the question of a hurried ceremony.

Cate crossed the room and opened the lid of the piano music box. The lilting tune filled the air. She sucked in a deep breath as she pressed the box to her chest and shuffled to the bedroom. She set the music box on the nightstand and kicked her shoes off, sinking onto the edge of the bed with a sigh.

How long would the farce continue? How long before Marcus tired of the games and left her to fight The Agency on her own?

She pursed her lips and closed her eyes, letting the music push out all the worry. They would solve this and The Agency would move on to a new target. And Marcus would move on.

Everything would return to normal, she assured herself. The situation was only temporary.

"And exhausting," she said as Riley tapped her knee with his paw.

"I'm tired, too, buddy," Cate said, lifting him onto the bed as Bailey scrambled onto the bed himself. "Wow, you're getting good at that, Bailey."

The little dog wagged his pigtail before circling and plopping down. Riley cuddled next to him with a sigh, laying his head across his canine companion's side.

"I really should change but I'm worn out. All that stress from Gianna did me in, boys." She leaned against the pillow, pulling her feet up onto the bed. "I'll go in just a few minutes."

* * *

Random images flitted across Cate's mind. Her heart pounded as she raced through the halls of the castle. A scream split the silence, and she froze, gasping before she plowed forward again.

As she rounded a corner, the world melted around her.

Cate gasped in a breath, her eyes fluttering open. Tinkling music still filled the air in the lit room. Her forehead wrinkled, and she pushed herself up to sit.

Two sleeping dogs curled at the bottom of the bed. Cate shifted her gaze from them to her own legs. She still wore her clothes.

A glance at the clock told her she'd been asleep for hours. With a sigh, she forced herself off the bed and changed into her pajamas before she slipped under the sheets. The music box continued to play in the darkness.

She closed her eyes, and let the music wash over her. Her mind returned to the reason she'd awoken. A nightmare had pulled her from her slumber.

Her pulse quickened. Nightmare? Nightmares had been what had kicked off the entire chain of events that landed them where they were now.

Why was she still having them? Cate rolled onto her side, tugging the covers higher. Her heart skipped a beat. Had her temporalysis resurfaced?

She swallowed hard as she snuggled deeper into the

pillow. Maybe it was just a normal nightmare. Probably prompted by Gianna's appearance today.

Yes, Cate thought to herself as she drifted back to sleep, *just a normal nightmare.*

When her eyes opened again, streaks of red painted the sky outside her window. She glanced at her clock and groaned, rolling onto her back.

Riley waddled up the bed, giving her a kiss on the cheek.

"Good morning, buddy," she said, stroking his head as he collapsed into her.

He yawned widely before snuggling his head into her arm.

"I feel the same way, Riley."

Bailey picked his head up and wagged his tail before letting it fall back down.

She lay in bed stroking Riley's soft fur for a few moments longer as random thoughts flitted through her mind. She wrinkled her nose as she recalled the nightmare she'd had. The thought drove her to rise.

"Okay, buddy, time to get up. We have to face the day, like it or not."

She wound the music box that had stopped playing at some point overnight and left it tinkling on her nightstand as she tugged on her robe and stretched.

She crossed the room and pulled open her door, finding Andrea waiting on the opposite side with her hands clasped in front of her.

"Good morning, Your Grace," she said with a broad smile.

Cate stood to the side and motioned for Andrea to enter. "Good morning, Andrea. I'm sorry, I overslept."

Andrea bustled past her, crossed into the bedroom, and tugged open a drawer to begin assembling Cate's clothes. "Quite all right, Your Grace. I did not hear anyone stirring so I waited."

"Sorry to have you standing out there."

"It's no problem at all," Andrea said with a smile. "I'm so pleased to hear that you slept."

"Yes, I did," Cate said as she sank into the seat at her vanity. "I fell asleep in my clothes."

"Oh, no. This is why you shouldn't have dismissed me after dinner. I would have made sure you changed."

Cate met her gaze through the mirror. "I know. But I survived, and look, I ended up in my pajamas anyway."

Andrea brushed through Cate's hair, an amused grin on her features. "Soon, you won't even need me, Your Grace."

"I used to change my own clothes once upon a time," Cate said with a chuckle.

"But now you have me."

Cate gave her a tight-lipped smile and a nod, staring down at the vanity top. She traced a scratch on it with her finger absentmindedly.

"Are you quite sure you slept well, Your Grace?"

Cate flicked her gaze up and nodded. "Yes. It's just this tension. It's killing me."

"I'm certain it's very nerve-wracking. I hope it's over soon."

"You and me both."

Andrea finished with her hair and assisted Cate with her dressing, folding her pajamas and stowing them away before hanging up her robe.

They parted ways at the foyer doors, with Cate taking the dogs out and Andrea continuing downstairs. After their stroll around the castle, Cate pushed through the door into the kitchen.

"Good morning, Your Grace," Mrs. Fraser said with a smile and waved a finger in the air. "I remembered this morning. See what a good night's sleep will do for you?"

"Good morning, Mrs. Fraser," Cate said, "though, again, the formality really isn't needed."

"Do you like Duchess Cate better?" Molly asked as she filled a bowl with brown sugar.

"I like just Cate. I hadn't even gotten used to Lady Cate yet."

"And the whole time you were holding out on us." Molly winked at her.

"And this is why," Cate said with a chuckle.

Molly wrinkled her nose in a silent giggle.

"Oh, Mr. Smythe requested a working breakfast in the library. He said it applies to Ms. Pearson, as well."

"Oh? He really feels quite terrible about all this, I think. I do feel bad that he's working over breakfast, though I'm surprised he's not skipping the meal entirely and leaving to make the train."

Mrs. Fraser wiped her hand against her apron as she set bowls on a tray. "There's been a change of plans on that front, too. He's asked to stay an extra day, possibly two."

"Oh!" Cate exclaimed. "That's perfectly fine. I hope he can enjoy a few days off."

Molly froze, her jaw hanging open. "Ahhh, I didn't get the impression he'd be taking any time off."

Cate raised her eyebrows, sticking a hand on her hip as Jack entered with Mr. Fraser. Greetings were given before Cate drove the conversation back to Mr. Smythe's change of plans.

"What gave you the impression Mr. Smythe is staying for work?"

Molly pressed her lips together and shot a glance at Mrs. Fraser.

The older woman finished transferring oatmeal into a server and set it on the tray. "He asked us all to be upstairs before breakfast for another announcement."

Cate's jaw flapped open. "*Another* announcement?"

"Mmm, that's what he said," Mrs. Fraser said with a nod.

"I'm not certain I can take another announcement," Jack said, running his fingers through his hair.

"You and me both," Cate said. "I suppose we should head up."

Mrs. Fraser nodded, lifting a tray filled with bowls and utensils. "I suppose. I personally miss the days when announcements were *not* made."

Cate glanced around the kitchen in search of the tea and teacups. "Is there something I can carry?" Cate asked.

"Nay, you know better than that. If it's tea you're in search of, it's already upstairs. Your husband is an early riser, and he's been with Mr. Smythe for over an hour."

Cate sucked in a deep breath as she shuffled behind the women carrying their breakfast. She shot a nervous glance at Jack.

"You ready for this?" he whispered.

"I don't know. But stay after. We need to talk."

Jack nodded as they paraded up the stairs and to the library. Mr. Smythe sat with paperwork spread around him. Gayle tapped around on her laptop in the chair next to him. Marcus stared out the window in front of the desk, sipping his tea.

"Breakfast, everyone," Mrs. Fraser announced as she bustled through the doors.

"Thank you," Mr. Smythe said without glancing up from his papers.

Marcus flicked his gaze to them as they entered, his lips curling into a smile as Cate entered. "Good morning." He set his teacup in the saucer and slid it onto the desk. "Good morning, Catherine, did you sleep well?"

"Yes, thank you."

He clasped her shoulder and rubbed it. "Good. There is news. Sit down."

Cate took a seat on the sofa as Marcus strode across the room, pouring a cup of tea and adding sugar before passing it to her. She accepted the drink, sipping at it as she studied the attorney.

He tugged off his reading glasses and set the paperwork aside. "I am sorry to have called you all together again, but there is news. And, as this affects everyone, I felt it easiest to tell you all at once."

"Yes, of course, Mr. Smythe," Cate said. "What is it?"

"Has there been any progress on verifying the marriage?" Molly asked as she sank onto the arm of the sofa.

"Nothing is open yet in the States, but I will call the moment it is," Gayle said with a smile and a flutter of her eyelashes.

The woman's second gesture made Cate's heart skip a beat. Bad news loomed. She flicked her gaze to Marcus, who, as always, appeared unflustered.

"What is the news, Mr. Smythe?" she asked.

Mr. Smythe pressed his lips into a thin line. "Assuming the marriage is verified, a new issue has cropped up."

"Which is?" Cate inquired with raised eyebrows.

Mr. Smythe licked his lips, scanning the group. "Ms. Caruso is challenging the claim."

"What?" Molly questioned.

"How?" Jack asked.

"Can she legally do that? We've met the terms of the codicil," Cate said.

"She isn't challenging the will," Mr. Smythe said, "she's challenging your marriage. She's suing you for fraud."

CHAPTER 6

*C*ate choked on her tea, sputtering a cough out as she lowered the teacup to the saucer. "Fraud?"

Marcus slid a hand onto Cate's shoulder and squeezed.

"Whoa," Molly shouted. "What? How?"

Mr. Smythe huffed out a sigh and shook his head. "She has managed to find an attorney willing to claim that your marriage is a sham. Preposterous, I know, however, they may convince a judge to take the case. Though even if they do, I would be surprised if it made it to trial." He lowered his gaze, flicking his eyebrows up and cocking his head. "Though stranger things have happened."

"How can she do this? On what basis?" Molly babbled.

Jack studied Mr. Smythe. "How likely is it that it *doesn't* make it to trial?"

"That's hard to say. I'm surprised any attorney would file this, though, some have no scruples."

"This is insane," Molly exclaimed, pacing the floor.

Cate grabbed her hand and squeezed it. She eased onto the sofa next to Cate, wrapping her arm around her.

"Mr. Smythe, can you explain what exactly she's accusing

us of?" Cate asked, patting Molly's hand.

"Simply put, she claims your marriage is fraudulent. Designed only to collect the inheritance."

Molly let her hand slap against her thigh. "How can that be? She was married five years before she inherited this place! How could she know?"

Mr. Smythe nodded at the statement. "The case could be made that she was aware of the familial connection, knew about the provision, and married to ensure her inheritance."

"But I didn't know," Cate said while Molly exclaimed, "That's ridiculous."

Jack sighed, scrubbing his face with his hands.

"I'm merely suggesting how the other side may frame this. It's my job to anticipate their next move and counter it."

"So, what do we do?" Cate asked.

"Yeah, how can you prove they didn't marry for money and that they really love each other?" Molly asked.

Cate shot Marcus an uncomfortable glance, heat rising in her cheeks. The corners of his lips turned up, and he squeezed her shoulder again.

Mr. Smythe slid several documents toward him and tapped his index finger against them. "We can make a strong case to ask for a dismissal."

Molly crinkled her nose. "How?" She flicked her gaze to Cate. "Oh, sorry."

"It's fine. Molly makes a good point. How?"

"On top of the fact that you married nearly five years before your inheritance, we have several other things that play in our favor. We can make the case that your separate addresses were due strictly to your employment. And, of course, His Grace's will can be used. We have not yet discussed your will and it would appear disingenuous to create it now, though we should deal with it after this matter has concluded."

Cate scrunched her eyebrows. "I'm sorry, Marcus's will?"

"Yes," Mr. Smythe said, retrieving the papers he'd patted earlier and waving them. "In most instances of fraudulent marriages, assets are kept separately, however, since yours are not, we have a solid case that the union is legitimate."

"What do you mean ours are not?" Cate inquired.

"Oh, my apologies, I assumed you were aware. Since one month following your nuptials, all estate assets are bequeathed to you and/or any children from your union, including..." He flipped through the document. "All monetary assets, which are substantial, the Stratfordshire estate, the Wintervale country estate, the London townhouse, the Maine estate, the house in Martinique, and Rosenberg Palace."

Cate's eyelashes fluttered as he read the list. Jack slow-blinked before flicking a stunned gaze in Cate's direction.

"Whoa," Molly murmured, "that's a lot of houses."

"Right, of course," Cate breathed out.

"Again, in situations where fraud is being committed, typically there is a separation of assets so that one party cannot benefit from the phony marriage. Or there is a pre-nuptial agreement in place to prevent the distribution of assets."

"And no such agreement exists," Marcus said. "Catherine and I wed for genuine reasons."

Mr. Smythe nodded. "Which is why I believe we'll have a solid rationale to request this claim be dismissed."

"Right," Cate said with a nod.

"What will happen if they don't dismiss the case?" Jack inquired.

"There will be a trial and the judge will make a determination," Mr. Smythe said.

"What are our chances in a trial?" Cate asked.

"Good, though I think we stand a good chance of avoiding that as well."

"Does it matter that no one really knew about our marriage?" Cate questioned.

Mr. Smythe knit his brow. "No. Obviously, some people knew. We can ask them for statements to present if we need them. The other side may try to argue that the secrecy indicates deceit on your part, but a statement from the dowager Duchess should put that to rest."

"Anna?" Cate asked, her eyebrows shooting up.

"Of course, dear. Mother would be happy to attest to our nuptials. You know how she feels about you."

"The dowager Duchess is fond of her?" Mr. Smythe asked, clicking his pen and pressing it to the paper.

"Mother adores Catherine. And of course, she would be happy to provide the necessary documents to prove that our little Riley," Marcus said, scooping up the small dog and stroking his fur, "was mothered by her beloved Athena and given to Catherine as a wedding present."

"Excellent, yes, that is excellent. It's those sorts of details that will make the authenticity of your union obvious." Mr. Smythe scribbled a few notes onto his legal pad before he clicked the pen again and stuffed it into his suit jacket pocket.

He gathered his notes and slid them into the briefcase. "If you don't mind, I will set up a temporary workspace in your office."

"Not at all."

Mrs. Fraser rose, adjusting her skirt and motioning to the oatmeal tureen. "And please take some breakfast. You'll need food to help with your work."

Gayle rose and smiled at the woman. "Thank you, Mrs. Fraser. I'll prepare food for both of us. Mr. Smythe, I will meet you in just a few moments."

He nodded at the petite blonde before scurrying from the room, already pressing his cell phone to his ear.

"I'll help you carry the meal, Gayle," Mrs. Fraser said, pouring more tea into their teacups and loading them onto a tray.

"Oh, thank you, that would be lovely."

Molly patted Cate's shoulder. "I should head downstairs and finish the breakfast clean up."

Cate rose as Molly did and offered her a hug. "Thanks, Molly."

"Stay strong, honey."

"Thank you," Cate said with a smile.

"You wanted me to stay?" Jack asked.

"Yes," Cate said with a nod. "If you have the time."

"I've got nothing but time. No one will let me do anything."

"Good," Cate said, raising her eyebrows. "You shouldn't be working yet."

"She's right. Better listen to the boss," Molly said with a grin.

"Guess I'll be down to sit around and steal cookies when we're finished. Better get some of those scotchies in the oven. They're my favorite. Don't tell Mrs. Fraser."

"I wouldn't dream of it. As far as she's concerned, you're a shortbread-or-die guy." Molly winked at him before she strode from the room with Mr. Fraser.

Jack smiled at her as she pulled the doors closed behind her.

Cate collapsed into the chair behind her, heaving a sigh as Marcus poured himself another cup of tea. He arched an eyebrow at her. "Drink your tea, Catherine."

Cate raised her gaze to him. "Don't tell me to drink my tea. We're being sued for committing fraud."

"Wrongfully."

Cate flicked her eyebrows up.

Marcus stirred milk into his tea. "We are being wrongfully sued."

Cate leapt from her seat. "Except we're not. We committed fraud. We didn't get married six years ago, we got married two days ago for the exclusive purpose of maintaining control of Dunhaven Castle."

"Yes, but only you, me, and the gardener know that."

Jack screwed up his face, snapping his gaze at Marcus. "Hey."

"He's not my gardener," Cate said through clenched teeth with her hands on her hips.

"My point, Catherine, is that to the rest of the world, we have not committed fraud. To the rest of the world, we have been happily married for nearly six years."

Cate rubbed at her temples, sucking in a deep breath. "What if we can't prove that?"

"We can. The burden lies on them. There is no way we could have known when Gertrude MacKenzie could die. If our marriage was fraudulent you'd likely not be named in my will as the sole beneficiary. There's the story about Riley. All the appropriate things are in place to assure a positive result."

Cate sank onto the sofa, blowing out a long breath. Her brow crinkled, and she glanced up at him. "Yeah, how is that working with Riley? How did he get to that pet store?"

Marcus rolled his eyes at her. "Honestly, Catherine. I took Riley to that store and paid the woman to sell him to you."

Cate arched an eyebrow. Jack shot her a glance, his features pinched.

"And when did you add me to your will?"

"One month after we wed. Have you not been paying attention, dear?"

Cate offered him an annoyed glance.

"What's the out?" Jack asked.

"Excuse me?" Marcus shot back.

"There has to be an out. Something that prevents her from actually claiming your estate in the event that something happens. I'm just trying to figure out what The Agency will throw out there next."

Marcus sipped his tea, stalking to the window and staring out at the rain that now steadily fell from the gray skies. "There is no such 'out' as you put it."

"So," Jack said, narrowing his eyes at the man as he tapped his chin, "if you were to drop over dead, Cate would inherit your entire estate?"

Marcus twisted to stare at him, arching an eyebrow. "You're cleverer than you look."

Cate shot Jack an unimpressed stare.

"I'm sorry, I'm a bit shocked is all," Jack said, flinging a hand in the air.

"I don't see why. It is, after all, my duty to ensure that in the event of my demise, my lovely wife is well taken care of."

"I suppose that makes it look legitimate," Cate said with a sigh, rising from the couch and stalking across the room. She rubbed a hand across her forehead. "Let's hope it works."

"It will work," Marcus assured her.

She nodded without speaking.

"Catherine," he said, approaching her, "it will work. You must stop fretting over the things we already have in hand."

She flicked her gaze to him. "Do we? We didn't expect to be sued for fraud."

"Yes, we did. I told you they would try multiple angles. This is a distraction. To stop you from tracking the source of the problem." He raised his eyebrows. "And it appears to be working."

"It isn't. But we have to deal with this unanticipated problem."

"It has been dealt with. And now we must focus on

others."

Cate furrowed her brow as she slid her gaze to the window again.

"Focus, Catherine."

"Ease off. Give her a minute," Jack shouted from across the room. He stormed toward Cate, wrapping an arm around her. "Why don't you sit down, Cate?"

Marcus huffed out a breath as Jack spun her away from the window.

"This is why I suggested you not be involved. The Agency will not attack you on one level. They will throw a dozen things at you at once. They have the resources to do so. And if you cannot prioritize you will lose."

"That's enough!" Jack barked.

Cate wrapped her arms around her midriff and shook her head, pressing her lips into a thin line. "He's right."

"Cate–"

Cate cut her gaze to Jack. "No, he's right." Cate sucked in a deep breath and shifted her focus to Marcus. "Okay, what do we need to do?"

"You need to stop fretting over our marriage and allow the measures already in place to do their work. Then we need to attempt to track down Gertrude and remove her from The Agency's reach."

Cate licked her lips and nodded. "Right."

"And how exactly do you propose we do that?"

"By following the clues," Marcus said after another sip of his tea.

"Which means what, exactly? And how does this solve our problem?"

Marcus narrowed his eyes and stared at Jack before he cut his gaze to Cate. "Must we include him?"

"Now, just a minute–" Jack began, wagging a finger at Marcus.

Cate pressed a hand against his chest, stopping him.

"Yes, we must," Cate answered.

Marcus arched an eyebrow, his lips forming a frown.

"Humor me," she said.

With another sigh, he nodded. "Fine. Let me explain it as though you were a child. We must determine where The Agency is holding Gertrude. She could be anywhere."

"Or in any time," Cate added.

"Correct, Catherine. We must begin with the limited information we have and use it along with my considerable skills and resources to continue to track the woman until we find her. Once we do, we must convince her to restore the original will."

Jack wrinkled his nose, frowning at Marcus.

"So, the intention is to return things back to normal. Back to Cate not being married to you."

"The intention is to restore history to the original version as closely as possible," Marcus answered.

The two men glared at each other.

Cate held her hands in the air. "Okay, what clues do we have?"

Marcus tore his eyes away from Jack, fixing them on Cate. He slid his phone from his pocket and toggled on the display. "We have this man leaving the offices of Smythe, Smith, and Smithon in 2009."

Cate stared at the pixelated image on the screen. "So, we go to 2009."

Marcus shook his head. "This man is in the employ of this man." He flicked to another picture.

Cate stared at the smiling face of a middle-aged man. She narrowed her eyes at the picture, cocking her head.

"So, we find this guy? How?" Jack asked.

Cate pointed a finger at the display. "Didn't we see him at The Business Summit?"

Marcus's lips curled into a smile. "Very good, Catherine."

"Arnold Chapman, oil exec," Cate said.

Marcus raised his eyebrows. "Very impressive, dear. Yes. Arnold Chapman."

"So, he's our first lead," Cate said. "How can we get access to him?"

"Now, you're focused," he said with a wink.

"If we know when the fake will was planted, why not just intercept it?" Jack asked.

"Because that does little to solve the overall issue, doesn't it?" Marcus answered. "We need to determine if they have Gertrude and where. We'll start with Arnold Chapman."

"And where will we find him?" Cate pressed.

"I happen to know he's hosting a party on May 15, 1956, at his London home."

"When do we leave?" Cate asked.

Jack rubbed his chin. "We need time to plan. And time to drive to London."

Marcus squinted at him before sliding his eyes to Cate. "Must we take him?"

Cate cocked her head, tugging back one corner of her lips.

Marcus rolled his eyes with a disgusted sigh. "Fine."

"There's no way you're taking Cate to London without me," Jack said, crossing his arms.

"I assume you have an invitation to this party," Cate asked.

"Of course. For myself and my wife."

"Whoa, just a minute," Jack said.

Cate fluttered her eyelashes at Marcus. "Surely you can manage an invitation for your good friend, Jack."

Marcus pressed his lips into a thin line. "I am a warlock, Catherine, not a miracle worker."

Cate crossed her arms, eyeing him with an unimpressed

stare.

He sighed, glancing at the rain falling from the skies. "I'm certain I will manage an invite for the gardener."

"He's not–"

Marcus held his hand up. "I know, I know."

Jack rubbed his chin. "That still doesn't solve the problem of driving. We'll need to go back, leaving time to drive, go to the party, investigate, and drive back. Now, we've done days in the past before, but we'll need to let everyone know we're unreachable for a few hours at least–"

"That's not necessary," Cate said with a shake of her head.

Jack furrowed his brow. "What do you mean? The party is in London."

"Marcus has the ability to open time portals that end up wherever we'd like whenever we'd like."

The confused expression on Jack's face morphed into astonishment. "So..." His lower lip bobbed up and down but no more words came out.

"We should talk about that because they're quite different than traveling through our time rips," Cate said.

"Obviously," Jack huffed out. "So, we'll only need the time for the party. We may be only gone for a few minutes then, right?"

Marcus groaned and rolled his eyes as he stalked away. "I'll leave you to explain this. We should leave as soon as possible."

"We'll be ready in a few minutes," Cate answered as he strode from the room. He offered her a nod and pulled the doors closed behind him.

Jack wandered across the room and collapsed into an armchair. He scrubbed his face with his hands. "This is insane."

Cate eased into the chair across from him. "And it's about to get crazier."

CHAPTER 7

*J*ack snapped his gaze to Cate. "What? Why?"

He let his head fall back onto the thick cushion behind him and covered his face. "Oh, maybe don't tell me. I don't want to know."

Cate sucked in a breath, allowing him a moment to settle.

He uncovered his face, sliding his eyes to hers. "The fact that you took me up on that is more disturbing."

Cate offered him an amused smile. "It's not that bad. It's just different."

Jack blew out a long breath before he pursed his lips. "Okay, so…no more time differential?"

Cate shook her head with a tight-lipped smile. "No."

"So, that's worse, right? Now we will be missing for however long this party is, at least. That could be hours."

With another head shake, Cate dismissed his concern. He crinkled his brow.

"Marcus can just return us to a few minutes after we left."

Jack lowered his chin to his chest. "Seriously?"

"Yep," Cate said, sucking in a deep breath. "The first time we traveled back to the 40s, we came back and I burst in here demanding to know how much progress Damien, Michael, and Celine had made. They looked at me like I was crazy. It had only been about five minutes since we'd left."

"Wow," Jack said, laying his head back on the cushion. "So, no more fifteen minutes to one, instead, just instantaneous return."

Cate bobbed her head up and down. "Yep. We can now live multiple days in the span of just minutes."

"Wonderful," Jack groaned.

"There's something else," Cate said.

Jack rolled his head toward her. "I'm afraid to ask."

"The time portals are quite different from ours, too. In addition to not being distorted–"

"And opening in any time *or* place," Jack said, wagging a finger at her, "which is still weirding me out, by the way."

"Right. In addition to those things..." Cate paused to suck in a deep breath and lick her lips. "When Marcus opens the portal, it's a bit...turbulent."

Jack's eyebrows shot up. "Turbulent? Care to elaborate?"

Cate chewed her lower lip, eyeing him for a moment. "It starts small. But...when the portal begins to open, there's a lot of wind and noise. A black hole expands until it's large enough to step through."

Jack slow-blinked. "A giant black hole with winds whipping. Sounds...wonderful."

"It's not so bad, but it can be nerve-wracking the first time it happens. Now, once the portal is open, and this is really important, when you go into the portal, do not stop walking until you come out on the other side."

"Don't stop walking. Why?"

"Because Marcus also enters the portal behind us. Once he steps out of the portal on the other side, it closes automatically. If it closes with you inside of it, you may get lost between times."

"For how long?"

Cate crinkled her nose. "Possibly forever."

Jack's eyes slid closed. Cate reached out and grabbed his hand, squeezing it. His eyes popped open, and he returned the gesture. "What in the world have we gotten ourselves mixed up in?"

Cate patted his hand and smiled. "I know it'll seem weird, but we'll get through it. It's not as bad as it seems, I promise."

"Says you. I can't believe you've done this before and were okay with it. You are definitely the braver one of us, Cate Kensie."

"I was far from okay," Cate said with a chuckle, "but I couldn't let them have you. You didn't deserve that."

"It's so bizarre."

"You'll get used to the portal."

"Not that," Jack said, leaning forward, still clutching Cate's hand. "The whole thing about me being missing. I was here one minute and just gone the next. But people think I was gone for a week."

"I know. When I found the newspaper, I couldn't believe it. And no one else remembered you being here. Not even Stanley."

"Thank goodness you did."

Cate offered him a tight-lipped smile and a nod. "And as much as you don't want to hear this, thank goodness for Marcus and his experience."

"You're right," Jack said, slumping in the chair, "I don't want to hear it."

"I know it's strange."

"No. It's more than strange. The last time I saw that guy he nabbed you from the castle and then put you in a...never mind. Never mind. Let's focus on moving forward. I'm going to need all my sanity to get through this time portal stuff."

"You get used to it. I've done it a dozen times at this point and look," she said, waving her hands in the air, "I'm fine!"

"A dozen times?" Jack questioned.

Cate nodded. "1942, 1955, 1965, 2013, 1810, and of course, 2014."

Jack batted his eyelashes at the list. "What?"

"We started in 1942 following Gianna. We went to 1955 where several Agency members were at a summit, then 1965 to warn my grandparents to leave. And by the way, I met my father when he was five." She grinned and chuckled as she recalled the memory. "Then 2013, and then 1810 where we found you."

"Why 2013? What's the connection?"

The smile waned on Cate's lips and she flicked her gaze to the floor. "Uh…"

"Cate?" Jack questioned, leaning forward and balancing his elbows on his knees.

"We followed Gianna around to multiple time periods in search of you. She…" Cate slicked a lock of hair behind her ear. "She said she'd tell us where you were if we went to 2013. She wanted…" Cate pressed her lips together, flexing her jaw as she kept her eyes trained on the area rug. "She wanted me to witness my parents' fatal accident."

Jack closed his eyes, shaking his head as he reached for her hand.

She grabbed it and squeezed it. "I'm okay."

"I'm sorry you had to go through that. And alone, nonetheless." He offered her a tight-lipped smile.

She snapped her gaze up to his face. "I wasn't alone."

"Cate, you may as well have been."

Cate shook her head, letting her gaze fall again. "No. Marcus was…kind and sympathetic."

"Two words I'd never have expected to hear associated with that guy."

"I know it seems weird, but...in that horrible moment, I was glad to have him there."

Jack heaved a sigh. "Well, I suppose we don't have much time to prepare."

"There's not much to prepare," Cate said.

"Well, I need to use the little time we have left to fret. I've lost a precious amount of time and I've got a lot to agonize over. The new time portals, working with the Duke..."

Cate chuckled as his voice trailed off. Before she could respond, the door burst open.

Marcus strode inside with Andrea in tow. "Has he been adequately prepared?"

Cate nodded as she rose to her feet. "Yes, he's aware of the new portal, what to expect, and how it works."

Marcus arched his eyebrows. "He knows the very important rule?"

Cate bobbed her head up and down, sliding her hand forward. "Straight through, don't stop until you reach the other side."

"Very good." Marcus glanced outside. "The weather is not suitable to leave from our usual spot."

"You mean you can't control that?" Cate asked.

He flicked his gaze to her, an amused smile playing on her lips. "I wouldn't want to show off. Perhaps another suitable spot?"

"The mausoleum?" Cate suggested with a shrug. "It's private and we can get there through the secret passage."

"Excellent suggestion. We should go now," Marcus said as he strode toward the door.

"Seriously? You're okay with going to the mausoleum with...him?" Jack thrust a finger toward him.

Cate glanced over her shoulder and nodded. "Yeah. It's okay. We've already been there together once before."

"After a minor tantrum, Catherine and I worked out our issues regarding that incident."

"It wasn't a tantrum," Cate said with a roll of her eyes as they stepped into the hall and crossed to the wall sconce that triggered the secret passage leading to the mausoleum.

"You raised your voice at me, and I believe you even stamped your foot," he said as she opened the passage.

They stepped inside with Andrea following them.

"Wait, is she going with us?" Jack asked, thumbing toward her.

"Yes, of course," Marcus answered, pushing the panel closed. "Catherine will need her ladies' maid."

"We should have brought a–" Jack began when Marcus conjured a fireball into existence. The ethereal blue light lit the passage, blinding Jack. "Flashlight."

"I come equipped with one," Marcus said as he pushed past Jack. "Come along."

Cate fluttered her eyelashes and shrugged as they fell in line behind Marcus.

Within minutes, they climbed the grade up to the secret entrance to the mausoleum. Damp air met them as they stepped into the crypt. Wind gusted outside already, blowing the rain around.

Thunder boomed overhead as Marcus spun to face them. "Are we ready?"

Jack glanced up, wincing. Cate wrapped an arm around his waist. "You'll be fine."

Marcus narrowed his eyes at them. "Catherine, you will go first–"

"No, Jack will go first, then Andrea, then me, then you."

Marcus puckered his lips and stared at her for a moment. "Fine. Mr. Reid, when I give you the word, straight through, understood?"

"Yes," Jack answered. Cate squeezed his shoulder as

Marcus spun away from them, raising his hands in front of him. A trace of a breeze tickled their skin, and a tiny black dot appeared in front of him. It grew larger and the wind swelled.

Cate's hair blew wildly as the twinkling black hole gaped open.

"It's open!" Marcus shouted over the din.

"Go!" Cate said, pushing Jack forward. "Remember, no stopping!"

He nodded, squinting against the wind gusts. "See you on the other side."

Cate smiled and waved him forward. He gave her one final glance before his chest expanded with a deep breath. He lifted his foot. It hovered in the air for a moment before he stepped forward, disappearing into the blackness. Andrea followed him.

Cate waited for a second after she disappeared before stepping into the darkness. She continued forward for a few steps before the blackness fell away.

Candlelight flickered in the small, windowless room as she stepped from the portal. Jack gaped around the space, his brow furrowed.

"Cate, thank God," he said, racing toward her and pulling her into a hug. "That was…odd."

"We made it. I told you it wouldn't be that bad."

"Bad enough," Jack said, letting go of her. "Where are we?"

"London house," Cate said as Marcus joined them.

"I see we've all made it," he said, adjusting his suit jacket. "Good. We should dress immediately. We leave in an hour."

"Right," Cate said with a nod. She stepped to the wall and opened the panel accessing the hall.

Dembe awaited them, offering a bow as they stepped into the foyer. "Duke," he said with another bow before he repeated the gesture to Cate. "Duchess."

Cate smiled at him. "Hi, Dembe."

"Good evening, Dembe. Is everything prepared?"

"Yes, Duke," Dembe said with a nod.

"Excellent. Will you assist Mr. Reid with dressing for the evening?"

Jack waved his hand in the air. "Oh, I don't need–"

Marcus twisted to face him, his eyebrow arched high.

"Thanks," Jack said with a nod and a hard swallow. "I'd be glad for the help."

"This way, Mr. Reid," Dembe said, waving his hand toward the stairs.

"After you," Jack said.

"Catherine, a moment," Marcus said.

"I shall wait in your room, Your Grace," Andrea said as she headed for the stairs.

Jack cleared his throat as he glanced between them before he grabbed the railing. With a huff, he followed Dembe.

Cate closed the gap between her and Marcus. "What's up?"

Marcus reached into his interior pocket and removed a velvet box. "Please wear this tonight."

Cate accepted the box, her eyes trained on it. "Is this the sapphire necklace?"

"Yes. We do not know what we will encounter. I'd like you to have the added protection."

"Okay, thanks," Cate said, smiling up at him. She pressed her lips together, not moving.

"Is there something you'd like to say?" he asked her.

She stared up at him through her eyelashes. "What about Jack?"

"I hardly think the necklace would suit him."

Cate pressed her lips together and shook her head. "You know what I mean."

"I will make every effort to ensure no harm comes to him."

Cate nodded, flicking her gaze down to the marble floor.

Marcus tipped her chin up. "I promise."

Cate offered him a tight-lipped smile. "Thank you."

She glanced over her shoulder at him as she strode toward the railing and climbed to the second floor, navigating to her bedroom and pushing inside. Andrea smoothed a sapphire evening gown across the bed.

"Ready, Your Grace?" she asked, straightening and clasping her hands in front of her.

"Yes," Cate said, handing off the jewelry case to her before she sat at the vanity.

"Your jewelry?"

"Yes," Cate said as Andrea approached.

"Is it a new piece?"

"No. My sapphire necklace."

Andrea offered her a coy smile through the mirror. "Oh, that's a lovely one."

"Yes, it is," Cate said as Andrea began to style her hair.

Within twenty minutes, Andrea had swept her hair into a style popular for the era, settling a tiara around the high bun. Cate rose from her chair to change.

"It's a lovely dress, Your Grace," Andrea said as she fastened the dress in the back. "You look beautiful in it. Blue is your color."

"Thank you, Andrea."

"It reminds me of the gown you wore to your wedding celebration in 1810."

Cate studied her reflection in the mirror as memories of the ball flitted across her mind, bringing a smile to her face. "Yes, the color is similar."

Andrea snapped open the jewelry case as Cate slipped into her shoes.

"Just a moment, I'll fasten them."

"I've got it," Cate said, sinking onto the bed and lifting her foot. The folds of fabric made it impossible to reach her ankle easily. "Okay, I need your help."

Andrea chuckled as she laid the sapphire necklace on the bed next to Cate and squatted to fasten the ankle straps of Cate's heels. "You should know better, Your Grace. This is what ladies' maids are for."

"Yes, I really should by now." Cate reached for the necklace next to her, her fingers caressing the blue gems. A shiver snaked down her spine, and she shuddered.

"Your Grace?" Andrea asked.

Her voice sounded miles away. Cate swallowed hard as she struggled to keep her eyes open. Her eyelids fluttered as images flitted across her mind faster than she could process them. She gasped in a breath and pressed her hands to her temples as pain shot across her forehead.

The pressure increased in her head before her eyes rolled back, and she collapsed backward onto the bed.

CHAPTER 8

"*Y*our Grace?" Andrea's voice called into the blackness. Warm hands tapped against Cate's cheeks as she flicked her eyes open.

With a moan, she pinched her features and fluttered her eyelids, trying to focus. The room filled in around her. She lay on her back in her bedroom at the London house with Andrea's concerned features hovering over her.

"Oh, Your Grace, thank heavens." Andrea pressed a hand against her chest and heaved a sigh of relief. "Let me fetch His Grace."

"No!" Cate exclaimed, reaching for Andrea's hand and squeezing it. "No, please don't tell him anything."

"But Your Grace–"

"Please," Cate said, pulling herself up to sit. "I'm fine. I just...I haven't eaten at all today. I got lightheaded."

Andrea stared at her for a moment, the concern still etched in her features. "I should fetch you something to eat, then."

"No, really. I'm okay. I'm sure I'll eat at the party."

Andrea flicked her gaze to the floor, chewing her lower lip.

"Really, Andrea, I'm fine." She glanced into the mirror and winced. "Oh, I've mussed the lovely job you did on my hair though. I'm sorry."

"Not to worry, Your Grace, I can fix that easily."

"Thank you," Cate said as she pushed herself to stand.

Andrea grabbed her hand, steadying her. "Are you quite certain you feel all right?"

"Yes, I'm perfectly fine," Cate answered, forcing a smile onto her face as she plopped onto the chair at the dressing table. Still clutched in her hands, the necklace clattered around the wooden top.

Cate uncurled her fingers, staring at the object. When she had temporalysis, it triggered her visions. Was it doing that again?

"Just set that down and I'll fasten it the moment I finish with your hair."

Cate dumped it on the table, pulling her fingers back with a frown before she quickly replaced it with a pleasant smile. "Thank you."

Within minutes, Andrea had her hair perfected and had fastened the necklace around her neck. Cate stared at it for a moment, afraid to touch it. Although the contact of the gems against her skin did not trigger anything wooziness at the moment.

Cate bit her lower lip and stared into the blue gems for a moment.

Andrea's voice pulled her back to reality. "Your Grace? Anything else?"

"Oh, no," she said, plastering a smile on her lips.

Andrea offered her a nod. "I will meet you downstairs with your gloves and bag."

"Thank you," Cate called as Andrea ducked out the door.

She spun to stare at the necklace again. First a nightmare, then another episode that seemed to be triggered by touching the sapphires. Her heart thudded against her ribs, and her stomach turned over. Something was amiss.

Her palms turned sweaty, and she wondered if another case of temporalysis may have infected her. Perhaps the last one never subsided. Her forehead pinched as she considered it. She shook her head, dismissing it from her mind. She had to get through this evening. She wouldn't mention it to anyone before then.

She pushed herself up to stand, her legs weak when she stepped away from the vanity. She closed her eyes, sucking in a steadying breath before she pushed herself forward to the door and slipped into the hall.

The sound of another door closing drew her attention across the hall.

Jack emerged in a tuxedo. "Wow, that's some dress."

"Thank you," she said with a smile.

His eyes landed on the ostentatious necklace, and he frowned. "Is that what I think it is?"

Cate glanced down before nodding. "Yeah."

"You've got to be kidding me. Turn around, I'll take it off."

"No," she said, waving the comment away, "it's okay."

"No, it's not. If this is some kind of weird power trip for him–"

"It isn't. The necklace has some sort of protective power."

Jack screwed up his face.

"Apparently, Marcus gave it to me so that nothing would happen to me in the crypt."

Jack wrinkled his lips into a disdain-filled frown. "I hate this."

Cate eyed him for a moment before she grabbed his hand and squeezed. "It'll get better. I promise."

Jack shook his head, avoiding her gaze.

"We'd better head down."

"Right," Jack said with a nod as they walked toward the stairs. "Let's see if we can get the world back to normal so we can end this charade."

Cate forced a smile onto her face before she picked up her skirts and descended to the first floor. Voices floated from the sitting room when she rounded the banister and stepped inside with Jack trailing behind her.

"Catherine, there you are. You look stunning," Marcus said as she entered. He crossed to her and kissed her cheek.

"Thank you. Hello, Mr. Smythe," she said to the other man in the room. "I don't believe you've met our friend, Jack Reid. Jack, this is Charles Smythe."

"Good evening, Your Grace," he said with a nod of his head before he swallowed the last of his brandy and set the glass on the bar. He thrust his hand out toward Jack. "Reid? Scottish?"

"You know it," Jack said with a grin as he pumped the man's hand up and down.

"I know a few Reids from Dunhaven. Any relation?"

"No," Marcus answered flatly.

Charles turned his head toward him with a nod. "I see. Well, I will messenger the paperwork to you tomorrow."

"Good."

Mr. Smythe offered them all a good night and strode from the room. Jack's brow crinkled. "Was that…"

"William Smythe's father, yes," Cate said with a nod.

"The resemblance is uncanny," Jack said with a flick of his eyebrows.

"I thought so, too."

"Are we ready?" Marcus asked, setting down his brandy glass. "The car is waiting."

"Yep," Cate answered as they shuffled into the foyer

where Dembe and Andrea awaited them with coats. "Do we know who else we may see at this event?"

"Undoubtedly several members of The Agency will be present. If we find no evidence within Mr. Chapman's home, perhaps we'll stumble upon another lead," Marcus said as Dembe slid his overcoat on.

"Stumble upon? That doesn't sound like you," Cate answered, pulling her gloves on after Andrea secured her capelet.

Marcus offered her a smirk. "There are several key people I would like to engage in a discussion."

Cate arched an eyebrow at him as she accepted her evening bag from Andrea. "*That* sounds like you. Do you think Gianna will be there?"

"If she's gotten word you will be, I imagine she'll put in an appearance."

"What does that mean?"

"It means she loves to goad you. And she will not miss out on the opportunity to do so."

"Wonderful," Cate groaned with a roll of her eyes.

"Do not let her provoke you. She's pushing you to make a mistake that she can capitalize on. Do not give her the opportunity."

"Right," she answered with a sigh, eyeing the swirls on the marble floor.

"Catherine," Marcus said, tipping her chin up, "keep your wits about you."

Cate nodded. "I will."

"Shall we?" he asked as he offered his arm.

She smiled at him as she slid her arm through his, flicking her gaze to Jack. He stared at them, an expression of disbelief on his features.

"Jack? Are you okay?"

"Uhh, yeah," he said, rubbing the back of his neck. "Yeah, ready. Let's go find some clues."

Cate smiled and nodded at him, reaching out to grab his hand and squeeze it before they strode into the spring night.

Cate slid into the backseat, gathering her skirts before the driver eased the door closed. Marcus entered next to her, leaving Jack in the front seat. The car eased away from the curb and snaked through the streets of London to the home of Arnold Chapman.

Cate stared up at the starry night sky as her fingers drummed the seat next to her. Her stomach jittered as the buildings rolled past her window.

Warm fingers wrapped around hers and squeezed. She cut her gaze to Marcus, and he offered her a smile. "Calm yourself, Catherine."

"I'm calm," she answered.

He arched an eyebrow at her. She pressed her lips together as she realized her pounding heart gave her away. Jack shot them a glance over his shoulder, his brow furrowing.

Cate sucked in a deep breath, trying to bring her heart rate back down. "There, see?" she asked as her heart returned to a normal rhythm.

The car slowed to a stop outside of a stately home. Marcus squeezed her hand again before he climbed from the car and circled it. He reached a hand inside to help her from the car as Jack stepped out, tugging at his collar.

Marcus scrunched his nose at Jack. "Stop fiddling with your collar like an ape."

"These are not the most comfortable things."

"You'll survive," Marcus shot back with a roll of his eyes.

Jack narrowed his eyes at the man. Cate stepped onto the pavement, and Jack offered his arm to her.

Marcus raised his eyebrows. "I think not, Mack."

"It's Jack, Pal."

Marcus frowned at him. "I am not your *pal*."

Jack inched closer. "Cate can make her choice."

"I'm not certain you will like the outcome of that," Marcus shot back.

Jack scoffed at the statement. "You don't know Cate Kensie."

Marcus stood taller, stepping closer to him. "*You* don't know Catherine Northcott."

Cate shook her head, stepping between them. "Enough. Let's go. We have work to do."

Marcus offered his arm as did Jack.

"This is ridiculous, Reid. It would look more than questionable for another man to escort her when her husband is available."

Jack puckered his lips. "It's your call, Cate. Whatever you're comfortable with."

Cate swallowed hard, flicking her gaze between them as heat rose into her cheeks. "Marcus is right. It would look odd and most of these people think we're married."

"We are married, dear."

Jack hesitated for a moment before he nodded. "As long as you're comfortable."

Cate forced a smile as she slid her arm into the crook of Marcus's. "I'm fine."

They strode to the door, pushing into the din of the party inside. Guests circulated in the nearby sitting room, talking and laughing.

Marcus surveyed the scene before leading Cate toward Arnold Chapman who already approached them. Cate glanced over her shoulder at Jack. "Stay close."

"Well, do my eyes deceive me, or is that Marcus Northcott I see," Arnold said with a broad grin, thrusting his hand out. "And here I thought there was a misprint on my final guest list. To what do we owe the pleasure?"

"Normally I wouldn't bother, but Catherine traveled with me, and I felt she deserved the night out."

"Ah, yes, the lovely Catherine," Arnold said, shifting his gaze to Cate. "A pleasure to see you again. I suppose we all owe you a debt of gratitude. After your marriage, the elusive Duke has become less elusive."

"I'm happy to be of service on that front," Cate said with a grin.

Arnold eyed Jack, his shoulders sliding down his back as an uncomfortable grin covered his face. "Have we met?"

"Jack Reid," Marcus said, "a...friend."

"Ah, you seem familiar," Arnold said as they shook hands.

Jack swallowed hard and licked his lips.

Cate noticed the discomfort building on his features. "I'm sure you've met at some point before. Well, I'm certain you have other guests to speak to, and we should say hello to a few other friends."

"Oh, before you go, my advanced apologies, Catherine, but I was hoping you, Marcus, might join us for a brief business discussion in about twenty minutes."

Marcus scanned the crowd before his focus centered on Arnold. "I would hate to neglect Catherine. We had planned for an uninterrupted evening together."

"I do understand. I would find it difficult to leave such a lovely woman, however, I do promise to keep it brief."

Marcus narrowed his eyes at the man as he mulled it over.

Cate patted his arm. "Go, dear. I'll be fine. Jack will keep me company."

Marcus huffed out a breath. "Well, I suppose I cannot say no."

"Certainly not or you may find yourself in the guest room," Arnold said with a hearty chuckle.

"I shall see you shortly," Marcus said with a curt nod before they moved away. They said hello to a few others before Marcus handed Cate a champagne flute and guided her toward a corner. Jack trailed behind, his hands shoved in his pockets as he surveyed the crowd.

"Are you okay?" Cate asked as they settled near the window.

"Yeah," Jack said after a hard swallow.

"Are you sure? Do you recognize some of these people?"

"Yeah," Jack said, rubbing the back of his neck.

"It's okay. You're safe now."

Jack nodded.

"But you may not be," Marcus said. "Catherine, I am not at all certain I should leave you for this meeting."

Cate sipped her champagne, scanning the crowd. "We'll be okay. This is the best way for you to get information."

"I had planned to do that with you at my side."

"They'll be far more candid without me. You know that."

He huffed, puckering his lips. Cate glanced over his shoulder at the front door. Her posture stiffened, and she took a long sip of her champagne. "Great."

Marcus glanced over his shoulder at the buxom blonde sauntering into the room. He twisted back to face Cate. "Now I know I will not attend."

"What?" Cate asked, her eyes wide. "No, you have to go."

"Not with Gianna here."

"I'll be fine," Cate answered, flicking her gaze back to the woman who leaned far too close to the married Arnold Chapman, laying a hand on his chest as she snorted a giggle. "Ugh, she does not know the meaning of holding back?"

Marcus arched an eyebrow at Cate. "What?" she said,

lifting a shoulder, "You know how I feel about her overly flirtatious nature."

"Yes, I do. And I know it drives you to make foolish decisions in an attempt to best her."

"I do not," Cate argued.

"Yes, you do. And after the physical fight with her in Germany, I would prefer not to leave you alone with her lurking around."

"You fought with her?" Jack questioned.

"He's making more of it than it was. Besides, she started it."

Marcus shot a glance at Jack before returning his attention to Cate. "I am not. In a misguided attempt to retrieve me from a locked cell in Eldinbury Castle, Gianna assaulted her violently. And she has physically attacked her on more than one occasion."

"Cate!" Jack hissed.

"It's fine," Cate said, her champagne swishing in the glass as she sliced her hand through the air. "I'm fine. Let's stick to the plan. You go get your information. Jack and I will wait here."

"Will you? Do you promise?" Marcus asked.

"I will be fine."

Marcus cocked his head, sighing as he arched an eyebrow.

"Yes, I promise. I won't go near her."

Marcus glanced at Jack. "Make certain she does not."

Jack nodded. "Of course."

With a sour expression, Marcus heaved another sigh before he squeezed Cate's arm and glanced at Jack. "Keep her safe."

Cate scoffed before taking another sip of her champagne. "She is unreal."

Jack followed the direction of her gaze as Marcus disappeared behind closed doors with a bevy of businessmen.

Gianna threw her head back, laughing as a group of men surrounded her.

Cate jabbed a finger in her direction, the champagne quivering in her glass. "Do you know she tried to convince Marcus to leave me stranded in 1942 and go with her?"

She downed another long sip.

"Maybe we should move somewhere away from her. I don't much like her either."

Cate puckered her lips as she stared at the woman.

"Cate?"

"Better to keep her in our sights. She's too dangerous to let slip away."

"Right," Jack said, tugging at his collar again. He stared at the woman again for a moment before he shifted his gaze to Cate. "This whole thing is too strange."

Cate let her shoulders slump. "I'm sorry. It must be so hard for you to see her and these people again."

"And this whole Duke thing." Jack shifted his weight from foot to foot before he spun to face her. "Cate–"

"Well, well, well," Elliott Stevens said, a grin on his oval face as he closed the distance between them, "if it isn't the Duchess herself."

"Mr. Stevens," Cate said, raising her chin as she stepped between him and Jack.

"Out on the town without your illustrious Duke." His eyes shifted to Jack. "And with the infamous Mr. Reid." He clicked his tongue at her. "Whatever will your husband say?"

Cate narrowed her eyes at him. "Oh, he's here. He's in a meeting."

"Oh, yes," Elliott said, rocking on his heels, "I believe Gianna just stepped inside with them. I'm certain she can distract him from any...shenanigans on your part. Though it still surprises me that he allows this to go on. He doesn't seem the type to suffer playing second fiddle."

Cate heaved a sigh.

"Oh, I don't mean to drone on about personal matters when there is business to discuss."

"I already told you, Marcus is–"

Elliott flicked a hand in the air. "Oh, no, not with the Duke. With you, dear Duchess."

Cate flicked her eyebrows up.

"We're prepared to give you one more chance."

Cate crossed her arms, staring up at the man. "One more chance for what?"

"To hand over Dunhaven Castle before we destroy everything you love."

Cate shook her head at him. "This conversation is over." She stepped sideways, but he blocked her way.

"I wouldn't be so hasty," Elliott said.

Cate bounced back a step, firming her jaw. "I will not give you my home."

"Then you'll give us everything else including your life."

CHAPTER 9

*H*eat seared through Cate as the man left the threat hanging in the air.

"Watch it," Jack hissed, pushing in front of Cate.

"Oh, I plan to," Elliott said, shoving his hands into his pockets. "I plan to watch as we dismantle everything you love."

Cate elbowed her way in front of Jack, her lips tugging into a grimace. "I will never let you take Dunhaven Castle."

She grabbed Jack's hand and tugged him away from the man as she stormed from the room. They ducked into a quiet hall. Cate collapsed back against the wall, blowing out a long breath.

"The nerve of that guy," Jack said, fidgeting with his collar again.

"He was the same way when we met him in 1955 while searching for you."

"What the hell have we gotten mixed up with?"

"Powerful and dangerous people," Cate said, pressing a hand to her stomach. She snapped her gaze up to Jack. "We need to look for more information."

Jack ran his hands through his hair. "I'm not sure that's a good idea."

"We need to get ahead of them any way we can, and we may never have an opportunity to search this house again."

"I'm pretty sure this is exactly what the Duke told me not to let you do."

"Since when do you follow Marcus's advice?"

Jack puckered his lips, sticking his hands on his hips as he considered it.

"Come on, Jack," Cate said.

"I don't know, Cate. I'm not sure we should risk angering these people on their turf. Or angering your esteemed husband."

"I will handle Marcus."

Jack shook his head, throwing his hands in the air. "Fine."

Cate nodded and grabbed his hand, leading him further down the hall and away from the party.

"I'm not sure which is more frightening. The fact that we may get caught by The Agency or the Duke. *Or* that you think you can handle it."

"I can. He's not an ogre."

"He's damned close," Jack said as they peered around a corner.

"It's clear, let's go," Cate said, picking up her dress and tiptoeing down the hall. "Try that door."

Jack swung it open, peering inside. "Billiards room."

Cate shook her head, continuing down the hall. She crossed to the opposite side and cracked a door open. She shook her head. "Nothing."

They continued down the hall to the next door. Cate flung it open. Moonlit lit the large desk across the room.

A smile spread across Cate's face. "Bingo."

She switched on the light, hurrying to the mahogany desk and circling it. "Check the file cabinet."

Cate pulled the drawers open on the left side of the desk, pawing through the items inside.

"What are we looking for?"

"Anything. Anything that may lead us to Gertrude or help us determine the other angles they'll be working," Cate said as she slid the middle drawer open. Pens rattled around as she swiped her hand inside, searching for any clues.

"I don't see anything," Jack said. "But I'm not sure I know what to look for."

Cate slammed the center drawer shut and tugged open the top drawer on the right. "When we were at Gianna's place in 1955, she had notes...photos...dates."

"Photos?" Jack asked, freezing with his hand still stuffed in the top drawer.

Cate's hand slowed as she pushed items around. Memories of the folder of Gianna's research filled her mind. "Me."

"What?" Jack questioned.

"The photos were of me. Me at Aberdeen. Me at Dunhaven. She's been watching me for years." Cate collapsed into the chair behind her, tears brimming in her eyes. "They killed my parents."

Jack slammed the drawer closed and hurried across the room, sliding his hand around her. "Cate..."

A tear slid onto her cheek, and she wiped it away. She sucked in a breath and blinked back the rest of her tears with a sniffle. "I'm not letting them take anything else from us."

She tugged open the bottom drawer and rifled through it. Her features pinched as she found nothing. "No!"

"Come on, Cate, let's get out of here."

Cate stared at the blotter on the desk. "Maybe if we–"

"No, there's nothing here. We should go."

Cate gripped the decorative edge, her knuckles turning white. She pressed her lips together in a thin line.

"Come on, Cate. There's nothing here."

Cate sucked in a breath and nodded. "You're right. Let's go."

She rose from the chair, and they hurried from the office and down the hall. The din of the party reached their ears as they turned the corner and continued toward the foyer.

Cate glanced into the library. "Arnold Chapman is in there. Their meeting is over."

She crossed to the sitting room and scanned the interior, finding Marcus where they'd been standing. She wound through the crowd toward him.

"Catherine, where have you been?" he asked as she approached.

"Sorry, we had to step out for a minute."

He grabbed her hands in his. "Are you all right? Have you been crying?"

Cate nodded at him. "Yes, we're fine."

"I told you not to move." He flicked his gaze to Jack. "Could you really not do what I asked for fifteen minutes?"

"Don't blame this on him. Blame it on Elliott Stevens."

Marcus refocused his attention on Cate. "What happened?" He shook his head. "Never mind. We'll discuss it in the car. We are leaving."

"Great idea," Cate said. "I've had as much as I can take of this party."

Marcus wrapped his hand around hers and led her toward the door. She grabbed hold of Jack's arm and tugged him along with them.

"Leaving so soon?" Gianna asked, stepping into their pathway. "The party's only just getting started."

"Stand aside, Gianna," Marcus said with a huff.

"Why? It appears you could use a fourth. You're a bit...unbalanced."

"We are leaving," Marcus said.

"The night is young. Jack, are you looking for a date?" Her lips curled into a smirky smile.

"Pass," Jack said, tugging at his sleeves with a grimace etched into his features.

Gianna pouted. "Boo. Well, looks like that leaves me with you." She slid her arms up Marcus's lapels.

Cate glared at the woman as Marcus wrapped one hand around one of hers and shoved it away. "For once, I agree with the Scot."

He tugged Cate closer and wrapped an arm around her waist. "It would be a terrible shame to downgrade when I'm already married to perfection."

Heat rose in Cate's cheeks as Gianna's features turned stony.

"Her supposed perfection may cost you everything, Marcus."

Marcus lifted a shoulder in a half-shrug. "I doubt it."

"We'll see," she snapped as Marcus led Cate past her.

Cate shook her head as she pulled on her capelet and stepped into the evening air, tugging at it. "She is something else."

Their car slid to a stop in front of the house. The driver popped out and raced around to open the door for Cate. She slid into the backseat with a huff.

"I certainly hope you got the information you hoped to find," Cate said as Marcus slipped into the car next to her.

"We can discuss it at home," he answered, "when you have cooled off. There is nothing further to do tonight."

"Cooled off?" Cate asked. "Are you kidding?"

Marcus slid his glance sideways to her as the driver pulled away. "I am not."

Cate crossed her arms, her foot tapping against the floor.

"You have every right to be outraged with her."

"I'm not outraged. I'm just…"

"Furious," he answered.

Cate pressed her lips together. "Okay, fine. Her behavior is outrageous."

"As are her threats."

Cate flung her hand out. "Yes, exactly. That's exactly what I mean."

Marcus's lips curled on the edges.

Cate wagged a finger at him. "Don't give me that look. Of course, I meant her threats. What else would I mean?"

Cate heaved a sigh, shaking her head. "First Elliott Stevens and now her."

The slight smile faded on his lips, and he twisted to face her more fully. "What? What happened with Elliott Stevens?"

"Nothing," Cate said, waving the question away before she pressed her hand to her forehead.

"Catherine–"

"He threatened her," Jack said, twisting to face them from the front seat.

Marcus's eyes went wide, and he flicked his gaze from Jack to Cate. "He what? What did he say to you?"

The car eased to a stop in front of Marcus's home. The driver hurried to open Cate's door. She climbed from the vehicle on her own and stomped to the house. She pushed through the front door, tossing her bag down and tugging off her gloves.

"What did he say, Catherine?" Marcus demanded as he stormed in behind her.

She tossed the gloves on the entry table before grabbing the edge, her biceps flexing as she slid her eyes shut.

Cate twisted to face him and Jack as he strode into the foyer. "He asked for Dunhaven Castle again."

"And he threatened to kill her."

Marcus snapped his gaze to Jack before he shifted his focus to Cate. "Is this true?"

Cate shook her head before she switched to a nod. "Not in so many words, but yes." She flicked her gaze up to his dark eyes. "Tell me you found something."

Marcus heaved a sigh. "This is becoming too dangerous."

"What?"

"You should not be involved. You are putting yourself directly in the line of fire. You shouldn't be exposed to these people."

Cate's jaw flapped open. "You don't get to make that decision."

"I feel I must. I have far more experience with them than you do."

Cate stuck a hand on her hip. "Sidelining me at Dunhaven Castle doesn't help to protect me at all."

"Cate, for once, I think he may be right," Jack chimed in.

"I can't believe you two."

Jack splayed his hands to the sides. "That man threatened you. He said you'd pay with your life. Maybe it's best if we don't push them while we sort this situation out."

Cate clamped her jaw closed as she glared at them both. "I am *not* stepping out of this fight. It involves my family and my home."

"Yes, but Catherine–"

Cate poked him in the chest. "Don't you 'but Catherine' me. You wouldn't be standing here right now if it weren't for me. Remember that next time you decide it's best for me to sit on my hands and do nothing."

Marcus puckered his lips, his annoyance obvious.

Cate picked up her evening bag from the table and waved it toward them. "I'm going to bed. We can discuss in the morning."

She spun on her heel and stormed up the steps to her bedroom. With a slam, she shoved the door closed and leaned against it.

"I assume the party did not go as planned, Your Grace?" Andrea inquired from her post near the vanity.

Cate heaved a sigh as she pulled herself away from the door and shuffled across the room. "You could say that."

"Perhaps some sleep will help."

Cate nodded as she plopped onto the bed. Andrea bent to unbuckle her shoes. Cate drummed her fingers on the bedspread.

"I'm sorry," Andrea said as she tugged one shoe off. "I'm nearly finished with the shoes."

"Oh, I'm not frustrated with you."

Andrea glanced up with an arched eyebrow. "I understand. Would you like to talk about it?"

Cate sighed as she slid onto her feet, and Andrea unfastened her dress. "No."

As Cate slid her pajama top on and buttoned it, she flung an arm out. "I just can't believe after everything, he thinks it's best for me to not be involved."

Andrea offered her an apologetic smile as she hung the dress.

"You know, I went to Eldinbury Castle for him. But he thinks I shouldn't be able to go to a party because someone may say something mean to me." Cate plopped on the vanity chair after tugging on her pajama pants.

Andrea pulled the tiara from her hair and set it aside. "I'm certain His Grace only wishes to protect you."

Cate flicked her gaze to Andrea through the mirror as she dismantled her hair. "Yeah, sure."

Andrea met her gaze. "He is quite protective of you."

"He likes to win."

"He likes to be certain you are safe," she answered as Cate's hair tumbled past her shoulders.

Cate blew out a sigh. "Gianna put an appearance tonight. *And* she threw herself at both Jack and Marcus."

Andrea offered a knowing glance as she slid the brush through Cate's hair. "That explains both of your consternation."

Cate's shoulders slumped, and she shook her head. "I don't understand why she has such an easy time provoking such a reaction from me."

"Because she is threatening everything dear to you. She has the upper hand because you care whereas she does not."

Cate studied the woman through the mirror. "You're right."

Andrea smiled at her as she set the brush down. "Of course, I am. Which is why you so enjoy my service."

Cate rose and pulled the woman into a hug. "Yes, it is."

"Do you think you will be able to sleep?"

"I think so. Despite the time change and all the excitement, my adrenaline is gone and I'm exhausted."

Andrea pulled back with a nod. "Oh, your necklace. Let me remove it."

"Oh, could you leave it?" Cate ran her hands over the jewels. "I'll get it, but I'd like to keep it with me."

"Of course, Your Grace. Sleep well."

"Thank you," Cate said with a slight smile as she pulled her robe tighter around her and fastened it.

Andrea squeezed Cate's hand before she slipped from the room, easing the door shut behind her. Cate wandered to the full-length mirror, sliding the robe collar open and eyeing the sapphires around her neck.

A knock sounded, drawing her attention away from the gems. Cate tugged the collar closed and inched the door open, staring through the crack.

"Hey, Cate," Jack whispered. "You okay?"

Cate swung the door open wider and motioned for him to enter. "Yeah, I'm okay. How are you?"

Jack stuck his hands on his hips, still in his tuxedo. His bowtie hung undone around his neck. "Nervous."

Cate sighed, pressing her lips together. "I'm sorry. I'm sorry to put you through facing them tonight—"

"It's not that."

Cate studied him for a moment. "Then what?"

"Do you think you may have painted a bigger target on our backs by marrying him?"

Cate arched an eyebrow. "I think if I hadn't married him, we would have already lost. So target or not, Marcus Northcott is the only thing standing between The Agency and Dunhaven Castle."

Jack crossed his arms, bobbing his head up and down. "I don't believe that. I think you're just as big a part of this fight as he is."

"I'm glad you realize that."

Jack closed the distance between them, reaching out to squeeze her shoulders. "I've always realized that, Cate. Like it or not, I'm not sure we can escape this and leave it up to someone else entirely."

"No, we can't. But after what happened to you, if you don't want to be involved, I get it."

He offered her a half smile. "No chance, Cate. We're in this together."

Cate patted his hand and smiled.

"Besides, I trust you a hell of a lot more than I trust him."

"We'll get through this," she promised. "Try to get some sleep."

Jack let his gaze roam around the room. "I hope I can. I'm not certain I'm comfortable sleeping in his house."

Cate raised her chin, offering him an amused grin. "Technically, it's also *my* house. So, if it bothers you too much, you can remind yourself of that."

"Oh, right," Jack said, smacking a palm to his forehead.

"You get all seven hundred houses including this one if something happens to him."

"Yep," she said with a giggle.

Jack smiled down at her. "Good night, Cate."

"Good night. Hope you sleep," she called as he slipped into the hall and pulled the door shut.

She sucked in a deep breath, shuffling around the bed and collapsing on the edge. She opened the lid of the music box, letting her eyes slide shut as tinkling music filled the air.

A knock interrupted her ruminating. She closed the music box as she rose before heading for the door. She pulled it open, expecting to find Jack unable to sleep.

"Did you even try to sle–" she began until she recognized Marcus. "Oh, sorry, thought you were Jack."

Marcus arched an eyebrow at her as she motioned for him to enter. "Mr. Reid visiting my wife in her bedroom at this hour. Should I be concerned?"

"Very funny," Cate said.

"Did I hear your music box?"

"Yes," Cate said with a nod. "I find it very relaxing. I really need to thank your mother for it again."

"She will be thrilled that you enjoy it."

They stood for a moment in silence before Cate spoke again. "If you've come to try to talk me into staying out of this again–"

"No, I haven't," Marcus said, clasping his hands behind his back.

"Good."

"I only wish to give you the option in the event that you'd prefer to exercise it." He studied her in the soft light. "I worry about you, Catherine."

"You don't have to."

"Of course I do. It is the duty of a husband."

She flicked her eyes up to him with a wry expression.

"I'm serious, Catherine," he said, sliding a lock of hair behind her ear. "These people are not kind. I do not wish to subject you to the depths they will sink to."

"I think I've subjected myself," she said, shambling across the room and opening the music box.

"That may be, but I will do everything in my power to shield you from any hostility if you prefer it."

Cate twisted to face him, knitting her brows. She studied him for a moment, her gaze settling on his dark eyes. "As easy as it would be to say yes, I can't. This is my fight."

Marcus reached for her hand, threading his fingers through hers. "Our fight."

Cate stared down at their clasped hands. "Right."

She raised her eyes to his, offering him a coy smile. "You need me to save you when you get captured."

"I will never live that down, will I?"

"No," she said with a chuckle. "But seriously...we're in this together."

"Together," he repeated, squeezing her hand. He studied her for a moment. "Will you be able to sleep?"

"I think so," Cate said, pulling her hand from his and shuffling to the bed. She collapsed onto it with a sigh. "Interacting with Gianna is exhausting. And that's not an invitation for you to shield me from harm."

"As long as you are committed, I will not question your involvement again. But I will not apologize for protecting you."

"I am. Together. We have each other's backs."

"Always," he answered with a slight smile. "Try not to let her upset you. She isn't worth it."

Cate offered him a curt nod.

"Good night, Catherine."

"Good night."

Marcus offered her one last smile before he strode from the room.

Cate let her shoulders slump, blowing out a long breath before she peeled off her robe and tossed it at the foot of the bed. She kicked her slippers off and crawled between the sheets.

With another long exhale, she stretched out on the comfortable mattress. She let her eyes slide shut as the music played.

Her mind went over the events of the evening, recalling first the conversation with Elliott Stevens, then the one with Gianna. As details raced by a new image replaced the one from the party.

Cate ran through the halls of Dunhaven Castle as a scream split the air. The image startled her, causing her to gasp and vault upright. She sucked in another breath as her eyebrows pinched together. *Did she have another case of temporalysis?*

CHAPTER 10

ate stared up at the ceiling as the music played. Light streamed through the window, announcing the new day. Worry coursed through her as the events of the past few days wandered through her mind.

The Agency proved to be as dangerous as Marcus said, but another issue weighed more heavily on her mind. Her nightmares and visions had resumed. The last time she'd had a similar experience, temporalysis had been the cause. An illness that could have killed her. Did she have it again?

Cate squeezed her eyes closed, her features pinching as she fought back tears. She should tell someone. She should tell Marcus.

Her gaze slid sideways to the piano-shaped music box. She narrowed her eyes at the drawer pull of the nightstand. She tugged it open, and searched the inside, hoping to find a Dragon's blood lozenge.

She found nothing useful. With a sigh, she collapsed back into her pillow. Her fingers found the necklace still around her neck. She unclasped it, laying it on the nightstand.

A knock sounded at the door and Andrea peeked inside. "Your Grace?"

"I'm up, come in."

"Good morning. Did you sleep well?"

"Well enough," Cate answered as she slid her feet into her slippers. She dressed for the day. As Andrea put the finishing touches on her hairstyle, she chewed her lower lip.

"All finished, Your Grace. Is there anything else?"

"Actually, yes. Could I ask you to ask Dembe for something? But I need you to be discreet."

"You mean, no one should know. Not even His Grace?"

Cate spun to face her. "Yes. I'm sorry. It won't be for long, and I hate to put you in this position…"

"Say no more, Your Grace. I am happy to help with anything you need. What is it?"

Cate licked her lips, her eyebrows pinching. "Can you find out if Dembe has any Dragon's blood lozenges?"

Andrea arched an eyebrow before returning her face to a neutral expression. "Yes, of course, Your Grace. Leave it with me."

Cate grabbed her hand and squeezed. "Thank you, Andrea. I'm so sorry to do this. And, please, don't worry. I'm being cautious is all."

"Of course." Andrea nodded as she clasped her hands in front of her before she spun on her heel and disappeared into the hall.

Cate drummed her fingers against the thick wooden top of the vanity. If she could get the Dragon's blood she could buy herself some time.

Cate pressed her lips together and sucked in a breath. "Please get them, Andrea," she whispered as she stood and crossed the room. She stepped into the hall, glancing at Jack's door and wondering if he slept.

She hastened down the stairs and into the dining room. Jack and Marcus leapt from their seats as she entered.

"Good morning, Catherine," Marcus said as she crossed to the table. He picked up a purple rose from her place setting and offered it to her.

She accepted it, smiling up at him. "Are these—"

"From Rosenberg, yes. I recall you enjoyed the last one I gave you. So, I had these flown in for you."

Cate studied the bouquet in the center of the table as she sniffed the single rose. "Thank you."

She eased into her chair as Marcus pushed it in behind her. "So," she said, setting the rose aside, "what information did you get last night? Jack and I found nothing."

Marcus froze as he returned to his seat. "What do you mean found nothing?"

She picked up her fork and draped her napkin across her lap as Dembe set a plate in front of her. "Thank you, Dembe. We searched the office and found nothing."

"You did what?" Marcus asked with his teacup halfway to his lips.

"We searched the office. I thought maybe we could find a clue like we did at Gianna's." Cate poked her fork toward Marcus. "We should try her place again."

"Because that turned out so well the last time," Marcus answered. "You should not have searched the office. I thought we agreed you would not slink about." He shot a disapproving glance at Jack.

"Don't blame Jack," Cate said as she slathered jam onto her toast. "It was my idea."

Marcus fidgeted in his chair. "Of course, it was."

"Anyway, we didn't find anything. So, I hope you came up with something in your meeting." She glanced over at Jack's full plate. "You're not eating?"

Jack frowned down at the food as though he didn't trust it.

Marcus took a sip of his tea. "I tried to tell him Dembe is an excellent cook. It did very little to convince him. The meeting produced a few leads we may follow up on. However, it will take a bit of work."

"What leads?" Jack inquired finally picking up his fork.

"The Agency has inducted several new members. Their properties would make an excellent location to hide a newly acquired asset."

"Asset?" Jack questioned after a sip of his juice.

"Gertrude," Cate concluded.

"Right."

"Where are the properties?" Cate asked.

"That is where the work comes in. I could not solicit the information without an investment in their group. I have called Charles Smythe to discuss it, and I have Stefano doing some legwork."

Cate sipped her tea, puckering her lips as she set the cup in the saucer. "You shouldn't invest with them."

"I would prefer not to financially tie myself to The Agency, but I do not see a way around it. It is the quickest way to find the locations."

Cate stared at the purple roses in the vase, her brow furrowing. "I know how we can get the locations."

"What?" Marcus asked as she slid the teacup and saucer onto the lace tablecloth. She held up a finger as she stood and tossed her napkin onto the chair. She hurried around the corner into the foyer and approached the phone. With the receiver cradled between her neck and shoulder, she waited to be connected after making her request.

Jack and Marcus followed her into the space as someone picked up the line on the opposite end.

"Hi! This is Catherine Northcott. I'm in town and was

wondering if you may be available for lunch...Yes, I'm free today...That sounds perfect. I'll see you then."

Cate replaced the receiver in the cradle and spun to face them. "Done."

Marcus narrowed his eyes at her. "Well done, Catherine."

"Someone want to fill me in on what just happened?" Jack asked.

"Last year, Catherine befriended one of the secretaries of a man involved with some members of The Agency. The woman is privy to much of the sensitive information handled by them including their properties." Marcus turned back to Cate. "At least I assume you called Ginger Fallinger."

"I did," Cate said with a smile and a nod.

"And this Ginger woman will tell you why?" Jack asked.

Cate lifted a shoulder as she searched for the words.

"Catherine and Ginger like to drink several martinis in one sitting which I'm sure helps loosen Ginger's lips."

"You'd think if she's working for The Agency, they'd want her to be more trustworthy."

"I may have allowed her to believe me to be a wronged woman which helped with her loose lips."

Jack pressed his lips together as he tried to hide a laugh.

"A clever ruse, though disingenuous," Marcus said. "Well, where are you lunching? We should make plans to accompany you."

The smile faded from Cate's face, and she shook her head. "No. You can't go. Ginger will never talk with you two around."

"You cannot go alone," Marcus argued.

"And I can't go with you."

"We'll have to follow you. Hide behind the fake plant at the restaurant or something," Jack said.

Marcus blinked several times as he shifted his gaze to Jack. "I don't hide behind fake plants."

Jack shrugged. "You will now if you want to keep an eye on her without blowing her cover."

"He's right," Cate said, "although…"

"What is it, Cate?"

"Are you sure you two can handle this without killing each other?"

Marcus scoffed. "I am in no danger of being killed. He couldn't even maim me."

Cate stared at him for a moment. "Let me rephrase. Are you sure you can handle this without killing Jack?"

Marcus sucked in a deep breath. "Of course."

Cate raised her eyebrows. "Jack, are you sure you can handle this without driving Marcus to kill you?"

"I'll do my best."

"Great," Cate said. "We have a few hours before lunch. Maybe we should go to Gianna's apartment."

"I am not certain that is wise."

"We found information there last time."

Marcus wagged a finger at her. "We found the information she wanted us to find. I am not certain it is helpful."

"Humor me. It can't hurt."

Marcus sucked in a breath and nodded. "Fine."

"All right. Let me just get my bag."

She hurried up the stairs, clinging to the thick wooden railing as she paused for a second. A clammy sweat made her dress stick to her back. She blew out a breath and resumed her journey up the stairs.

She pushed into her room, crossed to the bed, and collapsed on the edge. The door opened a moment later and Andrea slipped inside. She offered Cate an eager smile, dangling a small sachet from her fingers.

Cate leapt up, her eyes wide. "You got them."

"I did."

"Did Dembe agree to stay quiet about it?" Cate asked as she opened the pouch and fished out one of the drops.

"I asked him to remain mum about it. He did not disagree, though he advised this matter be brought to His Grace's attention."

Cate nodded as she winced from the bitter taste of the Dragon's blood on her tongue. She stuffed the pouch in her purse. "Yes, I don't plan on keeping it from him for long. Just long enough to make some progress on this situation."

Cate spun, nearly running into Andrea.

"Your Grace, are you certain you are all right? Perhaps it's wise to confide in His Grace sooner rather than later."

Cate's shoulders slumped as the words sank into her mind. Her lower lip bobbed up and down and her forehead pinched. "Yes, I know, I just...I'm not even sure it's what I think it is, and we really need to get this information."

Andrea pressed her lips together and nodded. "Perhaps, though, he can assess it better and put your mind at ease."

Cate flicked her gaze to the floor as her mind went in the opposite direction. *Perhaps he can put the final nail in my coffin.* "I'll tell him soon, I promise."

"Of course, Your Grace. And I shall say nothing further about it."

"It's okay, Andrea. I know you're trying to help. And you're right. I shouldn't hide it. I just...need some time."

Andrea nodded and squeezed Cate's arm. "Be safe, Your Grace."

"Thank you."

Cate hurried from the room and down the stairs. "Ready."

Marcus narrowed his eyes at her, cocking his head. "Are you certain?"

"Yep," Cate said, doing her best to hide the lozenge and her reaction to its bitter taste.

He stared at her for another moment before he nodded

and motioned for her to precede him to the door. Cate sucked in a breath as she stepped into the bright sunshine of the spring morning.

Within minutes the car eased to a stop outside Gianna's posh apartment building. Cate stared up at it, recalling their last experience there. Pictures of her with red Xs across her face danced through her mind. What would they find this time?

Cate climbed from the car, slipping her arm into Marcus's as they approached a figure leaning against the side of the building.

He straightened, bowing as they closed the gap between them. "Have you done as I asked?"

Stefano nodded. "Yes. The apartment is clear, and she has not returned. Hello, Duchess." He eyed Jack. "Did you find a new stray?"

"This is Jack Reid," Cate said.

Stefano's bushy eyebrows shot up. "Oh! The Scot that you didn't want to find."

Jack pulled his chin back to his chest, his eyebrows raising.

Marcus scowled at him. "That's not exactly what I said. Come along, we should not dally."

He tugged Cate along with him, leaving Stefano at this post. They entered the building, navigating to Gianna's apartment. With a flick of his wrist, Marcus unlocked the door and motioned for Cate to enter.

She sucked in a deep breath as she entered the lion's den. She grabbed Jack's hand as he crossed the threshold. "You okay?"

"Yeah, I'm good. You?"

She forced a smile onto her face and nodded. "Yep."

She pointed down the hall. "The last time we found evidence it was in the office."

Jack nodded as he stared around the posh space. "I'll check out the living room."

Cate took a step toward the office when Marcus tugged on her elbow. "Catherine, perhaps I should go first. The last evidence we found was quite disturbing."

She glanced over her shoulder as they wandered to the office. "Thank you, but I'm okay."

They stepped into the space. Her muscles tensed as memories of her previous experience here flitted across her mind again. She paused while another fleeting thought crossed her brain. With a sharp breath, she sucked harder on the dragon's blood lozenge and pushed herself to the desk.

She rifled through the folders on the top, wondering if she'd find more pictures of herself. Marcus slipped his hand onto her shoulder as he flicked open a folder and studied the contents.

"Anything interesting?" she asked while she shuffled to another folder.

"Not really, you?"

Cate lifted the folder closer as she flipped through the contents. "I don't know."

Marcus pressed closer to her, peering over her shoulder. He snatched one of the images from the folder.

"Who is this?" Cate asked, staring at the blonde in the photo.

"I don't know."

Cate flipped over the picture, searching for any other information. "Another victim?"

"Perhaps," Marcus said, folding the photo he held and shoving it into his pocket.

Cate eyed him. "You're taking that?"

"It may prove useful."

Cate searched through the other folders, finding nothing useful. "Doesn't look like we're finding a clue this time."

"Which may be a good thing."

"It's not," Cate said, dropping the last folder she searched. "We need a break." ·

"The last time we found a clue here it led to an extremely painful moment for you."

Cate pressed her lips together as she heaved a sigh.

"Though she underestimated you," he said, sliding a lock of hair behind her ear. "She underestimated your strength."

Cate smiled up at him. The sound of a throat clearing interrupted their conversation. Cate stepped back, shooting a glance at the door. "Nothing in here."

"Nothing out there either."

Cate grimaced and shook her head. "So much for that. Let's hope Ginger can help."

Marcus nodded, motioning for Cate to precede him around the desk. She took a step past him when the world around her melted for a moment. Random images of Dunhaven Castle's darkened halls fluttered through her mind.

She sucked in a gasp, grasping onto Marcus to steady herself.

"Catherine?" he asked, holding her from falling.

"Sorry," she said, licking her lips and sucking a breath in. "Lost my footing."

He arched an eyebrow.

She shrugged. "I tripped."

"Have you twisted your ankle?"

Cate pressed her lips together, waving a finger in the air. "No. I do *not* need to be carried."

"I shall be the decider of that," Marcus called after her as she stalked from the room.

Jack furrowed his brow when she passed him. "He has a real penchant for carrying me around like a damsel in a gothic novel."

She stepped into the hall, passing the open bedroom door. A whiff of Gianna's overpowering perfume floated past her nostrils. A blinding set of images spun through her brain.

The world swirled along with the memory-like pictures. The walls melted, and her vision blurred before she pitched forward.

CHAPTER 11

*I*mages sped through her mind faster than she could process. They settled into what seemed like a memory. She ran through the halls of Dunhaven Castle again. A scream sounded as she rounded a corner in a hall not currently used. Her stomach turned, and her heart pounded as she hurried toward her unknown destination.

She wrapped her hands around the doorknob. Before she could open it, the image faded away, replaced by blackness.

Cate's eyelids fluttered open, and she sucked in a sharp gasp. Two concerned faces hovered over her.

"Catherine," Marcus said, stroking her hair, "how do you feel?"

She crinkled her brow as she glanced around the room. "Fine."

Jack squeezed her hand. "Are you certain, Cate? You just passed out."

"I'm sure." Her lips tugged downward in a grimace. "Am I in Gianna's bed?"

"Yeah," Jack answered, nodding his head toward Marcus. "He carried you in."

Cate winced as she tried to push up to sitting. "I'm not surprised."

Marcus prevented her from rising. "You were unconscious. This was an obvious case for carrying you."

"I'm fine. Let me sit up."

"We have yet to assess that," Marcus answered.

"I hate to be a pain here, but I'm not comfortable laying in Gianna's bed. I'm perfectly fine."

Marcus arched an eyebrow at her. "Then explain your sudden fainting spell."

Cate tugged her lips into a grimace as she shrugged. "I–"

"Don't say you didn't eat enough because you had a healthy breakfast courtesy of Dembe," Marcus said, feeling her forehead.

"Maybe I ate too much," Cate suggested.

Marcus offered her an unimpressed stare. "Very funny, Catherine. Your pulse is slowing, though your heart was racing only moments ago."

"I'm fine. It was racing because I fainted, that's it."

"But what caused you to faint?" Marcus questioned.

Jack squeezed her hand. "For once, he has a point, Cate."

Cate flopped back into the pillows with a sigh. "I'm not liking the agreement between you two."

Marcus raised his eyebrows at her. "Well, that is simply too bad. We have–"

"Is that the time?" Cate gasped, swiping the clock off Gianna's nightstand.

"I have heard nothing from Stefano, so there is no need to panic."

"Yes, there is a need to panic," Cate said, pushing herself up to sit and trying to swing her legs over the bed's edge. "I'm going to be late for my lunch with Ginger."

"You are not going to your lunch with Ginger," Marcus answered.

"Yes, I am," Cate said as she pushed herself against the mattress in an attempt to stand.

"No, you are not," Marcus answered, pressing her back onto the bed.

Cate smacked a hand against the bedspread. "I'm not sick!"

"We have not determined that yet. We should go home and assess your condition."

Cate wrinkled her nose. "I'm not going home and being put to bed with a hot toddy like a Victorian housewife. I have important business with Ginger, and I'm determined to do my part."

"I said nothing about a toddy, though that could be arranged."

"It's not necessary. Now, let's go."

"Cate, maybe we should go back to the house," Jack said, clapping a hand on her shoulder.

Cate pressed her hands to her temples. "This is ridiculous. I'm fine. There is no reason to go back to the house and every reason to go to the restaurant. We'll discuss this all when we get home. And if I collapse at the restaurant, I'm certain you'll race in and carry me from the building."

"This is not a joke, Catherine. You collapsed."

"And scared the hell of out of us, Cate," Jack added.

Cate sucked in a deep breath, flicking her gaze to the floor. "I know. And I think I know what's causing it. And it's definitely something we can discuss as soon as I get this information from Ginger."

Marcus stared at her with a gaping jaw. "You know what's causing it?"

She flicked her gaze up to him before lowering it to the floor again. "I think so."

"And?" he prompted when she didn't continue.

"And we can discuss it when we're home. Getting this

information is vital. It could make the difference between success and failure." Cate flicked her gaze to his dark eyes again. "Please. This can keep, I promise."

"Tell me what you think it is," Marcus prodded.

Cate pressed her lips together, shaking her head. She sucked in a deep breath and flicked her gaze up to him. "I think it's temporalysis again."

"What?" Jack gasped, skirting the bed and kneeling in front of Cate. "Cate! This can't keep. It can be fatal."

Marcus narrowed his eyes at her. "Do you have–"

"Dragon's blood," Cate answered. "Yes, I got it from Dembe this morning. And I've used it."

Marcus heaved a sigh. "I shall need to speak to him about that."

"Don't punish Dembe for my choices," Cate said, pushing herself to stand. "I asked both Andrea and him to keep it a secret for a short time."

"Because of the lunch with Ginger."

Cate nodded at him.

"All right, Catherine. We shall discuss this further when we arrive home. But you are free to go to your lunch."

"Thanks for your permission," Cate said, patting his chest.

"If you feel ill–"

"I'll signal you. Though I hope to get through this. I'll use the dragon's blood." She pulled her purse open, retrieved another lozenge, and popped it in her mouth. "Let's go, we're going to be late."

"Cate," Jack said as they strode from the room, "are you sure this is a good idea? Temporalysis almost killed me."

"I know. But it didn't kill me the last time, and this is exactly like it was the last time."

"That doesn't mean it won't kill you this time," he answered.

"You don't know that," Cate said. "Maybe temporalysis is always non-fatal for me. We have no idea."

Jack glanced over his shoulder at Marcus. "Can it kill her?"

"If it is temporalysis, yes," Marcus answered. "Temporalysis can always be fatal. Surviving it once does not make you immune to fatalities."

"So, you can contract it more than once?" Jack asked as they slipped into the hall.

"Yes," Marcus answered.

Jack grabbed her arm and squeezed. "Cate, please, let's go back to the house and talk about this. We shouldn't dally. I nearly died from this."

Cate headed for the stairs. "I'm not going to die in the next two hours."

"You don't know that," Jack said as he hurried down the stairs after her. He pressed a hand to his forehead and shook his head. "Cate, please, reconsider this. It's not going to matter if we find Gertrude, and you're dead."

Cate pushed into the spring air, sucking in a deep breath. "I don't think two hours is going to make a difference, and maybe we can make some progress on this."

Jack stared at Marcus as he strode onto the sidewalk from the building. "Do you want to maybe weigh in here? I can't believe you're going to let her do this."

Marcus flicked his eyebrows up as he glanced between them. "I can't force her to do anything. She has her own mind."

The corner of Cate's lips turned up, and she cut her gaze to Jack.

Jack screwed up his face. "You're kidding. You carry her around like a doll, and you tell me not to let her get in trouble."

Marcus waved his finger in the air as they strode to the

car. "I take excellent care of Catherine. I protect her from harm as much as possible. But that does not mean I control her."

"Unbelievable," Jack said, flinging his arms out as he shuffled to the car and tugged the passenger door open. "The one time I need you to go all medieval on her plans and you refuse to do it." He slammed the door shut with a sigh before he twisted to face them. "Are you hoping she dies?"

Marcus shot him a surprised glance. "Certainly not. Catherine's well-being is of the utmost importance to me."

"So, you're going to let her go to lunch with someone from The Agency while she's dying so we can get a lead that may give us nothing while we delay her treatment for a potentially deadly disease? Smart."

"Ginger is hardly dangerous. I have my dragon's blood. And we're only delaying any other treatment for a few hours," Cate argued as the car wound through the streets of London toward the restaurant.

"I concur with Catherine. Believe me, if I felt she was in any danger, I would have argued the case myself."

"How about simply not allowing her to be this reckless?"

"Allowing me?" Cate cried.

"She is not a child, Mack. I cannot allow or disallow her to do things."

"Jack," he growled through clenched teeth.

"Rest assured, Mr. Reid, if I thought she would do herself any harm, I would have done whatever it took to convince her not to pursue the gambit with Ginger."

Cate snapped her gaze to him. "You wouldn't have carried me off like in a Victorian novel, though, right?"

"If circumstances warranted it," Marcus said as the car rolled to a stop outside the restaurant. "Have a nice lunch, dear."

Cate slid from the vehicle after the driver opened her

door. She poked her head back inside, flicking her gaze between the two of them. "Behave. Both of you. And don't come charging in and dragging me off unless my death is imminent."

She slammed the door shut and hastened to the entrance of the restaurant. The doorman pulled the door open for her, and she slipped inside. The maitre d' greeted her with a pleasant smile.

"Hi," Cate said with a smile. "Catherine Northcott. I'm meeting with–"

"Cate! Yoo-hoo!" Ginger waved from inside the restaurant. "I'm here."

Cate pointed at the bubbly blonde. "Found her."

"Ah, yes, Miss Fallinger," the man said with a wrinkled nose. He led her to the table, spinning to face her as they arrived. "May I take your coat?"

"Yes," Cate said, peeling the light jacket off and passing it over.

"Well, don't look at her like that, guv," Ginger said with a coy smile at the man. "She's a duchess you know?"

The man blinked his eyes at Cate as she settled in the chair. "Yes, Duke Northcott is my husband."

The man arched an eyebrow. "My apologies, Your Grace. Had I known–"

"You can make it up to her by bringing us two martinis to start," Ginger said.

"Right away," he answered, hurrying away with her coat in hand.

Ginger frowned at him as he scurried away. "Lousy sod. He's never nice to the mistresses."

"I'll bet he thought I was one."

"But you're not. And you're a whole duchess, too. That gave him a shock." Ginger stared after him for a moment more before she flicked her gaze to Cate, sliding an arm across the table to clasp her hand. "It's good to see you, Cate Catherine Northcott."

Cate squeezed her hand and smiled. "It's good to see you, too."

"And what have you been up to? Did you get your shopping spree?"

"I did," Cate answered, flicking her gaze to a plant that rustled nearby before she cleared her throat.

"Uh-oh. Tell me he did it again."

"No," Cate answered. "Nothing but good behavior."

Ginger arched an eyebrow over her expertly made-up eye. "Really? Are you sure?"

Cate clammed up as their martinis were delivered, studying the menu for a moment. Ginger picked her glass up and raised it to Cate. "To good times with the duchess."

Cate retrieved her glass, clinking it against Ginger's before taking a sip.

"Now, back to it. Are you certain? Because, let me tell you, Cate, once a cheater, always a cheater. I know. I'm a mistress. They tell their wives all the time that it's over and it never is. The first bad day at the office, or investment gone wrong, and there they are right back at your door looking for comfort."

The leaves of the plant rustled again. Cate did her best to ignore it, licking her lips as she set the menu aside. "I have no reason to suspect–"

Ginger wagged a finger at her. "Oh, that's the time he's doing it. When you don't suspect. Let me guess. Everything's going alone swimmingly at home. He's being overly nice. Helpful even."

Cate cocked her head. "It's like you can see into our marriage."

The leaves shook hard as she spoke.

Ginger took another sip of her martini. "You've got troubles, Cate. He's bouncing around with a mistress again. Mark my words."

Cate sipped at her drink. "You may be right." She furrowed her brow, but the appearance of their waiter prevented any further conversation. After placing their order, Cate sipped her martini again.

"Now, let's talk about more pleasant things like how big the necklace will be this time when he finally admits his nefarious ways."

Cate chuckled at her as Ginger waved for another two martinis. "That diamond necklace you were wearing the day we met was a dandy, Cate Catherine. I can't imagine what he'll give you this time."

"Well," Cate said as she finished her martini and handed the empty glass to the waiter as he replaced it with a fresh one, "that's something I was hoping you could help with."

Ginger flicked her eyebrows up as she studied Cate over the rim of her glass. "I vote rubies this time. No, no, sapphires. They'd look so beautiful with your eyes."

Cate waved the comment away. "I have sapphires."

"Oh, I bet they're dazzling."

"If you think the diamonds were incredible, you should see the sapphires."

"I may have to," Ginger said with a wink. "Okay, sapphires are out. So, rubies it is."

Cate leaned closer, tilting her head. "Actually, I was thinking something a bit different."

The corners of Ginger's lips turned up, and she leaned closer, arching an eyebrow. "Do tell."

Cate licked her lips as the waiter placed hot dishes in front of them. Cate poked at her chicken with her fork as she formed her request in her mind.

"You were saying?" Ginger asked as she stabbed a piece of pasta.

"I have a bit of money set aside. My own. Not his."

Ginger, chewed the pasta slowly, jabbing a fork at Cate. "No, sweetheart, you don't want to spend that on rubies. You spend *his* money on the rubies, and you keep that money for a rainy day."

"Well, that's the thing. I do want to keep it for a rainy day, but…"

Ginger sipped her martini, raising an eyebrow. "But?"

"I'd like to have more of it for a rainy day if you know what I mean."

"Oh," Ginger said, her chin raising higher, "you want to invest."

"Yes," Cate said, "I knew you'd understand. And I want to do it myself. Not with his investment people, I don't trust them."

"Oh, I understand. I've seen some of mine put their wives' money in low-growth deliberately. Why?" Ginger leaned closer, lowering her voice. "She can't leave him that way."

"Right," Cate said with a nod and another sip of her martini. "I want to make my own way."

"Oh, I'm not certain he's going to let you do that. The royalty is notorious for not wanting any scandal."

"Then maybe my investment will be a good reason for there not to be any more strife."

"So, you think having enough to leave him will keep him in line?"

Cate lifted a shoulder. "It can't hurt."

Ginger puckered her lips as she cradled the martini against her chest.

Cate slid her arm across the white linen tablecloth and grabbed Ginger's other hand. "Please, Ginger? I really want to stand on my own two feet and be proud of something."

Ginger eyed her for a moment before she twisted her arm

and grabbed hold of Cate's hand. She squeezed it as a smile spread across her face. "I'd be happy to help you."

Cate broke into a smile. "Thank you."

"What did you need? Typical investments made by some of the bigwigs in Arnie's office?"

"Actually," Cate said, "Marcus was in a meeting with some of Mr. Chapman's people last night. He mentioned something about newly acquired properties. He was considering investing, but he's still deciding. I'd like to beat him to the punch."

"Steal the investment right out from under him, huh?"

Cate raised her chin and nodded. "Yes. Though..."

"You're afraid?"

Cate winced, setting her fork on the plate. "I don't want to do anything foolish. I'm afraid Marcus may say I've jumped in without thinking if he finds out. I'd like to do a little research first."

"You want to see the locations and make sure they're worth it?" Ginger asked.

"Yes. But Marcus won't tell me anything about them."

Ginger's lips curled up. "Don't worry your pretty little head about that, love. I've got you covered."

Cate returned the gesture, picking up her martini and raising it toward Ginger.

With a giggle, Ginger lifted her glass and clinked it against Cate's. They finished their meal making light conversation about their lives. As Cate paid the bill at her own insistence, Ginger scrawled the addresses of the Chapman group's newly acquired properties on a cocktail napkin.

She slid it across the table toward Cate. "These are the ones that just came in during the last two months. Check them out and if you have *any* questions, you call me."

Cate smiled down at the napkin before she slid it into her

purse. "Thank you, Ginger. It was good to see you. I'll be in touch."

They said their goodbyes, exchanging a hug before Ginger offered her a wave and tottered off. Jack and Marcus circled around the large plant as Ginger disappeared through the door.

Cate pulled the address list from her purse and handed it to Marcus.

He perused it before pocketing it. "Well done, Catherine."

"Now, can we please discuss this temporalysis thing?" Jack asked.

"Yes, I think we should," Cate said with a deep sigh. "Because I think I'm getting worse."

CHAPTER 12

$\mathcal{C}$ate licked her lips, drumming her fingers against the seat of the car as they made their way home. The chicken she'd had for lunch threatened to reappear as worry over her condition consumed her. This time seemed worse. She worried it would be fatal.

Warm fingers slid around her hand, stopping their nervous movement. She glanced at Marcus who smiled at her.

She forced a smile onto her face as tears threatened. If she died, what would happen to Dunhaven Castle? Would it go to him? Would that spell disaster for her friends?

He squeezed her hand, sensing her apprehension. The car slowed to a stop outside the house. Cate climbed from inside, and they entered the house. They settled in the living room.

Jack collapsed onto the couch next to Cate, puffing out a sigh as he let his head drop into his hands. "Okay, can we finally address the temporalysis situation here before something terrible happens?"

"Yes, I think we should," Cate said with a shake of her head, her voice rising as panic laced it. "The dragon's blood doesn't seem to be working at all. The last time it helped with the symptoms, but this time it's not and I'm afraid–"

"Stop there," Marcus said, offering her a brandy. "Go back to the beginning and tell me what has been happening."

Cate grabbed the proffered beverage as Jack rubbed her shoulders. She took a sip, trying to steady her shaking hands.

"Take a breath, Catherine. There is no reason to panic," Marcus said, squeezing her shoulder.

Cate pursed her lips, sliding her eyes closed and sucking in a slow breath.

She opened her eyes, flicking her gaze up to Marcus.

"Ready?"

Cate nodded and took another sip of the brandy.

"From the beginning."

Cate sucked in a breath, crinkling her brow. "Wait, the beginning beginning, like the start of the original temporalysis, or the start of this one?"

"This one for now."

"Okay. Uh, it started the night Mr. Smythe made his announcement. I had a nightmare, very similar to what happened during the last bout of temporalysis."

"About?" Marcus asked as he poured himself a brandy.

"I was running through the halls of Dunhaven Castle. Someone screamed. I woke up."

Jack leapt from his seat, pacing the floor. "Bah, it's the same damned thing as it was last time."

"Let her finish," Marcus said. "I assume this was not an isolated incident?"

"No, it wasn't."

"But it's the same as last time. This started with nightmares." Jack jabbed a finger toward Marcus. "Nightmares of you chasing her all over the castle."

Marcus poured another brandy and held it out. "Try a sip for your nerves."

"I don't need a drink. I need everything back to normal. I need Cate not sick. Again. I need–"

"Take the drink, Mr. Reid. And let us finish our discussion."

Jack flicked his gaze to Cate. She gave him a nod. He grabbed the drink from Marcus's outstretched hand and took a sip, collapsing onto the couch next to her again.

"Continue, dear."

"Umm, I chalked the nightmare up to the stress of seeing Gianna, but…" Cate heaved a sigh. "I'm having the visions again."

"Of?" Marcus asked.

Cate lifted her shoulders. "I'm not sure," she said, her features pinching as she spoke, "they go so fast, I can't make them out. Sometimes it's the hall, sometimes it's other things. Last night before the party, I passed out as Andrea was buckling my shoes."

Her breathing turned ragged, and tears formed in her eyes. "It's the same as last time. It feels like memories, but it's not."

Cate pressed her lips together into a thin line as she held back the emotions welling inside her. Jack rubbed his hand across her shoulders again as he let out a sharp breath.

"And this happened earlier today while at Gianna's? This is the reason you fainted?"

Cate nodded as she sipped her brandy. "More visions. And a few almost came through at the restaurant. Now, I've had the dragon's blood. Two lozenges since I got them this morning but it's doing nothing to stop any of this."

Marcus nodded as he sauntered to the front window and stared through it.

"Oh, Cate, why didn't you say something last night?" Jack asked.

"I didn't think it was anything. I just wanted to get the

information at the party and today I thought the dragon's blood would help. I was going to tell you. I just wanted to get more information first."

Marcus sipped his drink before he spun to face them. "Tell me about the last time."

"Umm," Cate began.

Jack leapt from his seat poking a finger at the man. "The last time started with nightmares of her being chased through the castle by you."

Marcus flicked his gaze to Jack then returned it to Cate. "And then?"

"No," Cate said with a shake of her head. "It started with the hole in the library."

Marcus's eyebrows raised, prompting her to continue.

"I kept dreaming about a gaping hole in the library. I saw myself in clothing from the late 1700s. And I kept hearing a warning."

"And you found a passage there, correct?" Marcus asked.

"Yes," Cate answered with a nod. "In the spot it always appeared at in my nightmare."

"And did you have waking visions during that time?"

"No," Cate said. "I only had those later. After we met. Before that, I had dreams about you. Then we met. And then I had more dreams about you. Everything shifted to the dreams about the ball. That's when I started getting the visions."

"And that is when you started losing time. Wandering the castle, seeming to be in a different era."

"Yes," Cate answered.

"You did not have that before this?"

"The wandering? No, just recently."

"And are you suffering from the same now or just the visions and dreams?"

Cate crinkled her brow. "Just the visions and dreams so

far. They are fairly frequent, but so far, at least to my knowledge, no roaming around."

Marcus sipped his drink again, narrowing his eyes. Jack eased onto the couch, sliding an arm around Cate's shoulders.

Cate set her empty glass on the coffee table. "So, do I have temporalysis again? Am I going to get this every time I time travel now?"

Marcus heaved a sigh. "No, I don't believe you have temporalysis."

Cate flopped back against the thick cushions. "Great. What weird thing do I have this time and how deadly is it?"

Marcus finished his brandy and set the glass on the bar. "I am fairly certain I know, but I would like Mother to consult on your condition."

"Whoa, wait a minute," Jack said, leaping from his seat again, "we're not going anywhere until we get some answers. Cate could be dying."

"I doubt it, though providing answers is exactly why we should visit my mother. Besides, she would love to see you, Catherine."

"You doubt it? What if you're wrong?"

Marcus lifted his shoulders. "It's a sensation I'm not familiar with since I am never wrong."

"You're a real piece of work, you know that? I'm not willing to risk Cate's life–"

"Neither am I," Marcus growled with a curled lip.

"Stop it. Both of you. There is something far more important going on here," Cate said. "We need to follow up on those addresses."

Jack shot her a shocked glance. "Cate, we need to follow up on your illness which, by the way, no matter what the genius over here says sounds a hell of a lot like temporalysis."

Cate bit her lower lip, flicking her gaze to Marcus as she

rose to stand. "We need to find Gertrude before this gets any worse."

"Stefano can follow up–"

"No!" Cate said, balling her hands into fists. "I want to follow up."

"Fine. We'll do that first."

Jack scoffed, tossing his arms overhead. "You're joking! You're going to put this off to search these properties first?" He pressed his palms together, shaking them at Cate. "Cate, please, don't be so reckless. I nearly died from this. I know what it's like. You shouldn't ignore it."

"I'm not." She slid her gaze to Marcus. "I'm not dying, right?"

Marcus set his dark eyes on her. "No, I'm quite certain you are not. I would *never* risk your life, dear."

"That's good enough for me," she said with a nod. "Let's go."

Jack stuck his hands on his hips and shook his head. "I wish you'd reconsider."

"As much as I would love to see Anna again, we need a clue to Gertrude's location before she slips away from us entirely. We can't risk it, Jack."

"We can't risk your life either, Cate. I understand the current situation leaves something to be desired, but we've won for the moment. Maybe we should let it go."

"For the moment are the key words in that sentence," Marcus said as they made their way to the foyer. "The Agency is always seeking to find a new path forward. Any time we waste gives them an advantage. And while Catherine's condition is important, it can be dealt with after we find a path forward."

Cate pushed through the front door. Dark clouds sailed past, blocking out the sun. She hurried to the car, ducking inside as large raindrops pelted the sidewalk.

"So, can I stop taking these?" she asked, waving the pouch of dragon's blood lozenges in the air as Marcus slid in next to her.

"Yes, they will do nothing."

"Good," Cate said while stuffing them back in her purse. "I hate the taste of them."

Marcus passed along the first address and within half an hour they'd arrived outside of the apartment building.

"The address said Penthouse C," Cate said as she stared up at the posh building.

"Seems like it may be a logical place to keep her," Jack answered, studying the facade with his hands shoved into his pockets.

"Let's hope we get lucky on the first try."

They strode to the door where a doorman stood, his hands clasped in front of him. He stared down his nose at them, arching an eyebrow. "Visiting someone?"

"I'm considering buying Penthouse C," Marcus answered.

"Then you should get in touch with the Chapman group. They are handling the property."

"I'd prefer to see it prior to making an inquiry with them."

The doorman rocked on his toes. "Sorry, mate, viewings are only by appointment with the Chapman group."

Marcus offered him an unimpressed stare. He lifted his hand when Cate batted it down. "Hi, I'm sorry. Ginger Fallinger told us to stop by. She said it wouldn't be a problem."

The doorman raised his eyebrows, adjusting his cap. "You know Ginger?"

"Yes," Cate answered. "She's a friend. She passed along the address and told me to stop by if I'd like to see it."

"Oh, well, I'm so sorry to disappoint, but I don't have the keys, you see."

"Oh," Cate said, pressing her fingers against her forehead.

"I do." She patted her purse. "Silly of me. I forgot to say earlier."

"Ginger gave you a set?"

"Well, she let me borrow a set to look around. I'll return them when I see her later for dinner at the club."

"Right, well, if Ginger said it's okay, I guess it's okay. Go on up." He tugged the door open and motioned for them to enter.

"Thank you," Cate said as they filed past him through the door and pressed the button for the elevator in the lobby.

"Good going, Cate," Jack whispered as they waited.

Marcus flicked his eyebrows up. "I could have handled it."

"We didn't need anyone passing out from your weird sleep-touch thing," Cate retorted.

The doors whooshed open, and they stepped inside. "There's only one problem," Jack said as he pressed the button for the top floor. "We don't actually have the keys."

Marcus closed his eyes and shook his head. "You really are not all that bright, are you?"

"Look, mate–"

"I am not your mate," Marcus answered.

"Marcus can unlock the door the same way he did at Gianna's," Cate said, standing between them as the car continued its upward journey.

Jack furrowed his brow, scratching his head. "I thought the door was just unlocked."

"Why would Gianna leave her door unlocked?"

Jack shrugged. "I don't know. Felt invincible because of her ties to The Agency?"

Marcus clicked his tongue as Cate patted his arm.

"He's new to magic."

"Obviously."

The doors opened, and Marcus led them from the elevator, finding apartment C. With a flick of his wrist, he pushed the door open. An empty flat lay beyond it. Cate stepped inside, her heels echoing off the hardwood flooring.

"Do you think they moved her?" she asked, her voice echoing in the empty space.

"It's possible. Though it's also entirely possible that she has never been here."

Cate scanned the space again, bobbing her head up and down. "Okay, well, I guess we should have a look around."

"I'll go with you, Cate," Jack said, sliding his arm around her shoulders.

"Okay. We'll check the bedrooms."

Marcus nodded as he studied the empty bookcase.

Cate led Jack down a hall and entered the last door. She strode across the room and tugged open the closet door, searching the inside for any clues.

"Nothing," she said as Jack emerged from another door across the space leading to an en-suite bathroom.

"Me either."

"Let's try the room across the hall."

Jack nodded, and they hurried to the second bedroom. "I don't know how you can be so calm, Cate," he said as he swept a hand across the empty shelf in the closet, sending a spray of dust into the air.

"What do you mean?" she asked, spinning to face him after checking the corners.

"I mean all of this. Magic. Him." Jack pressed his lips together as his features pinched. "Your illness."

Cate shrugged as they crossed the hall to another bedroom. "As hard as this is for you to hear, I trust him."

She tugged open the closet door, and, upon finding it empty, pushed it shut, finding Jack on the other side.

"You can't be serious."

"I am."

"Do you really trust him or are you just going along with him because he's saying what you want to hear?"

Cate studied him for a moment. "He's not saying what I want to hear."

"How do you know? You wanted to look for clues. He says you're fine. How can you put your life in his hands, Cate?"

Cate shuffled around the room in search of anything that may be a link to Gertrude. She came to a stop before answering, sucking in a deep breath. "Because my life has been in his hands multiple times already, and he's come through every time."

She did a final scan of the space. "There's nothing here. Should we try the last door?"

Jack didn't answer for a moment, staring at her. "Did he put a spell on you?"

Cate burst into laughter. "What?"

"I'm serious, Cate. Did he put some sort of magical spell on you?"

"No," she said with another chuckle before her smile faded. "At least, I don't think so."

"So, you don't know," Jack answered, wagging a finger at her as she strode from the room.

"I do know. Mostly."

"Mostly?"

Cate switched on the light in the windowless room across the hall, finding a small bathroom. "He didn't, okay?"

"How can you be so sure?"

Cate glanced up at him, one shoulder rising toward her ear as she wrinkled her nose and prepared to answer. " Jack, I–"

"Catherine?" Marcus's voice called from the living room.

"Coming!" she answered. "We should go. We have three more locations to check."

She smiled at him and squeezed his hand before tugging him toward the door.

"Did you find anything?" she asked as she stepped into the square living room again.

"Nothing. There is no sign anyone has been here in the past several months since The Agency acquired it."

Cate frowned as she took a final look around the space. "Oh well. On to the next."

Marcus nodded as he placed his hand against her back and guided her toward the door. Voices sounded in the hall. Cate froze as a woman cackled before murmuring something to the man who had just spoken.

Her eyes went wide, and she snapped her gaze to Marcus. "That's Gianna! And it sounds like she's coming here!"

Cate bit into her lower lip as she realized they were trapped.

CHAPTER 13

*M*arcus pulled her closer to him. "We'll location hop to the car."

"No," Cate answered with a shake of her head, "we may overhear something crucial."

"We need to hide," Jack hissed. "Before they catch us."

Keys jangled outside the door as Gianna's voice became louder.

"Bedroom closet," Cate said, tiptoeing into the hall and hurrying to the master bedroom. She raced across the room and flung the door open. She stepped inside with Marcus and spun to find Jack grimacing on the outside.

"I'll go to the other one."

"No, Jack! There's no time. You'll get caught. Come on, there's room." She waved him inside and pulled the door shut behind them.

"This is not at all how I hoped the day would turn out," Jack whispered as the sounds of the door opening reached their ears.

Marcus slid his arm around Cate, pulling her closer to him. Jack frowned as she slipped her arm around his waist and leaned into him, knitting her brows as she concentrated on the conversation floating their way.

"Love the bookcases," Gianna said.

"I thought you would," Arnold Chapman's voice answered her.

Footsteps approached their location, stopping every so often. Cate's heart pounded against her ribs as Gianna's high heels clicked closer and closer.

Marcus tightened his grip on her when Arnold's voice echoed off the walls of the master bedroom. "What do you think?"

"Mmmm, it's roomy."

"You could do it up any way you'd like."

Silence met the statement for a moment before Arnold spoke again. "And look at that view."

"But I like my old flat."

"Then keep that, too. Whatever you want, Gigi."

Cate rolled her eyes. High-heeled footsteps shuffled across the room, sounding on the tiled bathroom floor before clicking back onto the hardwood.

"I don't know, Arnie. Perhaps the closet space can convince me."

Footsteps closed in on their location. Cate tightened her grip on Marcus as her heart pounded harder.

"Now, there's no need for that. I assure you it's adequate."

A giggle resounded as a thud jiggled the closet door. "Arnie," Gianna said with a chuckle.

"What?"

Another thud against the door. "You are insatiable."

"You're kidding me," Cate hissed.

Arnold's voice turned breathy. "I think you should take this flat. Think of all the new memories we can create here."

Cate wrinkled her nose at the statement as the sounds of lips smacking filled the air.

"All right, you've convinced me."

"Good. Let's properly christen the place, then, shall we?"

Cate grimaced, shaking her head. "Oh, gross."

"Perhaps we should leave," Marcus whispered in her ear.

Cate glanced up to answer when the conversation outside the closet changed.

"Just a moment. Let's save celebrating for the appropriate time."

"Appropriate time?" Arnold asked.

"My plan hasn't quite come off yet," Gianna said. Footsteps clicked away from the door.

Cate held a finger in the air, pressing her lips together as she listened.

"You're on track though, aren't you?"

"I've got some new tricks up my sleeve," Gianna answered. "I'm still working everything out, but this could be our ticket."

"And what of your nemesis?"

A sigh sounded and more high-heeled footsteps plodded across the room. "Cate Kensie is not my nemesis. Merely a thorn in my side."

"Quite the thorn, apparently."

"How that unalluring dimwit managed to convince a man like Marcus Northcott to marry her is beyond me."

Cate's jaw dropped open, and she stuck a hand on her hip.

"Yet she has. So, what is your play?"

Cate dipped her head forward, straining for the answer.

"I'm still working it all out. But as long as she continues to chase her tail looking for her benefactor and drag Northcott along with her, I have the advantage. I just need a bit more time to work out all the details."

"Can you string her along for that long?"

"I think so. She's rather stuck, isn't she? She has to find

Gertrude. Which gives me time to move forward with my next plan."

"I won't press you for details...yet. Though, what if the esteemed duchess gives up the chase? I assume you have her benefactor hidden quite well."

"She won't. I'll slip her a clue to keep her on the trail."

"And what if she finds the old biddy?"

Cate clamped her jaw closed, shaking her head.

"Let her. I've found a much more delicious angle to work that is guaranteed to bring us Dunhaven Castle."

"I like the sound of that," Arnold said before more lip-smacking replaced their conversation. A giddy moan escaped Gianna. "I like the sound of that even more."

The couple giggled for a bit more before the sounds of kissing replaced their laughter.

"Time to go," Cate said as Jack grimaced.

"I think we're pretty stuck," Jack whispered as the sound of a body smacking against the wall echoed.

"You really are ignorant," Marcus huffed as he pulled Cate close to him.

"Don't leave Jack," she warned.

Marcus pressed his lips together as he reached for Jack's hand. Jack pulled his back, screwing up his face.

"Give him your hand," Cate said as another moan cut through the air. "Quickly."

Jack eyed him suspiciously as he held out his hand. Marcus grabbed it and the dark room faded away, replaced by an overcast day.

Cate glanced around, finding their car on the side street they'd parked on earlier. "Thank goodness you got us out of there. I couldn't take much more of that."

Jack stood unmoving as his gaze slid around. He swallowed hard, wiping at his pale face. "What the hell just happened."

"Location hop," Cate and Marcus said simultaneously as they headed for the vehicle.

"What?" Jack questioned, hurrying after them.

"A location hop. Marcus can move from one location to another instantly. And lucky for us and our ears, he can take us with him."

"That was rather disturbing," Jack said with another gulp.

"I know," Cate answered as they slipped into the car. "Gianna and her shenanigans with any man who will look her way was something I never hoped to have first-hand knowledge of."

Jack slid into the front seat and twisted to face her. "I meant the location hop."

"Oh," Cate answered, crinkling her brow.

"One minute we were in a closet. The next we were on the street. I'm not certain I've fully recovered."

"I am no amateur, Mr. Reid. But if you prefer, I will gladly leave you behind the next time Catherine and I make a hasty exit."

Jack glared at him.

"I'm sure Jack appreciates your unique talent. Just give him a chance to take it all in."

The car merged into traffic and headed for the next location on the list.

"I hope we find something at one of these places. I did not like that conversation at all. What other things is she pursuing?" Cate asked.

"I'm afraid to find out."

"She's already kidnapped you, so it must be something else. But what? What guarantees her Dunhaven Castle? Especially if she doesn't care if we find Gertrude?"

Cate stared at her lap as she tried to parse through the meaning in her mind. "And what clue is she going to feed us?

How long is she going to have us following these leads around?"

"Until her next plan comes to fruition," Marcus answered.

"Which is what?" Cate asked again with a sigh.

"I don't know," Jack said, scrubbing his face, "but I hate this."

"Buck up, Reid. The Agency is not an easily surmountable enemy. This battle will rage for quite some time."

Jack shook his head before letting it fall into his hands. "I hope we can withstand it."

"Look to Catherine for a shining example. She has already spent time fighting them on your behalf. She has nearly died on your behalf. And now she leads the charge to save Gertrude MacKenzie from their clutches even as they move on to a new target."

Jack twisted to face them, his features pinching.

"So, dig deep and find your backbone. You'll need it. And Catherine will need your support."

"As long as we protect Dunhaven Castle and everyone in it, it doesn't matter how long it goes on," Cate said as she squeezed Marcus's hand.

Marcus kept his eyes trained on Jack as he tugged Cate's hand closer to him, patting it.

"We need to find a clue before Gianna leaks it to us. We need to give her less time for her plan than she wants."

"Excellent, Catherine. We should strive to keep them as off-balance as they try to make you."

"Easier said than done, I think," Jack answered. "How can we make that happen?"

"By looking for some sort of evidence and not worrying about things we don't need to worry about right now. We have to prioritize," Cate said.

"And we must trust each other," Marcus said, threading his fingers through Cate's.

"Right," Cate said with a nod. Both backseat passengers turned their gazes to Jack.

He paused for a moment before poking a finger toward his chest. "Oh, me? I trust you, Cate."

Marcus flicked his eyebrows up.

Jack switched his gaze between them. "Is that good enough?"

"It would be really good if you trusted both of us," Cate said. "We need to be a united front."

Jack frowned, his eyes sliding toward Marcus. "Okay."

"Okay, what?" Marcus asked.

Jack narrowed his eyes at the man. "I...trust...Cate and so by extension I...we are a united front."

"I think that's the best he can do right now," Cate said, patting Marcus's hand. "We'll take it. As long as we're all on the same side, we're good."

Marcus offered Jack a smirk as he clasped Cate's hand in both of his. Jack spun in his seat, blowing out a breath as he faced forward.

Cate cocked her head at his behavior. "Are you okay, Jack?"

"Oh, I'm just swell."

Cate fluttered her eyelashes as she stared at the back of his head. "I know the location hop is odd at first–"

"To say the least. I just location hopped with a guy who... never mind," Jack said, throwing his hands in the air. "We're all on the same side."

"That's right. And it's a good thing because we need everyone to figure this out."

"Let's hope there is a clue at this property," Jack said as the car rolled to a stop.

Cate stared up at the house. "Looks promising."

They stepped out of the car as thunder rumbled overhead. Cate hurried up the walk behind Marcus, pelted by large drops of rain falling from the overcast skies.

Marcus opened the door, allowing her to enter first before he stepped inside behind her. Jack brought up the rear, closing the door behind them.

They glanced around the empty space. Cate toggled the light switch on, but nothing bloomed to life. "No power."

Light sparked to life as Marcus conjured a fireball, leaving it floating above his hand. "Come along, Catherine. I shall accompany you this time."

Cate shook her head. "We should stick together. With no light, we could miss something." She flicked her gaze to Marcus. "Besides, we shouldn't leave him alone. The Agency has come after him once. We can't afford a second time."

"You are correct, dear. Come along, Reid. Keep your eyes open for any signs of the former mistress of Dunhaven."

Jack shuffled behind them into the room on their right. Cate stepped to the window, staring out of it for a moment as she tried to picture Gertrude here. An ache settled between her shoulders, and she wiggled them to relieve the pain.

By the time they worked their way through the downstairs, her temples throbbed. She lagged a step behind Marcus as they climbed up the stairs to the next floor.

Rain pelted the window at the top of the stairs.

"Catherine?" Marcus questioned as they reached the top. She stared out at the drops running down the glass.

"Cate?" Jack asked, his voice dull and echoing.

Thunder boomed overhead as images flashed through her mind. Her eyelashes fluttered. She turned, stalking ahead toward a bedroom at the back of the house. She hovered in the doorway as lightning lit the space.

Cate wandered into the middle of the room and stood for a breath before she spun in a slow circle. Her gaze fell to the floor. She took a few steps forward and dropped to her knees.

"Cate!" Jack shouted, racing toward her. "Are you hurt?"

Cate's fingers dug into the thick mauve carpet. She pulled up her hand. A gold chain dangled from her index finger.

She tilted her head, studying the medallion on the chain. "G.M.," she read.

"Gertrude MacKenzie," Jack breathed.

"She was here," Cate said, breaking into a grin. "She was here."

Marcus lifted the charm and studied it. "Excellent work, Catherine."

"Too bad she isn't still here," Jack said.

"No, they moved her when we arrived, I'd bet. But to where?" Cate questioned. She wrapped her fingers around the bracelet as she sat on her haunches. Images shot through her mind again.

She blinked her eyes as they flitted past. Thunder rumbled again.

"Catherine?"

"It's happening again," she said, her voice strained.

Marcus extinguished the fireball, dropping to a knee at her side and rubbing her back. "Breathe, Catherine."

Cate's features pinched as the pressure in her temples increased. She squeezed her eyes closed, grasping at the sides of her head. A tear rolled down her cheek. Her fists unfurled into shaky hands, and the bracelet fell to the carpet below.

Cate gasped in a sharp breath as her mind cleared in an instant. She braced herself against the rug with a hand as she tried to steady her breathing.

"Easy, Catherine. Tell me what just happened."

"Images. Lots of them. They just come in a rush, and it's painful. My head feels like it's going to explode."

Marcus rubbed her back as she blew out a long breath

and sat back on her haunches. Jack sighed and shook his head.

"All right," Marcus said with another rub of her back, "I think it's time we pay a visit to Mother. I don't think this can wait any longer."

She licked her lips, clutching his forearm as she cut her gaze to him. Her features pinched again as she fought back the emotion bubbling inside her. "Am I going to be okay?"

"Yes, dear, you are. I promise," he said, stroking her hair.

Cate nodded, climbing to her feet. Her knees wobbled, and she kept a firm hold of both men. Her stomach turned over. A lump formed in her throat. She tried to cling to Marcus's words, but she worried he'd underestimated her illness.

Not temporalysis, her mind repeated. But if not that, then what? And would she survive it?

CHAPTER 14

*C*ate's fingernails dug into the palms of her hands until they hurt. Rain pelted the car roof as she stared out the water-streaked window. She'd fought to keep her heart rate steady, and her hands from shaking, but the latest attack had rattled her.

More severe than the others, the intensity of the experience left her drained. She struggled to keep her eyes open as weariness wore her down.

She couldn't imagine an outcome where things turned out okay. Temporalysis could be fatal. And based on the severity of what she experienced now versus her previous illness, she couldn't fathom surviving this one.

Perhaps Marcus's mother had some sort of cure. She'd helped Jack, stabilized him when he almost died from temporalysis. Perhaps she could do something similar for her.

She wrung her hands in her lap as worry built. Warm fingers wrapped around her hand and tugged it away from the other. She offered Marcus a fleeting smile before she returned her gaze to the rain falling.

They arrived at the house, and Cate slid from the car, struggling to make it up the walk as tiredness coursed through her.

"I think you should rest before we go," Marcus said as they pushed into the foyer.

"Rest? Are you serious?" Jack questioned. "We should go right away. She's getting worse."

"A nap will not harm her. She is exhausted. This is wearing on her."

Cate heaved a sigh as she listened to the argument. An ache lodged itself between her shoulders again.

"It's fine," she said. "I'm going to lie down. We'll go as soon as I wake up."

"Of course, dear."

Cate waved to acknowledge the comment as she tugged herself up the stairs, clinging to the banister to avoid stumbling. She shambled to her room and collapsed on the bed. Her eyes closed as voices floated from downstairs. They grew more distant as she dozed off.

She startled awake, her eyes fluttering open to find only darkness. She rolled onto her side, scanning the room. A sigh of relief escaped her as she recognized her bedroom in the London townhouse.

She glanced at the clock, her eyes going wide. It read after eleven. She glanced out the window at the starry sky. Her features pinched as she hurried off the bed and scrambled down to the first floor.

Marcus read in the wingbacked chair near the fireplace. He glanced up from his book as she raced into the room, breathless from her dash. "I slept longer than I hoped. I'm sorry."

He closed his book and rose from his chair, approaching the drink cart. "How do you feel?"

"Fine. No nightmares. I'm sorry–"

"Catherine..." He squeezed her shoulder, passing off a brandy. "It's all right."

She sipped at it. "I really didn't mean to sleep this long. Where is Jack?"

"Asleep. I told him to rest, and for once he listened. Only after I assured him that we would wake him before we departed."

"I'm surprised he believed you," Cate said before taking another sip of the drink and settling back into the cushions behind her.

"As am I. Perhaps we should leave—"

"No," Cate said with a shake of her head, "absolutely not."

Marcus pressed his lips together. "Fine."

Cate let her head fall back against the pillow. "I'm worried."

"I know," Marcus said. "After we consult with Mother, I think things will become clearer."

"Can't you give me a hint?"

"I would prefer not to misspeak. And Mother is the best to assess your condition."

Cate chewed her lower lip before taking another sip of the brandy.

"You will be fine, Catherine. Mother can help."

Cate nodded without glancing at him. She stared at her shimmering reflection in the amber liquid.

He hovered over her, and his finger traced her jawline, tipping her chin up. "Trust me."

She offered him a fleeting smile. "I do. Mostly."

"Mostly?" he asked with a coy grin. "I will have to do something about that. That is the biggest obstacle we face at the moment."

She chuckled, and the corners of her lips turned up despite herself.

Marcus poured himself another brandy. "Stefano checked

the other two locations and found nothing. I thought you may want to know."

Cate sighed, shaking her head. "So, we're stuck again. So much for getting a step ahead of Ravishing Rita."

"Who?"

"Oh, Gianna. I nicknamed her Ravishing Rita when we met her in 1942. She couldn't keep her hands off Jack. Although, I never thought she'd actually nab him."

"Gianna will do anything she can to unnerve you," Marcus said, settling on the couch next to her.

"She seems to enjoy it."

"I'm certain she does. She loves to push your buttons. Don't let her."

Cate stared up at him through her eyelashes, clutching the brandy glass to her chest. "Easier said than done."

"Why does she bother you so?"

Cate let her head roll to the side. "Oh, let me count the ways."

Marcus arched an eyebrow at her.

"Seriously? You want me to name them?"

"I want you to stop allowing her to goad you. And to do that, you must understand why she does."

"She's a...she's awful," Cate said with a glance at him. "She's overly flirtatious. She uses her looks to get ahead. She takes pleasure in hurting other people. Especially me. The way she twisted the knife with everyone at Dunhaven was truly disgusting."

"She is jealous."

"Right. I'm sure she is."

Marcus sipped at his brandy. "I assure you she is."

"Oh, right," Cate said, wagging a finger in the air, "you're right. She would so love to woo you to her side and be a duchess."

"That will never happen. Though your excellent match is hardly the only source of her jealousy."

Cate fluttered her eyelashes as she considered the statement. "Right again. My husband and my castle."

Marcus slid a lock of hair behind her ear. "And many other things."

Cate twisted to face him.

"She can't hold a candle to you, Catherine, and she knows that."

Cate's forehead pinched as she stared into his dark eyes, contemplating the statement.

"Cate!" Jack's voice called from the entrance. "You're up."

Cate sucked in a breath, turning away from him to find Jack stumbling into the room, his hair mussed and his clothes wrinkled.

"Perfect timing, Mr. Reid," Marcus grumbled with a sigh as he rose to stand.

"I woke up a little bit ago. I hadn't planned to sleep that long. I guess the experience at the abandoned house wore on me more than I thought."

Jack collapsed onto the cushion where Marcus had sat a moment ago. "I'll bet. Do we have to wait until the morning to get answers?"

"No. We should go now. I'm certain Catherine would like to have this settled."

"You are correct," Cate answered, climbing from the couch. She finished her brandy and set the glass on the bar.

Jack rose, too. "Is she coming here or are we going to her?"

"We will go to Rosenberg. I think the atmosphere there will be conducive to setting Catherine's nerves at ease."

Cate set her hands on her hips. "Answers will be conducive to setting Catherine's nerves. Please say Germany isn't too far for a location hop because I don't think I can stand several hours on a plane in the 1950s."

"Of course not, dear. I am no amateur." He held out his hand, and Cate grabbed it.

"Mr. Reid," Marcus said, holding out his other hand.

Jack blew out a sharp breath. "Another jumpy thing. Just one minute we're here, and the next we're in Germany?"

Marcus stared at him, unblinking. "That is the plan."

Jack's lips form an O as he exhaled again. "Okay, right. Sure. Yes. Just…" He let out another breath, nodding his head. "Just one minute. I just…"

Jack bent over, steadying himself against his legs.

Marcus heaved a sigh, slipping his arm around Cate's waist as they waited.

"Sorry," he said, waving a hand in the air while still bent over.

"It's okay, Jack. Take your time."

"Is he always this much of a coward?" Marcus asked her.

"Hey, listen–" Jack said straightening.

"He doesn't like time travel either. Even the tame kind without the scary portal."

Jack held a hand in the air. "No, I don't. I don't, in general, like things that go against the natural grain of things like going to another time where you could kill your father or talk to yourself or instantaneously traveling from one location to another one thousands of miles away by some unknown means."

"The means are very known. Location hops are quite standard…for those capable, anyway."

"Well, they're not standard for me," Jack said as he straightened.

"Unsurprising. Have you collected yourself yet? I'm certain Catherine would like to get her answers sooner rather than later."

Jack stretched his neck, then shook his head. "No, but I'm ready."

Cate grabbed his hand and smiled. "It'll be okay. Marcus is an expert."

Jack grimaced as he grabbed the man's hand. "Right."

Marcus tightened his grasp around Cate and the room faded from her view, replaced by the foyer of Rosenberg Castle.

"There, made it, see?" Cate said, clapping Jack on the shoulder.

Jack scanned the space. "Yeah. I guess we did."

"There is no guessing about it, Mr. Reid. Welcome to Rosenberg Palace. Why don't you go into the sitting room, dear, and I'll wake Mother? Unless you'd prefer your room."

Cate squeezed his arm. "Sitting room is fine. Thanks. Please apologize ahead of time for waking her in the middle of the night."

She threaded her arm through Jack's and pulled him toward the large sitting room off the foyer. She pushed inside and led him to the sofa.

"I'm not sure I should sit. But I'm also not sure I can stand. These location hops are...unnerving."

"I know," Cate said, patting his arm. "Take a seat in the armchair. I'm sure this entire situation is wearing on you given your recent temporalysis."

"No more wearing than your current situation. Whatever that may be." He sank into the chair and shook his head, clasping his hands until his knuckles turned white. "Oh, Cate, I hope he knows what he's talking about."

Cate bit her lower lip, considering her answer when the door popped open across the room. Marcus strode in with Anna hurrying behind him in a dressing gown.

"Catherine," she said, rushing over with her red robe

flying behind her. She pulled Cate into an embrace, "how lovely to see you."

Anna leaned away from her, brushing a lock of hair from Cate's face. "Marcus says you're having some difficulties."

"A little," Cate answered with a nod. "We're hoping you can help."

"Of course, dear. Let me ring for tea." She glanced at Jack who stood near the armchair, her muscles stiffening. "Oh, Mr. Reid, how lovely to see you. You are looking quite a bit better than when I saw you last."

"I'm feeling quite a bit better. And I understand some of that has to do with your excellent care of me. Thank you for that."

"You're welcome." Anna offered him a curt nod as she led Cate to the sofa and eased her to sit. "Marcus, ring for tea."

"Oh, really, it's fine," Cate said. "No need to wake the household."

"There is every need, dear," Anna said, patting her hand. "Now, tell me what is happening with you."

"Well, as you know when I was here last, I had temporalysis."

"I remember, yes. It passed if I recall."

"I thought it did, however…"

Anna squeezed her hands as the housekeeper rushed in still in her dressing gown. "Oh, Mrs. Higgins. Tea right away, please."

The woman nodded and scurried from the room. Anna returned her gaze to Cate. "Continue, dear."

"The nightmares and visions have started again."

Anna narrowed her eyes at Cate.

"Tell her from the start," Marcus said as he settled into the chair next to Jack.

"The first start or the second start?" Cate asked.

"The first. Leave nothing out."

"Okay," Cate said, blowing out a long breath before starting. "I started having nightmares and visions about a passage in my library. I had them for a while before we found the secret passage there. Then..." She licked her lips, flicking her gaze to her hands. "Dreams about Marcus. After I met him, I began having visions of the ball."

"Your wedding ball," Anna clarified.

"Yes," Cate said with a nod, "and that's when I started wandering the castle, losing time, confusing where I was."

"That ended after the ball, correct?"

Cate swallowed hard. "Right, no more wandering around, but...I'm having dreams and visions again."

"Of?"

Cate's features pinched. "I'm not sure. It's random images. Sometimes I can't make anything out. They're painful. Crippling, at times."

"I see," Anna answered, flicking her gaze to Marcus. "And you assessed this?"

"Yes. But I wanted your opinion as you have first-hand experience with this."

"Quite right," Anna said. She placed a hand against Cate's cheek before moving it to her forehead. She cupped Cate's face in her hands and stared into her eyes.

Anna held a finger up, rising and kissing Cate's forehead. "Wait here."

The housekeeper bustled in with the tea, sliding the tray onto the coffee table.

"Thank you," Marcus said, dismissing her.

He poured a cup and passed it to Cate. Cate stirred in her sugar and sipped at the beverage, fidgeting in her seat.

"Almost, dear," Marcus said, rubbing a finger against her cheek.

She gave him a tight-lipped smile, taking another sip of tea as her leg bobbed up and down.

Jack poured himself a cup of tea and sank into the chair. He took one sip before he slid the saucer onto the table and leaned forward, balancing his elbows on his bobbling legs.

The doors to the room opened again and Anna hurried in with a glass case containing a floating purple rose. Cate's eyes went wide as she stared at it. Anna slid it onto the coffee table before she tugged Cate's teacup and saucer from her hands, setting them aside.

"I'm certain you recognize this," she said.

"One of the roses from your garden," Cate said.

"Not just any rose," Anna said as she lifted the glass. "The rose Marcus gave you before your ball on your first visit here. I had it preserved for you."

Heat rushed into Cate's cheeks as she shot a nervous glance at Jack, fluttering her eyelashes.

"Now, what I want you to do is touch the petals with your fingertips. You may need to use both hands. Give it a few seconds, and tell me what happens."

"Oh, uh, okay." Cate swallowed hard, staring at the floating rose. She slid her eyes sideways toward Anna, wondering what reaction the woman expected. She shot a glance at Marcus who poured a cup of tea, adding milk and sugar before passing it to his mother. He offered Cate an encouraging nod and smile.

Cate sucked in a breath and stretched her shaking hands forward.

Anna rubbed Cate's back. "Relax, dear."

Cate swallowed hard and let the fingers of both hands caress the rose petals. As her skin touched the silky softness, images flooded her mind, appearing and disappearing faster than she could process. She gasped, pulling her fingers away and cutting her gaze to Anna.

"Tell me what happened?" Anna prompted.

"Images again. Lots of them. I let go before it became painful."

The woman's lips curled on the edges, and she replaced the glass cover on the rose. "As I suspected."

Cate's crinkled her forehead. "What is it? What's wrong with me? Do you know?"

Anna sipped her tea, raising her eyebrows at Marcus. "Would you prefer to tell her?"

Cate's stomach turned over as she wondered what ailment afflicted her this time. Would it prove deadly?

CHAPTER 15

"*J* defer to you, Mother," Marcus said. "I am certain you will deliver the news in the best way for Catherine."

Anna slid her saucer onto the table and twisted to face Cate. She grasped her hands and smiled at her.

Tears shone in Cate's eyes, and her forehead pinched. "What is it? Just tell me straight out. Tell me what it is and how long I have."

"How long you have? Oh, darling." Anna caressed her cheek. "You're not dying."

Cate blinked back her tears. "I'm not?"

"No, of course not."

"You mean it's not temporalysis or something similar?"

Anna shook her head, smiling at Cate. "No, you're not ill."

Cate scrunched her eyebrows tighter. "Then what is wrong with me?"

"Nothing is *wrong* with you, Catherine. But you are having these experiences for a reason."

"Which is?" Jack prompted.

Anna's smile broadened. "You are clairvoyant."

Cate stared at her for a moment, unsure she'd heard correctly. "I'm what?"

"Clairvoyant," Anna said. She let go of Cate's hands and retrieved her teacup, sipping the warm liquid.

"Clairvoyant? Like a...fortune teller?"

Anna chuckled, shooting a glance at Marcus who smirked at the question. "Oh, I do love her, Marcus. No, dear, not like a charlatan with a crystal ball or a deck of cards. You are a true clairvoyant. You can see the future."

"See the future?" Cate shook her head. "No, I–I can't see the future."

"I assure you that you can, my darling."

"But...the visions and the nightmares...they were part of my temporalysis."

Anna shook her head, sliding the saucer onto the coffee table again. "No. Only the time losses and wandering were symptoms of the temporalysis. The dreams and visions are part of your gift."

"But..." Cate's scrunched up her face, blinking rapidly as she tried to make sense of it.

"I assure you that's what it is. You are not ill. Nothing is wrong with you. You are a clairvoyant. I know because I'm also somewhat of a clairvoyant myself."

"How did this happen to me? I've never had this before."

"You've never had it or you've never noticed it?" Anna asked.

Cate retrieved her teacup, staring into the amber liquid. "No, I've never had this."

"Think hard, Catherine. You may not have noticed it. Or you may have written it off."

"I have *never* had anything like this. It's crippling. These images flash across my mind faster than I can process. That's never happened to me."

"Maybe not. Your gift is stronger now. But you likely have had premonitions and dreams before."

Cate swallowed hard, heat washing through her body. "I dreamt about my parents dying before it happened."

"Yes, that's it. See? Clairvoyant." Anna wagged a finger at her before clasping her hands and circling them around her knees.

Cate pressed a hand against her forehead as she balanced the saucer in the other. "I don't understand any of this."

"And that is why I brought you to Mother," Marcus said. "She can help you."

"Yes, of course, dear. You need to learn how to process this."

"Obviously," Cate said. "I can't even begin to fathom how to wrap my head around this."

"Oh, no, no," Anna said with a chuckle, patting Cate's hand, "you misunderstand. You need to learn how to handle the images. How to make sense of them. And most importantly, how to ensure they are not crippling."

Cate sat motionless at the news.

"But I think this information is enough for today," Anna said. "You need to rest."

"Oh, no, I just woke up shortly before we came here. I'm fine."

"You need to let this sink in. And you need to sleep. You should do that more easily now that you know you are not sick." Anna smiled at her, rubbing her cheek. Her eyebrows shot up. "Oh, of course, you're worried about another nightmare. I have a solution for that. I'll make you a sleeping draught that will ensure you sleep soundly without any disturbances."

Cate nodded, her lips still parted as she tried to form words but found none. "Y-yes," she finally stammered, "that would be appreciated."

"It's all right, Catherine," Anna said as she rose. "Try to relax."

Cate scooted back on the sofa, drumming her fingers on the cushion. Marcus joined her, pushing a lock of hair behind her ear. "You see? I told you that you were not ill."

She shifted her gaze to him. "I'm not sure this is an improvement. It's worse than the temporalysis."

"It is not. And it is quite useful. Do not worry, dear, Mother will help you control it." Marcus took her hand in his and squeezed.

She nodded and offered him a tight-lipped smile. "Right. Okay. Yes. You're right. This is better than temporalysis. I'm not dying. I only feel like I am at times."

"And Mother will help you temper that."

"Right. Okay. Yes." She slid her eyes closed and drew in a deep breath. "I'm fine. It's fine. I'll be fine."

"I'm not sure I will be fine. I don't think I can recover from any of this." Jack's leg bobbed up and down frantically. "The portals and the location thingy and now this? Cate Kensie can see the future?" His jaw gaped, and he blinked hard.

"Maybe Anna should give you a sleeping draught, too," Cate said.

Marcus rolled his eyes as he rubbed Cate's shoulders. "You are far too needy, Reid. I'm certain you'll be fine."

Anna bustled back inside with a small vial of liquid. She dumped it into Cate's teacup and poured more steaming tea before dropping sugar cubes into it and stirring. "Drink this. It will help you sleep soundly, and we'll talk more tomorrow."

She passed the teacup to Cate. With a smile, Cate accepted it and sipped at the sweet liquid.

"I have assured Catherine that you will assist her in controlling her visions."

"Yes, of course. Do not worry, dear, we will make sure they are not as crippling. I promise."

"Thank you," Cate said as she finished the tea. "

"Now, you should go to bed. The draught will not take long to work. Marcus, you did not arrange for her ladies' maid to be here."

"My apologies, Mother, we came rather hastily."

Anna clicked her tongue. "That is no excuse. You should have planned ahead. No matter, I will help you, Catherine."

"It's not necessary, thank you. I can manage." Cate stood, her legs wobbly from the experience and the quick-acting sleeping potion. She glanced at Marcus. "You'll see to Jack?"

"Of course."

Cate smiled at him and took a step toward the door, one weak knee giving way as she stepped. Marcus leapt from his seat to steady her.

"Oh, that is fast-acting," she murmured, rubbing at her forehead.

He scooped her into his arms. "I shall return for you, Reid."

He carried her into the foyer and up the wide staircase as Cate shook her head.

"You will find any excuse to carry me around, won't you?"

Marcus smiled at her and winked as he climbed the stairs. "I asked Mother to make it extra strong just so I could carry you."

"I wouldn't put it past you," she said with a yawn. "Though this time I am rather grateful. Whatever is in this stuff is incredibly strong."

"I have no doubt Mother made certain it was strong enough to suppress any visions that may creep into your sleep."

"I hope you're right. I hope it's enough to let my mind wrap around this. I never imagined this was what I'd hear."

"And what did you think you would hear?" he asked as he strode past the statues lining the hall.

"Some weird illness that would slowly kill me. Or at least make life very uncomfortable until I survived it."

Marcus smiled at her as he strode toward the double doors of her room.

"Wait, I'll get the handle."

"Unnecessary, Catherine," Marcus answered. As the doors blew open in front of them, he wiggled his eyebrows at her.

"Showoff," she said with a coy smile.

He set her down inside, careful not to remove his hand until she was steady. "Are you certain you are all right?"

Cate yawned and nodded. "Yes, thank you."

"Good night, dear. Sleep well."

He stepped from the room, and she closed the doors behind him, leaning against them before she pulled her weary body away from them. She shuffled across the room, wondering if she could find her centuries-old nightgown.

As she approached the bed, she spotted a nightgown and robe laid out. The corners of her lips turned up. The housekeeper must have laid it out for her.

After changing, she slipped between the sheets, collapsing back against the pillows. Her tired eyes slid closed, and she relaxed into sleep.

When her eyelids fluttered open, bright sunshine streamed through the large window. She stretched and smiled at the sunny morning. She'd slept soundly with no nightmares.

A knock sounded at her door. "Come in!" she called.

"Your Grace, you're awake," Andrea said as she strode across the sitting room toward her.

"Andrea," Cate said with a broad smile, spinning to face her. "How did you get here?"

"His Grace fetched me last night. I'll ring for breakfast and set your clothes out for the day. We can dress whenever you're ready."

"I'm ready," Cate said, taking a seat at the vanity.

"I didn't want to interrupt your viewing of the garden."

Andrea fixed her hair and helped her change before another knock sounded.

"That must be your breakfast," Andrea said, rushing across the room to the door. She pulled it open, offering a quick courtesy. "Oh, good morning."

Anna bustled into the room with the tray. "Good morning, Andrea. Good morning, Catherine. I took it upon myself to wrangle the tray from the maid and bring it."

"Oh, thank you," Cate said as she settled at the table in the sitting room. "You didn't have to do that."

"In truth, I wished to check on you. Did you sleep well?"

"Yes," Cate answered. "No disturbances. Would you like to join me for tea?"

"Excellent. Ah, no dear, I just wanted to be certain you slept. I'm going to take in the gardens, but we will begin your training this afternoon."

"All right," Cate said with a nod. "Is Marcus up?"

"Out already," Anna said with a flick of her hand. "Though he assures me he will not be long. He is following up on something to do with a recent discovery you made. He said you'd know what that means."

"Oh, yes, I understand. Thank you."

"Of course, dear. Try to relax and we'll begin later."

Cate slathered jam onto her toast. "Actually, I hoped to do some reading on my condition."

"A wonderful idea. You are quite clever. It is no wonder Marcus adores you."

Cate swallowed hard as heat rose in her cheeks. Anna

patted Cate's shoulder, leaning down to kiss her forehead. Andrea curtsied as Anna strode from the room before she approached Cate.

"Is there anything else you need, Your Grace?"

"Yes, do you happen to know where Jack is?"

"I believe Mr. Reid is several halls over in the bachelor's wing."

"Of course. Would you mind waiting and showing me the way?"

"Not at all," Andrea said. Cate hurried to finish her breakfast, popping the last piece of toast into her mouth and standing as she wiped her mouth. "Ready."

Andrea led her through the halls of the enormous castle, leading her to a single door tucked at the end of an obscure hall. Cate thanked her and sent her on her way before she knocked on the door.

Jack yanked it open a second later. "Oh, Cate, thank goodness. I had no idea where to find you. I've been worried."

"I'm fine. I slept well. Did you get any sleep?"

"A little. Not much. I tried knocking on all of the doors in this hall, but nothing. I tried again this morning, too. Where is your room?"

"Oh, it's across the castle," Cate said, pointing in the general direction.

Jack stared in the direction of her finger. "Why would they put us so far apart?"

"Ahhh," Cate said with a wince.

"What?"

"I assume Anna put you quite far away from me because I'm–"

Jack let his head fall back between his shoulders. "Married to her son. Right. Wow, she's trusting."

Cate lifted a shoulder. "She's very protective of Marcus. I was on my way to the library. Would you like to come with me?"

"Beats staying here in my hole. Unless we'll upset Mama Northcott."

"I'm sure she'll be fine. She's in the garden."

Cate looped her arm through Jack's after he pulled his door closed and led him down the hall. He gaped around as they traversed the halls. "I thought Dunhaven was sprawling, but this…"

"Is massive," Cate finished for him with a chuckle. "Yes. I know. My bedroom alone makes mine at Dunhaven look shabby."

Jack sucked in a breath as they rounded a corner. "I guess we should talk about what I'm desperately trying to avoid talking about."

"My odd new gift?"

"Not sure I consider it a gift when it knocks you to your knees from the pain."

Cate arched an eyebrow as she approached a set of ornate double doors. "I'm really interested to see what Anna has to say about it this afternoon."

She twisted the knobs on the doors and pushed them into the room. "Until then, I was going to do a little research."

Jack strode into the library and scanned the space. "You really think you'll find a passage in the encyclopedia."

"I'm hopeful," Cate said, scanning the titles.

"I wasn't serious, Cate."

Cate snapped her gaze to him as she ran her finger along the books. "I was."

Jack scrunched his nose at her.

She stared at him for a moment before she waved him toward another shelf. "Look at these titles." She tugged them off the shelf one by one, stacking them in his arms. "Enchanted Objects and Their Uses, Basic Enchantments, Benson's Guides to Creatures."

Cate grabbed his book-laden arm and led him to the desk under the stained glass window. She tugged the top book from his stack and plopped it onto the desk. Dust swirled in the air as she thumbed through the book, finding the appropriate entry.

"Here. Look." She pointed toward a specific entry with an illustration next to it.

"Gobgoyle," Jack read, shooting her a brief glance before he read from the page, "A hairless, quadruped known for his characteristic triangular-shaped teeth and marble-like eyes. They are a popular pet among Dracopires."

Cate waved a finger in the air. "Which begs the natural question, what is a Dracopire?"

"There's nothing natural about that question, Cate."

Cate ignored him, flipping through to another passage. "Dracopires. Dragon-like vampires, some of which live in Romania. Surprise!" She offered him an amused stare. "But most of which live in Sangmond. So, then you wonder, what is Sangmond?"

"Not really," Jack murmured as Cate hurried across the room, pulling another book from the shelf and delivering it to Jack.

"Realms Beyond Earth describes it as another realm dictated by a blood-red moon that rises and sets like the sun." She handed it off to Jack, fanning the pages. "And there are hundreds of these. Look!"

Jack collapsed into the armchair opposite the desk. "I'm not sure how much more my brain can handle."

"And this entire library is filled with volumes like this. And don't even get me started on what's downstairs."

Jack snapped his gaze to her. "What's downstairs?" he whispered.

"Tons of magical stuff," Cate said with a grin as she returned to perusing the shelves. "A mirror that lets you pull your mirror image out of it."

"No," Jack said with a shake of his head. "No, no more. I officially can't handle anymore."

"Wild, right?"

"Wild is not the word, Cate. This is…insanity."

"We should have known, right?" Cate said, tugging a tome from the shelf and continuing to scan the titles.

Jack paged through the volume on his lap. "I don't know how we could have known any of this."

Cate shot him a glance over her shoulder. "Come on. Time travel existed and only at Dunhaven? We really had a narrow view of the world."

Jack studied her as she pulled another book from the shelf and carried them to the desk. "I think you're actually enjoying this."

"Enjoying what?" Cate asked as she paged through the book.

"All this. The new worlds, the odd creatures."

Cate scanned the entry she found. "It's fascinating."

"I will never understand how your mind works, Cate Kensie."

Cate offered him a smile before she returned to her book. She scanned the entry about the wide range of clairvoyants. Some only experienced feelings while others had vivid images of the future. Other psychics ranged in between, often their response depending on the severity of the situation.

While clairvoyants could experience any range of visions about the future, many of them centered around negative events such as deaths or other severe traumas.

Cate read the words again, her finger tracing the word negative. She stared into space as a shiver snaked down her spine. On what negative event did her mind dwell?

CHAPTER 16

Cate's features pinched as she squeezed her eyes closed. She stretched her mind to recall something from the visions she had. Something that would offer her a clue to what her mind wanted to show her.

"That face looks very worried, dear," Marcus said.

Cate snapped her eyes open to find him in the doorway.

"Are we learning?" he asked as he strode toward her.

"Yes," she answered. "I thought I might find some information on my condition here."

He leaned over the book, perusing the entry. "And what did you find that gave you such a distressed expression?"

Cate licked her lips and flipped the book closed. "Nothing."

"That's quite a bit of nothing to give you such a perturbed look, dear."

She tugged one corner of her lip back. "Did you find anything this morning? Your mother said you were out chasing down a lead."

"Nothing of promise," Marcus answered.

Cate's shoulders slumped, and she banged a fist against the desk's top. "We're not doing very well."

"We will persevere and triumph, Catherine."

She flicked her gaze up to him, pinching her eyebrows together. "I hope so."

"Perhaps a walk in the garden before you begin with Mother."

She sucked in a deep breath and nodded. "Yes. I think I need some air. Jack, wait until you see the roses."

Marcus sighed as he followed Cate from the room. "Come along, Mr. Reid. It seems you are invited, too."

They spent the time before lunch in the garden. Their meal was a quiet affair with stilted conversation as Cate's apprehension grew over her upcoming training session with Anna. What would she see? And how would she withstand it?

The meal ended with the servants carrying away all of the dishes. Cate traced the outline of her napkin, trying to control her heart rate.

Anna rose from her chair. "Come along, Catherine. Let's begin. If you gentlemen will excuse us, we have much work to do."

"I'll come with you," Marcus said as he stood.

"No, you will not."

"But Mother–"

"No, you will not." Anna wagged her finger at him. "Catherine needs space."

"She should not be alone."

"And she will not be," Anna answered, raising her chin. "I will be with her."

"But–" Marcus tried again.

Anna's eyes widened. "I said no. No means no. Perhaps a game of billiards or chess for you two whilst Catherine and I do our work."

Marcus puckered his lips, his displeasure obvious.

"Do not give me that face, Marcus. I will not stand for it. Kiss your wife goodbye and wish her luck."

"Yes, Mother," Marcus said with a sigh. He bent toward Cate, rubbing her shoulder while he kissed her cheek. "Good luck, dear."

"Thank you," she answered, sounding meeker than she'd hoped.

"Come along, Mr. Reid. We have a date with a billiard table."

"That sounds...worse than I expected," Jack murmured as he rose. "Good luck, Cate."

Cate smiled at him, offering a nod in silent thanks as her heart skipped a beat and her stomach turned over.

"Go," Anna said, shooing them away.

Cate swallowed hard as they left the room. Anna turned her focus to Cate, offering her a tight-lipped smile. "Come along, Catherine."

Cate forced a fleeting smile onto her lips as she rose, trying to hide her shaky hands.

Anna grasped them and squeezed. "There is no need to be nervous, dear. I understand how stressful this can be, particularly with your physical symptoms, but that is what we aim to temper."

Cate tried to smile, but her features pinched, and her lips quivered. She bit the lower one to stop the trembling.

Anna cupped her face in her hands. "Oh, darling, what is it?"

"It's less the physical symptoms and more..." She flicked her teary gaze away from Anna as she blinked them away.

"What, dear?"

"What is it that I'm seeing? The book said it's usually negative."

"The book?" Anna asked.

"I went to the library this morning, and I read about my condition."

Anna clicked her tongue. "I knew I shouldn't have left you alone. You're too clever for your own good, Catherine."

"I'm sorry. But I can't stop wondering what terrible event my mind is trying to show me."

"They're not all terrible."

"But most of them are," Cate said, her voice catching in her throat.

"Let's try to focus on teaching you how to make these less painful and debilitating first, shall we? And then we'll worry about what you see, and how we can use it to stop any tragedies."

Cate furrowed her brow, her lips forming a pout. "Stop them?"

"Yes, dear. We're shown things for a reason."

"So, we can avoid them?"

"Sometimes," Anna answered. "Or at the very least, we can prepare and minimize the damage."

Cate slid her shoulders down her back and raised her chin, pressing her lips together. "Okay. Let's do this."

Anna patted her cheek, smiling at her before she led her from the dining room. "We'll go to your bedroom. A space where you are comfortable. It will help."

They navigated through the castle's halls, pushing into the sapphire bedroom. Anna locked the doors behind them for privacy.

Cate wrung her hands, swallowing hard as she hovered in the space.

"Sit down," Anna said, motioning to the chaise. "And lay back. Try to relax."

Cate let her head rest against the thick cushion as Anna tugged a chair over toward her. "Now, your visions, the ones you have when you're awake...is there a trigger?"

"Umm," Cate murmured, "it seems to be random."

"Think harder, Catherine, because this can help you prepare for them. Talk through them with me."

Cate licked her lips, trying to recall the instances when she'd had the debilitating visions. "The first waking one I had was when I was dressing for a party. I picked up the sapphire necklace and experienced one. Another was in Gianna's apartment. And the third was in an abandoned house where we found Gertrude's bracelet. Oh, Gertrude is a relative."

Anna patted her hand. "I know. All right, were the visions always the same?"

"I don't know. They go by so fast, and my head hurts so much that I can't be certain."

"What does your gut say?"

Cate pressed her lips together. "That they were different. The one in the abandoned house felt different. Emotionally. I had a different response."

"So, they are of two different things most likely. Let's try to work on the one in the abandoned house. Given the other triggers, I'm afraid those may be more disturbing for you."

"Maybe we should start with those."

"No, you are still learning. You need to be able to access these and process them."

Cate's forehead pinched as she patted her stomach.

"Trust me, Catherine."

She offered a nod without making eye contact.

"Do you know why the visions are painful?" Anna asked.

Cate flicked her gaze to the woman and shook her head.

"Because you are correct. They are often of negative things. And because of that, your body fights them. Viciously, at times. Your mind wants you to see these things but a part of you is resisting them."

"Like an instinctual reaction to protect yourself from harm."

"Yes, exactly."

"So, how do I avoid that?"

"You must be open to them."

Cate barked out a harsh laugh. "I'm not sure I want to be."

Anna wagged a finger at her. "And that is why they hurt."

"Will I ever see anything good?"

"Yes, you may. I think you did last night with the rose."

Cate puckered her lips as she studied her feet. "Can we start with that one instead?"

Anna smiled down at her. "I'd rather start with something a bit more painful because conjuring happy future events will not teach you very much."

"Darn," Cate said with a wrinkle of her nose.

"I would very much like to help you with this. And I'm not doing it to be cruel. I want to be sure you don't suffer more than you have to."

Cate grabbed her hand and squeezed. "I know. Thank you."

"If it becomes too much, we'll try with a happy zerinnerung."

Cate snapped her gaze to the woman's face. "What?"

"Zerinnerung. It means future memory."

"Future memory," Cate repeated. "How odd, yet how right the description sounds."

"Let's get started." Anna shoved her hand into her pocket and pulled out an object. She dangled the gold bracelet from her fingers. "This seems to be a trigger for you."

"And you want me to touch it and see if I get a future memory."

Anna pulled it away, tilting her head. "Not just yet. I want you to prepare for it. Acknowledge that it may be painful. We cannot spare ourselves all the pain, but we can avoid much of it. If we're prepared, it is not as jarring."

"Right, okay." Cate stared up at the ceiling, trying to keep her breathing calm. "Okay, I'm ready, let me try."

"No, you are not," Anna argued.

Cate screwed up her face.

Anna's eyes traveled down to Cate's feet. They stuck off the chaise, pointing straight up in the air as she clenched her leg muscles.

"You're tense."

"I'm preparing," Cate argued.

"You're bracing. Which is a fear reaction. A fight or flight response and your body is preparing to do both."

"Fight and flight?" Cate asked.

Anna nodded. "Fight by causing you intense pain to prevent you from adequately understanding or responding to the images you're shown. And, if necessary, flight. You will pass out. We don't want either."

"Okay. Relax."

"Deep breaths. Think of happy things."

Cate closed her eyes, sucking in deep breaths as she tried to force herself to relax. She pictured Dunhaven Castle's library. Two furry pups lounged near the roaring fireplace. She lounged in her favorite armchair.

Cate licked her lips and flicked her eyes open. "Okay. Happy thoughts." She waved for the bracelet.

Anna arched an eyebrow, holding the bracelet out to her. Cate licked her lips as she reached for it. Her breathing turned ragged, and her hands began to shake as she reached for the bracelet.

"Sorry," she said, pulling her hand back.

"It's perfectly fine, Catherine. Take your time."

"The moment I reach for it all my happy thoughts disappear."

Anna smiled at her, setting the bracelet on the side table.

"That's normal. You're anticipating the terrible side effects. And that in itself is what exacerbates them somewhat."

"Only somewhat?" Cate asked with a chuckle.

"The visions will never be easy. But you can make them less taxing."

"By envisioning my happy place," Cate said.

Anna lifted her shoulders and fluttered her eyelashes. "Not exactly. But this is a first step. Catherine, you must understand, this will take quite a bit of work to learn to manage. You *can* do it. But it will not happen immediately."

Cate bit into her lower lip. "Patience is not my virtue."

Anna chuckled at her statement. "I understand, particularly when it comes to something like this. No one would *want* to experience this pain. And if I could take it away and teach you to manage this in one afternoon, I would."

Cate sucked in a deep breath, patting her abdomen as she tried to relax. "Can I ask how this step helps?"

"What do you mean?" Anna crinkled her brow.

"Well, I can't always anticipate when I'm going to have one of these. So, I wouldn't be able to think of my happy place or somewhere I feel safe before one occurs. They just sneak up on me. So, how would I use this to help?"

Anna pressed her lips together and nodded. "I understand. This will *not* help you with the ones we can't anticipate. What it will help you with is learning how to process the images by lessening the pain for those we can anticipate."

Cate furrowed her brow, her eyes falling on the gold bracelet. "So, in other words, instead of having them race across my mind faster than I can process them, I'll be learning to actually see them."

"Right, yes. Everything is jumbled right now because your mind is fighting against it. And because of the physical symptoms, it's really battling these visions. If you can control your physical reaction, we can make headway in processing these.

And if you learn to process them, you can master receiving them without much suffering on your part."

"Not much suffering sounds excellent," Cate said, shooting her a smile. "Okay, I'm going to try again."

"Whenever you're ready."

Cate sucked in a deep breath and licked her lips. She squeezed her eyes closed, bringing her cozy vision of Dunhaven Castle to the forefront of her mind.

She slid her eyes open to slits and reached for the bracelet. Her fingers touched the cold metal of the mono-grammed charm. A jolt shot through her body as images sped across her mind. Her temples ached and her muscles tensed as she struggled to make sense of the visions.

She fought to keep her hands on the metal for as long as she could. The comfy image of the library became lost in the fray. She struggled to keep her eyes open.

The pain became blinding, and the world closed in around her.

CHAPTER 17

Cate's eyelids fluttered open. Anna smiled down at her as she pressed a cool cloth against her forehead.

Cate fidgeted on the chaise. "That didn't go as well as I hoped."

"I did not expect you to accomplish it on your first attempt." Anna dunked the rag again and wrung it out before placing it on Cate's forehead again. "How is your headache?"

"Dulled," Cate answered. "I can try again."

"Don't rush it. Take time to recover from this one."

Cate shimmied up. "I can do it. I–"

"Catherine," Anna said, pushing Cate's shoulders back into the chaise, "do not rush. If you try again too soon, you'll only set yourself up for failure."

Cate settled back into the chaise with a sigh.

She let her eyes slide closed as she waited for the tension in her temples to release. After a few minutes, she opened her eyes. "Okay, I'm feeling a bit better now."

"A bit or better?"

Cate sucked in a breath. "Better. No headache. My stomach has settled."

"All right. Try again whenever you feel ready. Relax. Happy thoughts."

Cate closed her eyes again, conjuring her image of the dogs in the library. She snapped her eyes open, trying to hold on to the memory as she reached for the bracelet. The touch of the metal shoved the snug thought aside, replacing it with pain and nonsensical images.

She dropped the bracelet before she passed out, blowing out a long breath.

"All right, better," Anna answered. "Lay back."

"Better because I dropped the bracelet," Cate answered.

"Still progress."

"Debatable," Cate said as Anna pressed the cloth against her forehead.

After a few moments of resting, Cate stopped Anna from pressing the cloth against her forehead again. "I'm ready to try again."

"All right. Find your safe place," Anna said, dropping the cloth in the basin and settling back in the chair.

She brought her safe place into her mind again and reached for the bracelet. Her fingers brushed across the metal and the attack began. A cry escaped her, both from pain and frustration. She dropped the bracelet and flung herself back onto the chaise, blowing out a breath.

"All right, darling, it's all right," Anna said, pressing the cloth against her.

"It's not," Cate cried.

"Yes, it is.

"I'm not getting any better at this."

Anna pulled the cloth away and submerged it in the water. "You have tried three times. Mastery can take years. Don't be so hard on yourself."

Cate pushed herself straighter, blocking Anna's arm

before she could place the cloth on her head again. "I'm going to try again."

"No," Anna argued.

"Yes," Cate said, her jaw clenched.

"Catherine, you must wait before you try again. You're tired and weak from the last attempt. Rest."

Cate collapsed back onto the cushion, squeezing her hands into fists.

Anna patted her tight fists. "This is not resting."

Cate puffed out a sigh.

"Allow yourself to be cared for, Catherine. You do not need to take this all on yourself. You are not alone. I am here. Marcus is here."

Cate unfurled her hands, flicking her gaze to Anna. "Thank you."

Anna smiled down at her. "Of course. Now, I think that is enough for today."

"No, I'd like to try again. Maybe more than once. I can do it. I want to make some progress."

Anna grabbed her hand and patted it. "I know you do, dear, but I think–"

"No," Cate interrupted, "I want to try."

Anna sucked in a breath, arching an eyebrow before she nodded. "All right. Whenever you're ready."

Cate nodded and sucked in a breath as she prepared herself. She reached for the bracelet. Memories rushed into her mind, and she dropped the jewelry piece.

"All ri–"

"No, again," Cate said, grabbing the gold chain. Pain shot from temple to temple. She held on to the charm this time, forcing herself to focus. The images shot around her brain. She fought to control them as the pain forced itself further into her mind. If she could even make sense of one vision, she'd have made progress.

She bit into her lower lip until she tasted blood, refusing to drop the charm. Her limbs trembled with torment as her nerves burned. Tears welled in her eyes as the agony intensified.

"Let go, Catherine," Anna encouraged her.

She clung to the bracelet until tears rolled down her cheeks. Anna pried her fingers back. The visions ceased as she removed the charm from Cate's touch, setting it aside.

Cate's shoulders shook as she continued to cry. Anna shifted in her seat, perching on the edge of the chaise and pulling Cate into her arms.

"Shh, Catherine. It's all right."

The door unlatched across the room. "What's happened?" Marcus asked.

Anna waved him over. "She was a bit overzealous with her attempts. And you should not be unlocking doors with your magic tricks." She lowered her voice as he sank onto the edge of the chaise. "But I'm pleased you did."

Cate leaned away as she sniffled and wiped at her tears. "I'm fine."

Marcus pulled her into his arms. "You are not."

Cate relaxed against him, laying her head on his shoulder.

"She pushed herself a bit too hard. She is stubborn."

"Yes, I know," Marcus answered.

Cate's muscles relaxed, and the tension released in her temples. She pushed back, wiping at her cheeks again. "I am not. I wanted to make some progress."

"You did make progress, darling," Anna said with a rub of her back. "Tomorrow, we'll try again. You will learn how to manage this, I promise."

Cate sniffled again and nodded. "Thank you."

Anna stroked her hair. Suddenly, she froze. "Oh, Mr. Reid, I didn't see you there."

"Just wanted to see how Cate was."

Cate twisted to find him hovering inside the door. "Oh, Jack, I'm fine. Come in."

"Actually," Anna said, hurrying away, "she needs a bit of rest. We'll leave you alone. Mr. Reid, have you seen our gardens? I think you'll find them quite lovely. I understand you do a bit of gardening yourself."

"Oh," Cate said, her brow furrowing as Anna spirited him from the room, "but–"

"Leave it, Catherine. You will not convince Mother to bring him back."

"He's probably upset," Cate answered, still staring at the now-closed door.

"So are you. Stop worrying about him and start worrying about yourself."

Cate faced him, fluttering her eyelashes. "I'm fine."

"You are definitely not."

"I am," Cate insisted. "My heart is beating normally. You should know that."

"It is now. It wasn't moments ago. It felt as though it was ready to burst."

Cate sighed, clasping her hands in her lap. "This isn't exactly easy. It's a lot harder than I expected, actually."

"What did you expect?"

Cate shrugged, staring up into his dark eyes. "Magic."

The corners of his lips curled up, and she giggled. "Sorry, I couldn't help myself."

"Magic is not as simple as you may expect."

"You certainly make it look easy," she said, flopping back on the chaise.

He pressed her hand against his chest. "I am glad you think so. How are you feeling?"

Cate sucked in a deep breath. "Tired. I think the adrenaline is wearing off, and I'm realizing your mother was right."

"She usually is," Marcus said with a smirk. "You should rest."

"No, I'll never sleep tonight," Cate said, pushing herself up to sit.

"I think Mother will handle that for you. I'm certain she will not want you to experience any dreams during the night. It robs you of your strength."

"And I'm going to need that." She glanced back toward the door. "Maybe a walk in the garden."

"Are you going to the garden for you or for him?"

Cate snapped her gaze back to him. "Both."

Marcus flexed his jaw with a huff. "At least you are honest."

"He's in another time, in a foreign country, and he's worried about me."

Marcus rose to stand, offering her his hand. "As am I."

"I'm fine." Cate lifted a shoulder. "And I find the garden relaxing."

"Come along. At the risk of Mother scolding me, I will take you to the garden."

Cate smiled up at him as she slid her hand into his and stood. "Thank you."

"Of course. I cannot say no to you," he said as he wrapped her arm around his and patted her hand.

"Don't worry. I'll tell her it was my fault if you get scolded."

"It will not matter," Marcus answered, leading her from her bedroom into the hall, "she will blame me."

They strolled into the bright sunshine of the garden. Down the path, Anna pointed out a flowering plant with tiny pink buds.

She caught sight of them, her head tilting and her eyebrows shooting high. "What's this?"

"It's my fault," Cate answered. "I twisted his arm into bringing me. I needed some fresh air, and I love the garden."

Anna shot Marcus a glance before she returned her gaze to Cate. She felt her cheek, then her forehead, and finally her pulse. "Are you tired?"

"Yes," Cate said with a nod, "but I'm well enough to take a brief stroll."

"Make certain it is brief. You need your rest. You have been through a trying experience."

"I plan to rest after dinner," Cate answered before she turned to Jack. "How are you enjoying the gardens?"

"Oh, they're lovely. Are you sure you're okay?"

"I'm fine. Let me show you the roses." She grabbed his hand and tugged him toward the bush near the overlook. She pointed out the tiny purple buds.

"Cate, are you sure you're okay? I was worried sick."

"I'm fine," Cate assured him. "Really."

Jack crinkled his brow, staring into the distance.

"Jack, I'm fine. This is just...very new. And I'm not making much progress with it."

"What happened?"

Cate shifted her weight, pressing her lips together. "Anna gave me the bracelet. Every time I touch it, I get these visions. But I can't make any sense of them."

"And she hasn't been able to help you control them?"

"She says the first thing I need to do is learn to experience the ones I expect without pain. And then we can work on slowing them down and deciphering them."

"But you can't."

"Not so far. I've been trying to channel my happy memories but the minute I touch that bracelet, they all go right out of the window." She fluttered her hand in the air.

Jack sucked in a deep breath, shaking his head. "I don't know how you do it. I wouldn't want any parts of this."

"I have to. I have to figure this out before it destroys me. I hope to make some progress tomorrow."

"Cate–"

"I think that's enough for you, my dear," Anna said as she tugged Marcus toward them. "Marcus, take her back to her room to rest. And I think you should eat there tonight."

"Oh, I can–" Cate began.

"You will not," Anna said. "You must rest."

Cate pressed her lips together. "All right, but I'd like to grab the references from the library. I can't sleep all evening."

"Fine. As long as you don't stress yourself," Anna said.

"I promise."

"I'll walk you up, Cate," Jack said with a nod.

"Oh, but we haven't finished our tour," Anna said with a gracious smile at him, cutting between him and Cate and slipping her hand through his arm. "Come along, Mr. Reid."

Jack glanced over his shoulder as Anna led him away. Cate offered him a shrug and a wave.

"Ready?" Marcus asked as she turned back to face him.

"I'd better be before I get scolded," Cate said. "Did you get a tongue-lashing for bringing me down?"

"Nothing I couldn't handle. Though I will take you straight to your room and retrieve the book for you to avoid another."

"I can make it to the library," Cate said as they pushed back into the castle.

"You could and then I could carry you to your room or you could walk to your room and I can bring you the book."

Cate shook her head at him. "Fine, you can bring me the book."

"Are you certain? You know how I love to carry you about."

Cate rolled her eyes as a chuckle escaped her. They navigated through the halls to the sapphire bedroom. Cate pushed inside with a promise to rest as Marcus left to retrieve her book.

She stalked further into the room, blowing out a long breath. The trip to the garden had been more taxing than she was willing to admit. She craved stretching out in bed.

She drummed her hands against her thighs as she waited for Marcus to return. Her eyes fell onto the fine gold chain laying on the table.

Odd how such a tiny object could cause so much pain. She stalked toward it, staring down at it. Her hand trembled as she reached toward it again.

She snapped her hand back as the door clicked open behind her. "Your book, dear."

Cate spun to face him, accepting the thick tome. "Thank you."

"Do you need anything else?"

"Tea would be nice," she said. "And can you send Andrea?"

"Of course, dear," Marcus said. "I'll visit you later."

Cate smiled and nodded as he strode from the room. She flicked a gaze back to the bracelet before she left it behind in favor of staring out the window at the garden below. Anna continued to roam around with Jack.

Cate chuckled at the scene. Andrea arrived a moment later. Cate happily changed into her pajamas and settled in her bed with a warm cup of tea. Her mind wandered to her friends at Dunhaven. Their lives were almost frozen in time. Worried about their jobs and their home, they had no clue Cate and crew had left to try to solve the issue.

She traced the outline of the book next to her. She had to solve it. They deserved better than to be used as pawns in Gianna's game. She tugged open the tome, searching for the entry on clairvoyance.

She struggled to focus on the words written on the page. Her mind wandered to her experience earlier this afternoon.

Would she ever master these visions, or would they always defeat her? Would they always remain just beyond her grasp, warning her of something she'd never know?

Cate tossed the book to the side and threw back the covers. She slid her feet into her slippers and shuffled into the sitting room. She stared down at the bracelet on the side table.

Memories of her previous painful experience flashed across her mind. But it did not stop her from reaching toward it. Her fingers wrapped around the thin chain, and she rubbed the charm. Her fingernails traced the grooves of the monogram.

Her eyelashes fluttered as images began to flood into her mind. Pain throbbed at her temples as she fought to control the images and focus on something.

Her knees began to weaken, and she wobbled on her feet, stumbling forward. Her breathing turned raspy. She struggled to stay upright. A groan escaped her lips as the pain reached a fever pitch.

Cate unraveled her fingers, trying to drop the bracelet, but it tangled around her thumb. She shook her hand in a desperate attempt to free herself of the images, but she couldn't. She flailed her arm, but her vision began to close to a pinpoint.

She pitched forward, smacking her head off the edge of the side table before she collapsed to the floor.

CHAPTER 18

"Catherine?" Marcus's voice echoed in her head. "Catherine, open your eyes."

"What's happened?" Anna asked.

"I found her collapsed with the bracelet in her hand. She appears to have hit her head."

Footsteps scrambled into the room. "What can I do?" Andrea asked, breathless and panicked.

"Fetch a basin of water and a cloth. She's still bleeding," Anna answered.

Cate tried to force her eyes open, to tell them she was okay, but she couldn't. Her eyelids stuck closed as though glued. Her limbs would not respond. And she couldn't find her voice.

Warm fingers pressed against her wrist. "Her pulse is strong."

"Her heartbeat is normal," Marcus informed her.

"Good. With that prolonged exposure, she is likely exhausted. She will wake, darling. We must be patient."

Footsteps sounded again. "Ah, thank you, Andrea."

"May I stay?" Andrea asked.

Anna answered, "Yes, I'm certain she'd want you here."

Cool, damp fabric pressed against her forehead, gently wiping at the skin. It stung, but her muscles were too weak to wince.

Warm fingers threaded through hers. "Please wake up, Your Grace," Andrea squeaked.

Cate tried to squeeze her hand but found it impossible.

A finger traced the wound on her head, making it tingle.

"Cate?" Jack's voice exclaimed. "What the hell happened to her?"

"Calm down, Mr. Reid," Anna said. "She's fine. Merely exhausted."

"She doesn't look fine. She looks half-dead."

"Please stop your shouting," Anna answered.

"Will someone please tell me what happened to her?" Jack asked.

Anna heaved a sigh as the cloth pressed against her skin again. "She picked up the bracelet again. She must have held onto it for too long. She collapsed and hit her head."

"Oh, no," Jack groaned. "She needs a doctor."

"She will be fine," Anna argued.

"You don't know that," Jack shouted back. "And I'll be damned if I'm going to stand here, and let you two take care of her."

"Now, Mr. Reid, that is quite enough," Anna said, her voice turning heated. "I will not tolerate you speaking to me or my son that way. He is Catherine's husband, and I am her mother-in-law. There is no one more appropriate to care for her than those who love her."

Jack scoffed at the statement. "Oh, please."

"That is quite enough, Reid," Marcus said. "You can remain here only because Catherine would want you, but if you do not stop hurling accusations I shall remove you myself."

Silence pervaded the room for several seconds.

"Stay back and out of the way," Anna said. "I am less forgiving than my son."

What a nightmare, Cate thought. *If I could only open my eyes.*

Noises faded away as Cate drifted in and out of consciousness.

"...been hours. She needs a doctor," Jack said.

"What did I tell you, Mr. Reid? If you could not control yourself, I would ask you to leave."

"She hit her head. She could have a concussion."

Anna said, "She does not. She is perfectly healthy, merely exhausted."

"You don't know that," Jack responded.

"I do," Anna said. "I am quite experienced at this. She is perfectly fine. I would never risk Catherine's health."

"I've had enough of this," Jack answered.

A scuffle sounded, and her bed jiggled.

"Stop this right now," Anna shouted. "Mr. Reid, if you cannot control yourself, I shall ask you to leave."

"Oh, I'm not leaving her alone with you. No way."

"Then keep your mouth shut," Anna answered. A warm hand wrapped around hers. "You take your time coming back to us, Catherine. You get all the rest you need."

"This is ridiculous," Jack murmured.

Cate tried to force her eyes open but found the task impossible. *I'm okay, Jack.* Her lips would not form the words.

"Marcus," Anna's voice said a moment later, "open her music box."

The tinkling music filled the air a moment later. Her muscles reacted to it, relaxing more until she drifted away.

When her senses returned, the music still played. *The music.* Perhaps that was the key. Maybe the music could help her focus on the images her mind tried to send her. It helped her through temporalysis.

First, though, she had to wake up. She had to open her eyes. She tried to force them open again.

"How long do you plan on waiting until you realize she's not waking up?" Jack asked.

"Mr. Reid, how many times must I ask you not to interfere?"

"Enough," Marcus snapped, "we are all here for Catherine. We—"

Cate flexed her fingers.

"What is it, Marcus?" Anna asked.

"She is waking. She squeezed my hand." Fingers caressed her hair. "Catherine, can you open your eyes?"

Cate fought to force them open. Her blurry vision cleared a few seconds later.

"There she is," Anna said, patting her hand. She shot a glance at Jack who stood near the end of the bed with Andrea.

"I'm here," Cate whispered. "I've been here."

She tried to push herself up, but Anna and Marcus stopped her.

"Easy, Catherine," Anna said, "you are still weak."

Cate swallowed hard as she settled back into the pillows. "I couldn't let go of the bracelet. It got stuck."

"Why did you try it again?"

"I don't know," Cate admitted. "I just—thought I could make progress but it got tangled around my thumb."

"The prolonged exposure has exhausted you," Anna said. "You must rest. Do you feel strong enough to eat a little?"

"Yes," Cate said with a nod.

"I shall arrange it. Marcus, stay with her."

"I will do it," Andrea offered. "It's so wonderful to see you awake, Your Grace."

"Thank you, Andrea."

The blonde bobbed her head up and down before she spun on a heel and disappeared from the room.

"How do you feel, Cate?" Jack asked.

Anna flexed her jaw, her annoyance with him clear. Cate shifted her gaze from her mother-in-law to Jack. "I'm just a bit tired."

"Are you sure? You hit your head."

Cate raised a leaden arm, her muscles aching, and rubbed her forehead.

Marcus stroked the spot she'd smacked. "There is no scar."

"Thanks," she said.

"Cate, you should get checked out by a doctor."

"I'm fine," she said. "Just tired from the experience. I'm sure after some sleep, I'll be able to try—"

"No," Anna said with a shake of her head. "No more for at least a day."

"No," Cate said, shoving at the bed to try to sit straighter. "I can do it."

Anna raised her eyebrows. "I am the expert here. And I say you cannot."

"For once, I agree with her," Jack said.

"Well, I do not," Cate said with a shake of her head. She flicked her gaze to Marcus. "Do you want to help out here?"

"Mother knows best."

Cate huffed. "This isn't fair. You're ganging up on me."

"We will make progress, dear," Anna said. "I promise. But no more with the bracelet for now."

Cate heaved another sigh as Andrea returned with a tray of food.

"All right," Anna said as Cate polished off the meal, "now it is time for you to sleep."

She rose from the chair, shooing Andrea and Jack back.

"Time for us to leave. Marcus, if anything should change with her condition, you will let me know immediately."

Jack shook his head. "I'm staying, too."

"That is highly inappropriate, Mr. Reid. Catherine needs her rest. She does not need you hovering over her."

Jack shook his head, wagging a finger in the air. "I'm not–
"

"Okay, okay, that's enough," Cate said. All eyes turned to her. "I'm perfectly fine. You're all very kind to worry so much, but I'm okay. Have any of you eaten dinner?"

"There is no need for you to worry about that," Anna answered.

"I'll take that as a no. Why don't you eat, and Jack can stay with me and then switch."

Marcus stroked her hair. "There is no need for that, dear, I can stay."

Cate grabbed his hand and squeezed. "Go have dinner with your mother. Jack can wait with me, and then you can watch me sleep all night."

Marcus heaved a sigh and narrowed his eyes at Jack. "Fine. Come along, Mother, we shall eat quickly."

Anna arched an eyebrow and snapped her gaze to Jack. "Notify me if anything happens. And do not under any circumstances let her touch that bracelet."

Jack held his hands up in silent acquiescence. "Come along, Marcus."

"I shall stay, Your Grace."

"No, Andrea, please go eat," Cate said, waving her away.

"Are you certain?"

Cate nodded and smiled at her, sending her along her way.

Jack settled into one of the chairs near the bed with a sigh as the others slipped out of the room. He puffed out his cheeks and scrubbed his face with his hands before he focused on Cate.

"I thought we lost you."

"Nope, still here. Although, I'm starting to think this room is cursed," Cate said as she shifted around in the bed.

"Are you okay? Anything hurt?"

"No, nothing. I can't believe I cracked my head. That hurt. But it's fine now."

"Cate, I think we need to get out of here. I don't like this."

Cate crinkled her brow and shook her head. "I'm kidding. It's not cursed."

"Well, I'm not. The moment something happened to you those two closed ranks. They would barely let me anywhere near you."

Cate sucked in a breath, flicking her gaze to her lap. "I heard."

Jack arched an eyebrow.

"I was conscious for much of the time. I could hear you. I just couldn't open my eyes or speak. Or move. I fell asleep for a little bit, but I heard most of it."

"Then you know what I'm talking about."

Cate tilted her head, grabbing his hand. "They're just trying to help."

"Help? Cate!" Jack exclaimed, leaning forward toward her. "You hit your head, and they swept it under the rug. They didn't want to do a damn thing. You could have been hurt."

"That's not true. They're not inexperienced. And remember Marcus can feel my heartbeat."

Jack pulled his hand away, flicking his gaze out the window and flexing his jaw. "Cate..."

"Jack," she said, grabbing his hand again. She softened her voice. "Jack..."

He fluttered his eyelashes, snapping his gaze to her.

"Anna is very protective. When I was in a coma from the

snake bite, she accused Celine of poisoning me. Which is ridiculous," Cate said with a shrug. "But still…she is extremely protective."

Jack heaved a sigh. "I don't like it."

"I don't imagine you do. This is a tricky situation, though."

"Tricky isn't the word," Jack groused. "I hate this."

"I'm sorry," Cate said with a squeeze of his hand.

"It's not your fault. You did what you had to do to save Dunhaven Castle. And you know, I'd rather these two than The Agency."

Cate smiled at him. "Me too." She eased back into the pillows and shook her head. "Anna is going to be so disappointed when Marcus and I divorce at the end of all of this."

"She doesn't know?"

Cate shook her head. "No. She thinks we've been married since 1810."

"Ho," Jack hooted with a half-grin. "Two centuries of marriage, and then it all falls apart."

Cate giggled as she shimmied lower in the bed, letting her head rest on the pillow. "And then he goes back to Celine. Oh, the horror."

"What? She didn't like Celine?"

Cate rolled her eyes, sucking in a breath as she shook her head. "Uh, in a word, no."

"Really? The very alluring Marquis's daughter was not up to Anna's standards?"

"Not in the slightest. She told me during our first conversation that Celine was, and I'm quoting here, a most disappointing choice."

"Wow," Jack said, dropping his chin to his chest. "No wonder she hates me. I'm just a gardener."

"You're hardly just a gardener," Cate said.

"Yeah, well I'm not sure old Marc told her that."

Cate chuckled, slapping a palm against her face. "Call him that to his face and see what happens."

"Pass. I have no desire to live my life as a toad."

"A toad?" she said, laughing harder. "You think he'd be that kind?"

"Maybe I'd be a slug."

Cate burst into laughter as did Jack. They chuckled together for a few minutes until the door burst open and Marcus entered. His eyebrows raised high as he witnessed the scene. "How are you feeling, dear?"

"Much better," Cate said with a final laugh.

"It seems Mr. Reid is doing an excellent job at entertaining you."

Cate smiled at him and nodded. "As always. Thank you, Jack."

"Is the show finished?"

Jack flicked his gaze between them before he stood. "If you're feeling okay, Cate, I'll go eat."

"I'm feeling fine. Really, I don't need a babysitter. Neither of you needs to stay."

"I will be the judge of that," Marcus said as he settled into the seat Jack vacated.

"Are you sure you're all right?" Jack asked, squeezing her foot through the blanket.

"I'm sure. Have a good dinner."

"Mind if I check back before I go to bed?"

"Not at all," Cate answered as Marcus answered, "No."

Cate snapped her gaze to him. "Marcus, he can stop by."

"You may be asleep," he answered.

"Then you can tell him that."

"All right, dear. Please stop by on your way to retire," Marcus grumbled.

Jack smiled at Cate and mouthed the word "slug" before he turned to leave.

Cate hid a smile as he strode from the room. Marcus arched an eyebrow as he stared after him. He spun back to face Cate as Jack slipped from the room.

"And what funny jokes did Mr. Reid have that lightened your spirits so?"

"Nothing," Cate said as she adjusted her covers.

"A secret. Should I be worried?"

Cate offered him a coy glance. "No, though your mother sure was."

"Mother is extremely protective of you."

"And you."

Marcus cocked his head. "What did he tell you?"

"He didn't tell me anything. I could hear most of what went on."

"Then you know Mother said nothing out of bounds."

"I know," Cate said, tracing the edge of her blanket. "But Jack is extremely off balance. This is not normal for him. He's scared. He doesn't understand."

Marcus puckered his lips, crossing his arms. Cate reached for his hand, lacing her fingers through his. "I know you don't like him. I'm pretty sure the feeling is mutual at the moment. But you have the upper hand in this situation and that's what terrifies him."

Marcus narrowed his eyes at her.

"You understand so much more of this world than he does. He's running to catch up. Even I understand more than he does after our experience finding him. He's still learning to trust you, but every other second he learns something new and terrifying and he's struggling to keep up."

"I suppose I can understand how it may be difficult for his feeble mind to comprehend."

Cate tugged one corner of her lips back, glancing at him through her eyelashes. "Be nice."

Marcus heaved a sigh, squeezing her hand. "You know I would never harm him, Catherine."

"I know that. But he doesn't yet."

Marcus smiled at her. "I'm glad you know it. And that is all that matters to me."

Cate slouched further down the bed. "Does that include not turning him into a slug?"

Marcus flicked his eyebrows up, puckering his lips as he considered it. "Tempting as it may be, no, I would not."

"Good," Cate answered with a sigh of relief. She snapped her gaze to him. "Wait, can you actually do that?"

Marcus narrowed his eyes at her with a coy grin. "I must keep some mystery about me, Catherine. I wouldn't want you to become bored with me."

Cate shook her head at him.

"And now I think it's time for you to sleep."

"I am tired. But I'm fine. You don't need to stay. I am perfectly capable of sleeping on my own."

"That is my call to make, and I am perfectly happy to watch you sleep so that I may be here should you need anything." Marcus switched off the light, plunging the room into darkness. Moonlight shone through the window, illuminating some of the room as Cate settled back into the pillows.

Within moments she drifted off to sleep. When Cate snapped her eyes open, the room remained dark. "Marcus?" she called into the darkness, wondering what happened to the moonlight.

She turned on the light, finding the chair he'd sat in earlier empty. He must have gone to bed, convinced she was okay.

She shivered, rubbing her arms after she switched off the light again. A breeze tickled her skin as she settled back into the pillows.

196

With a start, she flicked the light on again, glancing around the room. Everything seemed normal. Cate crinkled her brow, clicking the light off. Just as she settled back into her pillows again, a shiver snaked down her spine.

She turned the light on again, searching her bed for a serpent. She found nothing. As she settled the covers over her again, movement caught her eye.

A cloaked figure stepped out from behind the wardrobe and stalked toward her. Cate's heart pounded as she stared at the person.

The figure tossed her hood back. Gianna smirked at her as she sauntered closer. "Hello, Cate."

"What are you doing here?" Cate demanded.

She swung her legs over the bed and attempted to stand. Gianna raced around the corner and shoved her down to the mattress.

"Marcus!" Cate called.

"He can't hear you."

Cate pressed her hand against her chest. "He'll know."

One corner of Gianna's lips tugged back. "I hope he does. We're going to take everything from you, Cate." She leaned closer, whispering in Cate's ear. "Everything."

"I won't let you," Cate said through clenched teeth.

Gianna grabbed a pillow, squeezing it between her hands. "You won't be able to stop me."

She pressed the pillow over Cate's face and smashed her against the bed.

CHAPTER 19

*C*ate startled awake, flailing her arms as she cried out.

"Catherine?" Marcus asked, leaping to his feet.

Cate gasped, her heart pounding. She squinted against the light as he flicked it on. She searched the room, her eyes darting around wildly.

"Catherine, what is it?" he asked, slicking a wayward lock of her hair behind her ear.

"I...Gianna...she..." Cate heaved a deep breath. "It was a dream."

"Just a dream or a vision?"

Cate crinkled her brow. "No, a nightmare, I think. She was here. She was..."

"She is not here. You are safe."

Cate grabbed his hand as she steadied her breathing. She slid her eyes closed, slowly sucking in a breath. Marcus wrapped his arms around her as he sank onto the bed next to her. She clung to him as her fear dissipated.

She pushed away from him a few moments later. "I'm okay."

"Are you certain?"

"Yes. I really wish I hadn't met her."

"But then we never would have reconnected, and I'm certain you'd agree that was a high point."

Cate chuckled as she settled back in her pillows. "Certainly the high point of the situation."

"Has Jack checked in?"

"Yes, dear, hours ago. It's nearly morning."

"Was I asleep?"

"Soundly. I sent him on his way to bed. I did not turn him into a slug."

Cate laughed at his statement before she sobered. "Oh, Jack!" She snapped her gaze to Marcus. "We need to check on him. What if it wasn't a dream? What if I misinterpreted it, and it was a warning? She said she'd take everything from me. What if she took Jack again?"

"Calm yourself, Catherine. I'm certain he is fine. Rosenberg is a veritable fortress."

Cate tossed her covers back. "And one where I was bitten by a poisonous snake."

"While it was open for a party. I'm certain no one could have entered."

"I want to be more certain," Cate said, pulling her robe around her.

"All right," Marcus said with a sigh as he rose.

Cate slid her slippers on and stood. "Please don't make me stay here alone."

"Certainly not. I am not letting you out of my sight."

Cate nodded, grabbing his hand and dragging him forward. They navigated the distance to Jack's room.

Cate pressed an ear against the door, knocking lightly. "I don't hear anything."

She banged against it again, shifting her weight from foot to foot. With a shake of her head, she grabbed the knob and twisted it. It didn't budge. "It's locked. Why would it be locked?"

Cate flung her hand toward it. "Open it."

"Catherine, I–"

"Open it."

Marcus sucked in a breath and flicked his eyebrows up. "Fine."

With a flick of his wrist, he unlocked the door and pushed it into the room. Cate crept into the dark room. "Where are the lights?"

"On the left wall. Wait!" He pointed a finger forward. Cate followed the line of his finger. A lump poked up the covers in the bed, limned in moonlight.

Cate crept forward, craning her neck to stare down at him. Jack lay on his side, sleeping soundly. She waited, counting his breaths. She blew out a sigh of relief.

"Satisfied, dear?" Marcus whispered as he wrapped an arm around her shoulders.

"Yes," she said, leaning a head against his shoulder as she patted his hand. Her brow crinkled. "Why was his door locked?"

"I'm certain he had his reasons."

"What reasons? Why lock the door?"

"I do not know, but I do not believe we should debate it here."

Cate stared down at him. "Was he afraid of something?"

"Catherine, it does not matter. He is fine. Let's get you back to bed."

"I'm just curious. I–"

"Whoa!" Jack shouted, drawing her attention from Marcus.

"Jack," Cate said.

Jack tugged the covers up to his chin. "What the hell is happening?"

"I had a bad dream. I wanted to check on you."

Jack's eyes slid to Marcus. "And him?"

"I was worried about you. We came to check on you together. And good thing, you locked your door. Why did you lock your door?"

Jack pressed his lips together, his eyes lingering on Marcus. "This is pretty close to the exact scenario I imagined when I decided to lock it."

Cate collapsed on the edge of the bed. "Very funny. Are you sure you're okay?"

Jack swallowed hard, lowering the covers with a nod. "Yes. I'm sure. I'm fine, Cate. I'm okay. How are you feeling? Have you gotten any sleep?"

Cate bobbed her head up and down. "Yes. Until I had that stupid nightmare. Don't worry, it wasn't a vision. Just a regular old nightmare."

"Are you sure?"

"I am. If you're sure you're okay, I'll head back and try to get more rest. I just wanted to check on you." Cate grabbed his hand and squeezed.

"Maybe I should come back with you. I can stay–"

"That will not be necessary," Marcus informed him, patting Cate's shoulder. "I will be with her."

"That's not comforting."

"I am not concerned about your comfort," Marcus retorted.

Jack pushed back his covers. "Which is why I should go with you."

"No," Marcus said flatly.

Cate patted Jack's hand. "No, you need your rest, too. It's fine." She stood and pulled his covers up over him.

"Cate–"

Cate pressed her hand against his again. "It's fine, Jack. I'm perfectly safe with Marcus."

Jack narrowed his eyes as he glanced up at the man. "If you're sure you feel comfortable."

"Absolutely," Cate said with a reassuring smile.

"Would you mind giving us a minute?" Jack asked Marcus.

"I would," he answered.

"Marcus," Cate said with a tilt of her head, "give us a minute."

Marcus puckered his lips, studying her. He traced the line of her jaw. "Do not be long. You need your rest."

She nodded in response as he strode from the room, twisting to give them one last look over his shoulder before he stepped into the hall.

"Cate…" Jack started, taking her hand.

She collapsed onto the edge of the bed. "I'm fine, Jack."

"Are you really? Are you sure it wasn't a vision?"

"Yes, because those make me tired, but I don't feel that tired. I just wanted to be sure."

Jack licked his lips, blowing out a sigh as he slumped back into his pillows. "And what about the rest?"

Cate crinkled her brow. "The rest of what?"

Jack nudged his head toward the door. "Him?"

"Marcus?"

Jack nodded at her question.

"He's fine. I feel safe with him."

Jack stared at her for a moment, studying her face. "Okay, as long as you're comfortable."

"He won't let anything happen to me," Cate said as she rose to stand. "Oh, and he promised not to turn you into a slug."

Jack's eyes went wide. "You told him?"

"No, I didn't tell him exactly. He promised he'd never hurt you. I felt it was prudent to ask if that included turning you into a slug."

"And he said he couldn't. That's a relief."

"Well, he didn't say he couldn't, just that he wouldn't."

Jack stared at her with a blank expression. "I don't know if I like this new world we live in."

Cate giggled at him. "You'll get used to it. Just like you did with time travel. Good night, Jack."

She shuffled across the room as he called after her, "I'm still not used to time travel!"

She spun, chuckling again. "Good night, Jack."

"Good night, Cate."

Cate waved as she slipped through his door into the hall.

Marcus pulled himself from leaning against the wall. "Have you settled his nerves?"

Cate slipped her arm into his and pulled him down the hall. "Yes."

"Wonderful."

"You could give him a break, you know? He's–"

"Struggling to keep up, I know. Though it is my duty to worry about you first. You, too, are struggling."

They turned the corner on the long walk back to her suite. "I'm not. We spent a lot of time together rescuing him. I'm way more used to this than he is."

Marcus stopped, turning her to face him. "You are still acclimating to this world and your new condition. And you are Gianna's main target."

Cate opened her mouth to respond, but he pressed a finger to her lips, silencing her.

"I understand your urge to protect him, but you must allow me to worry about you."

Her lips tugged up at the corners as she stared up at him. "I guess I can let you do that."

"Good," he said, flicking his eyebrows up. "Now, perhaps you'll allow me to carry you back to your room."

"No," Cate said, wagging her finger at him. "I can walk."

"But you're allowing me to worry about you."

"Worry, not carry. Those two letters at the start make a *big* difference."

Marcus chuckled at her as they pushed into her room.

"See, I made it," she said with a grin as she doffed her robe and climbed into bed. "I walked all that way on my own. Amazing."

"Yes, it is," Marcus said as she slouched down and pulled the covers over her. "You are an incredible woman, Catherine."

"Mmm-hmm," she said as he settled into the chair next to her bed. "Absolutely astounding. The real astonishing bit was the way I put one foot in front of the other over and over until we got here."

"That is not what I meant, and you know it. But it's time for you to rest."

Cate smiled at him as he turned off the light. She settled back in her pillows, letting the smile play on her lips until she drifted off to sleep.

When her eyes opened again, light streamed into the room from the large window. She squinted against it as she searched the chair for Marcus. Instead, she found Anna in his place.

"Good morning, Catherine," she said with a smile, patting her hand. "You probably expected Marcus and I am a poor substitute, but I sent him away early this morning."

"Oh," Cate said as she pushed up to sit, "certainly not a poor substitute. And I am glad you sent him, hopefully, to rest. He stayed all night."

"I know. He does worry over you so. Though I can see why."

Cate smiled at her, feeling heat rise into her cheeks. The thought of Anna's upset at their inevitable divorce raced across her mind. She licked her lips, searching her mind for conversation.

"The truth is I wanted to try something. I know Marcus would object, but I'm hoping you're game."

Cate flicked her gaze to the woman. "What is it?"

She offered her an amused smile and held a finger up before she hurried from the room. She returned with the purple rose.

"This should elicit a similar reaction as the bracelet, however, the future memory should be quite pleasant, I think. I thought we could try that and see how it goes. It should be a bit less taxing. What do you think?"

Cate stared at the purple rose floating in the case before she flicked her gaze to Anna. "I think I'm glad you sent Marcus away."

Anna chuckled as she slid the glass case onto the night table and eased into the chair. "There is no rush to try. Whenever you are ready, though perhaps after your breakfast."

Cate nodded in agreement, flinging off her covers.

"Oh, no, no, you remain abed. I shall ring for it."

"That's nonsense, I'm–"

"Recovering and hoping to try again today. Do not waste your energy traversing the halls for a meal that can be delivered to you."

Cate tugged the covers over her as Anna pulled the cord on the wall. "Marcus tells me your search for your ancestor took you to London."

"Yes, it did," Cate said, tracing the edge of her blanket.

"And how did you find the London home?"

"It's lovely and very convenient."

"I always thought it rather a bore. Possibly because Marcus's father typically left me there to do business. I do hope that isn't the case with you. I have warned him not to neglect you."

"He doesn't," Cate assured her as Andrea arrived with a breakfast tray.

"Shall I wait for you to dress, Your Grace?"

"No, no, Andrea, we'll manage," Anna said, shooing her away.

"And Marcus tells me you haven't yet been to Stratford-shire or Wintervale."

Cate scooped up a spoonful of porridge. "No."

Anna propped her head on her chin, staring into space. "How odd."

"I'm certain it's because we've been so busy–"

Anna waved a hand in the air, cutting off her answer. "There is no excuse. You really should view the properties at the very least so that you may begin making the changes you'd like to make it your home."

Cate shook her head. "Oh–"

"Do not be shy, Catherine, my son has a fortune and it should be devoted to making you happy. Make all the changes you'd like so you are happy there. It is your home now."

"Homes," Cate said with a shrug as she scooped up more of the porridge.

"Yes, dear, homes. Of which we have acquired many over the years. And they are all yours now. This palace included. I really should ask if there are any changes–"

Cate grabbed her hand. "No. That is where I draw the line. This is your home. I wouldn't change a thing."

Anna's shoulders slumped as she wrapped Cate's hand in both of hers. Tears shone in her eyes. "Oh, Catherine, Marcus could not have selected better in a wife."

Cate flicked her gaze to her bowl, pushing around the porridge.

"I don't mean to embarrass you, dear, but…" She heaved a sigh. "Well, I feel we have dodged a bullet. His near marriage to that…*woman* would have ruined him."

Cate forced a smile onto her face. "I'm sure–"

"Oh, please, you do not need to be gracious." She patted Cate's arm. "Admit it, Catherine, you are far better."

The smile on Cate's face broadened. "I'm not sure about that, but I am glad you think so."

"I know so. Now," she said, lifting the tray from Cate's lap, "let's get you dressed."

Cate climbed from her bed, trying to shake off the guilt building inside her over the previous conversation. She pushed it aside as they moved on to other topics.

When they finished, Cate's eyes fell on the rose across the room. "Would it be okay if we tried now?"

"If you're feeling up to it, dear, yes. Why don't you lay back in your bed and try to relax? Remember these will still be taxing, but I hope not as taxing."

Cate nodded, reaching for her music box. "I had an idea in the middle of the night, too." She lifted the box in the air, opening the top before she set it down on the night table. "I thought this may relax me. It helped so much during my temporalysis."

"Oh, I'm so glad you enjoy that little box."

"I cherish it," Cate answered as she settled into her pillows.

"Let me know when you're ready, dear, and I'll give you the rose."

Cate shimmied, trying to find a comfortable spot as she focused on the music. "How do you know these memories will be positive?"

"I do not know for certain, but since this object represents a positive moment for you in the past *and* you reacted to it once before, I believe this will show you positive future moments."

Cate nodded, recalling the moment when she'd received the rose from Marcus in the garden below. The memory brought a smile to her face. She sucked in a breath and flicked her gaze to Anna. "I'm ready."

Anna slid the glass off and set it aside. She retrieved the rose from where it floated and passed it to Cate. "Remember, still taxing so don't push too far."

"Right," Cate said with a curt bob of her head. Her heart beat faster as she reached toward the rose. She blew out a controlled breath, focusing on the music and the memory of the rose. Her fingers caressed the petals. Visions whipped across her mind in a blinding blur.

Her breathing turned ragged as she struggled to focus. Tension built at her temples. She fought against it, desperate to make some progress. The music tinkled in the background as her mind wrestled with the future memories.

"Catherine?" Anna questioned.

"Wait," she breathed. Her eyelids fluttered before sliding closed, and her forehead crinkled. She forced her heart rate slower and her breathing steadier. Her mind converged on one crystal clear image.

She sucked in a breath as she pulled her fingers away from the rose and flicked her gaze to Anna. "It worked."

CHAPTER 20

"*I*t worked," Cate repeated as she pinched her eyebrows together. The future memory danced across her mind.

Anna clapped her hands together with a grin. "Catherine! That's wonderful! And you could see the memory clearly?"

Cate matched her expression. "I did. Yes, crystal clear. Like I was standing right there."

"That is wonderful. Excellent progress."

Cate bit her lower lip as she reflected on the future memory she'd seen. Her forehead crinkled. "Are they real?"

Anna tilted her head. "What do you mean?"

"Are the future memories definitely going to happen?"

"Oh, yes."

"No way to avoid them?"

Anna narrowed her eyes at Cate. "I'm growing concerned this happy future memory was not quite so happy."

Cate chuckled. "Oh, no, it seemed very happy, but…I'm just curious to know how sure they are. Could my brain create something that won't happen? Has that ever happened to you? I want to know more for the bad ones."

"Oh, yes. Can your brain mislead you? Yes, certainly, but that's usually due to misreading the information you're given. You're fed things not to avoid them but to prepare to handle them in the best way possible. However, perhaps you witness your friend crying and interpret it as your friend being harmed when really she is crying happy tears because she is with child."

Cate sucked in a breath as she considered it. "I see. Okay. I'm ready to try the bracelet."

"Catherine! You can't."

"I can. I succeeded."

"Once. You succeeded once. You need more practice and more patience."

"But–"

The door to her suite burst open, and Marcus strode inside. "Good morning, Catherine. What does Mother have you doing that has your heart rate up?" He kissed her cheek before leaning on the bed to await her response.

"We are practicing," Anna said, waving the rose at him before she returned it to its glass case.

"And?" Marcus asked, directing the question to Cate.

"And it worked!" she exclaimed with a grin. She flicked her gaze up to him and raised her shoulders.

Marcus arched an eyebrow at her, smiling. "Excellent work, dear."

Anna patted her hand. "She did so well. And so quickly. You are an excellent pupil, Catherine."

"I want to try the bracelet again, but–"

"No," Marcus and Anna said simultaneously.

Cate's shoulders slumped as she flicked her gaze between them. "This is ridiculous. I made progress."

"And you are still learning. You managed to make sense of a happy future memory. The bracelet will be very different," Anna said.

"I will never learn how to tame the bad ones if I don't try."

Anna grabbed Cate's hand and rubbed it as she shifted her gaze to Marcus. "Oh, Marcus, I do like her."

"As do I."

Cate tapped her foot in the air as she puckered her lips. "I appreciate how much you both like me, but I still think I should try the bracelet."

"Tell you what, dear. You try the rose again in a bit. If you can easily focus on another future memory, I'll let you try the bracelet this evening." She held up a finger. "Just once."

Cate tugged back one corner of her lips and crinkled her nose.

"Mother is right."

"As I always am," Anna said, raising her eyebrows and smiling as a knock sounded at the door. "Come in." She snapped her gaze to Cate. "Oh, I'm sorry, dear."

"It's fine," Cate said as Andrea popped her head in.

"Your Grace? Just checking in to make sure you managed everything this morning."

"Yes, I'm fine, Andrea, thank you."

Andrea smiled and nodded, sliding her eyes sideways. "Also, Mr. Reid is here inquiring after you."

"We're busy," Marcus answered as Cate said, "Send him in."

Marcus huffed out a breath and nodded at Andrea.

Andrea smiled at them before she stepped back. Jack strode in a moment later. "Good morning, everyone," he said, his eyes darting around at the three of them. "Cate, how are you feeling?"

"Very well, thank you. We're making progress with my visions."

Jack flicked his eyebrows up. "Really? Did you see anything about Gertrude?"

Cate shook her head. "No, we're working on another angle that's less painful."

Anna tightened her fingers around Cate's hand. "We must be careful to not overtax her."

"Yeah, definitely," Jack said, sliding his hands into his pockets. "That sounds like a good plan."

He sucked in a breath and nodded, his head bobbing up and down over and over.

"Would you mind taking a walk with me to the garden? I could use some fresh air," Cate said.

A grin spread across Jack's face. "Of course."

Cate nodded and swung her legs off the bed. She patted Anna's hand. "We'll try again when I get back?"

"Of course, dear."

"I'll go with you," Marcus said as Cate rose from the mattress.

"Actually, darling, if you wouldn't mind staying, I'd like a word with you," Anna said.

Marcus pressed his lips together into a thin line as Cate slid her hand around Jack's arm. "Fine."

"We won't be long," Cate assured him. They left her suite behind and navigated the halls to the door leading to the garden. Cate squinted as she stepped into the bright sunshine, shielding her eyes as they wandered through the spring blooms.

"Glad I stopped by when I did," Jack said.

"Sorry to have kept you in the dark. When I woke up Anna was already there, and she wanted to try my visions with a different object, and–"

"You don't need to apologize, Cate. I know you're just doing what you have to. But I'm glad I came when I did to rescue you."

Cate sniffed at the purple rose buds. "Oh, I didn't need to be rescued. They're taking excellent care of me."

Jack furrowed his brow. "Oh, I thought...you seemed like you wanted to get out of there."

Cate sucked in a breath. "It has been a little uncomfortable."

"I knew it," Jack said, shifting his gaze out over the landscape. "As beautiful as this place is, we need to get out of here."

Cate fingered the delicate petals of the blooming buds. "No, we're so close to making progress."

"Cate, progress doesn't matter if you're–"

"I'm not. It's not what you think."

He gazed sideways at her. "Care to explain?"

Cate slid her eyes closed, her features pinching. She licked her lips before she fluttered her eyes open. She wandered to the stone wall circling the mountaintop garden and stared out over the rolling hills. "This is not going to end well."

Jack rubbed her shoulders. "I'm sure we can figure this out. We'll get the will fixed."

"No, not the will." Cate rolled her head to the side. "Anna wants to know when I'm going to start redecorating the houses. She's shocked that I haven't been to Havershire or whatever shire it is Marcus owns and the other one and the other one. And if I want changes at the palace to tell her."

She covered her face with her hands as she sighed. "I'm certain that's what they're talking about now. She's going to be so disappointed when she finds out the truth."

"Why does it matter?"

"I actually like Anna. I don't want her hurt in this charade."

Jack wiggled his eyebrows, shifting his gaze to the landscape again. "Hopefully, it'll all be over soon and you won't have to worry about it anymore."

Cate sucked in a deep breath and nodded. "With any luck. I

made some progress with the visions. But no one will let me try the bracelet again. It must have something to do with Gertrude."

"But you saw something, right?"

Cate nodded, avoiding his gaze.

"What?"

"What?" she asked.

"What did you see?"

"Oh, um, nothing to do with Gertrude. Nothing to do with anything. It was fleeting, but I could center on it. But I used the rose which brought a happy future memory."

"Future memory?"

Cate bobbed her head up and down. "That's what they are called. The visions. And they do feel like memories. It's weird. Anyway, I saw something obscure that doesn't help us at all. And no one will let me touch the bracelet."

Jack rubbed her shoulders again. "What do you think everyone's doing at home?"

Cate stared out at the bright blue sky as the fluffy white clouds floated across it. "It's kind of weird because the answer is nothing, right?"

"What?" Jack asked, his hand freezing on her shoulder.

"Well, think about it. We're here, living through days, but...Marcus will return us to almost exactly the moment we left. Only moments will have passed. So...at home, our friends are frozen in time."

Jack scrubbed at his face. "This is...weird. So, okay, how does this work? What if we fix all this? What if we fix the will? What happens when we get back?"

"Everything will be different."

Jack remained silent, rubbing his chin as he considered the statement. "Is that what happened when I went missing?"

"Yeah," Cate said with a nod. "I went to the library and you were gone but for everyone else, you'd be gone for a week. So, if we fix things, we'll go back and Mr. Smythe will be really confused about what's happened No one will know why the will is different."

"But we'll remember."

"We'll remember," Cate said. "Nothing will have changed for us. But everything will have changed for everyone else in the house."

Jack sighed, resting his chin in his palm as he balanced his elbow against his other arm. "I hope I can survive all this. It's just getting weirder and weirder."

Cate chuckled at him. "I mean, at least we can fix things, right? And then we'll just need to explain why things changed. Oh, maybe we can update the will after the last one with the codicil removed. That would fix it. I think."

"Right," Jack said, bobbing his head up and down. "Wait, couldn't you have brought me back early and stopped everyone from remembering I was missing?"

"We returned with you after we went searching. I guess we could have returned with you around when you disappeared, but..." Cate crinkled her brow. "Then there may have been two of you."

Jack's eyes went wide. "Two of me? That's..." He took a few breaths, his mouth hanging open. "So, I could, in theory, talk to myself."

"You could tell yourself how dashing you are. Or make bad puns to yourself," Cate said.

"Or make excellent puns," Jack pointed out.

"Either. Both."

Jack rubbed his chin again. "Can I ask you something?"

"Sure."

"Have you...talked to yourself?"

Cate shook her head. "No. I've never talked to myself, but I saw myself with you in 1942."

Jack's head slid forward as he stared at her. "You saw...yourself."

"Yeah. I saw myself with you. I wanted to grab you back then but it was the wrong you. The right you was with Gianna. It's really confusing, but yes, I saw myself."

"Did you see you?"

"No, the other me didn't see me."

"Whew," Jack said, rubbing his forehead. "Good thing. Or else the universe may have blown up."

Cate screwed up her face and chuckled. "What?"

"The universe will explode. It's like a basic tenant of time travel."

"I'm not sure that's true."

"I think it is. In Back to the Future, the lady couldn't handle seeing her older self. She passed out."

"I was only two days older."

"Still..." Jack said with a shrug.

"It's not a problem. Believe me."

Jack wagged his finger at her. "You don't know that, Cate. And as a Reid, I'm going to pull the safety card on this one and say just don't do it."

"But it's fine. Really, I promise."

"You can't know."

"But I do. In 1810, Marcus had an 1810 counterpart."

Jack's eyes went wide, and his jaw fell open again. "No. His eyes floated to the castle. Two Dukes?"

"Yep. And they talk to each other. They tell each other things. Like the future and what they should do."

Jack stared down at the ground, kicking the gravel around on the path. "I can't believe I'm going to say this, but...I'm kind of glad I was unconscious for that."

Cate pressed her lips together and shook her head as she playfully patted his arm. "Well, I am not. You were really sick. I would have preferred you to have been fully conscious."

"I wouldn't have stayed that way after I saw that," Jack answered.

Cate sucked in a breath. "Anyway, I guess we'll find out how things happen this time. If anyone ever lets me touch that bracelet."

"You're way braver than I am, Cate," Jack said. "I don't think I could do what you're doing. Scratch that. I know I couldn't do it."

"Yes, you could. You could do it for Dunhaven. For Molly, for the Frasers, for me."

"I think you're way braver than me."

Cate shifted her gaze to the palace's wall. "I guess we should head back."

"Yes, I'm sure Mama Northcott is pacing the halls because you've spent far too long away from her darling baby boy."

Cate giggled as they strolled back toward the door.

"You know, I never know what to call her. But I have a feeling if I called her Anna she'd faint dead away."

"Technically, you should call her Your Grace. She's the mother of a Duke."

"Technically, I should call you Your Grace. You're the wife of a Duke. Though it sounds so strange when that girl says it. Andrea, is it?"

Cate nodded as they pushed into the castle's hall. "Yes. Andrea. And Cate is just fine."

"You've never been one for titles," Jack said in his best Marcus voice.

Cate pressed her lips together as she suppressed another giggle.

"And are you certain you don't prefer Catherine?"

Cate shot him a sideways glance. "Yes, I'm sure. You're going to get yourself in trouble with your joking."

They wound through the halls to her bedroom suite. Cate pushed inside, finding the room empty. "No one's here."

Jack scanned the space before he slipped inside. "At the risk of being beheaded, I'll come in."

"They're not going to behead you."

"You don't know that," Jack said with a wag of his finger. "They must still be discussing all those renovations you're going to do at the house in Stratfordshire. Or perhaps the Mayberry estate. Or maybe the London home. And when you'll have tea with the Queen." Jack waved a finger in the air as he did his best Queen voice.

Cate shook her head as she giggled. "I'm glad the temporalysis has not dampened your sense of humor."

"Mrs. Campbell is going to be thrilled if you stay married through your one-year anniversary."

Cate sighed and sank onto her chaise. "I'm not certain what I dread more. Mrs. Campbell's one-year extravaganza–
"

"Don't forget The Presidents' Ball right on its heels."

"Right, and that, or touching that bracelet again." Cate slid her eyes sideways to the gold chain on the side table.

"The bracelet would win for me."

"I think it wins for me too." Cate stared at it before she glanced around the room. "And no one is here to stop me so…" She reached for the chain when Jack smacked her hand back.

"I'm here to stop you."

Cate snapped her gaze to him, her jaw hanging open. "Jack!"

"No, Cate. I'm not going to be turned into a frog because I let you pick that thing up."

"No one is turning anyone into a frog. And if you don't let me try, we'll never find out if I can do this. No one will let me try it."

"Well, you're not doing it on my watch. No way. I'm not going to let you do and get the wrath of the Northcotts while you lay unconscious. I had enough of that last night, and I didn't even do anything."

"Okay, fine. I'll wait until you leave."

Jack plopped into the armchair and flung his hands out. "Looks like you'll have a long wait. Because I'm not leaving."

Cate threw herself back onto the chaise, letting her body go limp. "Ugh. We'll never solve this."

Jack drummed his fingers on the arm of the chair. "I'll win favor with those Northcotts yet."

She poked a finger at him. "You should be worried about winning favor with me. I'm the MacKenzie."

"And I'm the Reid. I'm supposed to protect you. Always."

"Well, you are, by letting me pick this up, searching for information about Gertrude or whatever is happening with The Agency and defeating them!"

Jack wrinkled his nose. "Stop trying to convince me. I am not going to be the reason you're unconscious in the bed."

"You wouldn't be. I'm the one doing this. I know what I'm doing. And I was able to make progress this morning. My music box helps. I'm going to try that when I touch the bracelet and see if it works."

"And what if it doesn't? What am I supposed to do, just let you lay there unconscious until one of those two wander back in and say, 'Oh, hi, Cate's unconscious, don't know when she'll wake up.'"

"No, of course not. Hopefully, I won't be unconscious. I only passed out last night because the stupid chain got caught on my thumb."

Jack pursed his lips and clasped his hands in front of him, avoiding her gaze.

"Jack, you can monitor it. Pull it off me if I struggle too much. But let me try."

He slid his eyes closed and puckered his lips. "Damn it, Cate. If you get me turned into a dog, I'm going to bite you."

"Deal. You can bite me if Marcus turns you into a dog. Until then, grab that bracelet, and let's go."

Jack slid the jewelry piece off the table with a shake of his head as Cate hurried into the bedroom. She opened the lid of the music box before she stretched out on the bed.

"Okay, I need to prepare to touch that. I'll let you know when I'm ready. Lay it in my hand. It'll be taxing on me, but don't pull it away too quickly."

Jack huffed out a sigh, sliding his eyes closed. "Oh, Cate. I'm nervous."

"Don't be. It'll be all right."

"I really hope so."

Cate squeezed his hand and settled back into the pillows. She closed her eyes, letting the music wash over her. She steadied her breathing. She opened her eyes, staring at the bracelet. Her heart skipped a beat as she stared at it.

She shifted her gaze to the purple rose in its case next to the piano music box. The memory of receiving them along with her earlier future memory settled in her mind.

"Okay," she whispered. "Give me the bracelet."

With her eyes trained on the two gifts and the music playing, the metal, warm from Jack's skin, slid across her skin. She struggled to keep her eyes focused as memories raced through her mind. Tension twisted at her temples. Pain began to build. She winced.

"Cate?" Jack asked, leaping from his seat and hovering over her.

"Wait," she squeaked.

She gritted her teeth as she struggled to process the blur.

"Cate!"

"Wait," she said again. Her breathing turned ragged.

"That's it, I'm taking it," Jack said. He whipped the bracelet from her hand as she collapsed backward.

Exhausted, she struggled to suck in breaths. The doors to her suite burst open and Marcus raced in, followed by Anna.

"What's happened? What have you done?" he shouted at Jack.

"She wanted to try the bracelet. I–"

"She what? And you let her?"

"I'm fine," Cate whispered.

Marcus grabbed her hand, stroking her hair. Anna pushed past Jack, squeezing Cate's other hand in hers.

"I'm fine," she repeated. "And I think I know where Gertrude is."

CHAPTER 21

"ate, are you serious?" Jack asked from the foot of her bed. "You know where she is."

Cate struggled to push herself up. She made it as far as her elbows before Anna and Marcus stopped her.

"Easy, Catherine," Anna said.

"I'm fine, really. And I managed to get some clarity in my future memory that may help us."

"What did you see?" Jack asked, earning a glare from both mother and son.

"I saw a...house or something. It looked abandoned. I saw Gertrude there. She was..." Cate's features pinched. "Tied to a chair. It was dark. Ummm-"

"All right, easy, Catherine," Marcus said. "Take your time. There's no need to rush."

Cate struggled to sit up further. "There is. She's trapped there. We can solve this. We can-"

"Do you know the exact location?" Marcus asked.

Cate collapsed back into the pillows. "No."

"Then we have more work to do."

Cate covered her face with her hands.

Anna pulled them away, squeezing them in hers. "It's all right, Catherine. This is incredible progress. I'm amazed."

Cate sighed. "It's not enough progress."

"It's plenty," Marcus said.

"And each time you try, you'll get better. And you'll get more information," Anna said.

Cate nodded and waved at Jack for the bracelet. "Okay, I'll try again now."

"No," Anna and Marcus said simultaneously.

Anna shook her head. "You can't try again this quickly."

"Yes, I can."

"You're going to overtax yourself. You're still unsure, and you're going to hurt yourself," Anna answered. "You don't want to end up like you did last night."

Cate's shoulders slumped again.

"Maybe they're right, Cate," Jack said, squeezing her toes.

"Now, you're all ganging up on me," Cate said with an amused eye roll. "Fine, fine. Since everyone agrees, I'll wait."

Anna pulled a blanket over Cate's legs and tucked it around her.

Cate thrashed her head back and forth. "I feel like an invalid. I'm not sick. I'm perfectly fine."

Anna fussed more with the cover. "If you want to try again soon, you should not tax yourself now. In the meantime, perhaps you can recall more details from what you saw."

"You're right." Cate slid her eyes closed, trying to pull up as many details as she could from what she'd seen. After a moment, she clicked her tongue, pounding her fists on the bed. "It's all fuzzy now. It was so clear in my mind when I saw it."

"That's perfectly normal, Catherine. Until you can still speak whilst you have the visions, they will be vivid, then quickly fade. It is your body's way of protecting itself."

"I don't need to be protected from this. It's so frustrating." Cate patted the bed on either side of her. "You all don't need to stay. I'm perfectly fine."

"There is nowhere I'd rather be, dear," Marcus said as he stroked her hair again.

"Me too," Jack said with a nod. Marcus shot him an annoyed glance as he dragged another chair from the sitting room and plopped into it.

"Thank you all. I'm sorry this is going so slowly."

"There is no need to apologize," Anna said with a pat on her arm.

Cate puckered her lips as she bided her time to try again. "Did you say I'd be able to talk during these visions eventually?"

"Oh, yes. You should see them with just a tiny amount of pain and discomfort. You'll be able to speak while they occur. That should make them easier to decipher, although, as I mentioned, it can be incredibly tricky to attempt to pinpoint meaning."

"I have a feeling this one is fairly easy to pinpoint. It seems I'm seeing the place where Gertrude is being held captive by The Agency."

"And now we'll work to get more details on where that is. Are you ready to try again?"

"Mother," Marcus began, "are you certain it isn't too soon?"

Anna shot him a glance with her eyebrows raised. "Are you questioning me?"

"Of course not. Merely suggesting we err on the side of caution."

"I believe Catherine would like to try, and she won't rest until she does. So, she's not getting adequate rest anyway."

Cate pulled herself up to sit straighter, bobbing her head up and down. "I would very much like to try again."

"Mr. Reid, do you have the bracelet?" Anna waved her hand toward Jack.

Jack shifted around in his seat. "Uh, I'm kind of on his side on this one." He poked a finger toward Marcus.

"His timing is nothing short of amazing," Marcus murmured.

"Well, I think he makes a good point. I think it's too soon."

"And I say it's not," Anna answered.

Cate offered him a stunned glance. "I'm with Anna. And I'm the person experiencing it so my opinion outweighs everyone. Hand over the bracelet, Jack."

Jack eyed Marcus who glanced at him over his shoulder. "Don't look at me, Mr. Reid. We are outnumbered."

Jack pressed his lips together and shook his head as he dug the bracelet out of his pocket. "Can't believe this."

"Please keep your commentary to a minimum, Mr. Reid. While I appreciate your worry for your friend, I have things perfectly under control," Anna said as she accepted the bracelet dangling from Jack's fingers. "Catherine, whenever you are ready."

Cate nodded. "Okay, just give me a minute."

"Take your time," Anna said with a nod.

Marcus wrapped his hand around Cate's as she settled back into the pillows, allowing the music to relax her. She closed her eyes, letting her mind recall her happy moments at Rosenberg Palace as she'd done before and the seemingly happy future moment she'd witnessed when she touched the rose.

She pressed her lips together, preparing for the onslaught of painful images. Her heart skipped a beat, and she forced it to settle into a normal rhythm. With her palm open, she opened her eyes and slid them to Anna. "Ready."

"Good luck," Anna whispered as she dropped the bracelet into Cate's hand.

The metal hit her skin, cool to the touch this time, and the images began to rush through her mind. She fought to slow them, the pain building already.

She tried to speak as they floated past, but she found herself unable to make a sound. The tension built at her temples. Tears formed in her eyes as the visions showed no signs of slowing down.

"No," she cried as she dropped the bracelet on the bed. She blew out a shaky breath as a tear slid down her cheek.

"It's all right, Catherine," Marcus said, rubbing her arm.

"I didn't get anything this time. I got more *last* time. I'm going backward."

Anna scooped up the bracelet and set it aside. "You're not. These setbacks are normal. You're pushing yourself instead of letting them come to you. You are forcing things, and that is making this all the harder."

Cate heaved a sigh. "I just want to get more information."

"There are other angles we can try that don't involve your clairvoyance," Marcus said.

"Like what? An exhaustive search of all The Agency's properties in every time period?" Cate slapped a hand against her face.

"That was rather a dramatic way to put it, but yes," Marcus answered.

"I'm game. I can help. Just tell me what to do," Jack said, rubbing his hands together.

Anna sat back in the chair, furrowing her brow.

Marcus rose from his seat. "Their properties are extensive. It will take us days to comb through them and select potential locations to scout."

"Wait, wait, wait," Anna said, waving a hand in the air. She cocked her head, licking her lips and narrowing her eyes.

"What is it, Mother?"

"Surely, you can't want Cate to try again, can you?"

"I can do it," Cate answered.

"No. Not with the bracelet. But perhaps we can glean some additional details from the one clear memory she's had."

Cate bit into her lower lip, her features pinching. "Oh, but I can't remember anything else. I'm sorry."

"Yes, I know you said it's hazy now, but...what if we hypnotized you?" Anna asked.

Marcus cocked his head, flicking his eyebrows up. "Excellent idea, Mother. Perhaps that can help us narrow the search."

"I'm not sure I can be hypnotized," Cate answered.

"What makes you say that?" Anna asked.

"Well," Cate answered, tracing the blanket's edge, "I tried it once and it didn't work."

"When?" Marcus asked.

"When I had temporalysis, I–"

"Who performed it?" he interrupted.

"Ahhhh..." Cate stammered, avoiding eye contact with everyone.

Jack cleared his throat and waved a hand in the air. "Me. I tried it."

Marcus heaved a sigh. "Well, that explains it. User error. Mother is quite adept at it. I assure you she will have no issues achieving the hypnotic state with you."

Cate fluttered her eyelashes and blew out a long breath. "All right. Well, I'm willing to try. Will the memories hurt like they do when I touch the bracelet?"

"They may be frightening to you, but I am hoping they are not painful. Though hypnosis is not a standard technique for these situations, so we'll be feeling our way through."

"Wait," Jack said, "are you saying you have no idea what this will do to her?"

Marcus shot him an irked glance. "That's not exactly what she said, Reid."

"This is a controlled experiment. We can end it at any time," Anna added.

"I'd rather try this than the bracelet again. I mean, I'll try either, but this seems less taxing."

"Then that is what we will do," Anna said with a smile and a pat on Cate's arm. She waved at the window before she removed a pendant necklace from around her neck. "Marcus, close the drapes. Now, Catherine, lay back and try to relax. Focus on my pendant. Notice how it sparkles despite the dim light.

"Try to take deep breaths and feel your body relaxing. It's melting into the bed. You're beginning to feel very relaxed. Your eyes feel heavy as do your limbs. Your eyelids are starting to close.

"I'm going to count backward from three to one. When I reach one, you will be completely relaxed and asleep."

Cate's eyelids struggled to stay open as she stared at the pendant. Anna rolled it between her thumb and forefinger. It sparkled and glowed in the low light. Her limbs sank into the soft bedding, and her eyes slid closed.

She floated in darkness until Anna's voice spoke again. "Catherine, are you relaxed?"

"Yes," she answered.

"Where are you?"

"Nowhere," Cate answered as she spun in the black room.

"I'd like you to find a place where you feel safe. Where you feel happy."

Cate pinched her eyebrows together as she searched the darkness. Light pierced through it, and she moved toward the bright beam. She made out the outline of a partially open door. Cate grabbed the handle and tugged it open.

Her lips turned up at the corners as she recognized the

future memory she'd seen earlier. She walked into it, embracing it fully as she closed out the blackness.

"Have you found one, Catherine?" Anna asked.

"Yes."

"Good. If you feel any pain or become frightened, I want you to return here. Do you understand?"

"Yes," Cate said as her smile broadened.

"All right, Catherine. Now, I want you to search your mind to find the vision you saw earlier. The vision of Gertrude."

Cate's forehead creased. "No."

"I know you want to stay where you are, but I need you to find Gertrude. I need you to describe what you see when you find that vision."

Cate nodded, allowing the room to slip away from her. Images raced past her in the darkness.

"Have you found it?" Anna's voice echoed.

"No," she cried.

"Calm down, Catherine. You're fine."

Cate squeezed her eyes closed as images whizzed past her. "I can't make sense of anything. It's all moving too fast."

"Find the image you saw before. You recalled it after touching the bracelet. Find that image."

"I'm trying, but I can't." Cate pressed her fingers against her temples as she searched the buzzing visions for anything familiar. Voices floated around, the spoken words unintelligible. Her head swam as her senses overloaded.

"Catherine, go back…" Anna's voice trailed off, too soft for her to distinguish.

Cate wrapped her arms around her as she struggled to find a way forward. Nonsensical images surrounded her, voices overlapped, and a musty scent filled her nostrils.

In an instant, everything stopped. She found herself alone in the dark again. "Anna?" she called.

No one answered her. "Marcus?" Her voice echoed in the nothingness but no one responded.

"Jack?" she squeaked. "Anyone?"

Cate tightened her arms around her abdomen as she sank to sit. She stared into the blackness surrounding her. She was lost. And alone. And she had no idea how to find her way out.

CHAPTER 22

*C*ate shivered, rubbing her arms and letting her head fall back between her shoulder blades. She struggled to keep her heartbeat steady as she sat alone in the darkness.

"You can't sit here, Cate. You have to move," she said to herself. "You have to find a way out."

She rose to stand and spun in a slow circle. She slid her eyes closed and forced her mind to recall the safe memory she'd created earlier. When she opened her eyes, she spotted the light ahead of her.

Her lips turned up at the corners. Perhaps if she went back there, she could hear Anna again, and she could get out. She took a step toward it but stopped. If she went there, she may never be able to return for the information she sought.

She shook her head and turned away from the glowing light. She forced herself to move further into the darkness.

After a few steps, the light flickered behind her. Cate twisted to glance over her shoulder. It flashed again before it burned out, plunging her further into blackness.

She pressed her lips together and stretched her hands out

in front of her. She moved forward until she bumped into something. It screeched, and she stumbled back a step before she lunged toward it. Her fingertips explored the object.

A smooth surface with ornate edges. Cate used it to guide her steps forward. Muffled noises boomed overhead. She closed her eyes, trying to make sense of them.

"Voices," she whispered. She crept further forward. A man and a woman conversed, though she couldn't make out any of their words.

She continued forward. Her fingers scraped along a wall. She traced the edge of the picture frame molding.

"I'm inside a house."

She pushed herself forward, using the wall as her guide. She reached a corner and rounded it. Light glowed at the end. Her heart skipped a beat as she spotted it. She hurried forward toward it. The voices grew louder though she still couldn't make sense of them.

Cate tiptoed toward the doors, peering inside through the crack. Her pulse quickened. "Gertrude!"

Cate flung the door open and hurried into the space. Voices continued to babble from nowhere. She hurried toward the figure slumped in the chair. The woman's chin rested against her chest with her eyes closed.

Cate reached for her wrist, bound to the chair's arm. Her hand went through the woman. Cate rose and stumbled back with a gasp.

"It's not real. She's not here."

Cate straightened and spun, taking in the room. "This is the room I saw. Abandoned. Large. Yellow walls. Parquet floors. Tray ceiling. Large windows."

The couple spoke again. Cate struggled to make out the words, but she could not. She memorized as many details of the room as she could.

"Anna?" she called.

"Catherine? I'm here. We're here. Catherine, you need to go to your safe place."

"Okay," Cate answered.

She took a step toward the door when the voices started again. They babbled on with nonsense. "No," Cate said, shaking her head.

"Catherine, what's wrong? Talk to me."

"Someone's talking. But I can't understand it."

"That's okay, Catherine. Do not worry about that. Just come back to us," Marcus said.

Cate nodded and took another step to the door. "Okay."

The hairs on the back of her neck stood up, and her skin turned to gooseflesh. A shiver snaked down her spine. A low moan sounded behind her. She spun to glance at Gertrude.

"Gertrude?"

The woman moaned again. Cate took a step back toward her. "Gertrude?"

She took one more tentative step when Gertrude's head snapped up. Her muscles strained against the shackles around her legs and the handcuffs around her wrists. Cate stared into her wide crystal blue eyes, so similar to her own.

The women's gaunt face showed extreme shock. "Gertrude, it's okay. I'm Cate. I–"

"Cinderella," the woman said, her voice strained and hoarse.

Cate froze, her forehead pinching at the word. "What?"

"Cinderella," she repeated before she slumped in her chair.

Cate rushed forward toward her, kneeling in front of her. "Gertrude?"

With her eyes closed and her chin against her chest, Cate could solicit no further responses from her.

She rose, her features still pinched as she considered the strange event.

"Catherine?" Marcus called to her.

"I'm here. I'm coming back."

After one final glance over her shoulder, she hurried from the room and crept through the blackness until she found the other glowing doorway. She pushed inside, feeling the warmth of the future memory surrounding her. "I'm here."

Anna's voice echoed overhead. "Good, Catherine. You are safe?"

"Yes."

"All right, dear. I'm going to wake you. I will count backward and when I reach one and snap my fingers, you will awaken and feel refreshed. Ready?"

"Yes."

The countdown sounded as Cate smiled at the happy memory. Anna's fingers snapped, and the vision faded.

Cate fluttered her eyelashes open. Three concerned faces stared back at her.

Marcus stroked her hair. "Welcome back, dear."

Anna settled back in the chair with a sigh. "You scared us."

"Are you okay, Cate?" Jack asked.

"I'm fine. I just...I lost track of you. I heard you but when I tried to access the vision, everything went haywire."

"I told you to go back to your happy moment, but then we heard nothing from you for quite a while," Anna answered.

"Your voice cut off, and I was trapped."

"You were quiet for way too long, Cate," Jack said, grabbing her foot and shaking it. "And then you were murmuring, but we couldn't understand much of it."

Anna grabbed her hand and patted it. "I heard you call out for me, and then you seemed responsive again."

"I found the vision. I saw it again. I saw Gertrude. I saw

the room. I memorized as much as I could. It's definitely in a house of some kind. A big house. Old. Abandoned. Yellow walls. Parquet floors. Tray ceiling. Large windows."

"Could you see anything outside of the windows that could tell us where it was?" Jack asked.

Cate shook her head. "No." She flicked her gaze to Marcus, wrapping her fingers around his arm and squeezing. "We need to find her. She's not well."

"We will, dear. With the information you have, we'll look for houses controlled by The Agency. It will take a while to comb through the records." He straightened and flicked his gaze to Jack. "Come along, Reid, let's–"

"I'm coming, too." Cate pushed herself to sit, swinging her legs over the edge of the bed.

"No," Marcus answered as Anna grabbed her arm to pull her back.

"You've just been through an ordeal, Catherine."

"And Gertrude is going through a worse one. I'm not going to sit idly by resting from my tiny inconvenience while The Agency has her."

Marcus hesitated, glancing at his mother before he returned his gaze to Cate. She tilted her head, staring at him with a pout. "Marcus–"

"I will bring the property list here," he answered. "We will all take part in the search. Come with me, Reid, you can carry the files back."

"Thank you," Cate said, easing back into her pillows. Marcus strode from the room with Jack in tow.

"You are quite the fighter, aren't you, Catherine?"

"I hope so. We need this issue solved."

"I understand. When one of us is hurt, we must do all we can. I feel the same about my family. You included."

Cate licked her lips, avoiding Anna's gaze. She likely

wouldn't feel that way when they resolved this issue and she and Marcus split.

She raised her eyes to Anna's. She had to say something. To prepare her. It wasn't fair for the woman to assume their marriage was anything but a sham. Marcus had offered her a solution to save Dunhaven Castle from The Agency. He'd want his life back soon enough. She should be prepared.

Anna patted her hand again, stopping any statement on her part. "When you went to Eldinbury Castle in the middle of the night for Marcus, you revealed the depths of your strength. And I'm sorry to say, dear, but I think you will need that strength for this fight with The Agency."

Cate recalled the scene with Gianna when she asked her friends to repay their salaries to her. "They are terrible."

Anna offered her a tight-lipped smile. "Yes, I know. However, you and Marcus make an incredible team. You always support each other. And that is what will get you through this."

Cate swallowed hard again. "The thing is–"

"I know it sounds hollow, darling, but it's true. Marcus simply adores you, as do I. And we will both get you through this, difficult as it may be. We will stick together. Like family does."

Cate's features pinched. She opened her mouth to speak again when the doors opened. Jack hauled several folders overflowing with papers. He crossed to the bed and plopped them on the corner.

Marcus picked up one, thicker than an encyclopedia. "German holdings. Mother, this may be a good file for you to go over. You likely know many of these properties."

"Of course, dear," Anna said, accepting the folder.

He passed another thick folder to Jack who sank into the chair at the bottom of the bed and flicked it open. His eyes went wide. "They own *all* of this?"

"Indeed," Marcus said. "Their network is vast."

Jack wiggled his eyebrows as he fluttered his eyelids. "This will take more than a few days."

"We will mark anything that is not industrial and go from there," Marcus said, passing a folder to Cate before he eased into a chair with one of his own.

Several more remained stacked near Cate's feet. She stared at them before flicking open her own. The spreadsheet in front of her contained at least thirty properties per page. She shuffled through, finding similar content on the rest of the pages. "There are hundreds of these. Maybe thousands."

"This will take time," Marcus answered.

"They have more houses than you, Marcus."

"Than us, dear," he said with a wink.

Cate sighed. "My information isn't going to help us at all. This list isn't going to tell me that it has a yellow room with big windows."

"That's not true, Catherine," Marcus said. "We know it's not an industrial property or anything similar to it. We can rule out many of these."

Cate shuffled through her papers again and scoffed. "And still have thousands of properties to check."

Marcus shifted his gaze from his paper to her face. "We will find her, Catherine. I promise."

Cate let her shoulders drop, and she nodded. "Okay."

Jack caught her gaze, offering a tight-lipped smile before returning to his list.

Cate settled in, grabbing a pen and scanning the first page. She placed checkmarks near any property listed as residential. By the end of the first page, she had fifteen checks. Fifteen places to check on just the first page alone.

She flipped to the next page and ran the tip of her pen down the list, checking properties. After five pages, she tossed her pen down with a sigh. "Okay, I think I should try the bracelet again. Maybe I can get more details about this property."

"You do not need to do that. And we have no guarantees that it will help us," Marcus said.

"He's right," Anna agreed.

Cate heaved a sigh. "I've done five pages of this folder. And I have over fifty checkmarks already. At this rate, we'll each have hundreds of places to check. We'll never be able to check all of these."

"There is nothing wrong with identifying properties before we try another angle," Marcus said.

Cate puckered her lips, sucking in a deep breath before she picked up her pen and continued with her list.

She checked off a few more properties before she flipped to the next page. Her eyes glazed over as she hit page ten.

"I could use some tea," Anna said, rising from her chair and ringing the bell. The servants delivered it shortly after.

"How are you feeling, Catherine?" Anna asked as she checked off a few more properties while balancing her tea in one hand.

"Well enough to try that bracelet again."

Anna chuckled at her. "Perhaps after the tea."

"Sounds like a plan. I should be up to only one hundred and fifty properties to check then with hundreds of pages left to go." Cate took another sip of her tea as she scanned another page. She made a few checkmarks and turned the sheet over on the finished pile.

She browsed the first few properties on the page before she paused. She crinkled her brow and flipped back to the previous sheet. She searched it for the property that gave her pause.

The tip of the pen tapped it as she slid it down the page.

Her heart skipped a beat as she stared at the property description. Why did this property draw her attention?

Cinderella Chateau. Cate furrowed her brow. Was it the whimsical name that drew her?

Something niggled at her. Heat washed over her as the memory of her experience during hypnosis flitted through her mind. Gertrude had said Cinderella. Cate glanced at the title on the folder's tab. *French Assets.*

French. She'd heard people speaking in the background of her vision. They were speaking French. Gertrude had said Cinderella twice. This property fit.

She slid her saucer and teacup onto her nightstand. "I think I found something."

"What is it, dear?" Anna asked.

"The thousandth checkmark?" Jack joked.

"No. The place we should start, I think."

"Where and why?" Marcus asked.

"Cinderella Chateau. It fits, but more than that, in my vision, I heard people talking but I couldn't understand them. I realize now that they were speaking French."

"Based on that perhaps we should focus on the French properties. But why this one?" Marcus asked.

"Just before I left the vision to come back, Gertrude spoke to me. She said one word. I didn't remember it until I saw this description. She said Cinderella. She said it twice. I didn't know why she said it but seeing the name of this property, I think it may have been a clue."

Marcus studied the location. "It is remote enough. Abandoned for quite some time. It is an excellent possibility."

"Should we check it?" Cate asked.

"Yes, I believe so. It cannot hurt. Mother, would you mind continuing your work while Catherine and I–"

"And I," Jack added.

Marcus narrowed his eyes at him. "Perhaps you could assist Mother—"

"No, I think I'm best served going to the fairy tale chateau. No offense," he said, waving a hand at Anna.

"I disag—"

"Yes, Jack's right. He should go, too. In case I have another attack. I don't want you alone there with an unconscious me," Cate said, patting his arm.

He pulled his chin back as he glanced at her. "I am certain I will handle it, darling."

"I'm certain you can, too, but you shouldn't have to. Let's go. Can we do the location hop thing?"

"No," Marcus said with a pucker of his lips. "I can only location hop to places I am familiar with. I have never been to this property."

Cate let her head fall back between her shoulders. "Really? So, a drive? How long."

"Certainly not. We'll simply use a time portal."

"Oh no," Jack said with a sigh. "Not that."

"As I said, you may prefer staying with Mother."

Jack shoved his hands in his pockets and heaved a sigh. "I'll make do."

"How wonderful for us," Marcus grumbled. "Do you remember the rules?"

"Go straight through so you don't try to trap me inside," Jack answered.

"That's not exactly it, but it will do," Cate answered as Marcus narrowed his eyes. "Where should we leave?"

"Here is fine," Marcus answered, stretching his hands out.

"Marcus Benjamin Northcott," Anna exclaimed, slapping her hands against the stack of papers she perused, "how many times must I tell you not to open your time portals in the house?"

Cate's jaw dropped open, and she shot an amused glance at Jack.

"Mother–" Marcus began.

"Outside. I do not wish to spend the rest of the day picking up papers from your whirlwind. Now, out." Anna shooed her hands at them.

"Fine. We'll leave from the garden," Marcus said. Cate and Jack followed Marcus from the room and through the halls.

"So, have you opened many time portals in the house?" Cate asked, her words laced with giggles.

"I do not see the issue with it."

Cate offered him an amused grin as they pushed into the garden. "She has a point about the wind. With all those papers, it would take us days to clean up."

"At least we will save her that. Are we ready?"

Cate nodded as Jack answered, "Ready as I'll ever be."

Marcus arched an eyebrow and opened his mouth to answer.

"Just open the portal," Cate said before he could.

Marcus clamped his mouth closed and stretched out his arms. The sparkling portal appeared in front of them. When it opened fully, Cate pushed Jack forward, then followed behind him. Within seconds, they stared up at the red bricks of the rectangular house.

Black clouds painted the sky above it, and fog shrouded it. Cate shivered as she studied the facade. She wrapped her arms around herself as Marcus arrived.

"Are you cold, dear?" he asked, removing his jacket and slipping it around her shoulders.

"Thank you," she said, burrowing deeper into it.

"Should we go inside?" Jack asked.

"Stay here while I check it first," Marcus said.

"Check it first? We're not..."

Cate laid a hand on his arm. "Jack, let him check first."

Jack stepped back next to her and wrapped an arm around her shoulders. "All right. I'll stay with Cate."

"Make certain she is safe," Marcus said as he strode toward the house.

Cate pulled Marcus's jacket tighter around her as she glanced at the trees surrounding them. The remote property was the perfect place to hide someone. Would they find Gertrude inside or was this an ambush?

CHAPTER 23

Cate's breathing turned ragged as the loneliness of the area hit her.

Jack tightened his grip on her. "Cate, are you all right? Are you seeing something?"

She shook her head and stalked forward.

"Cate?" Jack called after her.

"He shouldn't go alone."

"Are you crazy? He's invincible. Let him go."

Cate shot him a glance over her shoulder as she hurried forward. "He's not invincible."

Jack huffed before he jogged forward. "Wait up."

Cate nodded at him as he joined her, matching her quick pace to the front door. She pushed inside, joining Marcus as he surveyed the entrance.

"Catherine, is something wrong?"

"You shouldn't be alone," she answered, threading her arm through his. "This could be a trap."

"Which is why you should have stayed outside."

Cate shook her head. "No."

Marcus smiled at her, tipping her chin up. "You are too stubborn for your own good."

"I don't want to have to save you again," she said with a coy grin.

"Let's hope it doesn't come to that." He scanned the space. "It appears abandoned. But we should still be on our guard. Catherine, let us know if you see the room from your visions."

She nodded. "I'm hoping we find Gertrude."

Marcus offered her a tight-lipped smile as he laced his fingers through hers and led her into the next room.

They explored the downstairs rooms, not finding Gertrude or the room from Cate's vision.

"Does anything look familiar?" Jack asked as they climbed the stairs to the second floor.

"The architecture looks similar to my vision, but I'm sure that's true for a lot of houses. I'm starting to worry this was a mistake."

"Well at least we can rule one of the million places to check off the list," Jack joked.

Cate offered him a half-hearted smile.

Marcus squeezed her hand. "There is no reason to worry, Catherine. There is a reason you were drawn here. You must learn to trust your gut."

Her half smile broadened to a full one. They searched a few of the rooms overlooking the front lawn, finding nothing. Cate chewed her lower lip as they stepped across the hall and into another room.

She scanned the room and shook her head as Marcus glanced at her. He wrapped an arm around her shoulders and guided her into the hall. She moved toward the next door, letting her fingers glide along the wall as she walked.

Her heart skipped a beat as it triggered a memory. While hypnotized, she'd experienced something similar to this.

"Catherine, are you all right?"

She nodded to him in silent response as she continued down the hall. They pushed into the next room, and Cate's pulse quickened.

Images raced across her mind, and she grabbed Marcus's arm. "This is it. This is the room I saw."

"Are you certain?"

"Yes," Cate said, taking a few more steps into the space. She spun, searching it. "She's not here. She was here in my vision. She's not here."

Marcus studied the room, shuffling further into it and tracing a hole in the wall.

Cate pursed her lips, her brow furrowing. "She's not here. My visions were useless. She's not here."

Marcus retreated to her, bracing her shoulders with his hands. "Your visions were not useless. They led us here. This is a clue. We must determine what it means."

"How?" Jack asked.

Cate's features pinched at his words.

Marcus glared at him. "There is a reason we were brought here by her visions. Trust me. I am far more experienced in these matters than you."

Cate pressed her lips together as she traced a finger along the picture frame molding. "There has to be a reason I saw this. You're right."

"Of course, I am." He offered her an amused smile, and she returned his expression.

"I hate to be the bearer of bad news, but I don't see any clues here. It doesn't even look like anyone's been here recently."

"Perhaps you should keep your opinions to yourself, Reid."

Cate glanced out the window, her finger tracing the dirty

and peeling sill. "He's right. There's nothing here. Maybe my visions aren't right. Maybe they're false."

Her forehead creased as she recalled the future memory she'd seen when touching the rose.

"They are not false, Catherine. There is a reason you saw this room. There is a reason you saw Gertrude in it. We are missing something."

"Yeah, Gertrude," Jack answered. "Maybe there's something in another room. There are two more up here that we haven't checked."

Marcus arched an eyebrow at him. "Perhaps you can check those instead of standing here making useless comments."

"We should all go together," Jack said.

"He's right. No one should go anywhere on Agency property alone," Cate said, wrapping her arms around herself again.

"Whenever you are ready, Catherine," Marcus said, sliding an arm around her shoulders.

"I'm ready."

Marcus nodded as he guided her to the door. She shuffled toward it, her mind aching from the disappointment. Her foot kicked something. The round object rattled across the floor, landing a few inches from her.

Her lips parted as she stared down at it. She leaned forward toward it. "What is this?"

Her fingers brushed it, and a plethora of images raced across her mind. She gasped in a breath as she snapped her hand back. "This was Gertrude's."

"Did you get a vision?" Marcus asked as she straightened.

She nodded. "I need to try again."

"No," he said, scooping it off the floor. "Just a moment. We should do this in a controlled way. We do not want you to pass out or suffer any ill effects."

"Maybe we should go back to the palace?" Jack suggested.

"That is the first excellent suggestion I've heard from you, Reid. Yes."

"No," Cate said with a shake of her head. "No, I want to try here. What if this leads us to another clue?"

"There is nothing wrong with getting that information at Rosenberg."

"Let me try again here," she said. "Maybe it'll tell us something about where else we can look."

Marcus heaved a sigh and opened his hand. Cate stared down at the green button. She reached out for it, but he closed his fingers around it. "Do not push things too far."

She nodded. "Okay."

With a shaky breath, she reached her trembling fingers toward the fabric-wrapped fastener as he held it out to her. She let her fingers graze it, and visions began almost immediately. Instinctively, she pulled her hand back.

"Catherine?" Marcus asked.

"I'm okay. It's okay." She blew out another breath as he wrapped his arm around her shoulders. She pressed her fingertips against the button again. Memories flooded across her mind, most of them faster than she could process.

Gertrude sat in a chair in the center of the room with her hands and feet bound. Her head hung down to her chest. The image changed before Cate could make out anything else. People entered the room, rushing around faster than she could make out clearly.

She tried to focus on details, to slow the images, but she struggled as pain grew across her forehead. She kept her fingers planted on the button as her knees grew weak. Hands grabbed her shoulders and pulled her back. Weakness coursed through her. Someone lowered her to the floor.

"Catherine," Marcus's voice said, floating in the air while

her vision blurred. She reached for him, and he wrapped his hand around hers.

She blinked rapidly, clearing her eyes until she could see her surroundings again. Marcus and Jack hovered over her.

"I'm okay. Just a little weak."

"You held on too long," Marcus said.

"I saw things. Some things, not many. Gertrude was here. Definitely."

"But she's not here now, so they're one step ahead of us again," Jack said.

"No," Cate said with a shake of her head. "No, I don't think so. I think she's here."

Cate shook her head and pressed a hand against her forehead.

"Easy, dear, we can discuss it further at Rosenberg."

"No, what I mean is I think Gertrude *is* here. Just not in this time. I think it was another time. The glimpses of clothing I saw in the visions looked older. Turn of the century maybe? I'm not certain. They went by too quickly."

"It's all right, Catherine," Marcus said. "We can work on it at home. That's excellent so far."

Cate nodded as she pushed up to her elbows. "If I can get one clear image, I may be able to pinpoint at least the decade."

Marcus rubbed her back as she sat up. "How do you feel?"

"Fine. I can stand."

Jack and Marcus helped her to her feet. She wobbled for a moment, grabbing Marcus to steady herself.

He clutched her hand, wrapping an arm around her. "Do you need to rest more?"

She squeezed her eyes closed for a second and shook her head. "No. I'm okay."

"Are you certain you can walk?" Jack questioned.

"Yes, I can. Let's finish searching the house." She took a step forward, struggling to stay upright.

"You need to rest for a bit more, then we can proceed." Marcus and Jack eased her back to the floor. Jack settled next to her while Marcus squatted on the other side. "Easy, Catherine, there's no rush."

She sucked in a deep breath and nodded. "Just a few minutes. I really want to make progress though. Even if it's just to finish the search here."

Marcus slid a lock of hair behind her ear. "And there will be no stopping you as soon as you've recovered your strength."

"You know it," she said with a wink and a smile. As she waited for her body to stop trembling inside, she attempted to recall any details from the visions driven by the button. They had already begun to fade from her mind.

She reached for details that she could not pinpoint. With a sigh, she let her head rest against her knees.

"Maybe I should try–"

A loud bang resounded, cutting off her statement. She startled, grasping hold of both men and snapping her gaze to Marcus. "What was that?"

"Stay here. I'll find out."

Cate grabbed his arm. "Wait, you shouldn't go alone."

"You are in no shape to go." He glanced at Jack. "Take care of her. Make certain she rests."

Jack nodded, sliding a hand around Cate's shoulders. "I will."

Marcus rose to stand and stalked from the room, pulling the door slightly closed behind him.

Cate heaved a sigh, her forehead pinching. "Go after him."

"Cate, no way, I'm not leaving you."

"He shouldn't be alone."

"Neither should you," Jack argued.

"Fine, help me up and we'll both go." Cate struggled to push herself up to stand.

"No," Jack said with a shake of his head. He pressed her shoulder down, planting her on the floor again.

"Jack, I'm fine. I feel better. I'll just sit here and fret."

"Then I'll distract you."

"How?" Cate asked flinging her hands out to her sides.

"We can talk."

"About?"

"Can we talk about how odd it is that you're fretting over him?"

Cate set her chin on her knees and wrapped her arms around her legs. "The Agency is not an enemy anyone should face alone." She picked her head up, shaking it. "No, I can't stay here."

"All right, easy, Cate, let me help you. If you insist on wandering around for Marcus Northcott, at least let me help you."

Cate allowed him to help her to her feet.

"You okay?" he asked as she stood for a moment.

"Yeah, I'm okay. I'm going to take it slow."

"Cate Kensie taking it slow? That's a first."

She chuckled at him before blowing out a sharp breath. "Okay, let's–"

The door creaked open on its hinges. Cate expected to see Marcus returning, but instead, another figure stood in the doorway.

She placed a hand against the jamb, cocking a hip and sticking her hand on it. "Hello, little mouse," Gianna said with a derisive grin.

"What are you doing here?"

"That's what I should be asking you," she said as she sauntered into the room and swung the door closed. "You found this place far faster than I expected. I'm starting to think I underestimated you."

"I know you did," Jack said with a glare at her.

"Well, I certainly did not expect you to get Marcus Northcott to marry you. And now this. How interesting." She spun on a high heel and raised her chin. "You are proving a worthy enemy, but I'm up to the task."

"Where is Gertrude?" Cate demanded.

Gianna puckered her lips, pulling them up into a satisfied smile. "I suppose I should tell you. Because it won't matter."

Cate's heart skipped a beat. "What's that supposed to mean? What have you done to her?"

"Oh, nothing, darling. Don't trouble your semi-pretty little head over it. It won't matter if I tell you she's in 1911 because you'll never make it there."

"Don't count on that."

"Oh, but I do. And that's because I have another present for you." She waved a ring in the air before she slipped it onto her finger. She lunged forward and grabbed hold of both of their arms.

Cate tugged at her arm but found herself unable to pull away. The room melted around them, disappearing from her sight for a moment. She tightened her grip on Jack's arm.

Bright light shone around them in the next instant. Cate squinted against it as the world filled in around her. She shivered, pulling Marcus's jacket tighter.

Gianna smirked at them as she let go of their arms and stepped back. "Have fun, Cate. I don't think you'll be alive much longer. Have fun with the three emperors."

With a chuckle, she disappeared from their sight, leaving them standing in a field.

"What just happened?" Jack asked.

Cate sucked in ragged breaths as she spun, searching the

surroundings with wide eyes. "I don't know but...I don't think we're in 1956 anymore."

"What?" Jack exclaimed, his voice shrill. "Where the hell are we? When the hell are we?"

"I don't know. But it doesn't look good." Cate stared at the thousands of tents set up on either side of them, shrouded in fog.

"Are we at some sort of campsite?"

The sun sat low on the horizon, still rising. "Okay, it's morning. There's the rising sun," Cate said, pointing at it. "So, that's east."

"East of what, we don't know," Jack said. "Is it a tourist site?"

Drums resounded, stopping Cate's heart. "Oh no."

"What is it?"

She pointed a finger toward a line of men marching from within one of the camps.

"What the hell?" Jack asked, screwing up his face.

"We're in the middle of a battle. She dropped us in the middle of a war."

Jack glanced back and forth between the two camps as soldiers lined up on either side. "Which side do we go to? Which side is ours?"

Cate glanced to her left, studying the flags whipping in the wind as the soldier rode in front of the troops. She glanced in the opposite direction, studying the flags and the uniforms.

"Cate? Do you have any idea? Because I think we should get out of the line of fire and fast."

She furrowed her brow, flicking her gaze between the two parties. On her left, a man rode up, yelling at his troops.

"Oh no," Cate said, covering her gaping mouth with a hand.

"What is it?" He followed the line of her gaze, studying

the man who rode back and forth, shouting in another language.

Cate licked her lips and pressed a hand against her stomach. "That…" She slid her eyes closed for a moment, swallowing hard. "That is Napoleon Bonaparte. She dropped us in the middle of the Napoleonic War."

CHAPTER 24

he color drained from Jack's face as he stared at the man racing up and down on a white horse regaled in battle colors. "I–I–I..." He scrubbed his face and tried again. "I've got nothing here. Nothing."

"We need to get out of here. The battle is going to start any minute now. He's whipping his troops into a frenzy."

"Do you know what battle this is? Which side should we go to?"

Cate spun in search of landmarks and the other generals. She snapped her fingers. "Wait. Gianna said to have fun with the three emperors. Three emperors. This is the Battle of Austerlitz."

"Who wins?"

Cate fluttered her eyelashes. "Napoleon. Definitively."

"I hate to sound like a fair-weather fan, but perhaps we should go to the French side then."

"Do you speak French?"

Cate shook her head. "Not a word. And he speaks Corsican. His troops are a mix, but I don't speak any of their languages. You?"

"No."

Cate flung her arms out. "Where's Celine when you need her?"

Jack's eyes went wide. "Do you think she's close?"

Cate shook her head. "No, she lives in Maine. Well, Massachusetts right now. And even if she was traveling, I doubt she's in Austria."

"Damn," Jack cursed under his breath. A shot rang out from the Allied side, announcing the first wave of battle. "French-speaking or not, I think we'd better go."

"You're right," Cate said. They joined hands and raced away from the center of the battle. "We need a place to think."

"In this battle? Are you joking?" Jack asked as he tugged her along next to him.

Cate's mind raced as fast as her feet as she tried to problem-solve her way out of the situation. She stumbled, falling forward onto her knees as more gunfire erupted. A sob escaped her.

"Cate, we can't stop."

"Where are we running to?"

Jack gestured toward the battle. "Not to. From. We're running from that."

"But to where? Jack, we're stuck here." She dug the timepiece from under her dress. "This won't work. We're in 1805. With no way back. Nowhere to go. We're nowhere near Dunhaven Castle to even try the watch, and I doubt it'll work anyway."

"Okay, you're right. We need to think. Somewhere without cannons and stuff."

Cate glanced at the encampment behind the French lines. "There. We'll sneak into one of the tents."

"Is that wise?"

Cate climbed to her feet. "There's nowhere else. We're in

clothes that don't fit the era. We can't possibly wander into town, a town that is under siege by the way, and ask if anyone minds giving us a place to think."

"Good point." A bullet whizzed by too close for comfort. "Tents. Yes. At least it's close."

They hurried further from the battle and ducked into the camp. A few men still milled around or hurried to join their units. Another outfit formed up, ready to head off into battle under their leader's orders.

Cate and Jack snaked through the haphazard placement of tents, using them for cover. They squeezed through a narrow passage between two tents. Jack inched to the corner and peered around them. Two men rushed past, carrying their weapons.

Jack ducked back, pushing Cate behind him. He peeked out again before he grabbed her hand and nodded. "Come on."

They hurried around the corner, past several other tents. "We need to find a place with few people. This is still too crowded," Jack said.

They turned another corner, coming face to face with a French soldier. Jack pulled Cate closer to him. The man pulled his chin back to his chest.

"Ahhh," Jack began.

The man babbled something in French that sounded like a question.

"Ummm," Jack stammered again.

The man stamped a foot on the ground and pointed to Cate, rambling more in French.

Jack wrapped his arm around her waist and tugged her closer to him.

The man spoke again, shaking his head and waving a hand toward a large tent. Jack glanced toward it, his forehead wrinkling. The man repeated his request, waving emphatically toward the tent again before he hurried away.

"Nice fellow. I think he was telling us to go to that tent. Maybe he wanted us to hide there."

"I'm not certain about that," Cate said. "But there aren't many people around here. Maybe it's not a tent housing soldiers."

"You mean like a place for eating or meeting or something."

"Right," Cate said with a nod as she yanked Jack forward. "Although, we probably should find some clothes and change if we can."

Jack nodded, pulling a tent flap open and staring inside. "Nothing obvious in there."

"Here!" Cate shouted, tugging pants, shirts, and jackets from a drying line.

"Stealing laundry during a war. What is happening?" Jack asked, grabbing the garments from her and leading her toward the large tent. He flung the flap back and scanned the inside. "It's clear."

They slipped in, closing the flaps behind them and securing them. Cate wandered to the cot and collapsed onto it. "This isn't a meeting tent," she said, patting the bedding, "but hopefully this is an officer's tent, and we'll be safe while they plan the battle and lead the charge."

Jack tossed the clothes on a nearby table and leaned against it, blowing out a long breath. "I can't believe this."

"Neither can I," Cate said, staring at the ground in front of her.

"She dumped us in the middle of a war."

"In another time period."

"To die," Jack said.

"To die," Cate repeated. She sank her head into her hands.

Jack shuffled to her and plopped on the thin mattress. He

rubbed her back for a moment until she pulled her hands away from her tear-stained face. She threaded her fingers through his and they sat in silence.

"We're stuck, right?" Jack asked.

"Yep," Cate answered. She opened the face on the time-piece and showed it to him.

"It's not slow," Jack noted.

Cate shook her head. "Because we didn't use it to go through a time portal. Which begs the question of what would happen even if we could make it to Dunhaven Castle. Could we find a time portal leading to our time and would this open it?"

Jack hung his head, shaking it. "I don't know. And how would we get to Dunhaven? We're in…Austria, you said?"

"Austria in this time. Even if this would work and could get us home. Or close. It would take months to get there. We can't live here for months."

Jack leapt from his seat and paced around the tent. "I don't even know what to say. I don't know what to do. I don't know…"

"Okay, calm down. We need a plan. We need to think. Vet options."

"What options?" Jack shouted, spinning to face her. His features pinched, and he slid his eyes closed. "I'm sorry."

"You don't have to apologize. I understand. This is a nightmare. And she knew it." Cate balled her hands into fists and pounded them against the cot.

"Do you think Marcus might…"

"How could he find us?"

"Maybe she'll tell him?"

Cate tilted her head. "Why would she do that? She wants me dead."

"I can't believe for the first time in my life I'm hoping to see the face of Marcus Northcott. And I'm sad that we won't."

"I doubt she's even spoken to him," Cate answered. "We're on our own, Jack."

"We don't know–"

Cate shot him a glance that stopped his words. She pressed a hand to her chest. "He's not upset. Not disturbed."

"You can still feel his heart?"

Cate nodded. "It's normal, steady, strong. He doesn't know yet. Or at least, if he does, he's not concerned."

Jack paced back and forth again, flinging his hands in the air. "This is unbelievable. I mean, what the hell are we supposed to do now? There has to be something. We can...Maybe..."

"I feel the same way. I don't know what to do. Going back and forth between one time period and another at Dunhaven Castle is one thing, but...we can't survive in 1805 for an extended period. We have no clothes, no money, nothing."

"Okay, we'll have to get money. And clothes. And try to find our way to Dunhaven Castle. At least there we'll know the family. They can help us search for a solution."

Cate let her gaze fall to her lap, tapping her toes on the floor.

"If it takes months, it takes months. We're not giving up."

"No, we can't. But–" Cate stopped mid-sentence, crinkling her brow.

"What is it?"

She pressed her hand to her chest.

"Cate? What is it? Are you sick?"

She shook her head, flicking her gaze up to Jack's face. "I think Marcus knows we're gone. His heart is pounding."

"Do you think they have him? The Agency?"

Cate slid her eyes closed, feeling the rhythm of his heart thudding against her ribs. She snapped them open and shook her head. "No. This is different from when they had him. This feels...agitated but not in pain."

"Do you think she'll tell him where she took us?"

"I wouldn't count on it. Not without some sacrifice on his part."

"Maybe he'll…"

Cate shook her head, clutching the edge of the bed as she fought the tears forming in her eyes.

"Damn it," Jack said, kicking the leg of the table near him.

Cate pressed her hand against her chest again, pinching her eyebrows. "Wait."

Jack spun to face her. "What is it? Did something change? Is he in pain or captured or back to normal?"

"No, none of those. His heart is still racing, but…it's 1805."

"Yeah?"

"I met Anna in 1810 at Rosenberg. So she's at Rosenberg. Maybe even Marcus." She flicked her gaze to Jack, the corners of her lips turning up ever-so-slightly. "We don't need to get to Dunhaven, Jack. We just need to get to Rosenberg Palace."

Jack stared at her, rubbing his chin. "Okay, so that's a far sight closer than Dunhaven, but…"

"But?" Cate prompted when he didn't speak.

He shook his head. "Cate, you're not married to him yet."

"I know. Anna doesn't think we were married until 1810, but maybe she'll listen. We can tell her I'm married to him in the future. She should understand. She's very much aware of time travel."

Jack blew out a long breath, setting his hands on his hips. "That's not a great plan, but at least it's a plan. And it won't take months. How far are we from Rosenberg?"

Cate shrugged and shook her head. "I'm not certain. In our time, a drive from what is now the Czech Republic to Germany would probably be eight hours, but we don't have a car."

"So, this is roughly six hundred miles."

"The average human walks maybe three miles per hour."

Jack narrowed his eyes, flicking his gaze up. "Which is two hundred hours."

"Eight days. Eight days of walking nonstop for twenty-four hours."

"So, in other words, weeks of walking if we're planning on sleeping at all."

Cate covered her hands with her face.

"This is a nightmare," Jack said, resuming his pacing.

Cate pulled her hands away. "Wait, horses. Horses can run pretty quickly. Maybe thirty miles an hour running, less trotting, but still quite a bit faster than walking. If we rode horses, we could cut this in half."

"Okay. There are horses here. We'll grab a few."

Cate pursed her lips, patting her hands against the cot's edge. "Great. So not only does this plan depend on finding our way to Rosenberg Palace, randomly showing up there, and convincing Anna that her very rich, very distinguished, very titled son married a common American in the future, but we also need to steal horses from the French army."

"I know it doesn't sound good, but it's the best we can do. We'll have to hope for the best."

"And steal food along the way." Cate doubled over with a groan. "Oh my gosh, our future depends on how good we are at being criminals."

"Thank Gianna. She's turned us into thieves."

Cate shook her head and held up the jacket she'd already grabbed. "I hate her so much."

"I'm not fond of her either. Even more so now. Every time I think that woman can't get any worse, she surprises me. First, she kidnapped me and held me in a dungeon. Then, she tried to make me repay my salary after she ripped away my job and your estate. And now she's stuck us in the middle of a war."

"I'm sorry, Jack."

"It's not your fault," he answered.

She stood and approached him. "It is. She's after Dunhaven. She's after me."

"She comes after a Mackenzie, she comes after a Reid. That's the way it is. We stick together."

Cate nodded at him as he pulled her into an embrace.

"We're in this together, Cate."

She pulled away and smiled up at him. Her grin faded, and she cocked her head. "Wait a minute. Technically, I'm a Northcott now. Do you think we can use that loophole to get out of this?"

Jack shook his head but chuckled in spite of himself. "I doubt it. Somehow that's made it worse."

"Infinitely. And you thought the time I got shoved into the loch was bad."

"Child's play compared to this," Jack said with a chuckle. "I'd give anything to fish you out of the loch again."

They laughed together for a moment before Jack offered a groan. "Oh, I guess we'd better change. Hey, how's his heart?"

"Not beating as hard as before, but it's not steady and strong like normal."

"But not captured or tortured or anything?"

"No, nothing like that. But normally his heart just beats in perfect rhythm. He is almost completely unflappable. But this is...different."

"I wonder if he senses yours is different."

"I don't know," Cate said, staring into space. "I hope we'll be able to ask him."

"We will. Think positive. All right, let's change and begin our Bonnie and Clyde lifestyle."

Cate shuddered and shook her head. "Right. I'll step out and keep watch while you change."

"Don't go racing off without me."

"I wouldn't dream of it," Cate said as she walked to the opening. "I'm counting on you to steal the horses."

"I suppose you'll expect me to saddle them, too."

"I can help. I helped the stablehand in 1810."

"Look at you, Cate," Jack said with a wink, "you're all ready for a life of crime."

She chuckled before stepping out of the tent. The sounds of the battle raged across the field. Cate wrapped her arms around her midriff and shifted her weight from foot to foot. Questions raced across her mind faster than she could process.

How would they navigate? How would they eat? What would they say when they got to Rosenberg? *If* they got to Rosenberg, her mind added.

She pressed her palms against her forehead as she paced in a small circle. Maybe they could steal a map before they left the camp.

Cate pressed a hand against her chest, focusing on Marcus's heartbeat. Slower than before, but different from the norm.

Something flashed across her mind, and her temples tightened. The tent flap fluttered open, and Jack stepped out in his French military uniform.

"It's a bit snug but it'll work," Jack said, tugging at the uniform. "Your turn."

"I think there are a few horses that way," Cate said, pointing them out.

"Okay, I'll think of a way to snag them while you change clothes."

Cate nodded and ducked into the tent. She hurried across to the cot where she left the clothes she's stolen. She unfastened her dress and shimmied out of it, tossing it aside. She glanced down at the slip, running a hand over the silky material.

She shook her head, deciding to keep it, and picked up the shirt. Voices sounded outside the tent. Her heart skipped a beat as she spun to face the opening. Had someone caught Jack?

The voice shouted again. What was happening?

She fiddled with the shirt, trying to find the opening with her shaky hands. The tent flap flew open and a man strode inside.

Cate held the shirt up in front of her as her jaw dropped open. She swallowed hard, staring into the eyes of Napoleon Bonaparte.

CHAPTER 25

The French military commander drew his chin back to his chest as he studied Cate. He raised his lower lip as he turned the corners of his mouth down and nodded his head. He waved a hand at her before he stalked to a container and pulled a bottle of wine from it.

"Ahhh," Cate murmured as she tried to cover herself with the shirt. Her heart pounded and her throat went dry. Could she make it outside without him catching her?

Probably not given that she'd need to cross the entire tent, and he stood halfway across it. Even if she could, she'd have no clothes.

He murmured something to her in another language again, but she had no idea what he said. His Corsican accent made it impossible to make out. He poured a glass of wine, sniffed it, and took a sip as he studied her again.

He waved a finger at her, trying to tell her to do something but she had no idea what. After another sip of wine, he spoke again, seeming to become agitated.

Cate swallowed hard again. She had to do something. "Uh, hi, I'm Cate."

"Américaine," he said, arching an eyebrow.

"Yes, I'm American. And I'm lost. And I'm very sorry to have wandered into your tent." It didn't matter what she said, he wouldn't learn any English until he was exiled ten years from now, Cate thought.

He grinned at her and spoke again. He twirled his finger in the air, signaling for her to turn around.

Heat rose in Cate's cheeks as the situation became obvious. "Oh, no, this is a mistake."

Napoleon took another sip of wine before he slammed the glass onto the table and stormed to her. Cate's eyes went wide as he grabbed hold of her cheeks and pressed his lips onto hers.

"Stop," she cried. "I'm not a prostitute." She pushed him back, showing him the ring on her finger. "Married, see?"

He furrowed his brow, reaching for her slip and tugging at it. "Prostituee."

"No," she said with a dramatic shake of her head. "Married." She pointed at the ring again. "Duchess." She pointed back at herself.

Napoleon drew his chin back before his face broke into a smile. He chuckled, doubling over. He grabbed her hand and rubbed a finger along the ring before he kissed it. He yanked her closer and kissed her cheek, tracing a line up to her ear where he whispered something she couldn't understand.

"You've got to be kidding me," Cate whispered.

His hands wandered down her back. She shoved him away before they cupped her somewhere she didn't want him touching. "Listen, Napoleon, I'm not here for this. I'm lost. My husband," she said, pointing to her ring, "is Marcus Northcott. Do you know him?"

"Marcus Northcott?" Napoleon repeated.

Cate nodded emphatically. "Yes. Oui. Si."

Napoleon slid his eyes sideways and shook his head. "Inno. Tu si mio."

He reached for her again, but she backed away, smacking into the cot and collapsing on it. With an arched eyebrow, he offered her a salacious laugh as he approached.

Cate gathered up the clothes she'd stolen and climbed to her feet. He reached for her as she tried to sidestep him, pulling her back against him and whispering something she couldn't understand in her ear.

He rubbed a hand along her belly, kissing her neck. She balled the clothes in her hand and spun to face him. "That's enough. I'm not here to be your prostitute!"

He stepped toward her, and she backed away from him. "No! I've had just about enough. First, the visions, then the hypnosis, then Gianna sends me here with no warning. I'm tired, I'm half-dressed, I'm a thief!" She waved the clothes in the air before she flicked a lock of hair away from her face. "And now Napoleon is trying to make me his latest conquest. No!"

She backed a few steps away. He called after her, but she ignored him. She spun away and lifted the tent's flap. Napoleon shouted behind her again, but she continued. She took one step outside of the tent when a harsh grip grasped her arm and yanked her back.

Napoleon tossed her down, shouting at her with a red face. She landed hard on her rear and the clothes she'd stolen spilled across the floor. He flailed his arms and wagged a finger at her.

She kicked her feet to propel herself backward as he chased after her. She smacked into a rifle, knocking it onto the floor. Napoleon grabbed her ankle and pulled her toward him. As she slid across the ground, she twisted to reach for the gun. Her fingers wrapped around the barrel, and she swung it behind her. The butt of the gun cracked him in the skull.

Blood bloomed from his temple, and his eyes rolled up in his head. He slumped forward, collapsing on her.

Cate sat stunned for a moment before she shoved his dead weight off of her and scrambled to her feet. She stared down at his limp form. Her eyes went wide, and her voice turned breathy. "Oh, no. I killed Napoleon. I can't believe this."

She dropped to her knees and pressed two fingers to his neck. She blew out a sigh of relief as his pulse thrummed against her fingertips. "He's alive."

Cate sucked in panicked breaths as her mind tried to recall all of the details of the battle. "Do they still need him?" she asked herself. "Uhhh, the battle started at eight. Forty-five minutes later, he orders a strike on the center. Then, later he moves the troops south. Did he do that already? Ohhh, if he doesn't wake up this could change the battle entirely."

Cate stood and paced for a few minutes, pressing her fingers to her forehead. She stared at the clothes strewn across the floor. With her eyes on the downed commander, she tugged on the pants and slid back into her shoes. She pulled the shirt over her head and stuffed both it and her slip into the pants before tugging the jacket over top. With a few twists of her wrist, she tamed her hair back and shoved it into her jacket. She snatched the gun from the floor before she grabbed the bottle of wine Napoleon had opened earlier.

She stepped to him and poured the liquid onto his face. He startled awake with a shout, wiping at his face.

Cate tossed the bottle down. "Wake up, Mr. Bonaparte. You need to win this battle."

She spun on her heel and stalked from the tent. She

pushed into the cold December air, shivering after the heated exchange in the tent.

The sounds of the battle raged behind her. She spun in search of Jack. "Jack?" she called, stalking a few steps forward.

Her breathing turned ragged as she spotted no sight of him. "Jack!" she called again. She tried to keep the panic at bay as the realization set in that he was gone. She was alone in a French military encampment in 1805.

"Jack!" she shouted again, her gaze shooting wildly around. A sob escaped her. She bit her lower lip and shook her head. "No. You can't panic. Find him."

She forced her breathing slower and searched in every direction. She peered around the corner of the tent. Two men walked with another man in front of them, nearing the line of soldiers preparing to advance. They shouted something at him as they shoved him forward.

"Jack," she breathed. They must have pressed him into service for the battle, likely assuming he was a deserter. She shook her head and hurried toward them.

Before she reached them the unit marched out. "Oh no," she breathed, trying to hurry forward to join them. The men marched out with Jack in their midst before she could. She cursed under her breath, following their direction as they advanced. There was no way she'd reach him before they entered the battlefield.

Cate's forehead crinkled as another regiment crossed in front of her, slowing her progress even further. An officer raced past her, shouting and waving at her. She stumbled away, but he grabbed her and shoved her into the lineup. She mixed in with the others, in the middle of the group as soldiers rushed to join them.

She tried to keep an eye on Jack's unit, but they were headed in the opposite direction. With a wince, she tried to fight through the soldiers and break free from them, but someone shoved her back into the line.

She marched forward toward the battle. The gunfire grew louder with every step. The regiment stopped marching. Cate stood in their midst, breathing hard from the walk and her nerves.

Orders were shouted. Mounted soldiers rode up and down. Banners flew, trumpets sounded, and drums beat. The unit lurched forward again, dragging Cate with them.

They swung to the left. Across the field, another unit lined up. Cate swallowed hard as the two sides came face to face.

One man across the battlefield raised a weapon and fired. The bullet struck one of the officers, knocking him from his horse. Fighting broke out around her. Gunfire exploded, deafening her. Men rushed forward with screams.

Cate stood still as the chaos erupted around her. The soldier-less horse reared up before racing wildly. Cate narrowed her eyes at it. She tightened her grasp on her rifle as she hurried toward the frightened horse.

With bulging eyes, the horse snorted and squealed. Cate raced to get in front of it. He barreled toward her, and she held her hand out to steady it. "Easy, easy, boy."

The horse skidded to a halt. The dead officer remained attached to him, his ankle twisted in the stirrup.

Cate reached out and rubbed the frightened horse's nose. "Easy, it's okay."

She wrinkled her nose as she freed the dead man's leg from the tangled stirrup. His open eyes stared widely at the sky. Cate closed them before she stowed the rifle in the saddle and stuck her foot in the stirrup. She swung her other leg over and mounted the horse, grabbing the reins.

"Okay, buddy, I'm scared, too, and I don't ride very well. So please don't kill me."

She tugged at the reins to turn the horse toward where she'd seen Jack marching. "Come on, buddy. Let's go get Jack."

The horse cantered across the field. She squeezed her knees against the animal to hang on. The ground in front of her exploded in a wide spray of dirt. It rained down around her as she tugged the horse to a stop.

A man rushed toward her with his weapon aimed. Cate smacked the horse's ribs with her heels, setting it into a gallop. The gun in the attacking soldier's hands fired, missing her widely. He tossed down the weapon and drew his sword.

Another cannon blast stopped her again. The man closed the distance between her. She spun the horse in a circle, seeking a way out. Her heart pounded as she reached for the sword stowed in the saddle. She withdrew it and slashed at the man, slicing his arm. He stumbled back a step, and she used the small window to set the horse to gallop toward Jack's unit.

She approached the group as they attacked the Allied units in the South. She scanned the chaos, searching for Jack. She slowed the horse and stood in her stirrups. "Where are you?"

She spotted him across the field. "Jack!"

She plopped into the saddle and signaled the horse to run. It charged into the fray, skillfully skirting fighting soldiers as he raced toward his destination. She ducked low behind his flying mane, clutching tightly to the reins and hugging the saddle with her thighs.

"Come on, boy," Cate whispered.

The man next to Jack took a bullet to the shoulder, falling backward with a bloodcurdling scream. The man on his right fell forward with a bullet to the skull.

Jack stood alone as one of the enemy soldiers rushed toward him. He struggled with his weapon, unable to fire it.

"Jack!" Cate screamed, freeing the sword again as she galloped toward him.

He snapped his gaze toward her, removing his eyes from the man who charged toward him. The soldier lifted his sword, ready to swing.

Cate urged more speed from the horse. If she didn't close the gap soon, the man would plunge his blade into Jack's chest. Jack wouldn't survive this battle. He'd die on the battlefield.

CHAPTER 26

"Jack!" Cate shouted again as she thundered toward him on the horse.

He stumbled to the side, and the man charging him thrust the knife into the air instead of Jack's chest. He whipped around to try for another attack.

The horse blocked him, racing between Jack and the foreign soldier. Cate slashed at him but missed.

She tugged the horse to a stop and swung him around. The man spiraled back as Jack wrangled a gun from one of the fallen soldiers near him. He aimed it at the man and pulled the trigger, but the weapon held no bullets.

Jack tossed it down and tried for another gun from the other soldier. His attacker slashed at him again. The blade sliced Jack's shirt sleeve but drew no blood.

Cate urged the horse forward, lining up her sword again. The man stumbled a few steps away as she swiped at him, avoiding her again.

Cate tugged the horse back again, spinning it around for another pass. The man spiraled and charged toward Jack who tried to pull another gun from a dead soldier.

"Jack!" she screamed again. She'd never get to them in time even on horseback. The man lifted his blade, prepared to strike when a gun cracked. Jack ducked instinctively. The man fell backward onto his back, an expression of shock on his features as a wound smoked between his eyes.

Cate set the horse in motion again, cantering up to Jack and easing to a stop. It trotted around him in a circle. "Need a ride?"

"Yes, please," Jack answered.

Cate grabbed his hand and helped him mount the horse behind her. She set the horse galloping across the field, heading toward the French encampment.

"We need another horse," Jack shouted in her ear as the battle raged behind them.

"I know," Cate called over her shoulder. "We should try to find some food, too."

She guided the horse through the camp as soldiers dragged hurt men for assistance. Blood oozed from a variety of wounds. Soldiers screamed in pain as their compatriots carried or dragged them for medical attention.

"Thank God I'm not one of them," Jack said as Cate slowed the horse to a trot and approached a hitching post with several horses. Jack dismounted, then Cate hopped to the ground.

"Listen, Cate," Jack said as he heaved a saddle onto one of the horses, "those guys grabbed me and—"

"I know. They probably figured you were deserting," Cate said as she helped fasten the saddle.

"I tried to get away, but…well, anyway, thanks for finding me."

"Of course," Cate said, catching his eye across the horse's broad back.

"I can't believe you charged into the battle like that."

"I was already part of it," Cate answered. "I got shoved into another regiment before I could catch up to you."

"Ugh, Cate, I'm sorry." Jack moaned, untying his horse. "That must have been frightening to walk out and find yourself alone."

"It was almost as frightening as what happened before," she answered as they pulled the horses along. She ducked into a few tents in search of food, stuffing the meager rations she found into the pouch dangling on the horse.

"What happened before?" Jack asked, adding food to their supply.

"Napoleon Bonaparte thought I was his call girl."

Jack stopped walking and shot a glance toward her. "Like *the* Napoleon Bonaparte? The one we saw earlier?"

Cate twisted to answer him as she continued with her horse. "Yep."

Jack led the horse faster as he jogged to catch up with Cate. "Are you okay? What happened? He didn't–"

"No," Cate interrupted. "I...hit him with the butt of a rifle and knocked him out."

Jack's eyes went wide.

"I thought I killed him. But I only knocked him out. Don't worry, I woke him up, so hopefully, I didn't change history."

Jack blew out a long breath as they threaded through the camp toward the edge furthest away from the fighting. "This is getting insane."

"Tell me about it. And now we're about to ride horses in a general, vague direction in the hopes of finding Rosenberg Palace." Cate stopped her horse as they reached the final tent and stuck her foot in the stirrup, grabbing the pommel.

"At least we know which way is west," Jack said as he mounted his horse.

Cate balanced herself on top of the animal, grabbing the reins. "We need to go southwest, technically, but let's just worry about getting away from this battle for now. I'd like to make progress before we have to search for shelter."

"Aye, I think we'll need it. It's a bit cold."

"It's December. I'm not surprised. The adrenaline helped before, but that'll wane now that we're not actively being shot at."

Jack twisted and stared out over the battlefield. "Yeah, I'm pretty glad about that, cold or not. Let's get out of here."

They set the horses to a quick trot and left the camp behind. They rode until the sounds of the battle died off before they slowed the horses to a walk.

"I can't believe Napoleon came on to you."

"In his defense, I was wearing only a slip. I think he took that as a sign. I tried to explain, I even brought Marcus's name into it, thinking he may know him, but he just wouldn't take no for an answer."

"Good for you clocking him like that."

"Let's just hope he's okay enough to win that battle before we accidentally change history."

Jack bobbed around as the horse meandered along. "Does it matter? Gianna doesn't care. They change history all the time."

"They are irresponsible." The corners of Cate's mouth turned up, and she started to chuckle. The giggle turned into a full belly laugh, and she slapped her thigh.

"What's so funny?"

Cate continued to laugh. "I remember you lecturing me about changing history, even subtly. And now we're faced with a situation where history is continuously changing." Another sharp laugh escaped her and tears fell from her eyes. "And I almost killed Napoleon."

Jack joined in, chuckling with her. "I never thought in a million years this would be happening. Napoleon hit on you."

Cate doubled over, tears still streaming from her eyes. "He did."

"We fought in the Napoleonic war. I nearly killed someone. Or he nearly killed me. And we stole two horses from the French army."

"Along with clothes and food."

"We're thieves," Jack said with a belly laugh.

"I'm a clairvoyant."

Jack pointed at her with a hoot. "Married to a warlock."

Cate chuckled a few more times before she sobered. "Yet we're still stuck in 1805. Too bad my clairvoyance didn't see this coming."

Jack blew out a long breath as his laughing tapered off. "That's still...odd to me, too."

"It's not any odder than it is to me. I can't believe it. But it's true. I can't deny that these images keep running through my mind."

"And you never had it before?"

"Well, I guess I did with the dream about my parents, but not to this extent."

Jack cocked his head, rubbing his chin. "I wonder why. What prompted it? The temporalysis?"

Cate rubbed at her palm. "Maybe the joined blood."

Jack crinkled his brow and shot her a glance as they continued along. "Explain this to me again."

"He sliced my hand and his and then did some sort of magic. After our blood mixed, he said he'd be able to feel my heart in his chest. And I could feel his in mine."

"That's so bizarre. But then, what about this situation isn't bizarre?"

Cate stared into the distance ahead of them. "Nothing. There is nothing normal about any of this."

"I honestly miss the days when the under-butler stole

some jewelry and our biggest problem was pinning the crime on him."

"Don't forget your genius legal maneuvering," Cate said, pointing a finger at him.

"Right. Back in the day, I sweated bullets over pretending to be a lawyer. Now, I'm hopping around in time with a warlock and a clairvoyant, and pretending to be a French soldier."

"Things certainly have changed and if Marcus is correct, they won't settle for quite some time."

"Let's hope he's wrong."

Cate shot him a sideways glance. "Sadly, he's not wrong often."

Jack pulled his lips back into a grimace as they meandered along. "That's scary."

"On all fronts." Cate glanced behind her then returned her gaze forward. "Maybe we should take a break and let the horses rest before we continue on the afternoon leg."

"You're right."

"I wonder if there's a barn or something around."

"Right," Jack said, rubbing his hands together. "I'm getting cold."

"Yes. I think we could use a break."

They found a shelter and spent a few hours allowing the horses to rest while they decompressed and warmed up. They avoided eating any of the food they'd grabbed, opting to ration it for when they felt hungry.

"Well, I guess we head west for a bit more before we try to get our bearings," Jack said.

Cate nodded as she mounted her horse and led it from the warmth of the barn they'd found. The cold air smacked them in the face as they headed into the gray day.

They set the horses to canter and made more progress toward Rosenberg Palace. After a time, they slowed the horses to a trot, continuing toward the now-setting sun. As they rode along the dirt road, a carriage approached behind them.

Cate and Jack pulled their horses to the side as the carriage whisked past them.

Jack waved a hand at it. "Aww, what I wouldn't give to be in a carriage. I can't believe how much I want to be in a carriage. My standards have really sunk."

"You and me both. No wind gusts chilling you to the bone. When Marcus and I came to 1810 for you, we took a carriage from Zurich. It wasn't a comfortable ride by modern standards, but it sure beats this."

"No kidding. I'm not sure how much more my rump can take."

"And we only have days more of this to look forward to."

"Fantastic," Jack groaned. "When we get to Rosenberg, I'm going to ask if they can magically fix my behind."

Cate chuckled as they continued, approaching the carriage that had passed them earlier. It sat in the middle of the road, unmoving.

Cate furrowed her brow, staring at the black carriage as she slowed her horse. "Umm, something feels off here."

"Maybe they're letting the horses rest."

"In the middle of the road?" Cate asked. She shook her head. "Something's wrong."

Jack pulled his horse to a stop as Cate did the same. "What do you want to do?"

Cate considered it, gnawing on her lower lip. "I hate to turn back. We have limited food and days to go before we even get close to Rosenberg."

"Keep going?" Jack asked.

Cate sucked in a breath and shrugged. "Let's pick up the pace and give them a wide berth. They should think we're

French soldiers. Hopefully, they're not from the other side and looking to snatch a few prisoners."

"Right." Jack gave his horse a nudge with his heels. Cate did the same, setting a quick pace as they moved forward.

They trotted toward the carriage, leaving the road to canter through the field next to it. The carriage shifted as they edged off the road.

Several people climbed from it. Two raised weapons, aiming them at Cate and Jack. "Stop!" one yelled.

"What should we do?" Jack asked.

"They're at pretty close range," Cate said, tugging on her reins. "I'm not sure we can get away without risking serious harm to us or the horses."

"Right," Jack answered. "I guess we'll hope for the best."

"If they plan to rob us, they will be sorely disappointed," Cate answered.

"Dismount," the man yelled.

Jack swung his leg over and climbed down from his horse. "We don't have anything of value. We're just soldiers."

"Step away from the horse and keep your hands up. Both of you."

Cate slid off her horse and held her hands in the air, stalking forward a few steps. The carriage shimmied again. The door opened and another man disembarked from the conveyance.

Cate's heart skipped a beat as she recognized Elliott Stevens dressed in 1805 finery.

He grinned at her. "Well, well, well, how interesting to meet you here, Duchess."

CHAPTER 27

$\mathcal{C}$ate raised her chin as she struggled to stop her knees from wobbling.

Elliott Stevens smirked at her as he stalked a few steps forward. "That is quite an interesting look for you, my dear Duchess."

Cate licked her lips as she considered her response. "We had to get creative after Gianna dumped us here in the middle of the Battle of Austerlitz."

"Creativity is something you seem to have in spades. You constantly slip through our fingers."

Cate flexed her jaw as her nostrils flared, and she crossed her arms. "I'm not going to apologize for making it too difficult for you to kill me or steal from me."

"I assume you have some sort of plan to get yourself out of this little pickle, Duchess?"

"It's none of your concern."

Elliott raised his finger in the air as he paced behind the carriage. "Actually, it is very much my concern. You see, I'm growing weary of this game."

"Then stop playing," Cate said, throwing her hands out to her sides.

Elliott chuckled at her. "It is almost a shame you won't join us. You are feisty, I'll give you that."

"I would never join your side," Cate spat at him.

Elliott squashed his lips together. "I figured as much. Unfortunately, you won't have many choices soon."

"Are we finished here?"

"Not in the slightest," Elliott said. He narrowed his eyes at her as he squared his shoulders, clasping his hands behind him. "Get in the carriage, Duchess."

"I don't think so," Cate said with a shake of her head.

His gun-toting goons shifted their weapons to Jack.

"I'm not asking," Elliott answered.

Cate swallowed hard, shifting her gaze to Jack. "Let's not do anything hasty."

"Oh, this is hardly hasty. You have been a thorn in my side for far too long. I'm ready for the endgame. Now get in the carriage."

Cate's knees wobbled as she took a step forward. Her heart hammered in her chest. Jack stuck close to her side, walking forward with her.

"No, no, no," Elliott said, waving his hand in the air. "Not him. Just you. We no longer need Mr. Reid."

Heat washed over her as she glanced at Jack. Her skin prickled, and the hairs on her neck stood up. She couldn't leave him here.

"Come along, Duchess, only you are invited."

"No!" Cate shouted, stamping a foot on the ground. "Both of us or neither of us."

Elliott barked out a laugh. "Oh, you are amusing. I can almost see the appeal. Though it's the fact that you have no ability to follow through that makes it rather ridiculous. Now, come along, or we'll shoot Mr. Reid."

Cate stepped in front of him, blocking him with her body. "Then you'll shoot me, too."

Elliott sneered at her. "Don't tempt me."

"You'll lose whatever leverage you think you have by kidnapping me."

"Oh, I don't think it. I know it. You, my darling Duchess, are going to bring us everything. Now, get in the carriage, or we will have to get physical, and I don't think you want that."

"I'm not going anywhere without Jack," Cate said through clenched teeth.

Elliott scoffed and shook his head. He waved a hand at the men. "Grab her."

"No!" Cate shouted as the men shouldered their weapons and stormed toward her. She backed away before she spun and ran toward her horse. One of them grabbed her roughly, tugging her backward before she made it to the animal.

"No!" she cried, trying to wiggle free.

"Cate!" Jack shouted next to her as the other man held him back. He fought against the larger man, trying to wrench his arms from the man's firm grasp.

"Jack!" Cate screamed, reaching for him. He tried to stretch his arms toward her, but the man held him back. Tears streamed down her cheeks as her attacker dragged her backward.

"Cate, no!"

"Jack," she sobbed as the man spun her toward the carriage. She dug her feet into the dirt, twisting to gaze at him as she struggled to break free.

Jack ripped his arms away from the man and raced toward her. "Cate!"

He dove for her as the man behind him caught up. He whipped Jack back, tossing him several steps away before he swung at him. He caught Jack in the jaw, knocking him to the ground.

"No!" Cate yelled. She kicked and flailed her arms as her attacker picked her up.

Jack recovered and swung a fist at the man, but Elliott's bodyguard blocked it, landing another blow against Jack.

It knocked him to the ground. The man strode toward the carriage, leaving Jack breathing heavily on the ground as his partner shoved Cate into the carriage.

They climbed inside after her, flanking her on either side as they shoved her into the seat across from Elliott.

Cate sniffled and wiped at her tear-stained cheeks. "Take him with us. We can't leave him here. Please."

Elliott sipped liquor from a glass, studying the amber liquid inside. He flicked his gaze up to her face. "Give me Dunhaven Castle."

Cate shuddered at the request.

"No? Too bad for Jack." He reached up to knock on the window.

Cate shot a hand out. "Wait!"

Elliott raised his eyebrows. "Are you willing to sign it over to me right now?"

Cate swallowed hard, her lower lip quivering.

"As I thought." Elliott rapped against the window, and the carriage lurched forward.

Cate spun to stare out the rear window of the carriage. Jack climbed to his feet as they rode away from him. He raced to his horse and mounted it. He grabbed the reins of her horse and set them both in motion as he followed behind them.

Cate kept her teary eyes on him as he rode behind them.

Elliott took another sip of his brandy. "Well, this is annoying." He knocked on the glass again. The carriage slowed to stop.

Cate sniffled, wiping at her tears and expecting Elliott to order the men to drag Jack into the carriage.

Elliott took another sip. "Tell him to stop following us."

"What?" Cate asked.

"Tell him to stop following us."

"No," Cate said. "You can't–"

"I can. Tell him to stop following us, or I will stop him permanently."

Cate's features pinched as she fought back another sob. The man next to her popped the door open.

"Go on," Elliott said with a wiggle of his eyebrows. "And if you try to run, I'll shoot you in the leg. In this time period, it will be extremely painful to live through."

Cate's lower lip trembled as she climbed from her seat. Her knees wobbled, and she clung to the carriage to stay upright. She spun to face Jack who slowed on his horse.

"Jack," she said with a sniffle, shaking her head, "you can't follow us."

"Like Hell, I won't. You tell him that."

The crease between her eyebrows deepened as tears spilled onto her cheeks. "You can't. He'll kill you."

"I'd like to see him try."

"Please, Jack," Cate said with a sob.

"Cate…" he said, his face scrunching.

Cate wiped at her tears. "Go to Rosenberg. Get help. Please don't take a chance. Please, Jack."

"Okay," he said, his voice cracking.

She wrapped her arms around her as her stomach turned over.

"Come along, Duchess," Elliott said.

Her lower lip trembled again as she gave him one final look before she stepped up toward the carriage.

"Cate!" Jack called.

She froze, flicking her gaze back to him.

"We'll find each other."

She nodded as more tears spilled down her cheeks. "Count on it."

Elliott tugged her into the carriage. She collapsed into the seat, and he knocked on the window. The carriage rolled forward. Cate twisted in her seat to stare behind her.

Jack stared after her. His horse pawed at the ground, nickering as he awaited the signal to continue.

Tears streamed down her cheeks as the carriage trundled away. She pressed her hand against the window as a sob escaped her. She pulled it back, covering her mouth as she continued to cry.

"Come now, Duchess," Elliott said behind her. "You cannot be *that* upset."

Cate twisted to glare at him. "You've left him to die."

Elliott narrowed his eyes at her as he poured another brandy. "You have very little faith in your friend. Oh, or is he more than a friend?"

He held the glass out to her. She settled into her seat with a grimace.

"I'm curious. My subsequent steps may need to change based on your answer." He waved the drink at her again, wiggling his eyebrows.

She smacked it from his hand. The displeasure on his face spoke volumes as he whipped a handkerchief from his pocket and wiped at the liquid spilled on his jacket. "What an interesting reaction. Should I be concerned that His Grace will not make an attempt to retrieve you from our clutches?"

Cate glowered at him as anger burned through her. She balled her hands into fists as the image of Jack stuck in 1805 in the middle of Austria danced through her mind. "He knows better than to make any deals with you."

Elliott cocked his head, arching an eyebrow. "Really? You don't believe he will come for you?"

"He'd be smart not to. You can't be trusted."

A slow smile spread across his features. "Do you realize what we can offer you?"

"Nothing," Cate spat.

Elliott leaned forward toward her, his grin broadening. "That's just not true. Join us. Convince your husband to join us. You would be surprised at the perks."

"I don't think so."

"I understand he is a very wealthy man. I'm certain you want for nothing. But I assure you the rewards will be vast."

Cate cocked her head, flexing her jaw. "Go back for Jack, and I'll consider it."

Elliott snorted a laugh. "You have no bargaining power here, Duchess."

"Then why ask me for help with my husband?"

He shrugged, refreshing his own brandy and taking a sip. "I'm offering you an opportunity. A chance to do things the easy way. Do not misunderstand, we do not *need* you to bring him to our side."

"Then let me go," Cate answered.

Elliott laughed again, raising his glass in a silent toast to her. "Again, you misunderstand. We do not need you to convince him. We can do that ourselves. Though it will be far more painful for you and him than if you were to volunteer."

"I will never give in to you."

Elliott fluttered his eyelashes, flicking his gaze out the window. "More's the pity. I fear you will regret that decision, but it will be far too late then. Now, I am tiring of this conversation. Fletcher, if you would be so kind?"

He waved a hand at Cate. She furrowed her brow a second before his meaning became clear. A sharp, shooting pain slammed through her head. Her eyes rolled back into her head and her world went black.

* * *

Cate's eyes fluttered open. A dark room surrounded her as she lay on her back on a soft mattress. She gasped for breath before she pressed a palm against her aching head, squeezing her eyes closed. The memory of being knocked unconscious flooded back to her.

She forced her eyes open and allowed them to adjust to the darkness. "Where am I?" she whispered.

She slid her hands along the silky material enveloping her. With a furrowed brow, she reached for the curtain hanging from the tunnel and eased it open a smidge. She peered through the slit, searching the large room beyond.

With a shaky breath, she tried the other side, finding a window. She scrambled from under the covers and hurried to it, staring out into the late evening sky. Purple streaked it as the sun set behind her.

She searched the landscape for anything she recognized, but she found nothing. "It doesn't matter. I need to get out of here."

She spun to face the room in search of her shoes. After finding them near the bed, she tugged them on.

How far was she from Jack? Could she find him again? Her heart broke as she recalled leaving him on the road.

"I'm coming, Jack." She glanced around for anything useful but found nothing.

With a deep swallow, she wiped her sweaty palms against her pants and hurried toward the door.

She cracked it open and peered into the hall. Candelabras flickered up and down its length, revealing nothing. Her heart pounded as she swung it open. A shadow passed in front of her, and a figure blocked her way forward.

Cate stumbled back a step, her eyes wide. Her throat went dry, and her heart stopped.

Gianna sashayed into the bedroom with a cat-who-caught-the-canary grin on her features. She lifted the candelabra in her hand. The flickering candlelight twisted her smile into an evil mask. "Hello, mouse."

CHAPTER 28

Cate balled her hands into fists, ready to fight the woman to free herself.

"Don't bother to make a fuss, Cate. You won't get very far." She waved toward the hall. Two bulky bodyguards entered, closing the door behind them and blocking it.

Cate's stomach turned as she realized she was trapped.

Gianna set the candelabra on a dresser before leaning against it and setting a hand on her cocked hip. She stared at Cate with a smirk. "If it was up to me, I would have left you in 1805 on your own."

"I wish you would have," Cate answered.

Gianna's grin broadened. "But this will be so much more fun."

Cate struggled to stop her knees from wobbling as her body threatened to tremble all over. "I don't agree."

"Oh, I do. We have big plans for you, Cate."

"I'm not joining you," Cate said with a shake of her head.

"Good!" Gianna said, her eyes going wide. She pulled herself off the dresser and sauntered forward. "I hope you don't. In fact, you agreeing now is my worst nightmare."

Cate pulled her chin back as the woman closed the gap between them. She narrowed her eyes, staring at the dark marks rimming her neck.

"Admiring my necklace?" Gianna inquired.

"What happened?" Cate asked, flicking her gaze from the black marks to Gianna's face.

"Your husband happened."

Cate swallowed hard, narrowing her eyes.

"He nearly killed me when I told him what I'd done to you. Lucky for me, I escaped with my special trinket. Just a flick with a time period in mind and poof!"

Cate furrowed her brow. The pounding heartbeat she'd detected earlier must have been caused by his anger.

Gianna reached out to trace a finger down Cate's cheek. "And I am so looking forward to doing even worse to you."

Cate snapped her head away from Gianna's touch. "You'll never get the chance."

"Oh, don't tell me you're going to give in and join us now," Gianna said with a pout.

"Marcus won't give in to you."

Gianna's eyes went wide, and she leaned closer, inches from Cate. "Oh, but he will. He won't have any other choice."

Cate shook her head. "No."

"Oh, yes, dear Cate. He won't be able to stand watching us torture you." She leaned forward and whispered in her ear. "He will break. And then we will own him."

Cate shoved Gianna away from her. The men across the room rushed forward. Gianna tossed a lock of hair back. "It's fine. I'm fine."

She raised her chin, the sneer returning to her features. "Oh, I am going to enjoy breaking you."

She stalked to the door, yanked it open, and waved her slender fingers at an unseen person. A box appeared, and she grabbed it, spinning and tossing it across the floor. "Get dressed. Elliott wants to dine with you in thirty minutes."

The men stalked from the room. The door slammed behind them, startling Cate as she stood in the center of the massive, dark space. Only the candelabra kept the blackness at bay.

Cate wrapped her arms around her midriff as she wandered to the bed and eased onto it. She needed a way out. And she needed it fast. She couldn't risk staying here.

At worst, no one would come for her, and she'd die a slow, painful death at the hands of Gianna. At best, Marcus came for her and she'd die a slow, painful death at the hands of Gianna. Cate wrinkled her nose at her prospects or lack thereof.

She forced herself off the bed and hurried to the window again. The cold glass sent a chill through her body as she pressed her hand against it. Darkness grew with each passing moment. She glanced down at the ground below her. She needed to get to the first floor. Unless...

Cate grabbed hold of the handle and flung the window open. She leaned out as the icy wind chilled her further. The ground swayed below her while she pondered leaping. Could she make it?

She straightened, gasping for breath. She'd try another way. This would be a last resort.

She swung the window closed and hastened across the room, bypassing the crushed white box on the floor. She eased the door open a crack and peered in the hall. Nothing. She waited for several breaths before she let go of the ornate knob.

The candelabra glowed on the nearby dresser. She grabbed it and returned to the door, pulling it open further before she leaned into the hall and glanced up and down.

"Which way?" she questioned as she eased her door closed behind her and flicked her gaze back and forth.

On her left, the hall disappeared around a corner. On her right, it continued straight before branching.

Cate chewed her lower lip before she darted to the left and hurried to the corner. Holding her breath, she peered around it. Empty.

She let out a breath and scurried down the hall, holding the candelabra high overhead. Her heart pounded so hard, she worried someone would hear her coming. She rounded another corner, spilling into a wide hall that led to a grand set of stairs.

Her heart skipped a beat, and she raced forward, grasped the thick, wooden banister, and rushed down to the marble floor below. She flung the wide wooden door open.

A dark figure filled the opening as she attempted to take a step into the night. Cate stumbled back a step, her jaw falling open. Slow and steady footsteps approached from her side.

"You are meant to be dressing for our dinner," Elliott said as he strode from one of the rooms tucked to the side of the foyer. "Not racing into the night."

"I told you she couldn't be trusted," Gianna added, joining him and swirling her sherry in her glass.

Cate raised her chin. "Let me go. I can't do anything to help you."

Elliott let out a loud, belly laugh. "I disagree. But we should discuss that over dinner. Now, please, go change."

"No," Cate answered.

Gianna clicked her tongue against the roof of her mouth. "There is no point in refusing."

"I won't help you. I can't help you. There is nothing I can do for you."

"You can't or you won't?" Elliott questioned, signaling for her to follow him into the sitting room.

"Both," Cate said as she stalked in behind him with Gianna following her.

"I very much disagree," he answered, pouring a brandy and offering it to Cate.

She shook her head, refusing the beverage.

Elliott's shoulders slumped, and he heaved a sigh. "Are we going to go through this again? Just take the drink. Duchess. It seems like you could use it."

Cate grabbed the glass from his hand as Gianna circled around her and draped an arm over Elliott's shoulder. "Oh, please let me kill her, Elliott. She's useless."

"That's enough, Gianna. Our dear Duchess is quite useful in one capacity or another. But that we shall discuss over our meal. Now, run along and dress. I do not want you at my table in that uniform."

Cate slammed the brandy glass on the nearby table, rattling the empty vase on it. "I'm not certain I care what you want."

Elliott sipped his drink as he leaned against the mantel and stared at the roaring fire under it. "I admire your tenacity, but I grow weary of your refusals."

"This is why I wish you would let me finish her. She is useless to us. A thorn in our side."

"I thought you wished to break her?" Elliott questioned.

"I vacillate between the two desires. At the moment, I prefer a swift death at my hands."

Elliott waved his hand at her, dismissing the conversation. "Not now." He spun to face Cate. "I will not ask again."

"Bring Jack here, and I will."

Elliott narrowed his eyes at the statement. "There is so much I cannot wait to dig into at our dinner. I so hope I will not need to put a gun to your head."

"Ohh, let me do it!" Gianna said, clasping her hands together.

Cate firmed her jaw but spun on her heel, grabbed the candelabra, and stormed from the room.

"I expect you to be prompt. Do not dally!" Elliott shouted as she mounted the stairs.

Her blood boiled and heat washed over her as she made her way back to the room she'd left behind. She curled and uncurled her fists with each step. She held back the tears filling her eyes, refusing to cry over The Agency no matter how grim things appeared.

She reached the room she'd awoken in and pushed through the door. Her breathing turned ragged as she collapsed back against it. She was stuck. She couldn't get away.

Her mind stretched as she vetted through options. Her choices were few. She couldn't run. She couldn't hide.

She had to stay alive long enough to find her way out of the situation. Perhaps she could sneak away in the dead of the night. She would have to endure the dinner first.

With a tensed jaw, she stalked across the room and collected the box. She picked at the collapsed corner, trying to peel the lid off.

She found a lilac evening dress inside in the typical style for the era. A grimace formed on her lips as she tugged her jacket off and stared down at the dress.

A knock sounded at the door. "I'm not ready yet!"

A woman pushed inside with a nod. "I will assist you, Your Grace."

Cate bit her lower lip as she nodded, acutely aware of how much she missed Andrea. She peeled off the stolen clothes and slipped into the dress, allowing the maid to fasten it.

"Your hair, Your Grace?" the girl asked.

"Leave it."

She shook her head and pulled a long plume from within the box. "Mr. Stevens insisted."

Cate sighed as she shuffled to the dressing table and collapsed on the chair. She stared at the wooden top without seeing it as the woman pulled her hair into an upswept style, affixing the feather to it. The fluffy plume cascaded onto her shoulder as the girl finished the style.

She hurried across the room and retrieved gloves from the box. "Your gloves."

Cate pulled herself from her rambling thoughts, flicking her gaze up to her through the mirror. She sucked in a deep breath, rising to stand. The woman approached her, holding out the first glove. Cate slipped her hand inside as the woman shimmied the garment to her elbow. She slid the other on.

"Anything else, Your Grace?"

Cate shook her head.

"Mr. Stevens asked that you present yourself in the sitting room downstairs when ready."

Cate licked her lips and nodded. The maid scurried from the room, leaving Cate standing in the center. Her head pounded, her muscles ached, and her stomach rolled.

She slow-blinked as she forced one foot in front of the other. Her train dragged across the floor behind her as she stalked from the room and down the hall. She followed the route she had taken when trying to escape, plodding down the stairs and into the sitting room.

Elliott sipped at his brandy from the wing-backed chair near the fireplace, his gaze shifting to her as she entered. The corner of his lips turned up at the edges, and his eyes sparkled as he studied her up and down, rising from the chair. "Well, I am beginning to understand exactly what it is our intrepid Duke finds so alluring."

Gianna glanced at Cate, rolling her eyes. "I still don't see the appeal."

"That's your jealousy speaking, Gianna, dear." He approached her, his eyes never leaving hers. "Would you like a cocktail or would you prefer to go straight to dinner?"

"Dinner. I prefer to get this over with."

Elliott offered his arm to her. Cate stared down at it with a frown before she flicked her gaze to his and slid her hand through the crook of his elbow.

He patted her hand. "I admire your spirit. I will so enjoy having you on our side."

"I will never be on your side," she said as he led her down the hall toward the dining room.

Gianna trailed behind them, her hips slowly rolling side to side as she down the rest of her sherry. "Don't be so sure, princess."

"Ignore her," Elliott said as he led Cate to a high-backed chair and tugged it away from the table. Cate sank on it as he pushed it under her. She startled, her shoulders rising to her ears when he cupped her arms in his hands. "She's jealous."

Gianna sauntered around the table and plopped into a chair, whipping a napkin onto her lap. "I'm not. I'm frustrated."

"Behave, Gianna," Elliott said as he sat at the head of the long table. Servants descended on them and poured their wine.

Elliott swirled it in the glass before sniffing it and taking a sip. "Now, tell me, Duchess, what is your relationship with Mr. Reid? It seems rather...complex."

"That's none of your business," Cate answered.

"Oh, come now. You are his employer, but what else are you? A friend? A lover? How does your husband feel about that?"

Cate flicked her gaze to him, her jaw flexing as her hand

slid onto the table. Her fingers wrapped around her knife as she answered him. "It's none of–

"My business," he finished, waving a hand in the air. "Of course. You've said. Though I really need to know. You see, I need to understand how valuable you are."

Cate slid the knife under the overlay fabric of her dress and into her pocket. "I don't understand."

"Don't you?" Elliott questioned. "You continue to tell me you are not valuable, but I don't believe that."

"I'm not," Cate said with a shrug as servants delivered their first course. She stared down at the liquid in her wide bowl.

Elliott stirred his soup before lifting his spoon to his mouth. He settled it back in his bowl and eyed Cate again. "I disagree. Please, eat, Duchess."

"I'm not hungry."

"You are really trying," Gianna said. "The food is not poisoned."

Cate flicked her gaze over the floral arrangement separating them and narrowed her eyes at the woman. "I wouldn't trust anything you said."

"She is quite right. At this moment, you are much more valuable to us alive. I am not certain what game you think you are playing, but I'm fairly certain if we apply the appropriate amount of pressure to you, your husband will give us what we want."

"I doubt it," Cate said. She sipped at the soup, sickened by how good the food tasted after having none all day.

"I don't. After what he did to Gianna when he found out you were in 1805, I'd wager he will move heaven and earth to ensure no harm comes to you."

"He will never join you."

"Respectfully, I disagree again. The question is how much

will you need to survive before he does. That should be the only question burning through your mind."

Cate slid another spoonful of soup into her mouth, letting the warm liquid roll across her tongue.

"You don't enjoy being harmed, do you, Duchess?" Elliot asked.

"Please say yes, because I cannot wait to try a few things," Gianna said with a smirk.

"Does it matter what I answer?"

"Yes," Elliott said after another sip of his wine. "It very much does. You are in complete control of this situation."

Cate's forehead crinkled as a servant collected her bowl.

"Don't play coy, mouse," Gianna said with a roll of her eyes. "You cannot possibly be that stupid."

"Gianna," Elliott said, his voice filled with restraint, "behave." He flicked his gaze back to Cate, his eyes gleaming in the candlelight. "Think, Duchess."

Gianna clicked her tongue and shook her head as the servants appeared with the next course. "Really, Elliott. Do you see now? She is far too simple to be of any good to us except as a pawn."

Elliott held up his hand to shush the woman as he kept his eyes trained on Cate. "We want your husband on our side. You can bring him around."

"And why would I do that?" Cate asked.

"Because, dear Duchess, if you don't, we will make your life a living Hell."

CHAPTER 29

The words echoed in Cate's mind as she stared at the food on her plate. She swallowed hard and flicked her gaze back to Elliott.

"You don't want that, do you? You don't want us as your enemy."

"I can't help you," she answered.

Elliott cut into his beef and popped a piece in his mouth, flicking his eyebrows up. "Can't or won't?"

"Can't," Cate answered, stabbing a green bean with her fork.

"You're lying," Gianna spat.

Cate focused her gaze on the woman across from her, studying the dark bruises around her neck. "I'm not. I can't do what you're asking."

"Elaborate," Elliott said as he sawed at his meat again.

"I have no control over Marcus's decisions." She poked at a potato cube before she slid the fork into her mouth.

"Oh, come now, Duchess. You're being far too modest."

"I am not."

Gianna arched her eyebrows and fluttered her eyelashes

at Cate. Elliott's utensils clattered onto his plate, and he clasped his hands together, resting his elbows on the pristine white tablecloth. "Do you mean to tell me that a man who reacts as violently as Marcus Northcott did to his wife's disappearance gives her opinion no credence?"

Cate chewed the inside of her lower lip, attempting to come up with a response.

"I don't believe that," Elliott said with a shake of his head. He grabbed his wine glass, taking a sip before he tipped it toward Cate. "I believe he will do anything you ask."

Cate sighed. Marcus hated The Agency. And their less-than-real marriage wouldn't live up to Elliott's expectations.

A cackle erupted from across the table. Gianna bent forward over her plate as she laughed. She slapped the table before she rested her chin in her palm and eyed Cate with a few more giggles escaping her. "I think, Elliott, what has our dear little Cate all twisted in knots is that her marriage isn't real."

Elliott flicked his eyebrows up. "You've mentioned this theory before. I disagree. Care to settle a bet, Duchess?"

Cate flicked her gaze up from tracing the pattern of the lace tablecloth. She studied Gianna's features in the flickering candlelight.

"Come on, Cate. What's the harm in admitting the truth?"

Cate slid her trembling hand into her lap. She fought to stop her entire body from shaking, pressing her fingernails into her palms.

Gianna tugged one of the flowers from the arrangement in the center of the table and twirled the stem between her thumb and index finger. She tugged a petal from it, dropping it to the linentablecloth. "He loves her." She yanked another petal and let it flutter down. "He loves her not. Which is it, Cate?"

Elliott studied her from the head of the table. "I find it so interesting that you will not answer. Is there some truth to Gianna's accusation?"

Gianna smirked at her. "Come on, Cate. Admit it. What would it hurt? You married him just to keep Dunhaven Castle safe. How you knew our play, I haven't yet worked out. But I imagine that has something to do with your illustrious husband's intricate network of connections."

Cate focused on her breathing, unwilling to admit anything.

"Now, wait just a moment, Gianna," Elliott said, wagging a finger at her. "You see, that is something quite different than what I am asking."

Gianna tossed the flower down and snapped her gaze to Elliott. "How so? I maintain they married for legal reasons only."

"No. You said she married him to keep Dunhaven Castle safe."

Gianna offered him an unimpressed stare. "Same thing."

"Oh, no," Elliott answered, waving a finger in the air. "No, no. Not the same thing at all." A smile spread across his face, and he studied Cate. "Perhaps our dear Duchess married for legal reasons, but the illustrious Duke did not. Oh, how interesting. Who is in love with whom?"

"You think he loves her?" Gianna questioned. "I honestly cannot see how. She's nothing. Certainly not his type if his previous fiancee is any measure. And he can surely attract far better."

"The heart wants what the heart wants. And I still maintain his throttling of you speaks volumes."

"Marcus Northcott does not like to lose," Gianna shot back with a shrug. "It may not speak to any emotional connection."

"We shall soon find out, I think. Much to our Duchess's chagrin." He flicked his gaze to Cate, his features lit by the flickering candlelight giving them a more sinister appearance. "Unless you are willing to convince him. But before that, I am very curious to know your answer, dear. We can solve that mystery here and now."

"Admit it, Cate. Your marriage is a sham," Gianna said. "I'd love to know I'm right. I'd love to know if my case in the future has merit."

Cate flexed her jaw, her nostrils flaring as heat rose in her body. "Your case will be right where it deserves to be. In the trash."

Gianna scoffed. "Perhaps Mr. Smythe's legal maneuvering will see my complaint thrown out, but, again, that's not what I've asked. I asked if the case had merit because you have perpetrated a fraud."

Elliott leaned forward, his lips parting, as the tension between the two women hung heavy in the air.

Cate swallowed hard, narrowing her eyes at the blonde across from her. Her lips twisted as she pushed her anger down. "Your case has no merit. Our marriage is real."

The smirk on Gianna's face faded, replaced by a scowl. "I don't believe you."

"I'm not asking you to believe me."

"Oh, goody," Elliott said with a clap of his hands. Cate snapped her gaze to him. "I was rooting for you as a couple. It will make our job so much easier."

Cate shook her head. "I told you already. I do not control my husband's decisions. Real or not, I cannot force Marcus to join you."

Elliott smiled at her. "You do not need to force him, dear. You only need to ask."

"I'm afraid you will be sorely disappointed by my ability to change my husband's opinion of your organization." Cate stood and tossed her napkin onto the table. "And now, if you'll excuse me, I am the one who has grown weary of this conversation."

Gianna slapped a hand against the table, rattling the dishes. "You have not been dismissed from this table."

Elliott sucked in a breath. "I had hoped to share a dessert and an after-dinner cocktail, but if you are too tired, I understand."

Cate nodded and took a step toward the door. She restrained herself from slipping her hand into her pocket and wrapping her fingers around the knife she'd sneaked from the table.

"Just a moment," Elliott called after her.

Cate froze, her muscles stiffening and her shoulders rising to her ears. She held her breath as she twisted to glance at him.

"You haven't given me an answer. Can we count on your cooperation, Duchess? Will you bring us Marcus Northcott?"

She let her shoulders relax and raised her chin. "I'll give you my answer in the morning."

"I look forward to it."

Cate turned away from him and strode from the room. She held her breath as she continued down the hall, rounding the banister and sliding her hand onto the smooth wood. She tugged herself up the stairs and navigated to the bedroom.

Tension grew at her temples. She pushed through the door, slammed it shut, and collapsed against it. The emotions she'd held in check until now bubbled to the surface.

A sob burst from her as tears rolled down her cheeks. She slid down with her cheek pressed against the polished wood. Her shoulders shook as she cried, releasing the tension she'd experienced through the meal.

She twisted to press her back against the door. She tried

to steady her breathing, sucking in shaky breaths as she struggled to control her emotions.

A knock at the door startled her. She wiped at her cheeks and climbed to her feet. After a few more sniffles, she inched the door open.

The maid who had assisted her earlier peered in. She curtsied. "Your Grace, would you like to change now?"

"Yes," Cate answered, opening the door further.

The girl carried in nightclothes. Cate slid the knife from her pocket as the maid laid out the nightgown and robe. She tugged open a drawer on the nearby dresser and slipped the weapon inside.

The girl spun as she slid it closed and waited for Cate to cross the room. Within twenty minutes, she had Cate readied for bed. The girl disappeared from the room after another curtsy. Cate retrieved the knife from the dresser and slid it into her dressing gown pocket.

She settled at the window, staring out at the moon overhead. Frost tinged the edges of the window. She pressed her hand against it, feeling the coldness of the night through the glass. Her mind wandered to Jack. Where was he? Would he survive the night? Would she ever see him again?

Likely not, she thought as a shiver shook her. She pulled her hand away from the pane, rubbing it against the velvety material of her robe. She stayed at the window for another hour, waiting for the house to settle.

Her best chance at making it out of this house was in the wee hours of the morning. Restlessness coursed through her as she paced the floor of the room. Her adrenaline waned, but she feared falling asleep if she sat.

She couldn't risk sleeping through the best time for her to escape. Her mind spun out of control as she planned beyond her escape. What would she do? How far was she from where they'd left Jack?

She wondered if there were stables on the property. There must be. They'd arrived by horse-drawn carriage. She should steal a horse. And she shouldn't go far in any direction because she had no idea where she was or which direction to go.

Her features pinched as the realization of how dire her situation was crashed down upon her. Where was Rosenberg from here? How far had they traveled?

She squeezed her eyes closed, settling against the window again. "Think, Cate. You couldn't have gone too far. Rosenberg is likely still to the west."

She sucked in a deep breath. She'd ride in the opposite direction of where the sun rose.

Cate licked her lips and raised her chin, happy with her plan. She could do this. She could find her way home. She had to. She'd find Rosenberg first, then search for Jack.

She blew out a long breath, resuming her pacing back and forth. A knock startled her. She wondered if the maid had returned to check on her before retiring.

"Come in," she called.

The door swung open, and Gianna sashayed into the room, still in her evening clothes. "Still awake?"

Cate swallowed hard, balling her hands into fists. "Like I could sleep while under the same roof as you."

Gianna's lips curled at the corners. She strode past Cate to the dressing table, picking up the brush and running her fingers over the soft bristles. "I feel as though our conversation at the dinner table was unfinished."

"I don't. I've said all I care to say."

Gianna puckered her lips, letting the brush fall back onto her shoulder as she stalked closer to Cate. "What a shame. I would very much love to continue, so I think we will. You claim your marriage isn't a fraud, but I disagree."

Cate breathed out a sigh. "I don't care."

"I do. It affects all of my plans, you see. So, I would appreciate some clarification."

"This conversation is finished," Cate said, stepping to the side to skirt around the curvaceous blonde.

Gianna grabbed her by the wrist, yanking her back. "And I said it's not."

Cate tried to wrench her arm from the woman's grasp. "Let go of me."

"Not until we've got a few things straight. I have a different request than Elliott."

Cate tugged at her arm again. "I've given you the only answer I can."

"Then answer this question. What is more important to you? Dunhaven or your husband?"

Cate scrunched her eyebrows together. "What do you mean?"

"Which is more important to you? Your home and your friends or your husband?"

Cate narrowed her eyes at the woman, finally ripping her wrist free. "What kind of question is that?"

"A fair one. I have an offer for you."

Cate stalked away from her, staring out the window. "I already know the offer. Bring Marcus to your side or face the consequences. I told you I'd let you know in the morning."

"Oh, I have quite a different deal. One that you may find appealing."

Cate twisted to stare at her, bringing a smile to Gianna's face. "I see you're sufficiently intrigued. Good."

Gianna rubbed the bristles of the brush against her other palm as she stalked across the room in one direction. "Elliott wants everything. I'm willing to give you something back."

Cate raised her eyebrows, prompting the woman to continue.

Gianna spun and retreated the way she'd come. "I'm

willing to allow you to keep Dunhaven Castle. You keep your home. Your friends keep theirs. Everyone is happy."

"And what are you asking in return?"

"Marcus. Lure him here. Hand him over to us. Leave. Simple." She waved the brush in the air. "Oh, one more pesky detail. You will need to divorce him. We need him completely free for our purposes."

Cate stared at the woman as she cocked a hip and eyed her.

She flicked the face-framing lock of blonde hair back. "I think it solves all our problems. What do you say?"

"Get out," Cate answered.

Gianna slid her head forward, fluttering her eyelashes. "Really? You are willing to lose everything for him?"

"I'm losing nothing. You can't be trusted. I'd never make a deal with you."

Gianna sighed, flicking her gaze to the floor. "You really are stupid."

Cate raised her chin. "You'll never live up to your word."

"Neither will he. Let him go, mouse. Give him to us and save yourself."

Cate shook her head slowly.

Gianna puckered her lips, her nostrils flaring with irritation. "Well, I suppose I should thank you."

"Thank me?"

The blonde lifted her shoulder in a half-shrug. "Now I get to break you."

She stalked forward toward Cate. "And while Elliott gave you until the morning, I'd prefer to be ahead of the game."

She brandished the heavy silver brush, flicking the bristles again. "Let's start now."

CHAPTER 30

*C*ate's heart skipped a beat as Gianna stalked toward her, smacking the heavy silver brush against her palm.

She shook her head and pressed herself against the window sill. "I don't think Elliott will be pleased with your decision to up the timeline."

"I don't really care. I'm *sick* of the adoration of Cate Kensie. A few extra bruises won't hurt. There will still be plenty left to torture for your husband's benefit."

"No," Cate said with a shake of her head.

"Consider this payback for what your husband did to me for sending you to this time." Gianna raised the brush overhead.

Cate wrapped her fingers around the knife in her pocket and pulled it from the folds of fabric. She thrust it forward. "I don't think so."

Gianna stopped with her hand raised behind her and cocked her head. "Well, well, well, the little mouse roars."

"Leave, Gianna."

Gianna narrowed her eyes at Cate. "I don't think so. Let's

have this out. At least now I have an excuse for attacking you."

Gianna widened her stance and wiggled her fingers. "Make your move, Cate."

Cate lifted her chin, fighting to steady her shaking hand. "No. Either make yours or leave. But I'm not attacking you."

"Afraid?"

"I'm not going to be goaded into a fight with you. Get out or attack me."

"With pleasure," Gianna growled at her. She lunged toward her, swinging the heavy brush. Cate skirted to the side, still holding the knife out.

Gianna spun to face her with her nostrils flaring. "Come on," she said, encouraging Cate to make her move.

Cate shook her head. "No."

"You are maddening," Gianna answered. She sliced the hairbrush through the air. "Fight, Cate."

"Leave, Gianna."

"After I've bruised that pretty little face a few times." She pounced forward, pummeling Cate and knocking her into the bed.

They struggled against each other as they slammed into the mattress. Cate flopped onto it, fighting to keep Gianna from cracking her with the brush. The knife slipped from her hand, thudding softly against the bedspread.

She twisted to find it. Gianna tossed the brush away and wrapped her hands around Cate's throat. "Perhaps I'll skip the small stuff and just go for the big finish."

Cate gasped as the pressure increased against her windpipe. She ignored it and reached for the knife behind her. Her fingers grasped clumsily for the metal object.

"Say goodnight, Cate," Gianna growled.

Cate winced as Gianna's fingers tightened around her

neck. Her vision blackened on the edges, and her lungs burned for air.

Her fingers finally latched onto the cold metal handle. She gripped it and swung it blindly overhead.

Gianna shrieked, releasing her grasp on Cate's neck and stumbling backward.

Cate sucked in a breath with a groan and pushed herself up to sit. Gianna leaned against the wall, a hand pressed to her cheek. She glanced incredulously at Cate as she pulled her fingers away. Blood tinged the tips.

Cate swallowed hard as she stared at the large gash running from her lip to her ear. Blood ran from it, dripping off her jawline.

Cate's eyes went wide, and she launched herself off the bed. She grabbed the post on the corner and flung herself around. She needed to escape before the shock wore off Gianna.

She lifted her robe and nightgown, keeping tight hold of the knife, and started toward the door. Gianna plowed into her from the back, knocking her to the hardwood floor. Her chin smacked against it and split open. The jarring pain jounced the knife from her hand again. It skittered across the floor.

Blood pooled underneath her jaw, and tears stung her eyes. Gianna's weight pressed against her. Her head lifted as the woman grabbed a fistful of Cate's hair and yanked back.

She pushed it forward, attempting to bang her forehead off the floor. Cate flailed her arms behind her as she lifted her hips. Gianna toppled to the floor, tugging Cate back with her.

Cate kicked and thrashed her arms, striking Gianna in the face again. She yelped in pain as Cate hit the wound she'd sliced into her cheek.

Cate used the temporary pause in the fighting to

scramble to her feet and race to the knife. She snapped it up and continued to the door.

She flung the door open and raced through the doorway, smashing into an individual in the hall.

She took a stunned step back, raising the knife in the air.

Elliott held two glasses and a decanter of brandy. "Well, Duchess, this is not the way I had hoped to meet."

Cate backed up a step, gasping for breath.

Gianna shouted from inside the bedroom, "Restrain her. She attacked me."

Elliott's eyebrows shot up as he studied Gianna's limping form. He flicked his gaze to Cate. "What happened?"

Cate's features pinched as she sucked in another shaky breath.

"Well? Isn't anyone going to tell me what just occurred between you two?"

"I told you. She attacked me. Lock her up until Northcott is here. She does not deserve the treatment you are offering her."

"What were you doing here, Gianna? I asked you to stay away from our dear Duchess whilst she considered my proposal."

Gianna flexed her jaw, wincing as the wound on her cheek oozed more blood.

Elliott breathed out a sigh. "You should have that tended. Go now and see to it."

"Elliott…"

"I said go," he snapped.

Gianna offered Cate a disdainful glare while she pushed past her, knocking her back a step as she strode down the hall. Elliott waved the glasses toward Cate's bedroom. She raised the knife at him.

"You won't make it further than the next hall, Duchess. Do not jeopardize what little goodwill is left on my behalf."

Cate swallowed hard as she considered her options. She let her hand fall to her side and stalked into the room.

Elliott followed her into the bedroom, swinging the door closed behind him. He set the glasses and decanter on the tall dresser near the door.

"I'll need the knife."

Cate slid her eyes closed as she held it out in front of her. He pulled it from her hand and set it on the dresser. He poured brandy into both glasses before he held one out to her.

She wrapped her arms around her midriff and shook her head.

"Take it, Duchess. You need it."

Cate accepted the drink from his hand, pressing it against her arm as she tightened her fingers around the glass and stared into the amber liquid.

"Tell me what happened."

She flicked her gaze to him, his face lit by the melting candles of the candelabra. "Does it matter?"

He sipped at the brandy. "It does to me. What brought Gianna here? And what started the scuffle?"

Cate barked out a laugh as she paced the floor. "It was a bit more than a scuffle."

"It appears she got the worst of it. How intriguing you are to me. It seems when you are backed into a corner you become quite fierce. What prompted such a reaction from you?"

"She attacked me."

"Unprovoked?"

Cate shot him an irked glance. "She didn't like my answers to her questions."

"Which were?" he asked after another sip of brandy.

"She offered me Dunhaven Castle in exchange for Marcus."

Elliott puckered his lips, stalking closer to her. "And you refused?"

Cate nodded. "And she did not care for my response."

Elliott sucked in a deep breath. "Well, I hope my offer is still in contention. It will make things much easier for you. I can assure you Gianna will have no mercy when it comes to using you to convince your husband to join us. Especially now. I cannot imagine this latest incident will earn you any generosity on her part."

Cate swallowed hard, giving him no answer.

"I'll take that as a yes." He raised his glass. "Again, I prefer you as an ally."

He studied her for a moment before he sucked in a breath. "Well, I shall leave you to your thoughts. I only dropped by to inform you that your husband has been sent for."

Cate snapped her gaze to him, her eyes searching his face for more information.

"I expect him to arrive early tomorrow morning. I shall expect my answer from you over breakfast." He offered her a tight-lipped smile, his eyes lingering on her for a moment before he spun on a heel to leave. "I'll send someone to attend to your chin."

"It's not necessary," Cate said. "I'm fine and prefer not to be disturbed."

"As you wish." He offered her a final nod, collecting the knife, decanter, and his brandy glass and leaving the room. The click of a lock announced the end of any escape attempts through the door.

Cate stalked to the vanity and collapsed onto the chair. She took a long sip of the liquor before she set the glass on top. She studied the cut on her chin in the mirror before she wiped the dried blood away.

She sank her chin into her palm, wincing as the touch

stung the scrape. Weariness crept over her. She fought her heavy eyelids, forcing herself to her feet. She crossed the room and twisted the doorknob. It did not give way. With her hopes of the lock failing dashed, she spun and studied the room. Could there be a secret passage?

She sucked in a breath and pushed off the door. After an hour of searching, she collapsed on the bed. She buried her head in her hands. With a deep sigh, she kicked her shoes off and lay on her side. Despite her agitation, her eyes slid closed in minutes, and she drifted to sleep.

When she opened her eyes, she found herself in her room at Dunhaven Castle. She gasped, scanning the room as she tossed back her covers. How had she gotten here? Had Marcus come in the middle of the night?

She slid from her bed and crossed the room, peering into the sitting room. A scream stopped her heart. Cate swallowed hard, racing to the doors to the hall and flinging them open. Another shout echoed through the halls.

She hurried toward it, racing past Molly's room and rounding the corner. Before she took another step, the image faded around her.

Cate's eyes fluttered open. She tugged her eyebrows together as she tried to place herself. Her heart sank as she found herself in the bedroom she'd fallen asleep in. No one had rescued her. She remained with The Agency.

She turned over to stare out the window. Streaks of light brightened the early morning sky. Cate let out a long sigh as a knock sounded at her door.

She pushed up to sit, clearing her throat. "Come in."

The lock disengaged and a maid scurried in, holding a dress. "Good morning, Your Grace. Your clothes."

Cate dragged herself from the bed and slogged to the dressing table. "Thank you."

The maid styled her hair and helped her change into the

blue dress she'd brought. "Mr. Stevens has asked that you join him for breakfast in the dining room."

"Thank you," Cate said, dismissing the girl.

The maid scurried from the room, pulling the door shut behind her. Cate sucked in a breath as she attempted to prepare herself for the encounter. He'd demand an answer. He would not like her response. How long could she refuse before they harmed her? How long could she refuse before they realized she held no value?

She stared at herself in the mirror for a moment before her eyes fell on the empty brandy glass on the vanity. Her fingers traced the rim before she grasped it and smashed it against the heavy wood. It shattered into pieces. She carefully picked up one large shard between her thumb and forefinger and slid it into her pocket.

With her chin raised, she sucked in a deep breath and strode from the room. She snaked her way through the halls and down the wide staircase. Her gaze lingered on the double doors leading outside.

"Duchess," Elliott said before she could consider it any further, "I hope you slept well. I was just coming to check on you."

Cate snapped her gaze to him, her heart dropping as any chance of escape diminished. He offered his arm, and she reluctantly accepted it.

"Did you sleep? You did not answer," he asked as he led her down the hall.

"I managed a little."

Elliott offered her a smile as they entered the large room, lit by the morning sun. A groan sounded from the table.

Gianna sat in the same seat she'd had the previous evening. She slammed her teacup into its saucer and whipped her napkin onto her lap. "Maybe now we can eat. I'm starved."

"Good morning, Gianna, dear," Elliott said as he seated Cate.

She flicked a less-than-impressed gaze at him, the bandage on her cheek wrinkling. Cate stared at it. "Admiring your handiwork?"

She glanced sideways at the servant who poured her tea and nodded.

"Please, Cate, have a good look." Gianna peeled the bandage from her face, revealing the long slice. She slammed a fist on the table, rattling the dishes.

Cate startled in her seat, sliding her eyes closed before she flicked her gaze back to the angry gash.

"Gianna, please," Elliott said after a sip of his tea. "Let's not make a scene."

"She has disfigured me. I–"

"Enough," Elliott said flatly. "We have discussed this."

Gianna's nostrils flared as she shot a glare in Cate's direction. "You'll pay for this."

Elliott's teacup clattered back into his saucer. "That is quite enough. I hoped to enjoy a pleasant meal."

A footman delivered a steaming bowl of oatmeal to Cate. She picked up her spoon and pushed the thick, warm paste around before she raised a spoonful to her lips.

Gianna ate some of her meal before her spoon clattered into her bowl. "I cannot do it. She should not be treated this way."

"If you cannot manage to contain your animosity, please take your meal elsewhere."

Cate swallowed another mouthful of oatmeal, flicking her gaze to Gianna who sneered at her.

"I will not be chased from my rightful place."

"Your rightful place is where I say it is. Remember that," Elliott answered.

"I have done more for you than–"

"I will not discuss this here. You have been handsomely rewarded and will continue to be so. But you do not make the final decisions here, Gianna. Accept that."

Gianna sucked in a long breath, her nostrils flaring as she blew it out. "You're going to regret this, Elliott. Mark my words."

"So noted," he said as he lifted his teacup to his lips and shifted his eyes to Cate. "And how is your breakfast, Duchess? Up to your standards."

"Yes, thank you," Cate answered.

Across the table, Gianna offered a frustrated sigh, flicking her gaze into space. A butler hurried into the dining room and hastened to Elliott. He bent to whisper in the man's ear. Elliott's eyebrows shot up, and his lips curled on the edges. "Ah, thank you, Belmont."

Elliott dabbed at the corners of his mouth with his napkin before discarding it on the table. "Well, it seems your husband has arrived, Duchess. So, I will need an answer to my question from last night. Can I count on your support? Will you deliver us Marcus Northcott?"

$\mathcal{C}$ate chewed her lower lip as her heart thudded in her chest, and her pulse quickened. She flicked her gaze to Gianna, her eyes falling to the laceration on her cheek. She flexed her jaw, feeling her own cut stretch and pinch. Her eyes lowered to the brown liquid in her teacup. Could she continue this war?

"Duchess? I'm afraid I will need your answer immediately."

"She's too stubborn. Time to make her pay."

Elliott shushed his female compatriot. "I would like to hear our dear Duchess's answer."

Cate sucked in a breath, pulling her gaze from the tea and twisting her head to stare at Elliott. His lips parted as he awaited her answer, one eyebrow arching in anticipation.

"I'll see what I can do."

A tight-lipped and triumphant smile crossed his face. Gianna let her hand slap against the table. "Oh, Elliott, please don't tell me you believe her. She's lying."

"We will take the appropriate precautions. And we will

know soon enough if she is. I can assure you, Duchess, if you are lying, the repercussions will be immediate and severe."

"I can't guarantee you anything," Cate said.

"Because you won't even try. You're bluffing," Gianna said, crossing her arm over her chest.

"Oh, don't discount yourself, dear. I have every faith that the request of your husband will not fall on deaf ears."

Gianna pressed her lips into a thin line as she stared at Cate. "Let's stick with our original plan. I have more faith in that than in Cate Kensie."

"Come now, Gianna," Elliott said as he rose, "I think we can all agree that this course of events is preferable. Recognizing the mutual benefits we can provide each other is far better than forcing one's hand into agreement."

Gianna glared at Cate. Elliott fluttered his eyelashes at her. "Are you still to be counted on?"

She flicked her gaze at him through her eyelashes before she balled her napkin and tossed it onto the table. She rose from her seat with another glare at Cate before she stormed from the room.

Elliott approached Cate and offered her his arm. "Ignore her. She is jealous."

Cate stood and slid her hand around his elbow.

"You are making the right choice," he said, patting her hand. "The benefits of The Agency are vast, even for someone as privileged as yourself and your husband."

"Gianna's attitude suggests I'm not making a wise choice."

Elliott smiled down at her as he led her down the hall. "Gianna is jealous. Between us, I believe she had her sights set on your husband."

Cate sucked in a deep breath as he pushed open the doors to a large library. "Wait here. I shall bring your husband to you soon."

She nodded and stepped inside. The doors thudded

closed behind her. She wrung her hands in front of her as she paced the floor. What had she done?

She settled on the window seat overlooking the cold landscape. Her heart pounded against her ribs, and her stomach turned over. She licked her lips as she wiped her sweaty palms against her dress.

She couldn't deliver what she'd promised. The only question that remained was whether she would face The Agency alone or if Marcus would help her.

Voices sounded in the hall. Cate rose from her seat, squeezing her hands into fists until her nails dug into her palms. The doorknobs twisted, and the doors pushed open.

"I think you'll find her quite well," Elliott's voice said. He paraded into the room with Gianna. Marcus followed behind them.

Tears filled her eyes as she spotted him. Her gaze fell on the odd-looking shackles around his wrists. They glowed with a blue, pulsating energy.

"Catherine," he breathed as he pushed past Gianna and hurried to Cate.

She blinked up at him before she settled her gaze on the shackles.

"Are you all right?" he asked her.

She swallowed hard and flicked her gaze up to him. "More or less."

He narrowed his eyes at her chin, lifting his bound hands to raise her jaw. "What is this?" he demanded, twisting to glance at Elliott over his shoulder. "You assured she was unharmed. She is not." He turned back to Cate. "What happened?"

"A small, unfortunate accident. She is quite well, I assure you. Duchess, perhaps you can attest to this."

Cate glanced around him. "We need some time alone."

Gianna barked out a laugh. "I think not. Come on, then, Cate, I'm dying to hear your appeal."

Cate kept her eyes trained on Elliott. "I can't work miracles. This is not a stage play."

Elliott narrowed his eyes at her. "I think we can allow them a private moment. It may prove most effective."

Gianna snapped her gaze to the man, but he held a hand up to silence her. "You have fifteen minutes, Duchess. Then I want a progress report."

Cate sucked in a breath, drawing her chin to her chest as she waited for them to shuffle from the room. "Fifteen minutes. I expect to be impressed."

The doors swung shut behind them with a bang, and Cate's features pinched.

Marcus lifted his bound hands to caress her cheek. "Catherine, are you all right?"

She sucked in a shaky breath and nodded. "Yes," she squeaked out.

"That sounds less than convincing. What happened to your chin?"

She flicked her gaze up to him. "Gianna attacked me. I fell trying to get away."

Marcus huffed out a sigh, his irritation obvious.

"I gave as good as I got," she assured him.

He flicked his eyebrows up and returned his gaze to her. "The wound on her cheek?"

Cate nodded.

He cocked his head and sucked in a breath. "This will end today for you. I will ensure that they return you to Rosenberg and–"

"What?" Cate asked, cutting her eyes up to his. "No."

"Catherine, I will not allow them to harm you."

"No," she repeated with a shake of her head. She wagged her finger at him. "No, you're not doing that again."

Marcus sighed, pressing his lips together. "We have few other choices."

"We have some. We'll make some options. You can't sacrifice yourself again."

"I can, and I will. I will not allow this treatment of you to continue."

"I will come back here for you."

"No, you will not."

Cate offered him a stubborn glance through her eyelashes.

"Catherine, this cannot continue. Gianna is dangerous–"

"Exactly," she interrupted. "What do you think they'll do if you are no longer in the picture?"

"I will make sure that does not happen."

Cate tilted her head and puckered her lips. "You are always saying we cannot trust them. Why would we trust them now?"

"We are wasting time. I will not allow them to do what I know they will do to you."

"Neither will I. We need a way out of this. And then we need to find Jack. We were separated again when Elliott Stevens ripped us apart." Her eyes fell on the pulsating shackles. "I assume these stop you from doing any magic."

He nodded. "Who has the keys?"

"Who do you think?"

Cate pressed her lips together. "Gianna."

"Catherine, you cannot get the key. It is impossible. We must make certain you are safe first."

Cate sliced a finger through the air, her other hand on her hip. "I am *not* telling your mother that you are property of The Agency."

"Mother will understand that I–"

"No! I refuse to do it. We are not leaving here separately."

Marcus drew in a deep breath and shook his head. "This

is not a discussion, Catherine."

"No, it isn't," she agreed. "You are not sacrificing yourself for me. It's nonsense."

"I have never once made a nonsensical judgment in my life."

"There's a first time for everything," Cate said with a flick of her eyebrows.

"This is not a game."

"No, it's not. It's my life and your life and a lot of other people's, too. There's no margin for error. We have to find a way out of this, and we have to do it together."

"You will not take no for an answer, will you?"

Cate shook her head. "And you'd better not do what you did the last time. I'll come back for you so I can kill you myself."

One corner of his mouth tugged up. "While I appreciate your sentiment, there is no good option here. They will not simply allow us to refuse them. Not when they have the upper hand."

Cate rubbed her chin. "No, I'll have to get my hands on that key."

"Catherine!"

"I can do it," she promised, snapping her gaze up to his face. "I just have to get close enough to Gianna to use this." She pulled the glass shard from her pocket. She whipped the handkerchief from his pocket and wrapped the glass in it before hiding it again.

"No, we'll find another way."

"This is the easiest way. I'll easily be able to get close to her, she's been chomping at the bit to put the screws to me. All I need to do is tell them I failed."

"Failed at what?"

Heat rose in her cheeks as she eyed him. "I may have told them I'd try to convince you to join them. Once they realize I can't do that, Gianna will try to force you to their side. And that's when I'll steal the key."

"Catherine, this is the worst plan I've ever heard. No."

"There are no other plans, Marcus. This is the best we have."

"There are other options."

"Like what? You can't trade yourself for me. That's worse. That means I need to come back here for you instead of just getting the key from Gianna."

"Or you could simply move on. Mother will help you get back to your time and to Dunhaven Castle. I'm certain she'll also help you locate Jack."

"No," Cate growled between clenched teeth. "I didn't survive the Battle of Austerlitz and nearly kill Napoleon for nothing."

Cate took a step toward the door when Marcus grabbed her by the elbow and tugged her back. "You did what?"

"It was an accident. I didn't have much choice. Anyway, he's fine."

A knock sounded at the door. Cate twisted to eye the barrier, her heart skipping a beat. She spun back to Marcus. "We can do this. Together."

She slid her hand into his and nodded. The door creaked open behind her. His hand tightened around hers as she glanced over her shoulder. Elliott stepped inside with two bulky guards, and Gianna hovered in the doorway.

"Well, have we made any decisions?"

"Sadly–" Cate began when Marcus tugged her behind him and stepped forward.

"Yes, we have," he answered.

Cate's eyes went wide as she stumbled back. "Marcus, no."

"I want Catherine returned to Rosenberg immediately. I demand a cessation of all hostility against her."

"This is not what we discussed," she whispered.

Elliott cocked his head, puckering his lips. "There seems to be some misunderstanding. The lovely Duchess is most welcome in our membership. If she has managed to convince you to join–"

Marcus held up his hands. "I'll stop you there. She has not."

"Oh?" Elliott said with a frown. "But–"

"I demand Catherine be let go immediately."

"I don't think so," Gianna said, stalking into the room. "She is far too great of an asset to us. She allows us to keep you in control."

"My apologies, Duke, but I am still quite lost in this conversation. Why not simply accept the deal on the table? We take both you and your lovely wife into our fold and–"

"No. Catherine is not to be subjected to any of what The Agency offers."

"Marcus, this is not what we discussed," Cate said, grabbing hold of his arm. "Don't do this."

"It seems your wife is not in agreement. Perhaps you would like to–"

"That won't be necessary. We do not agree on the subject. I am currently in your custody. I am trading myself for her."

Cate slid her eyes closed and shook her head. "Marcus, no."

"The discussion is over, Catherine. I have made up my mind."

Her heart thudded as her mind shot in a hundred directions. Could she get the key before they escorted her away? Would she be able to return here and rescue him?

"So have we," Gianna said as she stalked forward. "And it appears we do not see eye to eye either."

Elliott stared at the floor for a moment, his hands clasped behind his back as he frowned. "This is a most disappointing turn of events."

"Speak for yourself, Elliott," Gianna said with a smirk made even more sinister by the slice across her cheek. "I'm about to have the time of my life."

"Elliott, I expected more from you," Marcus said as he sidestepped to block Gianna from Cate.

Elliott shot him a confused glance. "As did I of you."

The man spun on a heel and disappeared from the room. The guards crossed toward them.

"Elliott!" Marcus shouted after him as Gianna lunged for Cate with an evil laugh.

"You should have agreed, Marcus."

"Take your hands off her," he shouted as Gianna yanked her toward the door. The two men restrained him from following.

"This would have gone so much easier if you'd only agreed. But then again, I do appreciate your stubbornness. It gives me the opportunity to alleviate so much stress." She chuckled again with a tiny squeal of excitement as she dragged Cate from the room.

"Come along, my dear little Cate. We are going to have so much fun."

Cate sucked in a shaky breath as Gianna paraded her down the hall toward a closed door. She flung it open when they reached it and forced Cate down the wooden stairs.

Candelabras lit the space below as Gianna continued to push her forward until they reached the bottom few steps. With one rough shove, she sent Cate tumbling down to the ground. She landed on her hands and knees.

Gianna stomped down the remaining stairs and yanked Cate up by her hair. She paraded her toward a chair with leather straps next to a table of instruments. Cate eyed them, swallowing hard.

She had to escape before those wrapped around her wrists. Before she became a prisoner, or worse, a victim.

ate gritted her teeth as Gianna forced her across the room. She dug her feet into the floor, trying to stop her progression. Pain shot through her as the woman twisted her hair tighter.

Cate clawed at Gianna's hands, trying to break free of her. They reached the chair. Cate arched her back away from it as Gianna tried to shove her toward it. She released her grasp on Gianna's hands and reached into her pocket. She wrapped a sweaty palm around the glass shard and pulled it out. Blindly, she swiped it behind her, slicing through the fingers that held her hair.

Gianna screeched, releasing Cate's hair as she stumbled back a step. Cate fell forward, smacking into the chair. She grasped it and pushed herself up.

"You bitch!" Gianna spat at her. "You'll pay for that."

Cate twisted and sliced the shard through the air again, narrowly missing Gianna as she leaned away.

Gianna shook her bloody fingers as she winced. "Come on, then."

"Give me the key to those magic handcuffs," Cate said.

Gianna barked out a sharp laugh. "I don't think so. If you want it, come and take it."

Cate's nostrils flared as she sucked in sharp breaths. Gianna inched to the side. Cate circled away from the chair, keeping the glass shard at arm's length.

"Come on, Cate. Make your move." Gianna signaled her to come closer.

Cate's heart pounded as she tightened her fingers around the glass.

"Here, let me make it easy." Gianna pulled a glowing key from her dress pocket and dangled it in the air. She tugged her lips back into a grin as she tossed it across the room.

Cate followed the key's path until it clattered to the floor and rolled across it. Gianna lunged forward, and Cate snapped her gaze back to the women, waving the shard again.

"Give it up, Cate. You're not going to win. I'm going to take everything you have. After I ruin that pretty little face of yours."

"I told you before I wouldn't let you have anything of mine."

"You won't have a choice, sweetheart." Gianna launched herself at Cate, plowing into her and knocking her to the ground. Cate struggled to keep hold of the glass shard as her shoulder slammed into the cold, hard floor. Gianna reached for her wrist and pressed it into the ground.

Cate fought to hang on to the makeshift weapon as the woman pounded her arm against the stone floor again and again. With her free hand, Cate clawed at her face.

Gianna released the pressure on her wrist as she fended off Cate's attack. Cate used the opportunity to wiggle free and slash at her again. The rough glass caught her sleeve, tearing into it and her flesh underneath. Blood bloomed from the slice, soaking the thin material.

Gianna sucked in a gasp as she grabbed at the fresh wound. Cate slid her heels toward her rear and braced them, shoving her hip in the air to topple Gianna from straddling her.

The blonde rolled to the floor next to her. Cate scrambled to her feet, still holding the shard. It pressed against her fingers, drawing blood. She shifted her gaze toward the key glowing in a dark corner of the room.

Gianna shot her an angry glare and climbed to her feet before Cate could cross to the key. "Going somewhere?"

Cate snapped her gaze back to Gianna, trying to antici-pate the woman's next move. "Go for the key, Cate," she dared her.

Cate backed away from her and the key.

"What's the matter? Chicken?"

Cate circled behind the chair, keeping the heavy wooden object between her and Gianna. She inched toward the corner opposite the key.

Gianna grabbed the tray of tools from the table and flung it toward Cate.

She held her hand up, blocking the sharp instruments from hitting her face. When she lowered her arm, she found Gianna inches from her face. The woman slammed her into the wall. The air rushed from Cate's lungs.

She struggled against the woman who pinned her. Gianna wrapped a hand around her throat and squeezed. Cate strug-gled to draw in a breath. She clamped a hand over the blonde's face and shoved her back, pressing the shard into her neck.

A droplet of blood dripped down her neck before Gianna backed away. Cate wrapped a leg around Gianna's, tripping her. She fell backward, smacking into the chair.

Cate raced past her and scooped the key up from the ground before hurrying toward the stairs. Gianna crashed into her as she reached them. Cate crawled up a few of the steps, their edges poking into her ribs.

"I don't think so, Cate," Gianna growled as she elbowed her in the back.

"I do," Cate grunted back. She rolled onto her side and drew her leg to her chest before she kicked it out. Gianna slid down a few stairs.

Cate clamped onto the handrail and tugged herself up, clambering up a few more steps. She reached the door, her fingertips caressing the knob when Gianna wrapped her arm around Cate's neck. Cate squeezed the shard tighter at her side before she shoved it backward. It stabbed Gianna in the gut.

The woman gasped, releasing her hold on Cate. She stared at her with wide eyes before she fell backward, tumbling down the stairs and landing in a heap at the bottom.

Cate swallowed hard, unsure if Gianna remained alive or not. She sucked in shaky breaths, unfurling her fingers and staring at the glowing key. She curled her fingers around it again before she twisted the doorknob and climbed to the hall.

She eased the door shut and hurried forward. Elliott Stevens rounded the corner. He froze as he spotted her. Cate's heart stopped, and her blood ran cold. She couldn't make it to the library first.

She swallowed hard as she hurried forward to him. "Mr. Stevens, please, I just need a few more moments with my husband to convince him."

"Where is Gianna?"

Cate ignored the statement, clamping onto his arm with a hand. "He is extremely stubborn, but I'm certain I can achieve the result I had hoped to earlier. Just five minutes."

"The time for negotiations has ended, Duchess. I—"

"This is not the way you hoped things would go. And I must admit, it's not the way I had either. What can it hurt?"

He glanced over her shoulder at the closed door leading downstairs.

"Please," Cate said again, tightening her grip.

"I suppose five minutes will not hurt. Though I am quite perplexed that Gianna agreed to this."

Cate swallowed hard as she fluttered her eyelashes at him, refusing to answer the statement. He wrapped an arm around her shoulders and led her to the library doors. He pushed them open. Marcus twisted to face them, his eyes going wide. The two men still on either side of him reached to restrain him.

Cate pushed past Elliott and hurried across the room.

"Catherine, are you quite all right?"

Elliot waved the men back. "Five minutes, Duchess."

She reached Marcus and threw her arms around his neck, tugging him closer to her.

"Catherine, what's happened?"

She pressed her cheek against his, whispering in his ear, "I have the key."

His muscles tensed, and he leaned into her. "Touch it to the shackles, and they will open."

She squeezed her eyes closed and nodded. She pulled away from him, staring up into his dark eyes as she slid her closed hand down his arm.

"Elliott!" Gianna's voice screamed.

Cate's heart stopped, and she gasped for breath. The voice called out again, this time closer. Cate's knees trembled as she slid the key between her thumb and forefinger.

"Gianna?" Elliot questioned as she appeared at the door. A bloodstain marred the front left side of her dress.

She pointed a blood-soaked hand at Cate. "Stop her, she has the key!"

Elliott snapped his gaze at them. Cate pressed the key against the shackles. They snapped open, falling from his wrists. The corners of his lips turned up as electricity crackled between his fingers. He leaned forward toward her and whispered, "Get down."

Cate swallowed hard, crouching low as he swung his hands out. Two white-hot fireballs slammed into the guards on either side of him. They fell backward, stunned and unmoving. With a stomp forward, an arc of energy buzzed over her head, shooting toward Gianna and Elliott.

A shriek split the air as firm hands grabbed hold of her and an arm wrapped around her. Her surroundings turned black.

Details filled in around her seconds later. She sucked in shaky breaths as she recognized her room at Rosenberg. She let out a sob as the pressure released around her shoulders.

"Catherine," Marcus began.

She interrupted him, spinning to face him and swallowing hard as she threw her arms around his neck.

He pulled her closer to him and stroked her hair for a moment before he pulled away. "Are you all right?"

She bit her lower lip and nodded, sniffling and wiping a tear away from her cheek. "Yeah, I'm fine."

He tipped her chin up, studying the scratch at the tip. With a swipe of his finger, he healed it. "Anything else?"

"No. I escaped pretty unscathed." She pressed a hand to her forehead as her heartbeat steadied along with her breathing. She flicked her gaze up to him and offered a weak smile. "I told you I'd get the key."

He offered her an amused smile with a shake of his head. "We really must stop finding ourselves in these situations."

"I agree."

"You must learn to defend yourself."

333

Cate flicked her eyebrows up. "Hey, I think I did pretty well. I drew blood three times and knocked her out again."

"That is not what I am referring to. We must stop her from doing what she's done to you this time around. I will not have you stranded in time again or worse."

Cate chewed her lower lip. "We need to find Jack. He's still stranded."

"I have search parties already looking for him."

"And we need to free Gertrude. I know where she is. Or when, rather. But I'm certain they will be moving her soon. We need to find both her and Jack as quickly as possible."

"We need to ensure your safety first."

"No!" Cate argued. "There's no time to lose. After what we just did, they will move Gertrude. And I'm sure they'll attempt to find Jack."

"Catherine, I will not go after either of them until I have given you the ability to protect yourself. Now, come along. This time there is no room for discussion."

Cate heaved a sigh, opening her mouth to argue. He flicked his eyebrows up. "I will not take no for an answer."

"Fine," she said with a huff, "but I fail to see how you're going to prevent this, short of never letting me out of your sight."

Marcus led her from the room, sliding his gaze sideways to her as they strode down the hall. "That can be arranged."

"That's ridiculous. I wasn't actually suggesting that."

"Have you forgotten, dear, that I have a magical menagerie at my fingertips?"

Cate snapped her gaze to him as they rounded the corner, heading for the library housing the books on magic. "Do you have something to prevent unwanted time travel?"

"No. But I have something that can return you no matter where you are."

Cate fluttered her eyelashes as he pushed the doors

open to the library and waved her inside ahead of him. "That would have been more than useful yesterday morning."

He crossed the room and opened the secret passage behind the bookcase. They descended into the darkness. Marcus lit the sconces around the massive chamber before he crossed to a shelf. He snapped open a small wooden box and retrieved the item inside. After uttering a few words Cate did not understand, he held it out to her.

"It's a button," she said, holding up the round brass object to the flickering firelight.

"A very powerful button."

"It can return me to where in time?"

"Wherever I am," Marcus said.

Cate stared down at the item laying in her palm. "Really?"

"Should you ever need me, you can return immediately to my side."

Cate stared down at it, cocking her head. "How do I use it?"

"Just a simple rub with your thumb will return you."

She closed her fingers around it and nodded. "Okay."

"Shall we try it?" Marcus asked.

Cate's heart skipped a beat, and she swallowed hard, suddenly uncomfortable being sent away alone.

"We do not need to if you prefer not to."

Cate licked her lips and slid her shoulders down her back. "I'll try."

"All right. I'm opening a portal to Dunhaven Castle in April 2019. You should arrive in your bedroom. Use the button to return here."

Cate nodded, and he stretched his hands out in front of him. "Wait," she said, tugging at his elbow.

He arched an eyebrow as he twisted to face her. "Changed your mind?"

She shook her head. "No, but you're not supposed to open time portals in the castle."

Marcus tugged a corner of his lips back and thrust his hands out again. "Mother is not home."

Cate clicked her tongue as the winds began to swirl around her. The candlelight on the sconces flickered wildly as the portal sparkled in front of him. He gave her a nod. She swallowed hard and stepped through the portal. Moments later, she appeared in what was now her bedroom.

She stepped forward, glancing around the space. She hadn't arrived at Dunhaven yet. She wouldn't for almost two months. The dog beds were missing along with her personal items.

She eased onto the edge of the bed, recalling the first moments she'd seen the room. How naive she had been then. So much had changed. The sun coming through the windows glinted off her wedding ring.

She rubbed a thumb along it before she opened her hand and studied the thick, brass button. She stood and stalked forward. "Let's see if you work."

With a rub of her thumb across the round button, the room began to disappear around her. A tingly sensation shot through her body, and she experienced the sensation of falling.

A moment later, she stood in the dimly lit magical menagerie.

Marcus smiled at her. "Welcome back."

"It worked," she said, squeezing it in her hand.

"Of course, it did. I am no amateur, Catherine." He snapped the wooden box closed and slid it back on the shelf. "Now, shall we proceed with the other matters at hand?"

Cate lifted the timepiece from around her neck and unclasped it, sliding the loop of the button through the chain before she re-clasped it and hung it around her neck.

"Yes, we should search for Jack and–"

"No," Marcus interrupted as he led her up the stairs. "We should find Gertrude first. If she is moved, we risk losing her."

"But…" Cate said, her heart sinking as they reached the library, "Jack is out there all alone."

"And I have people searching for him."

"We can't leave him here."

Marcus pushed the bookcase closed. "I am not suggesting we do. But we have to make a choice."

"Jack," Cate said.

"You are sharper than this. Think, Catherine. If we lose track of Gertrude, it may be forever."

"What about my clairvoyance? Maybe I can track her–"

"You are still learning how to use that. Let's not pin our hopes on something that may not pan out. I prefer a sure bet. And so do you. We must leave Jack behind."

CHAPTER 33

"*N*o!" she shouted, her features pinching. "We can't."

"It's not forever. We will bring him home, too, but we must take the opportunity for Gertrude before it's gone."

Cate licked her lips, pressing them together. She hated leaving Jack, but he made an excellent point. He also likely preferred to ensure the reason for their marriage ceased to exist. She only hoped he'd keep to his word to rescue Jack after they no longer needed to stay married. "You're right. As much as I hate this, you're right."

Marcus squeezed her shoulder. "We will find him, Catherine, I promise. But we must save Gertrude first before we lose the chance."

She nodded, taking solace in the words. He'd helped her find Jack once. They could do it again.

"Okay, so 1911. We need to go to the Cinderella Chateau then."

"What date?" he asked.

Heat washed over her. "I don't know. She didn't tell me."

"It's all right–"

"No, it's not!" Cate said, pressing a hand to her forehead. "We can't check every day in that year." She slid her eyes closed and stalked away, pacing the floor. "I should have known she wouldn't have given me enough information."

Marcus stopped her roaming. "Easy, Catherine, what do you remember from your visions?"

"Nothing. I couldn't remember anything until your mother hypnotized me."

"You saw the window. What was outside of it?"

Cate closed her eyes and tried to recall the vision. "I can't. It's all fuzzy." She flicked her gaze up to him, tears welling in her eyes. "I'm sorry."

"There is nothing to be sorry for, dear. We will find another way."

"Take me back to 1956," she said.

Marcus flicked his eyebrows up.

"I can try again. I can pinpoint something that can help us. At least narrow it down to the season."

"You do not need to put yourself through that."

"I want to."

"Catherine–"

"Marcus...we don't have time to waste. You said it yourself. Now, take me back to 1956, and let me try to find out where she is."

Marcus heaved a sigh as he pressed a hand against her back. "Come on."

"Where are we going?"

"I had better not open the portal in the library even if Mother isn't home."

Cate suppressed a giggle as they stepped into the hall and snaked their way to the garden. He stretched his hands in front of him once they were safely outside of the castle.

Cate licked her lips, hoping she'd be able to find some clue before it was too late. Marcus dropped his hands and twisted to face her. "That button does not work inside the portal. So, do not dally."

"Right," Cate said, pushing two pointed fingers ahead. "Straight through, no stopping."

"Exactly."

She smiled and nodded as he spun away and stretched out his hand again. Within moments, she stood in the same garden over a century later. Marcus arrived seconds after her, and they made their way to her bedroom suite.

Anna pursued the stack of papers they'd left her with. "Ah, there you are. Any luck?"

"Yes and no," Cate said, wringing her hands.

Anna tugged the reading glasses from her face and set them aside. She stood, frowning at Cate before she took hold of her hands. "What's happened?"

"We need more information," Cate answered.

"No," Anna said with a shake of her head. "Something has happened. What is it?"

"Mother, we need—"

Anna waved his comment away as she kept her eyes focused on Cate. "Marcus, go fetch tea."

Cate sucked in a breath. "That's not—"

"I shall decide what is necessary and what is not. And right now, tea is necessary. Marcus will fetch it whilst you and I have a conversation."

Marcus offered Cate an apologetic glance. She smiled at him and squeezed his hand before he strode from the room, leaving them alone.

"Now, come and tell me all about what's happened," Anna said, leading Cate to the bedroom and easing her onto the bed.

"Gertrude was not at the chateau, but we found her bracelet. She's there…just in another time. We've narrowed it down to 1911, but I need to determine if I can glean any additional details about when in 1911 she is taken there before–"

Anna held up a hand, stopping her. "Just a moment. More happened."

Cate pressed her lips together. "Not much. I–"

"Catherine, dear, you are in a dress from a completely different era. And whatever happened to you during that time has frightened you terribly. Now, what happened?"

Cate squashed her features as she struggled to control her emotions. "We…Gianna found us at the chateau. Jack and I were alone, and she sent us to 1805. In the middle of the Battle of Austerlitz." Her eyebrow arched, and she fluttered her eyelashes as she remembered the surreal experience. "I almost killed Napoleon. Oh, speaking of, did he win the battle? I'm afraid I may have changed history."

"Don't worry about that now, dear. You must have been terrified. Marcus did not take the news very well either."

"I surmised as much based on the last encounter I had with Gianna."

Anna patted her hand. "He returned here after her confession. There was no consoling him."

Cate pinched her forehead. "I assume the impending confrontation with Gianna was not something he looked forward to."

"Losing you is the thing he fears the most."

Cate flicked her gaze away from the woman, certain color rose in her cheeks at the misstatement.

Anna pushed a lock of hair behind Cate's ear. "What happened next, dear?"

Cate nodded and sniffled. "After Gianna dumped us, we managed to escape. We planned to come here and hoped to get your help to return to this time, but…"

Anna rubbed her arm. "Go on."

"The Agency found us and separated us. They took me to a house. I don't know where."

"And that is where Marcus disappeared to earlier. I figured as much."

"I'm the cause of this." Cate pressed her lips together as she rubbed her forehead. "They want Dunhaven Castle. And now Gertrude has been taken, and Jack is missing again. And Marcus is–"

"Right where he wants to be." Anna squeezed her hand and grinned.

Cate forced a weak smile onto her lips.

"Oh, Catherine, I realize this is quite difficult. The Agency is not an enemy I'd wish on anyone. They are cruel and spiteful. But Marcus will do what is necessary to protect you." She flicked her eyebrows up. "And from what I've seen you make quite a formidable adversary for his enemies. It is quite refreshing how devoted to each other you are."

Cate swallowed hard at the words. She blinked a few times before he changed the subject. "We had to leave Jack somewhere in 1805. We cannot waste a minute in retrieving Gertrude before they move her again."

"I understand. How trying, though I assure you Marcus will not rest until both are found."

Cate pressed her lips together as she considered it. She could understand his reasoning to find Gertrude. But Jack? He had no motivation to retrieve her friend.

"He would do anything for you, Catherine. Do not fret."

Cate forced another smile and nodded. He must have really laid it on thick with his mother about their marriage. The truth would crush her. But she had larger things to worry about.

"I need to try the bracelet again."

"I had an idea about that. You're still struggling to make sense of the visions even with our strategies. But what if you touch the bracelet again, and then I hypnotize you? You were able to detect things using that strategy the last time."

Cate sucked in a breath, her fake smile turning genuine. "Yes. Okay."

"Excellent. Then we shall use that tactic for now."

"For now?" Cate asked, crinkling her brow.

"Well, yes," Anna said as she rose and retrieved Gertrude's bracelet. "We will continue our work after you have settled this matter. It may even be easier given that your nerves should be somewhat settled. At least, I hope so. But if I know The Agency, they will not allow you much downtime."

Marcus returned with a maid scurrying behind him carrying a tray of tea. "Ah, here is the tea. Let's have a sip before we begin."

"Oh," Cate started.

Anna cupped her chin. "It will settle your nerves, dear."

"I could use that," she answered with a sigh as Anna passed her a steam cup. She inhaled the aroma and took a drink. She let the warm liquid wash over her tongue and tried to let her muscles relax.

Anna flicked her gaze to her son. "Marcus, may I have a word with you?"

"Now is not the best time," he said, pouring a cup of tea and handing it to her.

Anna accepted it, her eyes unwavering. She raised her eyebrows toward her hairline.

Marcus took a sip from the cup he had poured for himself before he settled it back into its saucer. "Of course, Mother."

"Excuse us, Catherine, we won't be more than a moment. Enjoy your tea, dear, and try to relax."

Cate sipped at the warm drink again as they stepped from the room. She sighed as she considered the task ahead of her. She would be better prepared for it this time. Even if she became lost during her hypnosis, she knew how to come back.

She could do this. She would do it. She had to. Her mind wandered to the conversation occurring beyond her doors. What had Anna wanted to speak to Marcus about? A cold sweat beaded on her brow. Had she realized their marriage was fake? Had Cate tipped her off somehow?

The opening door interrupted any further thoughts. Marcus and Anna strode back in.

Anna set her saucer on the tray. "Shall we begin?"

Cate passed her teacup back to Anna and nodded. She lifted the lid on her music box, flicking a glance at the purple rose in its glass case. She conjured the future memory she'd had when she touched it.

Holding it in her mind, she swung her legs onto the bed and settled into the pillows.

"Are you ready?" Anna asked.

"Yes," Cate answered with a nod.

"Not too long. You must have the energy for the hypnosis after."

"I understand," she said, holding her palm out for the bracelet.

Anna dangled it from her fingers. "Good luck." She dropped it into Cate's palm. The cold metal smacked onto her skin and images began to form.

They fluttered through her mind faster than she could process. Her breathing turned labored, and tension formed at her temples. She tried to focus on the images as they rushed past.

The memories slowed, and she focused on one vision. Gertrude sat in the yellow room. Her head hung down to her chest. Voices rambled in another language. A piano played a song. She tried to focus on it when voices shouted over it.

The pain in her temples became blinding. If only she

could spot one more detail. She flicked her increasingly blurry gaze to the window. With a flutter of her eyelashes, she tried to clear her vision, but the task proved impossible. Blackness crept from the edges of the room until it consumed her.

She snapped her eyes open with a gasp.

"You did quite well that time," Anna said as she hovered over her.

"I don't feel like I did well. I didn't get any additional details that can help us."

"But did you get any additional details overall?"

Cate squashed her eyebrows together. "Yes, I think so. More details than the blurry images."

"Then you have improved," Anna said as she dangled a medallion in front of her. "Now, let's try the hypnosis to clarify some of those details further."

Cate nodded and settled into the pillows, focusing on the sparkling gold pendant as Anna swung it back and forth.

After a few seconds, her eyelids grew heavy and her muscles relaxed. When Anna finished her countdown, her eyes drifted closed.

When she opened them again, she found herself in her sitting room. She smiled as she recognized the warm future memory the rose had shown her.

A moan emanated from behind her. She snapped her gaze toward it before she pulled the doors open. Blackness yawned in front of her.

"Catherine," Anna's voice echoed overhead. "Can you find the vision of Gertrude?"

"I'm trying," Cate said. "I'm searching through the darkness."

"Remember when you find it to focus on some clue about the date."

Cate stepped into the black hall with a nod. "Okay."

She crept forward until the warm light from her suite disappeared. She glanced over her shoulder, resisting the urge to turn and run back to safety. She needed information. With her shoulders squared, she continued forward until she struck something. She explored it with her fingertips.

The picture frame molding ran up the plaster wall. "I'm close. I feel the molding I ran into the last time."

"Good, Catherine. Excellent."

Cate pressed her fingers against the wall and used it to guide her. She reached the corner. Light bloomed from an open door. "I see light."

She moved toward it and peered into the room. Gertrude sat in the middle of the room, tied to a chair.

"I found her."

"What do you see, Catherine? Can you tell the season through the window?"

Cate flicked her gaze to the window. "It's snowing. It's winter."

"Good," Anna answered her. "Now, come back."

"No," Cate said, shuffling further into the room. "I can find more. There was music and a voice. I'll try for more."

"Be careful, Catherine. You do not want to become lost again. Keep in contact with me."

Cate continued around the room, approaching the limp form of Gertrude again. She knelt in front of her. "Gertrude? Can you hear me?"

She pushed the dirty blonde hair from the woman's face, cupping her chin. "Gertrude?"

The woman moaned in response, but she did not open her eyes. From the door, music floated into the room. Cate furrowed her brow as the piano music continued.

"Christmas. Someone is playing Christmas music."

"That's excellent, Catherine. Excellent work. Now, come back."

"Wait, there's something else. They're speaking again." Cate inched back toward the door. "They're speaking French. I can't understand it."

She licked her lips, closing her eyes as she tried to pick out any words. She recognized two. It was all she needed. A smile spread across her face. "I know what date this is. I know where to go."

"That's excellent, Catherine," Anna said. "Now, make your way to your safe place, and I'll bring you back."

Cate nodded and took a step toward the door when it slammed shut in front of her. She stumbled back a step, her lips parting as she stared at it.

"Catherine? Have you made it?"

"No," she answered. "The door is closed."

Cate hurried toward it and twisted the knob pulling on it. It didn't budge. "I can't open it. I'm trapped."

"It's all right. It doesn't matter. I'll bring you back from where you are."

"Okay," Cate agreed. Anna's voice echoed overhead, informing her that when she snapped her fingers Cate would awaken.

The countdown progressed. Anna finished it. The sound of fingers snapping reverberated around the room. But Cate did not leave.

She stood in the center with an unconscious Gertrude.

"Anna? I'm stuck. That didn't work."

Cate dug her fingernails into her palm as she flexed her fists. "Anna?"

She received no answer. "Anna? Hello?" she called again.

No one responded. She spun in a slow circle, realizing she was trapped.

CHAPTER 34

"*H*ello?" Cate called again into the silence.

Anna's voice no longer guided her. She had been cut off from all communication. She remained stuck inside her mind.

"Anna? Marcus?" she shouted.

She wrapped her fingers around the doorknob again and twisted it. It didn't budge. She banged against it with a fist, jiggling the handle as she tried to force it open.

"I'm stuck," she said, her voice laden with panic as she pressed her back against the door. "If you can hear me, I'm stuck. I can't get out."

She left the door behind and crossed to the window. She peered outside, finding nothing beyond it. "What happened to the outside?"

Blackness surrounded her. She spun to face the room again. Her heart skipped a beat as she stared at the now-empty chair in the room's middle. "Gertrude?"

The woman no longer sat in the room. The yellow walls darkened, beginning to turn black on the top and bottom.

Cate pressed her fingertips to her temples as tightness

twisted them. She squeezed her eyes closed. "Go back," she told herself. "Leave."

"I don't think so," a new voice said.

Cate snapped her eyes open. Gianna sashayed from a dark corner. In the shadows, the red gash on her face appeared even more menacing. Cate went stiff, squeezing her palms into fists again.

"You are stuck here, mouse."

"I'm not a mouse," Cate answered through clenched teeth.

"Oh, but you are," Gianna said as she sauntered closer. "You're such a nothing. A nobody. You may as well be stuck here. You're useless."

She circled around Cate as she continued her taunting. "You got away from me, but I am working on something bigger. Something you won't get away from."

She stopped as the finished her loop, pressing closer to Cate. "Something that will destroy you and your Duke."

"I'll never let you have Dunhaven Castle."

Gianna threw her head back with a laugh. "Never say never, Cate. I have plans for you that may change your mind."

Cate scowled at her, throwing her shoulders back. "No."

"Don't be so quick to reply. You've yet to see the true power of The Agency. And you've yet to see the lengths I'll go to in order to crush you. You'll wish you had given in long ago when I'm finished."

"And you don't know how far I'll go to protect my friends."

Gianna arched an eyebrow as she circled in the opposite direction. "Oh? Does that include your husband? Because I doubt he'll go that far for you."

Cate bit her lower lip.

"No answer?" Gianna completed her arc and set her hands on her hips. "Aww, poor mouse. She's just realizing how right I am. Tell me, what are you going to do when he drops you? You can't win alone."

Heat washed over Cate as the words stung. She'd face this situation soon enough. Likely as soon as they found Gertrude. Which they couldn't do until she found a way out of her own mind.

Cate glanced around the room again in search of an exit.

"There's nowhere to go, Cate. You're here all alone with me." Gianna laughed at her again. "Maybe we'll win out sooner rather than later."

Cate hurried across the room to the door and tugged at it again. It wouldn't budge.

"There's no way out. Poor Cate. She's trapped in her own mind."

A wave of panic washed over Cate as she wrapped her arms around her midriff. Her eyes settled on the window. Blackness lay beyond it. But was there also a way out?

She crossed to it and tried the latch, finding it stuck.

"Oops, that won't work either."

Cate took a few steps back from the glass. She backed into the wooden chair Gertrude had occupied moments ago, sending it screeching across the parquet. Her eyebrows furrowed as she placed a hand against the back.

She flicked her gaze back to the window.

"Have a seat, Cate. Take a load off. You're stuck."

"Not if I can help it," she answered, grabbing hold of the chair. She hurled it toward the window. It smacked into the pane, cracking it.

Gianna studied her blood-red nails as she cackled again. "Oh, the little mouse roars again. Too bad. Still not working."

Cate retrieved the chair as it clattered back to the floor and tried again. The crack in the glass widened. She lifted the wooden object a third time and smashed it into the pane. The glass broke away, leaving sharp shards stuck.

A burst of icy air swept inside the broken window. Cate held her arms up against it as it tossed her hair wildly. Bits of glass dislodged as the gusts grew stronger. She collapsed to the floor, covering her head with her hands as the assault continued.

Gianna's laughter stopped, replaced by a gurgle. Cate risked a glance, finding the large fragment of the razor-sharp glass poking from Gianna's abdomen. She shot Cate a shocked glance before she slipped to the floor.

The wind continued to pound, shoving her limp form into a wall. The yellow-black barriers began to melt. Cate squeezed her eyes closed again as dust and debris floated around the room, carried by the gale-force winds.

A voice called to her, but she couldn't hear it over the clamor. The voice called again as the wind came to a sudden stop.

Cate fluttered her eyes open.

"There you are," Anna said with a smile as she stroked Cate's hair.

Cate sucked in a sharp breath as she forced a nod and reached for Marcus's hand. "I made it." She tried to sit up, but Anna eased her back.

"No, not yet. Rest a moment."

"I'm okay." She flicked her gaze to Marcus. "I know the date. We should go."

"You can rest for a moment. Then we'll go."

"How do you feel?" Anna asked as she poured Cate another cup of tea.

"Okay, I'm just…confused," she answered as she accepted the saucer and sipped from the cup.

"About the visions?"

Cate shook her head. "Why do I get stuck? In both instances, I've gotten stuck."

"As I said, we've never used hypnosis to clarify clairvoyant visions. I'd wager it's one of two things. Either your mind is trying to show you something else, something it considers more vital than what you are seeking."

"Or?" Cate asked.

"Or there is some sticking point that blocks you from returning. A fear reaction, for example."

Cate pinched her eyebrows together.

"It may help to know what happens when you are stuck."

Cate shimmied up higher on the bed. "The door closed, and I got stuck. Gertrude disappeared. The walls started to turn black." She shifted her gaze to Marcus before sliding her eyes back to Anna. "Gianna came."

Anna drummed her fingers against her teacup. "Heavens, it could be either. Given your tumultuous relationship with that woman, you may have some fear of encountering her."

"Or your mind may be trying to show you a future threat," Marcus said.

Cate set her teacup on the saucer and slid it onto the night table. "We should go. I know what date. December 20, 1911."

Marcus stood and stalked to the end of the bed. "All right. I will retrieve her."

"What? No!" Cate shot up to sit and swung her legs over the bed. "I'm going, too."

"That is not necessary. You should rest. I will handle this."

"Definitely not. You are not going alone. No way."

Marcus heaved a sigh. "Catherine, I will be fine. I think Mother will agree you should rest."

Anna rose from her seat and waved her hands in the air. "Don't use me as your excuse, darling. This is between you and Catherine." Anna approached and pinched his chin. "And if it's all the same to you, I'd prefer her to go. I don't like the idea of you heading to an Agency stronghold alone."

Cate raised her eyebrows at him and offered a triumphant smile. "Let's go, dear."

Marcus huffed and took her hand. "I cannot believe you two continue to band together to defeat me."

They wound through the castle toward the garden. "You shouldn't go alone. She knows that. And I know that."

"I am perfectly capable of retrieving a woman from captivity."

Cate stepped into the bright sunshine. "I'm certain you are. But you shouldn't do it alone. And you don't have to." She offered him a smile.

The corners of his lips turned up before he let go of her hand and stretched his out. "Ready?"

She nodded. He opened the portal, and they traveled to the French Chateau in 1911.

Cate shivered as she arrived in the cold. Snow fell around her, and she wrapped her arms around her midriff. Marcus arrived a moment later. He removed his jacket and draped it around her arms.

"Thanks," she said, thrusting her arms through the sleeves and wrapping tighter in the folds of fabric as they stalked to the front door.

"Stay behind me."

"With your track record with The Agency maybe you should stay behind me."

Marcus shot her a glance, and she grinned at him. "I will never live down these instances, will I?"

"No. I feel pretty good about rescuing you twice," she said as they stepped into the empty house.

"Do you think anyone is here? In my visions, I heard things."

"It appears not," Marcus said as he scanned the rooms.

"Can you see through walls?"

He shot her a confused glance. "No."

"Oh, it would have been convenient."

"Sorry to disappoint," he said, leading her past a doorway as he peered inside.

"It's okay. I'll forgive you."

"The house seems empty," Marcus said after a glance into another room.

"Should we head up to the room?"

"I don't like this."

"You think it's a trap?" Cate inquired as they stared up the stairs leading to the second story.

Marcus narrowed his eyes. "I don't know, but I want you to stay close to me."

Cate looped her arm through his and nodded. Together, they climbed the stairs. Marcus glanced down both sides of the hall before he inched toward the room where they'd found Gertrude's bracelet in 1956.

Cate swallowed hard, tightening her grip on his arm as she glanced up at him.

He stopped. "Do you sense something?"

She shook her head. "No."

He tugged his arm from her grip and slid it around her shoulders, pulling her closer to him. She leaned into his chest as they approached the yellow room. They crept toward the partially open door. Cate peered in through the crack. A woman sat slumped in a chair in the room's center.

"There she is."

Marcus held her back. "Wait."

Cate's heart thudded as she stared at the woman. So close, yet still so far. She pressed her lips together as Marcus reached for the door. It creaked on its hinges as he pushed it open. Cate held her breath as she scanned the room, then flicked her gaze to him.

He nodded, and they proceeded inside. Cate hurried toward Gertrude and knelt in front of her. "Gertrude?"

She pressed two fingers to the woman's neck. "She has a pulse."

She glanced down at the ties around her wrist before she tugged at them. "We need to get her out of here."

Marcus crossed to the window and peered out before he approached Cate. With a touch, he burned away the rope holding Gertrude. She flopped forward, nearly toppling out of the chair before Cate righted her.

"Do you think she'll be okay?"

"She is likely drugged. We can take her to Rosenberg to assess her before returning her to Dunhaven."

Cate nodded as she stood. Footsteps sounded in the hall. Cate snapped her head toward them as Marcus tugged her back and shoved her behind him.

"Well, well, well," Gianna said as she strode stiffly into the room, "if it isn't our little mouse who could roar."

CHAPTER 35

*M*arcus wrapped an arm around Cate and reached for Gertrude.

"I wouldn't do that if I were you," Elliott said before he could touch her.

Marcus flicked his eyebrows up in question. "I don't see why not. We've won."

He pressed a hand against the woman as he held Cate tightly. She expected to disappear from the room and reappear in Rosenberg, but they remained at Cinderella Chateau. Marcus's brow furrowed slightly.

"She's laced with anti-magic powder," Gianna said. "If you touch her, you're rendered powerless for a few moments."

"I tried to warn you," Elliott said. "But you did not listen. As you did not earlier, Duchess."

Cate glared at him as he stepped toward the window and stared outside. "Though despite all that, I am quite glad to have this opportunity to speak again."

Gianna offered a less-than-impressed glance at him as she settled her arms over her chest. "I'd rather just kill you and be done with it."

Elliott twisted and wagged a finger at her. "Gianna."

"Is that not your plan?" Cate questioned.

"It is not. Your earlier escape coupled with the coup you pulled at Eldinbury Castle only makes me want you in our fold more. Between your husband's power and your resourcefulness, you'd make quite a strong addition to the team."

"I think not," Marcus answered.

"Let's let the past be the past, shall we? Surely, we can find a way to work together toward a common goal."

"There are no goals The Agency has that Catherine and I wish to be a part of."

"Are you going to let him speak for you?" Gianna asked Cate.

"I agree completely with his statement."

"Do you?" she asked as she sauntered around the room. "Are you certain? Perhaps you'd like to reconsider. It is likely you who will suffer the most in this war."

Cate lifted her chin and sucked in a breath. "I am certain."

"I guess stranding you in 1805 wasn't severe enough. Don't worry, I'll find something that is."

"Is there really no way to convince you?" Elliott asked.

"None," Marcus assured him.

"I wouldn't be so sure. People can do all sorts of things when they are pushed to their limits," Gianna taunted.

Elliott spun to face them, his hands clasped behind his back. He sighed and shook his head. "I suppose then, there is nothing left to do here. Go ahead, Gianna, finish her."

Gianna lifted her skirt and withdrew a knife from her boot.

"No!" Cate shouted, tearing herself away from Marcus and standing between Gianna and Gertrude.

Gianna's lips curled into a smile. "Oh, you've made this

easy." She reached out and grabbed hold of Cate's wrist, flicking a finger across the ring she wore on her right hand.

The room disappeared from sight, replaced by a barren landscape lit only by a cold winter sun.

"Welcome to the 1600s, Cate. Have fun. Ta!" Gianna backed a step away, waving a hand at her as she giggled and disappeared.

Cate scrunched her nose as she fished the timepiece from under her dress. The button dangled on the chain next to it. With an annoyed sigh, she grabbed it and rubbed a finger across it. She reappeared in the room next to Marcus as he launched a fireball at Elliott.

"Ah, there you are, dear. Just in time."

"What?" Gianna questioned as Marcus tossed a fireball at her, knocking the knife from her hand. It skittered across the floor, landing in a dark corner as she cried out from the sting.

She wrinkled her nose and set her jaw, diving at Cate again. They disappeared from the room and reappeared in a new location.

"Let's try the 1500s and see if that sticks." Gianna shoved her back a few steps before she disappeared.

Cate shook her head, scrunching her features as she used the button to return to Marcus. "That's becoming tedious."

"Why are you back?" Gianna growled through clenched teeth as she dove toward Cate again.

They disappeared for a third time. When they reappeared in their new location, Gianna shoved Cate backward. She stumbled a few steps before plopping on the ground. "Perhaps 1743 will suit you better."

She disappeared again, leaving Cate in the middle of another time period. With a grumble, she climbed to her feet and returned to 1911.

"Really, you should stop this, Gianna," Marcus said as he

pinned Elliott against the wall with a beam of light. "You can't win."

"I'm not a quitter," she said, reaching for Cate again. Marcus shot a fireball her way, and she danced backward away from it.

Cate narrowed her eyes at the woman before she reached for her. "My turn." She slid the ring from a still-stunned Gianna's finger and flicked a finger across it. The room faded, replaced by a field overlooking a small town. Cate stepped away from her. "Welcome to Spain circa 1492."

She rubbed her hand across the button and snapped back to the room with Marcus. Elliott gasped out a breath as Marcus let up on his assault.

"Catherine? Are you all right?"

"Yes," she said, tugging the ring from her finger and placing it in his palm. "You can add this to your collection. Now you have two time-travel devices."

"Where is Gianna?" Elliott gasped.

Cate flicked her gaze to Marcus. "Did she tell you where I was?"

The corners of Marcus's lips curled up. "No."

"Then I won't tell you," she said to Elliott. "Open the time portal. Let's go home."

"You can't," Elliott said with a groan as he tried to climb to his feet. Marcus dropped him back to his knees with a small fireball. "You can't touch her and open it. You're stuck. Stranded here with only conventional means to travel."

"Open the portal," Cate said as she tugged Gertrude up to stand. "I'll take her through myself."

"There's too much danger of you becoming stuck inside."

"Then location hop to Rosenberg, and I'll follow with this," she said, dangling the button on the chain.

"I will not leave you alone with him."

Cate sucked in a breath and stared at him. "We have to do something. Can I get rid of the anti-magic stuff?"

"I am beginning to understand why you married her," Elliott said as he used the windowsill to climb to his feet.

Cate shook her head at the man.

"I would suggest you take your leave, Elliott. We are finished here." Marcus lifted the man from his feet and tossed him out the door before slamming it shut.

Cate followed the man as he flew by before she flicked her gaze back to Marcus. "Now what? We have to do something."

"There is no good option," Marcus answered.

"Well, we have to pick the best option," Cate answered, tapping her foot on the floor. "We can't leave her here."

"Yes, I know, but I am not willing to risk your safety to take her. You cannot carry her through the entire portal, and I will not leave you here alone."

"I can do it. Just give me a little extra time before you come through."

"Catherine–"

"Marcus, there is no other choice. We have to–" Cate dropped Gertrude into the chair and grabbed her forehead.

"Catherine? Are you all right?"

Images flashed in front of her again as she groaned and sucked in a sharp breath. "Yes. I'm fine, but I'm having another vision."

Marcus pressed his lips into a thin line. "We cannot stay here much longer."

Cate squeezed her eyes closed for a moment before she righted herself. "The time portal is the best option. Just hold it open long enough for me to get through with her."

Marcus shook his head. "I don't like this, Catherine."

"Neither do I. In fact, I'm a little worried, but there isn't another option. And I trust you."

He narrowed his eyes at her as he outstretched his arms. "Flattery will get you nowhere."

"Seems like it got me a portal back to Rosenberg Palace," she said with a cheeky grin.

He clicked his tongue at her. "Be careful, Catherine. One slip—"

"I know," she said as she tugged Gertrude up and slipped her arms around her chest.

The winds began to whip in the room as the portal opened. Cate glanced over her shoulder at the black opening. She dragged Gertrude backward into the darkness.

The absence of light surrounded her for far longer than she was used to. She bit into her lower lip as she hauled the limp woman through the portal. She continued backward, worrying that she might be stuck when warmth finally heated her back.

She twisted, squinting at the bright sunshine overhead when she stepped into the garden. She dragged Gertrude back a few more steps away from the portal and laid her on the lawn.

With a press of her two fingers to the woman's throat, she detected a pulse. Cate blew out a sigh of relief and turned to eye the portal. Where was Marcus? Another moment passed, and she rose to her feet. Still nothing.

Her heart pounded harder as the portal continued to swirl. She clasped her hands, wringing them. A moment later, he stepped through and the portal snapped shut behind him.

She heaved another sigh. "There you are."

"I wanted to leave you plenty of time."

"I had more than enough time. Then I started to worry you weren't coming."

"How is she?" Marcus asked as he dropped to a knee next to Gertrude.

"Her pulse is still weak, but she seems okay."

"We'll have Mother look at her," Marcus said as he scooped Gertrude into his arms.

Cate followed him inside. "I'll find your mother."

"Tell her we are in the crystal room."

Cate nodded as they parted ways. She hurried through the halls and down the main stairs, pushing into the sitting room. Anna sipped tea as she continued to peruse The Agency's properties.

"Catherine," she said with a flick of her eyebrows toward her hairline. "Is everything all right? Did you find Gertrude?"

"Yes. She's been drugged. Could you have a look?"

"Of course," Anna said as she slid the saucer onto the coffee table. "Did you run into any trouble?"

Cate swallowed hard and fluttered her eyelashes as they strode into the foyer. "A little. You can always count on Gianna to make trouble."

Anna stopped on the first step and grabbed Cate's hand. "Are you all right?"

"Yes," Cate said with a nod, "we are both fine. I..."

"Yes? What happened? Did she harm you?"

"I stranded her in 1492."

Anna slid her head forward as her jaw fell open. "You did what?"

"I know I shouldn't have, but–"

"But nothing. Bravo, Catherine. You really are quite clever. I am so pleased with Marcus's choice in you."

Heat rose in Cate's cheeks as Ana tugged her up the stairs. She changed the course of the conversation. "They're in the crystal room."

Anna pulled her along through the halls before she pushed into a bedroom. Gertrude lay on the bed as Marcus stared out the window.

"Careful," he said as they entered, "she is covered in anti-magic powder."

Anna's eyebrows shot up. "I suppose that explains some of what I've heard about your trip to rescue her."

Cate crossed to him, slipping her hand in his as Anna assessed Gertrude.

"Mother, perhaps gloves would be appropriate."

She fluttered her hand at him. "I am not planning on doing magic in the next quarter of an hour."

Anna peeled up an eyelid and studied the pupil. "Would you care to share how you stranded Gianna in the 1400s, Catherine?"

Marcus arched an eyebrow. "Is that where you put her?"

"Yes. She kept using that ring to dump me in various times and locations. I finally got it off her hand and stuck her in the 1400s."

"Excellent work. She is undoubtedly resourceful enough that she will find her way back. She is like a cat," Marcus answered.

Anna straightened and faced them. "Gertrude is merely asleep. I'll remove the anti-magic and monitor her. You two should go back for Mr. Reid."

Cate crinkled her forehead.

"She will be fine here. Go find your friend, dear."

Cate grabbed her mother-in-law's hand and squeezed. "Thank you."

Anna kissed her cheek and pulled her into an embrace. "Be careful, dear." She flicked her gaze to Marcus. "Take care of her."

"Always," Marcus answered as he took Cate's hand in his and led her from the room.

Cate blew out a breath as they snaked through the halls for yet another trip to the past. "I hope we find him quickly. Then this whole mess can be over."

Marcus offered no comment until the stepped into the garden. "Ready?"

She nodded, and he opened the portal. They arrived in the same garden over a century earlier and entered the castle. "Why don't you wait–"

"No," Cate said with a shake of her head.

Marcus drew in a breath as he considered his response.

"I'm not going to wait in my bedroom. You said you had people looking for him. When can we expect to hear from them?"

"I returned us to a few moments before Stefano is due back. He should meet us in the sitting room."

"Okay, let's go." Cate led the way down the hall as Marcus hesitated. She spun to face him. "You coming?"

"Catherine, I think you should wait for me to discuss this with Stefano and then we'll–"

"No. You can't cut me out of the information. We've discussed this."

He closed the gap between them and slid a lock of hair behind her ear. "I don't wish you to be upset."

She furrowed her brow. "Upset?" Her eyes grew wide, and tears stung them. "You think…"

"With any luck, he has been found. If not, we will find him. But there is no need for you to know the details of it if you find it worrisome."

She set her jaw and blinked her tears away. "I'll be fine."

She took a step away from him before she twisted to face him again. "We'll find him, right? You promised."

He offered her a half-smile. "I did. And I always keep my promises."

She returned his expression and slid her hand into his. They made their way downstairs to the sitting room. Stefano paced the space, already awaiting them.

"News?" Marcus asked as he strode inside.

Stefano clutched at his hat. "There's a problem."

Cate's heart sank, and her stomach turned.

"I do not like to hear those words," Marcus answered as he stalked to the drink cart and poured two brandies. He handed one to Cate before he took a sip of his own. "What is it?"

"He's gone."

Cate stiffened at the words.

Marcus slipped an arm around her and rubbed her shoulder. "Explain."

"We searched near where you told us. We found the horses. But no Reid. He's gone." The man winced as he raised his eyes to Marcus. "He's gone."

CHAPTER 36

"What?" Cate questioned, her eyes wide. "What do you mean he's gone? He can't be gone."

She snapped her gaze to Marcus, her features pinching as she stared at him.

"We'll find him," Marcus said, rubbing her shoulder.

"How? I'd like to believe that, but..." She pressed a hand to her forehead as her features pinched. "How?"

Marcus tugged her brandy glass from her hand and set it on a side table before guiding her to the sofa. "Sit down, dear." He offered her the glass again. "We will find him."

Cate popped up a moment later, the liquid in the glass sloshing wildly enough to nearly spill over the top. "Again, I ask how? What if he's gone? What if The Agency took him again? What if they moved him to another time period?"

"Catherine, you are panicking over what may be nothing. The Agency seemed fully interested in you alone. I doubt they bothered with Mr. Reid after they abandoned him."

"Then where is he, Marcus?"

"Wandering. Perhaps the horses got away from him whilst he slept."

Cate's shoulders slumped, and she collapsed onto the sofa. "Oh, Jack."

Marcus rubbed a hand across her back. "We will find him, Catherine." He cut his gaze to Stefano. "You checked the area near the horses?"

"In a fairly wide radius. Nothing."

Cate groaned, letting her head fall into her hand.

"Do you have the horses?"

Stefano nodded. "We brought them back with us. Why?"

"They may offer us some clue. Take me to them."

Cate rose to her feet.

"You wait here," Marcus said.

"No, I want to go."

"Catherine, there is no need. You are upset. I can look over the horses myself."

Cate slammed the brandy glass onto the side table. "I'm going, too."

Marcus fluttered his eyelashes. "All right. Come along."

Stefano led the group from the room to the stables, speaking to one of the stablehands who showed them to two stalls with the horses.

Cate stared at the steed that had carried her through the battle before she moved on to the next one. "This was Jack's."

"Where are the saddles?" Marcus asked the stablehand.

He pointed to them, and Marcus squatted to study them. Cate looked them over from above while petting the horse's nose. "Nothing is missing. None of the weapons. Nothing."

She pressed a hand against her head again. "He's out there with nothing."

Marcus heaved a sigh as he rose to stand. Cate reached for the saddle to double-check the weapons. Her hand swept across the fastener, and a rushed image formed in her mind. She snapped her hand back.

"Catherine? What is it?"

"There's something on the saddle that's giving me a vision." She dropped to her knees and reached for it again.

"Careful, Catherine. We do not want you to overdo it."

"This could be Jack's life."

He squatted down, knocking her hand away. "I understand, but it does us no good if you are unconscious and cannot communicate anything about his location."

Cate sat back on her heels as he searched the saddle. He tugged a scrap of fabric from the clasp and held it up.

"It must be a piece of his uniform. Well, his stolen uniform. I hope that doesn't matter."

"It seems your visions are tied to people you care for, so I would highly doubt it's about a random French soldier. It must relate to Mr. Reid."

Cate reached for it, and he tugged it away. "Do not overdo it."

She nodded. "I won't. But we need a clue."

Marcus set the shred of fabric in her palm. Images began to form in her mind, racing past as she tried to focus on any details. They rushed past too quickly for her to make sense of. The tension built at her temples. She dropped the fabric before she passed out, gasping for breath.

"Anything?"

She shook her head as a lump formed in her throat. "It was too fast. I'll try again."

"No," Marcus said, grabbing the fabric piece before she could. "You cannot try again yet. You'll exhaust yourself and find nothing."

"We don't have time for this," she said, clenching her fists.

"What we do not have time for is you to pass out trying to find him. The search will stall, and we will waste precious time."

Cate's face fell as she realized he was correct. "Maybe your mother can hypnotize me."

"That would be an option if I knew where exactly my mother was at the moment."

"You don't know?"

Marcus rose to stand. "She is traveling. She could be anywhere."

Cate pounded a fist against the ground. "You hypnotize me."

"Hypnosis is not one of my many skills."

Cate buried her face in her hands. "We have to do something."

"Let's return to the palace and discuss our options." He offered her his hand. She heaved a sigh before she accepted it and climbed to her feet. Tears stung her eyes as they returned to the castle and pushed inside.

"You should–"

"Don't even say rest. I can't rest. I have to keep trying."

"Catherine," Marcus began with a sigh, "you cannot continue this until you pass out or worse."

She pressed a hand against his lapel. "Trying in the stables was probably a terrible idea. I can do better. I just need to relax and remember my happy memory. And my music box would be nice."

"I will retrieve it for you."

Cate nodded as he stepped away. She grabbed his elbow before he took another step and winced. "And my rose."

He smiled at her. "Of course, dear. I won't be but a moment."

Cate offered a fleeting smile before he strode away before she wrung her hands as she paced the floor. She made two passes before her nervous energy drove her to the upstairs library. She pushed into the room and crossed to the book with information on her condition.

She pulled it open as she wandered to the desk, skimming

the information in search of best practices or tips she could use to make the process easier.

Her finger traced the words as she whispered them aloud. "Remaining calm and relaxed when the visions press in is vital to information processing. Yeah, right. Easier said than done."

She continued to scan down the page. "Beginner clairvoyants often find visions painful as their mind attempts to block them. Even happy memories can be taxing on them. With practice, visions can become less frenzied."

She let her hand thud against the desk. "Yes, but how much practice? And how can I make it less painful?"

She flipped the page in search of more information. "Reminding oneself of happy memories, in particular, happy future memories can ease the pain of visions. When the visions push in, forcing your mind to turn to a happy vision can slow them and make processing easier."

Cate raised her eyes from the book and stared into space. She had one happy vision she could use. In her hypnosis, it was her safe place. Would it matter if the event would never occur?

The doors creaked open and Marcus strode inside. "I thought I may find you here."

"I was looking for more information to help with my visions."

"I expected nothing less," he said with a smile as he crossed to her. "Are you ready to try again?"

"Yes," she said as she slammed the book shut. "Did you get both the music box and the rose?"

"I did, yes. I put them in your room."

"Okay. Let's see if I can make sense of any of these visions."

They traversed the halls to the sapphire room. Cate pushed inside, finding her music box and her rose on the nightstand. She studied them as she eased onto the bed and opened the lid of the piano. Tinkling music filled the room. She lifted the glass off the top of the display case and grabbed the rose.

Her fingers caressed the petals, and she slid her eyes closed. Memories floated by as tension built at her temples. She sought the one clear memory she'd conjured previously. It floated by and her mind slowed. The tension released in her temples.

She opened her eyes as the vision continued. She'd managed to control this one. Could she do it again with the fabric scrap?

With a reluctant sigh, she returned the rose to its case and slid the glass over it. She settled back into the pillows and held out her hand. "Okay, I'm ready."

"Do not push too far. You can try again later if you must." He dangled the fabric over her upturned palm before he dropped it into her hand.

Memories rushed past and tension built in her as she struggled to make sense of them. Images stormed through her mind. She tried to find the happy memory. She forced her mind to search for it. Pain built across her forehead. She fought to ignore it, searching for one detail that could lead them to Jack.

Loud noise deafened her as she sought information. She gritted her teeth as the pain ramped up. The visions stopped suddenly, and everything went black.

She snapped her eyes open and shifted her gaze to Marcus. "You're pushing too far," he said as he slid the fabric into his pocket. "Did you see anything we can work from?"

She shook her head. "It went too fast. I heard something like thunder, but I couldn't make out what it was."

She slammed her fists against the bed. "Okay, let me try again."

"Absolutely not," he answered. "You must wait longer."

"We don't have time to wait," Cate insisted. "I can try again."

"Catherine, this is not a discussion. You will wait." He settled into the chair next to her bed.

She collapsed back into the pillows with a sigh, drumming her fingers against the bed. She banged her head into the soft pillow. "Just let me try again."

"No. You will not convince me. Why don't we have tea?"

Cate huffed as he pulled the cord on the wall to summon the servants. "Tea is not going to help."

"Tea always helps. Ask Mother."

"Millions of Americans would disagree."

"Too bad you married a Brit," he said with a cheeky grin. The maid hurried inside and Marcus requested tea. She curtsied before she scurried from the room, returning shortly after with a tray.

Cate sipped the warm liquid as anxiety built in her. She polished off the drink in a few sips and slid the saucer onto her nightstand. "Okay, I'm done. Let me try again."

"I have barely taken one sip, Catherine."

"I can't help that you're a slow tea drinker."

"Tea is meant to be enjoyed not inhaled." He poured her another cup and handed the saucer to her.

She snatched it from him and sipped it. "Happy?"

"Infinitely," he answered.

She sucked in a breath, taking another sip and forcing the warm liquid down as she waited to try again. Her muscles relaxed, and her apprehension eased. Perhaps Marcus was right about the tea.

He finished his cup, and she took the last sips of hers.

"How are you feeling, dear?" he asked as he set their saucers on the tray.

She fluttered her eyelashes and yawned. "Tired."

"Perhaps you should sleep before we try again."

"No, I–" she said as she struggled to keep her eyes open. The music box played as she let her head fall back into the pillows. "Maybe just a few minutes."

Her eyes slid shut and blackness replaced her view of the room. Music droned on, sounding further and further away until she slipped to sleep.

* * *

Images floated past her as she stood in a dark space. "Hello?" she called out, her voice echoing off the emptiness.

Loud noises whisked by along with more blurry visions. "Where am I?"

She tried to make sense of the things that scurried along but she failed.

"These are visions," she said to herself. "I need to see them."

She chewed her lower lip, attempting to make the pictures move slower. She couldn't. Her breathing turned ragged and her heart pounded. She recalled the passage in the book. She closed her eyes and forced her mind to recall the happy visions. Her breathing slowed, and her pulse returned to normal.

The image of her suite at an unidentified moment in the future appeared. She smiled as the memory filled her with warmth. Her eyes slid open, and she stared at the image stuck in front of her.

"Jack," she breathed. Her heart skipped a beat, and the image skittered. "No!"

Her hands shook as the image flickered again. She pressed her lips together, forcing her mind to the happy vision.

The picture of Jack glowed to life again. She blew out a slow breath as she stepped toward it. "Where are you?"

She studied the details. He wore the French uniform. He stood inside a tent. His hands were bound. She reached a finger toward him. The image rippled as she touched it before it sprang to life. She stumbled back a step as it played like a movie.

"No, I don't understand. I can't understand you. I'm not French," Jack shouted.

Someone spoke in another language.

Jack shook his head. "I can't understand. I'm not French. I stole these clothes. I'm sorry, but I'm not French."

A new voice entered the conversation, unseen to Cate. Someone spoke French again, and the new voice replied in English. "You have been found guilty of deserting the army with stolen arms. The crime is punishable by death. You will be hanged at sunrise."

"What? No!" Jack began when the memory began to fade.

Cate's eyes went wide as she stared at the paling vision. "No! No!"

It disappeared as her body shook. She tried to search for the future memory again but it was gone. Her body shook again, and the blackness around her faded.

"Catherine, wake up," a voice called.

She snapped open her eyes, finding the sapphire room around her, and Marcus hovering over her, his hands wrapped firmly around her shoulders. "Catherine? Are you all right?"

She grasped his lapel, balling it in her fist. "I know where Jack is and if we don't hurry, he's going to be killed."

CHAPTER 37

"Slow down, Catherine," Marcus said. "What did you see?"

"Jack. I saw him. I saw a vision. It worked." She sat up, her heart racing from the experience.

"Easy, dear. Take a deep breath, then tell me what you saw."

Cate swallowed hard, grabbing his arm. "The visions came when I fell asleep. They were racing, but I slowed them. I saw him. I saw Jack."

"Where?"

"He's with the French army again. They must have found him. They accused him of deserting." She gripped his arm tighter. "Marcus, they're going to hang him at daybreak."

She flicked her gaze outside to the setting sun. Her stomach turned over.

"All right. I will find him."

"I'm coming, too."

"I would argue, but I doubt I'll win."

"You won't," she said as she swung her legs over the edge of the bed. "And I'll be fine. I'll be with you, right?"

"Is that trust I detect in your voice?"

She offered him an amused smile as she rose. "It just might be. Come on, let's go."

"We'll use a portal to go to Austerlitz after dark."

"After dark?" she asked as she hurried along with him to the garden. "Why not now?"

"I would prefer not to appear on the fringes of the French army in nearly broad daylight."

Cate arched an eyebrow at him. "Good point. Okay, night it is."

They strode into the garden. Instead of opening the portal, Marcus spun to face her. "Before we go, there are some rules."

"Rules?" Cate asked, furrowing her brow.

"Stay with me at all times. Do not go off on your own. Do not disappear anywhere out of my sight. I don't care how strong of an urge you have to find Mr. Reid, we do not separate."

"Okay," she said with a nod.

He arched an eyebrow.

She lifted her shoulders in a partial shrug. "I said *okay*."

"I want to be sure it sinks in."

Cate tugged her lips back in a grimace. "The last time I was in that camp, Napoleon thought I was his prostitute, and then I got shoved into a regiment to fight. I have no desire to go anywhere alone while there."

"Good." Marcus stretched out his arms and opened the portal. Cate stepped inside once it opened, walking through the blackness into a dark night. She wrung her hands as she waited for Marcus.

He appeared moments later, and she breathed a sigh of relief as he wrapped his arm around her. "How will we find him?"

An owl hooted in the distance. Marcus pulled Cate closer

to him before he stalked toward the noise, calling back to it. Cate squashed her eyebrows together as the bird landed on his outstretched arm.

"Why?" she managed.

He tugged a feather from the bird before he whispered a few words in its ear. When he lifted his arm, the owl fluttered off and sailed into the camp.

Marcus waved the feather in the air. An image formed in the air. Cate's eyes went wide as she stared at the bird's eye view of the camp.

"Is that..."

"Yes," Marcus answered. "Our feathered friend can spy for us."

A smile crossed her lips as she glanced up at him before refocusing her attention on the aerial image. "Too bad he can't see in the tents."

"Jack is a criminal. He will be guarded. We look for the tent with soldiers stationed in front."

"Right," Cate said as she leaned closer to him.

"Are you cold, dear?" He removed his jacket and wrapped her in it before he pulled her closer to him.

"There," she said after tugging her arms into his jacket. "A tent with guards."

"So it is. Come along." He wrapped her hand in his and tugged her toward the camp. They snaked through the tents, careful to remain unseen.

"What's the plan when we reach the prisoner tent? Are you going to blast them or what?"

"Blast them?"

Cate flicked her gaze to him, mimicking his summoning of a fireball with her hand. "You know, with the fireball thing."

"That would draw far too much attention. I shall need to be more subtle."

She nodded as they approached the tent. "Oh, the magic sleep thing."

"Go into the tent as soon as I disable the first guard and find him. I will join you as soon as I've disposed of the second."

"Okay." She followed Marcus as he darted around the side of the tent and knocked one guard out with a touch. Cate slipped into the tent as the other guard shouted. His voice cut off as she scanned the dark space. "Jack? Jack, are you here?"

"Cate?"

"Jack!" she exclaimed, following the sound of his voice.

"Cate! How did you get here?" he questioned in the dark.

Bright light bloomed a moment later as Marcus stepped into the tent and lit it with a fireball that hovered above his hand.

"Oh, good, you found him."

Cate hurried to Jack's side as he rose to sit on his cot. She stared at the shackles around his hands and feet before she flicked a glance at Marcus. "Can you get rid of these?"

"Of course."

With one quick blast, both sets fell away, freeing Jack. Cate threw her arms around him. "I was so worried when they found the horses without you."

"How did you get away?"

Cate pulled away from him. "Carefully."

"We should go," Marcus said.

Cate nodded and stood, tugging Jack up with her.

"I assume you took care of the guard outside, though I'm not certain what will happen if I wander through the camp like this again. Maybe no one will recognize me, but–"

"I think we'll take the shortcut." Marcus extinguished the fireball before he wrapped an arm around Cate and clamped a hand onto Jack's wrist. The confines of the tent faded away, replaced by momentary blackness before Cate's room at Rosenberg replaced it.

Cate breathed a sigh of relief, letting her head rest against Marcus's shoulder for a moment as she stared at Jack. "Thank goodness that's over and you're safe."

"You, too. Cate, when they took you, I–"

"I know. I felt the same way. But it's over now."

"Thank heavens. We can't waste any more time. We need to find Gertrude."

"We did," Cate said as she righted herself. "She's safe. She is with Anna in 1956."

"You found her? How?"

"Her bracelet," Cate explained. "I figured out the date, and we managed to rescue her from The Agency."

Marcus's lips curled at the corners as he stroked a lock of her hair. "After Catherine stranded Gianna in the 1400s."

Jack's eyes went wide. "You did what? How?"

"I took her little time travel ring that she used to maroon us here off of her finger and left."

"Good going, Cate," Jack said with an amused grin. "Let's hope that's the end of her."

"I would highly doubt that. As such, we should return to 1956, return Gertrude to Dunhaven, speak with her about the importance of not changing her will, and then go home. Undoubtedly, The Agency will already be concocting the next plan."

"These people are like cats. They never stop."

"And I doubt they will for quite some time," Marcus said. "They did not grow into the organization that they are by giving up."

Jack blew out a long breath and frowned. "Right. I guess we'd better get at it then."

"Are you sure you can manage it?" Cate questioned. "This

must have worn you out. You're still recovering from the temporalysis."

"I'm okay," Jack said with a nod. "It's fine. I can make it."

"Are you sure? Jack, I don't want to risk your health."

"I'm sure. I'm strong as an ox, I promise. I've been milking it at Dunhaven so I don't hear it from Molly and Mrs. Fraser."

Cate chuckled.

"Then we should go," Marcus answered. He stretched his arms when Cate batted them down.

"Stop opening time portals inside."

Marcus heaved a sigh and shot her a sideways glance. "You are as bad as Mother."

"I don't want the room wrecked. Oh, wait, my rose and music box. I should take them back." She crossed to the nightstand to retrieve both before they made their way to the garden. Marcus opened the portal, and they returned to 1956.

After snaking through the castle halls, they arrived in the crystal bedroom. Cate set her keepsakes on the dresser as she walked in. Anna still tended to Gertrude who remained asleep.

"Ah, Marcus, Catherine, you have returned triumphant."

"Yes," Cate said as she approached the sleeping woman. "We found him. I managed to work through a vision while asleep that led us to his location."

A smile spread across Anna's face. "Progress. Excellent. You are a fast learner."

Cate returned her expression before she sank onto the edge of the bed and pulled Gertrude's hand into hers. "How is she?"

"Perfectly fine. I have kept her asleep until you returned, however, I can wake her if you'd like to speak with her."

"Yes, I would like that very much," Cate answered.

Marcus kissed the top of her head. "I will leave you to discuss the matter with her alone, dear."

"Ah, I'd like to stay," Jack said, stepping forward. He glanced down at his clothes. "Oh, I hope I don't frighten her."

"She's a time traveler, I think she'll be okay," Cate said with a chuckle. "And I think you should stay. She should know both of us still protect the secret."

Jack nodded as he hovered behind Cate.

"Come along, Marcus. There are a few things I would like to discuss with you."

Marcus gave his mother the slightest of flinches before he grabbed Cate's hand and squeezed. "Good luck."

Anna slid her arm around Marcus's and tugged him away. "She will awaken in a few moments."

"Thank you," Cate said before the door clicked closed. She turned her attention to her ancestor. Jack slid his hand onto her shoulder and squeezed.

She reached back to grab it, threading her fingers through his as Gertrude's eyes fluttered open. She sucked in a gasp, a fearful expression twisting her features.

"It's okay, Gertrude," Cate said, squeezing her hand. "You're safe now."

"Who are you?" the woman demanded. She flicked her gaze to Jack, her brow furrowing. "Is that...is that Jackie Reid?"

"Aye," he said, circling the bed and plopping onto the side across from Cate. "It's me, Lady MacKenzie."

"But you–"

"Left, I know. My father died, and I came back. I worked for you for the last six months of your life." He flicked his gaze to Cate. "Cate's the owner of Dunhaven now."

Gertrude studied her. "And you know the secret."

"I figured it out pretty quickly, actually," she said with a slight chuckle.

"So did those people," Gertrude said, her face pinching again.

"The Agency. I know. They were at Dunhaven in 1942 during the war. They have been trying to get control of the castle ever since."

Gertrude licked her lips, her brows pinching.

"Which is why we need you to change your will again. There's a clause that requires me to be married–"

"I know. I didn't want to put it in, but they forced me. It was all I could do to resist giving in to that wretched woman's so-called agency."

"I understand. But when we return you to Dunhaven, you must call Mr. Smythe and change the will. Please."

She snapped a panicked glance at Cate. "Has Dunhaven been lost?"

"No," Cate said with a shake of her head. She lifted her left hand. "I'm married. But I wasn't. We nearly didn't catch it in time to correct things."

"I'm sorry, dear. I tried my hardest–"

"It's not your fault," Cate said, patting her hand.

Gertrude shifted her gaze to Jack. "Are you…"

"No," Jack said, understanding the question without her needing to finish. "She's married to someone who can help us win against these horrible people."

"I see. Dunhaven must never be lost to them."

"We're working on that," Cate said with a smile.

Gertrude tugged one corner of her lips back as she cupped Cate's face in her hands. "You look so much like a MacKenzie. I am sorry we never met. Your father thought keeping you away would protect you."

Cate grabbed her hand and squeezed. "We're meeting now. And I'm glad for it. I just wish it had been under better circumstances."

Gertrude smiled and pushed herself higher on the bed as

she glanced around the room. "Where are we?"

"Rosenberg Palace in Germany," Cate answered.

"Germany?" she questioned. "However did we get here? I believe they held me in France."

"They did. This is my husband's home. One of them," Cate answered.

Gertrude arched an eyebrow at her. "I see. Well, it seems you have the matter well in hand. I suppose we should return to Dunhaven, and I should get on with my end."

"There's no need to rush. If you feel tired..."

"I'm not ancient. I'm still in good shape. I do not need to rest like a child," Gertrude said.

Cate suppressed a chuckle at the woman's words, so very like her own protestations at times. "All right. I'll find Marcus. He can return us to Dunhaven."

Gertrude offered her a sharp nod of approval as Cate and Jack rose to stand.

"She reminds me of someone," Jack whispered as they made their way across the room to the door. "Where do you think your loving husband is?"

"Sitting room, maybe?"

"Wonder what mummy dearest wanted to talk to him about?" Jack asked as they snaked through the halls toward the foyer.

"Maybe about not opening time portals in the house."

Jack arched an eyebrow. "Wonder how Gertrude will take the time portal trip."

"She doesn't seem afraid of much, so likely better than you," Cate said, shooting him an amused grin.

"Very funny. Maybe if it wasn't *him* opening them, I'd feel better."

"Doubt it," they said at the same time as they reached the foyer floor.

Cate crossed to the closed doors and knocked before they pushed inside. "She's ready."

"Excellent," Marcus said. "We will return her to Dunhaven at once."

Anna rose and crossed to Cate, pulling her into an embrace and kissing her cheek. "Be safe, dear." She turned to Marcus as he strode across the room. "Take care of her. And think about what I said."

"Of course, Mother," he said, kissing her cheek before they left the room.

They collected Gertrude from the crystal bedroom and took her to the garden. After she confirmed the date of her disappearance, Cate explained the new time travel portals to her.

"The portal we use to access other locations is a bit different from the ones you are used to. They are quite chaotic," Cate explained. "But once you enter, do not stop walking until you see Dunhaven Castle. Otherwise, you may become trapped."

"I understand, though I do not see the appeal in time travel whatsoever, particularly in this form."

Cate suppressed a giggle at the statement, shooting a glance at Jack as Marcus opened the portal. When the gale-force winds swirled around them, Cate signaled for Gertrude to enter. Jack followed behind her, then Cate.

Within seconds, bright sunshine surrounded her. She stepped forward to join Jack and Gertrude in the back garden at Dunhaven Castle.

"I never thought I'd see it again."

Marcus joined them seconds later. "I will wait for you here."

Cate nodded, and they set off toward the castle. They pushed in through the front door and escorted Gertrude to her bedroom.

"I will call Mr. Smythe today. I hope when you return, everything is corrected." Gertrude pulled Cate into an embrace.

After a few more words, they parted ways. Cate and Jack hurried from the castle and returned to the garden.

"Finished?" Marcus asked as they rejoined him.

Cate nodded and sucked in a deep breath. "Time to find out if this worked."

CHAPTER 38

"I hope so. I am afraid to go back and find out. I'm afraid something else will be haywire," Jack said with a shake of his head.

"I guess it's better to know as soon as possible," Cate said with a squeeze of his hand as Marcus opened another portal to their time.

"See you at home, Cate," Jack said with a nod before he stepped inside.

Cate followed behind him, arriving at Dunhaven Castle nearly fifty years later. She stared up at the relatively unchanged castle with a tentative gaze.

"Time to face the music," Jack said.

"After we change, of course.

"Of course," he said with a laugh. "I can't very well talk to anyone like this."

"Everyone should still be downstairs. We should have a clear path upstairs," Cate answered as Marcus joined them.

They closed the distance to the castle, entering through the front door and hurrying up the steps and to their bedrooms to change. Cate eyed the music box on her nightstand as she tugged a cardigan over her tunic. Would she have any more visions, she wondered.

She slid her fingers across the piano's tiny lid. "I sure hope not. They are not pleasant."

With a smile at the small box, she spun on a heel and crossed to the sitting room. As she reached the door, she doubled over.

Pain shot across her forehead as images flooded through her mind. She fought to steady them and herself but lost the battle. She collapsed to her knees, clutching her head. Tears formed in her eyes, and her hands trembled as the visions continued. Voices murmured, but she couldn't make sense of them. Blurry figures moved around, but she couldn't make them clear.

As quickly as the sensation hit her, it passed. She sucked in a shaky breath and opened her eyes. She pressed her lips together, struggling to calm her nerves and slow her pounding heart.

A knock sounded at the door, startling her. "Coming," she called, forcing herself to her feet.

The door inched open. "Catherine? Are you all right?"

Cate took a steadying breath as she pulled the door open. He must have detected her pounding heart. "Yes, I'm okay."

"Really?" he asked.

"I had another vision. It took me by surprise. I wasn't prepared for it."

"Did you manage to make sense of any details?"

She shook her head. "No. It was all a blur. I guess I haven't quite caught on to this whole thing yet despite the strides I've made."

He offered her a tight-lipped smile. "I'm certain you will."

"Have you spoken with Mr. Smythe?" she asked as she joined him in the hall.

"Not yet."

"We should find him. With any luck, this whole mess is over."

He offered her another fleeting smile as they strode through the halls and down to the foyer.

Gayle hurried toward them from the library. "Oh, there you are. I'm so glad I found you. Mr. Smythe has requested to speak with you immediately. If you don't mind, I'll fetch the staff as well."

"Thanks, Gayle. Are we meeting in the library?"

"Yes, Jack's already there. I just need the Frasers and Molly." She squeezed Cate's arm before flitting past her to find the other staff members.

"Moment of truth," Cate said with a weak smile as they walked toward the library. She pushed inside, finding Jack in his usual armchair. Mr. Smythe sat opposite him, shuffling papers.

"Oh, good, Gayle found you. Excellent," he said as Cate and Marcus entered.

She shot Jack a hopeful glance, flashing her crossed fingers as she patted his shoulder before making her way to the sofa and perching on it.

The others joined them a few moments later.

"What is it now?" Molly asked as she took a seat next to Cate. "She wants me to also pay for the time I stayed here on vacation?"

"No, thank you all for coming," Mr. Smythe said. "When I first announced the change in the will, I must admit to having been puzzled to have missed it. After a thorough investigation, we have found that this was *not*, in fact, Gertrude MacKenzie's final will and testament. She updated it several years later and removed the marriage clause. The will is identical to the one I presented to you when we met in the States. You are, indeed, the rightful heir to Dunhaven Castle, married or not."

A collective sigh of relief went up through the room, and Molly rubbed Cate's shoulders. Cate pressed her lips together as she sucked in a breath and nodded. "Thank you, Mr. Smythe."

"What about the lawsuit?" Mrs. Fraser asked.

"I am certain that will be dismissed given the new evidence that has come to light. It has no merit whatsoever now as the challenge is meaningless."

"Oh, thank heavens. So, we are all safe."

"Indeed, you are. And once again, I must apologize for the situation. I do not know how this could have happened, but I am pleased that we were able to rectify it quickly and as easily as possible despite some trepidation on your part for which I profusely apologize."

"There's no need to apologize, Mr. Smythe," Cate answered. "I'm glad the matter is cleared up. Thank you for your diligence."

"Well, I suppose this calls for a celebratory dessert tonight," Mrs. Fraser said as she rose. "You and I had better get baking, Miss Molly."

Molly sprang to her feet with a grin. "Definitely." She turned to face Cate. "Congratulations. I'm so glad we don't have to move."

"Thank you," Cate said with a smile.

Mr. Smythe stuffed papers into a folder and rose as Mr. and Mrs. Fraser and Molly left the room. "If you don't mind, Gayle and I will stay on one more night and head back tomorrow morning."

"Of course," Cate answered, "stay as long as you'd like."

He offered her a slight smile and a nod before he collected his briefcase, and he and Gayle departed.

"Well, I guess it did work," Jack said as he climbed to his feet. "I can't believe it, but it did."

"Thank goodness. One bullet dodged."

"I don't want to know what they'll throw at us next."

A shiver ran down Cate's spine as the memory of her vision crept back into her mind. She suppressed a shudder, wrapping her arms around herself as she forced a smile onto her face. "Whatever it is, we'll face it together."

"Sounds like a plan." He shot Marcus a glance before he sucked in a breath. "I think I'll go snag some biscuits from Mrs. Fraser while I still am considered ill enough to get away with it."

Cate offered him a genuine smile and a nod. "Okay. Enjoy."

He shot another glance at Marcus before he strode from the room, pulling the doors shut behind him. Cate blew out a long sigh as she collapsed onto the sofa.

A brandy glass waved in front of her. She accepted it and smiled up at Marcus. "Thanks." After a sip, she sucked in another breath. "Well, I guess you're off the hook."

"Off the hook?" he asked.

"Yeah. I mean, we don't need to be married anymore. And I'm sure you'd very much like to carry on with your life uninterrupted by the wife you never planned to have." She forced a smile onto her face and flicked her gaze to him.

He narrowed his eyes at her as he studied her over the rim of his glass.

"Thank you. You didn't have to do this, but I'm glad you did."

"You are welcome, Catherine."

She licked her lips, drumming her fingers against her thigh. "Anyway, I will speak to Mr. Smythe in the morning. He can draw up whatever paperwork is needed, and we can part ways." She chewed her lower lip as the last words left her lips.

"Catherine–" Marcus began when a knock sounded at the door.

"I should get that," she said, leaping to stand and setting the brandy glass on the table. She scurried across the room and flung the doors open, racing into the hall as she tried to steady her nerves.

Another knock sounded at the front door. "Coming!" she shouted down the hall.

She rounded the corner and opened one of the doors. Her heart skipped a beat, and she slow-blinked at her visitor who grinned at her.

"Hello, dear," Anna said as she rolled her bag across the threshold and pressed into the house. "Oh, what a lovely little castle. It's very cozy."

Cate stared at the woman, finding no words as she eased the door shut.

Anna studied her expectantly. "Oh, no, I've interrupted something."

Cate recovered her senses, shaking her head and swallowing hard. "No, not at all. I just…"

"Just what, dear?"

"Was in the library, and it took me a minute to get here, is all," she fibbed before offering a nervous chuckle. "Let me get someone to take your things up to your suite."

"Oh, lovely, yes, I would like to lie down after that long trip."

"Right, of course."

Marcus strode from the hall before she could leave, his brow furrowing. "Mother?"

"Yes, dear. I've made it."

"I see. For what?"

"Catherine's training, of course. You didn't think I would abandon her, did you? She is far from mastering these visions. She needs help. And I am here to provide. I'll stay as long as it takes." She grinned at them both before she lifted her bag. "Oh, Catherine, never mind the help. I can carry it. If you'll just show me the way. I hate to be a bother."

"No bother," she answered with another nervous giggle. She slicked a lock of hair behind her ear and motioned for Anna to follow her.

"I will take your bag, Mother," Marcus said, pulling it from her hands and following them.

Cate wound through the halls, leading her to a large suite two halls away from hers. "I hope you'll find it comfortable."

"Oh, how lovely. Violet is my favorite color. Thank you, dear. Now, I'd like to rest. If I could just have a tray for dinner, that would be appreciated. I do not wish to cause a ruckus."

"I will let Mrs. Fraser know. And it's no bother at all. You're welcome to join us for dinner."

"Oh, no, dear, but maybe tomorrow. I'm quite tired."

Cate smiled and nodded at her before Anna pulled her into another embrace. "Oh, it's so good to be here, Catherine."

"It's good to have you." She smiled at her and squeezed her arm before she and Marcus left the room.

Cate sucked in a shaky breath as she pulled the doors shut to Anna's room and took a few steps down the hall. She planted a palm against her forehead. "I can't believe this. Did you know she was coming?"

"No, I did not," Marcus said.

Cate let her shoulders slump and squeezed her eyes closed as she shook her head. "What are we going to do?"

"About?"

"Our divorce," Cate said. "We can't get divorced with your mother here."

"I would prefer we did not."

Cate huffed. "She will be devastated. She thinks we're really a couple."

"Technically, we are."

"That's not helpful." She breathed out another sigh as they reached the top of the stairs. "I'm sorry."

"Whatever for?"

She plodded down the stairs next to him. "You're stuck with me for who knows how long now."

"Catherine," he began as they reached the foyer floor, "we should discuss–"

Another knock interrupted his statement. Cate let her head fall back between her shoulder blades as she flung her hands out. "What now?"

She stomped to the door and flung it open, staring at the next visitor on her doorstep. Her brow crinkled as the blonde flipped a lock of hair over her shoulder and slid her sunglasses down. She looked familiar, but Cate couldn't place her.

"Hi," she said in a British accent with a grin as she chomped on her gum.

"Hello, can I help you?"

"I'm here to see Jack Reid."

"Oh," Cate said, the crease between her eyebrows deepening as she stepped back from the door and motioned for the woman to come in. It hit her why the woman appeared familiar. The pictures in Gianna's flat. This was the woman from the pictures. "Come in. May I ask your name?"

"Of course," she said with another grin as her heels clicked across the marble floor. "Amanda Reid. Jack's wife."

Cate stared at the woman as her stomach turned over. What had The Agency done this time?

The End
To be continued…

Want to Read More About Cate?

Look for more Cate Kensie in November 2024

Until then, check out another Scottish mystery series!

Unlock the secrets of the Duchess of Blackmoore's enigmatic past with Lenora, a gifted but lonely orphan. When a Scottish duke's proposal reveals dark mysteries, Lenora's journey into the eerie castle unveils chilling secrets. With her life in peril, she races against time to solve a twisted mystery. If you crave strong heroines, family secrets, and intricate mysteries, immerse yourself in Book 1 of Nellie H. Steele's historical series—where the past holds deadly secrets and heroines rise to face them.

Find out what happens in *Death of a Duchess* available on Amazon Now! **Click HERE to get your copy now!**

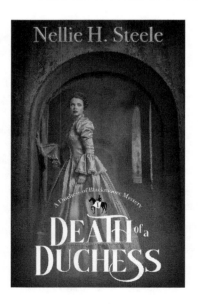

Click HERE to get your copy of Death of a Duchess!

Get THREE FREE Books!

Let's keep in touch! Join my newsletter and receive three free books!

Read on for a sneak peek of *Death of a Duchess*

ABOUT THE AUTHOR

Award-winning author Nellie H. Steele writes in as many genres as she reads, ranging from mystery to fantasy and allowing readers to escape reality and enter enchanting worlds filled with unique, lovable characters.

Addicted to books since she could read, Nellie escaped to fictional worlds like the ones created by Carolyn Keene or Victoria Holt long before she decided to put pen to paper and create her own realities.

When she's not spinning a cozy mystery tale, building a new realm in a contemporary fantasy, or writing another action-adventure car chase, you can find her shuffling through her Noah's Ark of rescue animals or enjoying a hot cuppa (that's tea for most Americans.)

Join her Facebook Readers' Group here!

OTHER SERIES BY NELLIE H. STEELE

Cozy Mystery Series

Cate Kensie Mysteries
Lily & Cassie by the Sea Mysteries
Pearl Party Mysteries
Middle Age is Murder Cozy Mysteries

Supernatural Suspense/Urban Fantasy

Shadow Slayers Stories
Duchess of Blackmoore Mysteries
Shelving Magic

Adventure

Maggie Edwards Adventures
Clif & Ri on the Sea